Humphrey

& Jack

Humphrey

& Jack

Ian Thomson

Quirinal Press
LN2 5RT

Copyright © Ian Thomson 2018

Ian Thomson has asserted his right under the Copyright,
Designs and Patents Act 1988 to be identified as the author of this work

All rights reserved

*This book is sold subject to the condition that it shall not,
by way of trade or otherwise, be lent, resold, hired out or
otherwise circulated without the publisher's prior consent in
any form or binding or cover other than that in which it is
published and without a similar condition including this
condition being imposed on the subsequent purchaser*

This book is a work of fiction. The characters within it are not intended
to represent any persons, living or dead. Any apparent resemblance
is purely coincidental.

In Memoriam
Stuart Skinner
1975 - 1995

By the same author

Martin, a Novel

The Mouse Triptych

The Swan Diptych

Come Away, O Human Child

Cherries, and Other Tales

monachopsis

> n. the subtle but persistent feeling of being out of place, as maladapted to your surroundings as a seal on a beach—lumbering, clumsy, easily distracted, huddled in the company of other misfits, unable to recognize the ambient roar of your intended habitat, in which you'd be fluidly, brilliantly, effortlessly at home.
>
> *The Dictionary of Obscure Sorrow*

HUMPHREY

1. Doctor's Orders

'Ah, Humphrey, good to see you. Take a seat. What can we do for you today?'

'Nothing, I hope, James. I'm fine. You sent for me.'

'Sorry?'

'Letter from your receptionist. Annual review.'

'Of course. Of course. Now we'll need to do some blood tests as a matter of routine before…'

'Yes, James. I know. I booked myself in with the phlebotomist a couple of weeks ago. You should have the results by now.'

'Well, let's have a look.'

He swivelled round to check his computer.

'Because there's no point in me making an appointment to see you,' Humphrey said, 'only to have to make an appointment to see the practice nurse who will only tell me to make an appointment to see you, is there? Waste of everybody's time.'

Dr Bell looked hard at Humphrey for a moment or two.

'Well, no, I suppose not,' he said.

Humphrey & Jack

'Quite,' said Humphrey smugly.

Humphrey had known Dr Bell since they were at school. They were not friends exactly. James Bell was a year younger than Humphrey. According to the brutal etiquette of public schoolboys, it was considered improper for boys of different years to consort with or even to acknowledge each other. However, by the time they were in the sixth form, Humphrey in the upper sixth and James in the lower, there was a certain relaxation of the protocols and even the use of Christian names might be permitted within the precincts of the sixth form common room.

So now, decades later, there was an easy familiarity between them, though Humphrey really didn't 'do' friends.

Actually, that one year's difference, even now, led to an infinitesimal superiority of tone on Humphrey's part whenever they were engaged in conversation, just a minuscule hint of condescension. Neither of them was particularly conscious of it, but it meant that Humphrey did not hold his GP in awe, as some do.

'How have you been since last time?'

'As I said, absolutely fine.'

'Splendid! Now then…' He consulted the computer screen. 'Cholesterol down. Excellent. Statins doing their job then.'

'Good,' said Humphrey.

'Kidney function fine.'

'Good,' said Humphrey.

'Liver function fine.'

'Good,' said Humphrey, who was rather surprised.

'Uric acid under control. Any gout attacks?'

'Not a twinge. Not had an attack in fifteen years.'

'Excellent. Now, let's check your blood pressure. If you could just take your jacket off.'

This was the bit Humphrey hated. Dr Bell put the cuff around his upper arm and Humphrey felt it tighten. It was most uncomfortable. Then the doctor released the pressure.

Humphrey & Jack

'Well?' said Humphrey. 'I expect it's a touch high. I got a bit stressed on the way here. Bloody traffic. Will they ever finish that bypass? And this city must have more than its fair share of clowns who don't indicate on roundabouts.'

'Well, it's more than a touch high, Humphrey. 160 over 90. Are you still drinking a lot?'

Here we go, thought Humphrey. Here comes the lecture.

'I've cut down,' he said.

'How much would you say you drink in a week? In units?'

'I can't be bothered with units,' said Humphrey airily. 'Apparently, years ago the government asked the BMA boffins to come up with safe levels and some policy wonk made the figures up in his head.'

'Where did you get that from?'

'Oh, I don't know. *The Daily Mail* probably.'

'No wonder you have high blood pressure if you read *The Daily Mail*.'

'I don't take *The Daily Mail*, James. I probably found a copy lying about in *someone's* waiting room.'

Humphrey put on an 'I rest my case' face.

'Be that as it may, Humphrey, you're trying to avoid the question. Can you give me some idea how much you drink each week?'

'Well now, I probably have a glass of the old rouge with lunch. And then, in the evening, a dry Martini or two before supper and then perhaps half a bottle of wine.'

'No more than that? Are you sure?'

'Are you suggesting I'm fibbing?'

'Studies do suggest that most people understate how much they drink when asked by a doctor.'

'Is that from *The Daily Mail*?'

'Well no, a bit more reliable than that. *The British Medical Journal*.'

'I've read that alcoholism is common in medical doctors. Drug abuse too.'

Humphrey & Jack

'And suicide. It's a stressful occupation. But this isn't about my health, Humphrey, it's about yours.'

'I know. I know. It's just that every time I have to see you chappies, I get *The Lecture*. The dentist's the same. Every time it's: "Do you floss?" "No," I tell him, "life's far too short to be messing about with flossing." Do you floss, James?'

'No, as it happens.'

'Well, there you are then.'

'Where? Where am I?'

'Well, if most doctors are suicidal alcoholics who don't floss, why should I worry?'

Once again, James gave Humphrey a long hard look.

'Right. Well, what I'm going to do is to increase the dosage a little on your hypertension meds. And what I want you to do is to cut down little by little on the booze intake. Try to stick to just one Martini and perhaps miss out on that glass of red at lunchtime, or a glass less in the evening. Try and have at least one alcohol-free day each week. Can you do that?'

'I can but try,' said Humphrey lugubriously, already planning to pick up a nice Chénas or a Fleurie from Waitrose on the way home.

A prescription popped out of the printer and Dr Bell signed it.

'There you are then. Anything else I can help you with while you're here?'

'Well, the old knees are creaking a bit. Pretty painful going up and down stairs. I suppose you can expect that as you get older?'

'Well, there's a certain amount of wear and tear, yes. But, to be candid, Humphrey, you're carrying rather more weight about than you should. That doesn't help. How many pounds do you weigh?'

'Pounds? I couldn't tell you. I'm not an American. About fifteen stone. You do the sum.'

'Two hundred and ten, Humphrey. It's too much for your height. What's your diet like?'

Humphrey & Jack

'Well, I happen to rather like cooking, you see. So I would rather not have you put me on a diet of roots and berries. Actually, it's rather healthy. Lots of salads. Chicken…'

'Red meat?'

'About once a week. A grilled steak, perhaps.'

'Fish?'

'On Fridays. Religiously.'

'Seriously?'

'No. Joke. Any day really.'

'Well, it does all sound rather healthy, I agree. You're not telling me porkies, are you?'

Humphrey hadn't mentioned his predilection for pork pies, it was true, nor for chocolate, but one must be allowed the occasional treat, mustn't one? And besides, he wasn't under oath.

'You might consider cutting down on portion size perhaps. Smaller plates are a good little psycho-con. Brain thinks you're eating more than you are. But it's the booze really. The alcohol prevents the body from burning fat that's already there. And, it may also interfere with the feeling of satiety, so you eat more than you might otherwise. But you know all this, Humphrey.'

Oh, I do, I certainly do, thought Humphrey. He had heard this part of the lecture innumerable times.

'Well, we'll see,' he said. 'I will have to balance certain innocent gratifications against the puritanical benefits. Anyway, you said my liver function was fine.'

'For now,' Dr Bell said.

'Ah well,' Humphrey sighed. 'It's my life, after all.'

'But you don't want it cut short prematurely. *On mourra seul.*'

'What? Oh yes. One dies alone,' said Humphrey. 'Pascal. Miserable bugger.'

2. The Bees, the Blackbirds, and the Cat

It was too much to hope that the peace would last. The noise would start up soon and one day he would lose control and kill somebody.

Humphrey was enjoying a June evening in his garden, two days after his visit to the doctor. It wasn't silent. You can't find silence in England nowadays. Even on the top of Scafell Pike the purr of distant traffic wafts over Wastwater. Even in the wastes of Exmoor a faraway police siren moans through the heather.

The noise of traffic in Humphrey's urban garden was a roar rather than a purr but it was a muted roar and Humphrey had learned to edit it so that it remained in his auditory hinterland. The same with the whining of ambulances and fire engines and police cars across the city. The noise could be pushed away, almost out of mind, like the commonplace daily tragedies which had summoned them. Someone else's misery, muffled and indistinct.

For the moment, however, everything in Humphrey's garden was lovely.

He had been watching the bees. They were busy in the lavender just by the garden table where he was enjoying his permitted Martini. The bees weren't noisy, despite their reputation for buzzing. In fact he couldn't hear any noise from them at all.

He had seen quite a lot in the papers about declining bee populations as a result of pesticides or global warming or fracking or 'this Tory government'. He was rather sceptical about this but began to fear it might be true when they had not put in their usual appearance as spring turned to summer. He rather liked bees and wanted them to hurry up and prove the doom-mongers wrong.

Humphrey & Jack

Then, one June morning, there were two of them - then four, then two dozen. The golden rod would be out soon and his garden would be alive with bees. Wonderful.

Humphrey was fascinated by their movement. A bee would land on one of the lavender spikes, gathering nectar and picking up pollen, then it would rise a little, twist and move on to another spike, and so on, seemingly at random. However, Humphrey knew from various television programmes, that bees didn't do things at random and wondered what secret algorithm controlled their restless activity. Except when one of them came whizzing past his ear they went about their work in silence.

The garden was alive with birdsong. He could hear the chattering of finches, the cheep-cheep of sparrows, the moaning of pigeons, and best of all there was the glorious descant of the blackbirds with their ravishing trills. Humphrey thought he should go on some sort of course so that he could distinguish the other melodies that filled his garden with such simple delight: the calls from tree to tree, from the hidden recesses of flowering bushes, and from the shadows under the hedges.

Out of the corner of his eye, Humphrey saw that a blackbird, a young male, was hopping about near his table. Along with his Martini, Humphrey had brought out some olives and some Carr's Table Water Biscuits. He saw now that he had dropped one and that it had broken on the paving of his terrace. This was what had attracted the bird. It was pecking at the biscuit and, now and then, it would fly off with quite a large fragment, taking a wide but shallow curve over the surface of the lawn, to disappear under the broad leaves of the rhubarb patch. Quite soon, it would return from under the leaves for more.

Humphrey was quite taken by this audacious little chap. He crushed another biscuit in his hand and threw a little trail of crumbs leading from the original biscuit almost to the table leg, reckoning that the bird might be attracted by crumbs of a more manageable size.

Humphrey & Jack

It seemed to be working. On each foray, the delightful little creature would land a few yards away and then, in a series of little runs, come closer and closer to where Humphrey was sitting absolutely still.

He thought the blackbird must be very young because he was quite small and his feathers were perfectly black and glossy and his beak was very orange. Occasionally, he would cock his head on one side and it looked to Humphrey as if the bird were examining him. Humphrey wondered if he could tame him. Perhaps, if he were quiet and persistent he could get the bird to come up onto the table. He thought he might buy some bird seed next time he was in Waitrose.

He was delighted when he saw his winged friend take a different arc from the terrace with a sizeable fragment in his beak. This time he landed at the bottom of the stone steps which led down to the lawn and fed the morsel to his mate who was waiting there. Then together they flew off into the rhubarb patch. Did they have a nest nearby?

Soon the bird was back and very nearly at Humphrey's feet.

A shift in the light, as the westering sun slanted through the leaves of the huge ash tree by the house, caused Humphrey to change focus and he saw with horror that he and the little blackbird were being watched.

It was Aristotle, next door's cat. It was sitting at the end of his terrace contemplating the bird with greedy malevolence.

Humphrey loathed cats. To be fair, he had a suspicion that he might be allergic to them and that a chance encounter could result in a rash and hideous sneezing fit. However, he reserved a particular detestation for this cat - a cat which he sincerely believed lived only to annoy him.

There had been the occasion when it had left a mangled partridge on his doorstep and Humphrey had nearly trodden on the carcass from which a cloud of nasty flies arose and settled. Recently, it had taken to parading back and forth along the terrace at night, turning the security light on and off and waking him up. He had seen the animal do it. Padding across the paving with its tail in the air, flooding his bedroom with orange light and returning when it went out. Finally, there had been the occasion on an insufferably hot night last August when Aristotle had got into his downstairs bedroom and sat on his head whilst he slept. Naturally it had frightened the hell out of him and he had grabbed the thing and flung it back out of the open window. He had not slept again that night.

Humphrey shifted slightly in his seat. Simultaneously, the blackbird flew off in his curve to the rhubarb and the cat streaked across the lawn and under the leaves.

'Aristotle, NO!'

Humphrey rose to his feet, knocking over his Martini.

He was relieved to see that almost immediately the blackbird and his mate had flown out from the other side of the rhubarb patch and both of them had glided into an azalea bush on the other side of the garden hotly pursued by the cat which was now crouching low and stalking towards the bush.

'Aristotle, sod off! Go on! Shoo!' Humphrey bellowed, trying to pelt the cat with olives which fell far too short.

'Leave them alone, Aristotle! Bugger off!'

He was suddenly aware that anyone in the public park which lay just beyond the low hedge at the bottom of the garden might have looked up and seen a sixty year old man waving his arms about and seemingly swearing at a Greek philosopher who had been dead for two and a half thousand years.

The cat, however, was blithely ignoring him and lay on the grass, head on front paws, staring into the bush.

There was nothing for it but for him to go down the stone steps on his creaking knees and chase the creature away. He picked up a stone on the way and threw it. Bingo! It hit Aristotle on the haunch and the cat turned with a yowl and sped in the opposite direction to the fence which ran between Humphrey's garden and his neighbour's. There, it looked back at Humphrey with a baleful stare, and then slipped like a black liquid through the narrow gap in the palings.

Humphrey & Jack

As Humphrey slowly climbed the steps back up to the terrace, the noise started up.

First there were the yippy dogs. Humphrey did not despise dogs as much as he did cats but he had no time for the little varieties with their high-pitched *yip-yip-yip* which set his teeth on edge. He abhorred these Yorkshire terriers and King Charles spaniels and dachshunds and corgis and other little rat-like lap dogs that no grown man should be seen with in public. Yet here they were, with their masters, out for their evening walk, and as soon as they were let off the leash, off they went, chasing each other in frenzied circles, and yipping away till Humphrey physically felt the noise as a tautening of the skin across his temples.

Then there was the screaming girl.

At the bottom of the park, near Prior Ingham's Road, out of sight of Humphrey's house except from upstairs, there was a children's playground. Now, the sound of children playing didn't unduly upset him. He wasn't an ogre. The swings and slide and climbing frame were sufficiently distant for their cries to come to him on the evening breeze like childhood memories, dimmed and subdued by time.

Apart from the screaming girl.

He assumed it was a girl because no self-respecting boy would make such a racket and then keep it up, sometimes for almost an hour at a time, every blessed evening. It was an attention-seeking scream, a phoney distress scream, a diminutive diva scream. It made him want to find the child and say: 'I'll give you something to scream about', and then strangle her so she couldn't.

As usual, a game of football had started up near the bandstand and local oiks were uttering their oafish cries with every thump of the ball.

Lads on motor bikes with their silencers removed were roaring up and down Prior Ingham's Road.

A neighbour had started up a strimmer.

Worst of all, the gang with the boom box were back. The amplified music with its thudding bass and moronically banal lyrics invaded the evening and took possession of it completely.

Humphrey righted his Martini glass on its little tray and went back inside the house.

'Just one Martini,' his doctor had said but Humphrey set about mixing another. After all, he had spilt his first one. It's true that there had been very little left in the glass but Humphrey was quick to persuade himself that he deserved another because of the din outside. He could still hear the banging bass rhythm in the kitchen even though it was at the other side of the house. He could actually feel the vibrations. They seemed arrhythmic and were very unsettling. He would have to tackle these youths, he thought. He could not endure this racket every night.

A second Martini led to a third and he was feeling defiant and courageous when, at about half-past nine, he set off down the garden with a walking stick to berate these selfish hoodlums over the low hedge.

It was not a success.

3. What's in a Name?

What indeed? Humphrey Icke hated his name.

Whatever had possessed his parents to condemn him to such a lumpy, soft, upholstered sort of a name? Were they mad? There was no family tradition, no genealogical obligation to uphold. Had it been sadism? Had they been drunk? Was it a joke?

He had once asked his mother.

'The minute I saw you, I knew it was right,' she had said. 'We had a number of other names in mind, your father and I, but you were so plump and sweet and…and… edible, that it had to be Humphrey.'

'What other names?' he'd asked.

'Well, George, of course, and John - though that seemed a bit ordinary, and your father liked Thomas, and I wondered about Henry for a

Humphrey & Jack

while, but when the midwife handed you to me, I was sure it had to be Humphrey. You were so chubby it was just right. Humphrey of Gloucester was Henry V's brother, you know.'

His mother was a historian. She taught at the Tech.

'But babies just aren't called Humphrey,' he'd said.

'Well, the Duke of Gloucester must have been a baby once, darling. Now, what do you want for lunch?'

And that was that. There was never any point in arguing with her.

George! now there was a right regal name. And so was Henry, and even John, ordinary or not. He would have loved to have been called Thomas.

His name had been a nightmare during his schooldays.

At his prep school, it had been 'Humpy' or even 'Humpty-Dumpty,' justified a little by his rather tubby shape. He had shed many a tear in the boys' cloakroom sitting alone on a bench near the boiler.

Fortunately, these nicknames did not follow him to his public school where masters and boys used surnames. Christian names were only used in private between intimate friends and Humphrey had no intimate friends.

Icke generated 'Spike' and this was his appellation for most of his school career. Puberty had not burnt off his puppy fat; he was still rather plump, but the nickname was ironic, in much the same way a tall boy might be called 'Tiny'.

There was a brief period in the Upper Fifth when he acquired a terrible new nickname. For no reason that he could remember, he had become engaged with Roman Catholicism. It didn't last but he had become quite fervent. It was a faith that seemed to offer solace to the solitary and a transcendent mystery in place of the platitudes of this world. He had begun to take instruction at the Priory of St. Sebastian on the edge of town.

All this was very secret and intense. It would have appalled his Presbyterian parents. At school, you could be a Buddhist, or a communist, and nihilism was fashionable, but to be RC was beyond the pale. So he said nothing.

Humphrey & Jack

However, the game was up one Tuesday evening at prep. He entered the classroom to hoots of derisive laughter. The other boys had discovered a devotional card of the Blessed Virgin Mary taped to the underside of his desk lid and, for a time at least, he became BVM. It was intensely mortifying.

A less feral atmosphere prevailed in the Sixth Form. Most of the time he became Spike again, though Pushbike and Hitchhike had their brief vogues and were forgotten.

At university people usually called him just Humphrey though it felt a bit less stigmatic. Although the institution was not as multicultural as it is now, there were still a good many foreign students so that, amongst people with names like Amandeep or Jean-Marie or Xavier or Xiang, Humphrey's name didn't stand out so much. He still hated it.

It occurred to him nowadays that his name might have been the root cause of many later miseries: his sexless loneliness, his cantankerous eccentricity, maybe even his neurotic noise aversion.

He once looked up the etymology of the name: Humphrey - Norman in origin, derived from 'Hunfrith', Old English, 'peaceful warrior'. His very name marked him out as a ludicrous oxymoron whose terms cancelled each other out.

In short, Humphrey felt he added up to - well, nothing very much.

4.   Neighbour

'How many times do I have to tell you?' Humphrey said. 'I do not want your mangy cat marauding all over my garden.'

'Aristotle is not mangy, Mr Icke,' said Mrs Bellingham with equal force. 'He is in the peak of health. And cats do not maraud.'

'Yours does.'

'Don't be ridiculous. You don't even know what the word means.'

'Give me strength. I was a university lecturer for thirty years, woman; of course I know what the word means.'

Humphrey & Jack

'Don't you "woman" me.'

'That's what you are, isn't it? A woman? Or are you some sort of camel? I confess there is some sort of resemblance.'

'Now you're just being rude.'

'I am trying to make you see sense. Your cat marauds: that is to say, it plunders, pillages and ravages. It makes forays into my garden and murders birds.'

'Well that's Nature, isn't it? That's what cats do.'

'Not in my garden they don't.'

'You can't stop Nature, Mr Icke. Who do you think you are? God?'

'"And the Lord God was walking in the garden in the cool of the day" and there was not a bloody cat to be seen. Genesis.'

'That's not true.'

'The first bit is.'

'Well then, it's blasphemy. You should be ashamed.'

'And not only does it maraud, it defecates in my flowerbeds. Or, since you have but a stunted vocabulary, it craps on my land. It crouches there like some kind of incubus; it looks at me defiantly right in the eye and it craps.'

'Incubus?'

'Oh, never mind. The point is, what are you going to do about it?'

'About what?'

'Angels and ministers of grace defend us. The cat. The bloody cat.'

'What do you expect me to do?'

'Keep it in. You love it so much. Keep it forever by you, next to your heart. Keep it indoors.'

'You can't keep a cat indoors.'

'Why not?'

'It's unnatural. It would be cruel. They like to roam.'

'Into my garden. They like to roam into my garden.'

'Oh, this is ridiculous.'

'Your malevolent cat likes to maraud into my garden.'

Humphrey & Jack

'Aristotle can't help it. Cats are territorial creatures.'

'But my garden is not Aristotle's territory. It is my territory. To Aristotle my garden is out of bounds; off limits; access is denied; trespassers will be prosecuted - and what sort of name is Aristotle for a cat?'

'He's a very clever cat.'

'He's a sly cat, I grant you. Look, if you won't keep it in, how are you going to prevent its unlawful entry on to my premises?'

'I say again, Mr Icke - and this is getting very tedious by the way - what do you expect me to do?'

'You could start by mending the fence. Look. Down there. The broken slat. That's where he comes and goes.'

Humphrey and Mrs Bellingham were having this conversation over the very fence through which Aristotle was wont to gain admittance to Humphrey's garden.

'Ah,' said Mrs Bellingham with a note of triumph in her voice. 'The slat sticks out on your side. It is your responsibility to maintain the fence.'

'Ah, but that is precisely where you are wrong, Mrs Bellingham,' said Humphrey, equally triumphant. 'I have checked the deeds and the responsibility lies firmly in your court, as it were.'

'Oh, now you're really being ridiculous. I don't have time for this, Mr Icke.'

'It's Doctor Icke, as you very well know.'

'Yes, yes, yes, whatever you say. Now, I shall wish you a good morning. I have things to do.'

And she turned to go.

'You can expect a solicitor's letter.'

'Good morning,' said Mrs Bellingham firmly and she went into her house.

'You haven't heard the last of this!' shouted Humphrey to a closing door.

***

Humphrey & Jack

Fifteen minutes later, Humphrey was at Mrs Bellingham's front door clutching a sizeable document. When she opened the door and saw him struggling to open the plan in the stiff breeze, she closed her eyes for a moment and sighed in frustration.

'What is it now, Mr Icke?'

Humphrey ignored her deliberate repeal of his doctorate and held up the plan of the properties.

'Look,' he said. 'Here is the fence. It is a boundary fence. Now, you may think it's a party fence, which we would have equal responsibility to maintain. But it is not so.

'If you look here, there is a mark that looks like a T on your side. Now to these surveyor chappies that means that the responsibility for maintenance lies with you.'

Mrs Bellingham was unimpressed.

'And if you look here…' she said tracing a fingernail down the diagram of the boundary fence, '…you will find another T mark on your side of the fence. So where does that leave you? It looks like we have joint responsibility and I don't propose to do anything about it.'

Humphrey hadn't seen the other mark but he was only mildly abashed. He had another card up his sleeve.

'Be that as it may,' he said, 'if you will not do something about it I really will have to involve my solicitor.'

'And he will laugh in your face,' she said. 'Honestly, Mr Icke, for a man of your education, you can be remarkably childish. All this fuss about a cat going about its business and a broken slat in a fence. You must have too much time on your hands. Now go away and leave me alone. I have plenty to do even if you don't.'

'Don't think this is the end of the matter,' said Humphrey, trying to fold the plans along their original folds. 'And I swear, if your murderous feline keeps on marauding in my garden, I will poison it.'

Mrs Bellingham slammed the door shut.

5. The Unremarkable Sex Life of Humphrey Icke

The only extraordinary thing about Humphrey's sex life was, he supposed, that he had never really had one. Everybody else had one, or that's how it seemed. He had spent a large part of his life living among males who talked about sex most of the time. He suspected that those who boasted most - about their conquests and the frequency and quality of their erotic contortions, and how they attracted women like moths to the light - were simply lying. But there was no way of proving it.

Their boasts were also diminished by the fact that, as far as Humphrey could see, most people seemed to find a mate if they wanted one. Of course there was the Darwinian fact that beautiful people attracted other beautiful people but that was not all there was to it. When Humphrey was forced by necessity to go into town, something he avoided whenever possible, it was clear that even the most ill-favoured were able to find a mate, to nest, and even to breed, though it's true that their offspring were usually pretty unlovely, if not actually hideous.

This was not always the case of course. It was eternally puzzling how a beauty could often be enthralled by a beast and an Adonis enter into matrimony with an unsightly crone. Wealth and power were aphrodisiacs, it was true, but that did not explain some of the more bizarre and ungainly pairings you saw in the High Street.

But the thing is: Humphrey didn't want a mate, and, what is more, he couldn't understand for the life of him why there was so much fuss about it. Why did this illogical passion take such control over people's lives? Why were people prepared even to kill each other, or to kill themselves, over this thing called love? Wars have been fought over women. Cities have been razed to the ground. Empires have fallen. Troy, Gaza, Carthage, Alexandria.

Humphrey & Jack

And yet, viewed objectively, it was all utterly risible. All this pother about putting a swollen bit of your body into a hole in someone else's anatomy. Ludicrous (and insanitary), Humphrey thought.

He had been put off it all from a very early age.

When he used to go to the Saturday matinées at the Essoldo as a child, he would, like all the other pre-pubertal boys in the stalls, make dire vomiting noises whenever there was a kiss on screen. Whenever the hero rescued the heroine, whether it be from Indians or aliens, it seemed obligatory for him to start snogging her. The cartoons were snog-free territory, of course, apart from Pepe le Pew, the amorous skunk. Humphrey hugely admired Superman's good sense in resisting the blandishments of Lois Lane in favour of duty and celibacy. On the way home, Humphrey would fling his gaberdine raincoat over his shoulders, doing up just the top button so that it was like a cloak, and 'fly' home, arms stretched out like his hero.

Later, when he was in the fourth form at school, there had been an incident involving another boy which still had the power to make him blush if he inadvertently recalled it. It had occurred at the Pocklington Street Swimming Baths and the boy was called Rupert Knight.

For a long time games afternoons were a torment to Humphrey Icke. In winter it was rugby, like it or not, but in summer he had had to endure the humiliations of cricket. His feeble eyesight made the game impossible for him. Though he wore spectacles with lenses so thick that they could have done service in a small observatory, he couldn't even see the sodding ball. If his side were in to bat, he would be put last in the batting order.

On the rare occasions he had to trudge to the crease he would be out first ball. If his side were fielding he would be sent out somewhere near the boundary where he hoped the ball would come nowhere near him. He had visions of himself with a skull split open after being struck by his invisible nemesis. Most of the time he would stand there beseeching the rain gods to send a deluge beyond Noah's imagining.

One spring in his second year, he was standing out there bored silly as usual. There was a line of cherry trees just beyond the boundary and a brisk breeze was causing a blizzard of blossom to swirl about him. Some wag had later written in the school magazine: 'Icke lounged at fine leg like a Dresden shepherdess - and was about as much use.'

What a relief it was then, when, in his O level year, Humphrey was allowed to go swimming on games afternoons. All the better that they had to use the nearest municipal baths because the school's pool was being rebuilt. Its Victorian original had become host to dubious forms of botanical life and besides, it was utterly freezing. Instead the boys were bussed into town and then left to their own devices because there were not enough games staff to supervise them off-site. They had been told that a master would call in on them from time to time to ensure that there was no untoward behaviour, but it never happened.

The town baths were Victorian too but had been carefully maintained. The pool was heated and so heavily chlorinated that your eyes would become irritated if you stayed in the water too long. Around the pool on three sides there were changing cubicles with half doors and above them a viewing gallery.

Usually Humphrey would find himself sharing a cubicle with Rupert Knight, not through choice, but because all the other boys had paired off naturally with friends and he and Knight were the residue, as it were.

On the day in question, Humphrey had come out of the water and returned to the cubicle early because there was horseplay starting up and he did not wish to be involved. He thought nothing of it when Knight joined him shortly afterwards. They grunted at each other in lieu of conversation and that was that.

Humphrey fished his watch out of his trousers and saw that there was a good while yet before the school bus came to collect them. He leaned on the half door to watch the others splashing and ducking each other or trying to pull each other underwater from below. It was a nuisance that his glasses kept misting up and he had to keep taking them off to wipe them. Knight was sitting on the bench behind him and Humphrey was vaguely aware of him fidgeting.

Humphrey & Jack

Knight was an anaemic-looking boy with pale eyelashes and thin fair hair that looked almost pink in certain lights. He was bullied cruelly by the other boys because of his prodigious member which they referred to as 'Knight's lance'. Humphrey had seen this appendage for himself because they were obliged to shower naked after rugby and, although he tried to keep his eyes straight like a guardsman, there was no avoiding the thing. It forced one to look at it. It hung out of the boy like some kind of alien contrivance or like a thick pink length of garden hose.

For the moment, Humphrey was hardly aware of Rupert Knight's existence. He was watching his classmates depth-charging each other from the side. One of them would clamber out of the pool, run along the side, leap into the air, and plunge into the water, arms around his knees, in order to cause the maximum splash and the maximum alarm to the other swimmers. It was dangerous but that was the point. Humphrey half-deplored and half-admired this athleticism. There was envy and self-loathing too as he wiped away the spray as well as the steam from his specs.

Suddenly, he was very much aware of Knight indeed. As he stood there, leaning on the half-door with his backside protruding into the cubicle, he found that Knight had moved up behind him and was stroking his bottom. The sensation was totally novel and not at all unpleasant. What was going on could not be seen by the others and this added to the strange frisson. He felt disinclined to object.

Nor did he protest when Knight began to peel down his wet swimming trunks till they were just a thin band halfway down his thighs. Then, quite slowly, his seducer's fingers traced around his hip until they closed on his growing erection.

And still Humphrey did not demur. He was in a sort of swoon.

It was only when Humphrey felt himself being prodded, first in the buttocks and then at the top of his thighs, that he realised that Knight was trying to penetrate him with…that thing.

He twisted in panic, slipped on the wet duckboard on the cubicle floor and banged his hip quite hard. Knight recoiled, bent forwards and sat down abruptly on the bench, trying unsuccessfully to cover his burning lance with both forearms. To no avail. There was just too much of it.

He burst into tears.

'You won't tell anyone, will you?' he pleaded.

Humphrey ignored him and struggled to his feet. His bruised hip hurt like hell. As quickly as possible, he wrapped a towel around his waist and removed his trunks under cover so as not to inflame his assailant's lusts any further. He dressed quickly and left the cubicle door wide open so that anyone who chanced to look could see Rupert Knight, stark naked, crouched over his subsiding apparatus and keening softly.

6.   In The Seven Stars

When Humphrey peeped round the door of the saloon bar of The Seven Stars the others were already there.

'Hail to thee, blithe spirit,' Garth Porter said.

'*Ave Domine*!' Hector Podowski said.

'Are we well met here?' Norman Retford said.

'We are well met,' Humphrey Icke said. 'What can I get you, gentlemen?'

'No, no, no, honey child,' Hector said in a grotesque parody of a Creole accent. 'I is in da chair. I'se just got a round in. What is you 'aving?' Humphrey asked for a pint of Doom Bar Ale.

At last they were settled. They called themselves the Evangelists because there were four of them. Not because they brought good news - quite the contrary. They had met on Mondays and Thursdays for some years in order to have a good whinge: Mondays, because it was pie and pint day, Thursdays because it was curry day.

They always convened in the same ritualistic way though now they would all be rather hard put to remember quite how their association began and how their rites developed. Norman and Humphrey were retired lecturers from Radcester University around the corner, Norman in English and

Humphrey & Jack

Humphrey in medieval history. Garth was a lecturer in Early Modern History and still in post. Hector was the Head of Art at the Grammar School across the road and, though he had been the last to join the fellowship, he had evolved quite naturally as their president.

'Now, my masters, I declare this meeting of the Radcester Guild of Backbiters and Defamers (Seven Stars Chapter) well and truly open, Hector Podowski, Chief Bitch, presiding. If there be any here present who know of any let or hindrance why Master Humphrey, Lord High Flinger of the Ordure and Chief Scourge, should not nominate today's target, let him speak now, or forever hold his peace'

'Just put the pies down, Cora, and stop trying to eavesdrop.'

Cora was the landlady who did as she was bid, putting the food on the table and returning to the bar. She replied to Hector with her middle finger.

'Humphrey, you have the floor.'

Humphrey began to tell them about the bees, the blackbirds, and the cat. And about Mrs Bellingham and the fence.

The Seven Stars was a proper pub. There was no juke box, no piped music, no television, no gambling machines. It had seen better days but it was clean if a little dingy. There was a whole set of those pictures of dogs playing snooker, with the bulldog about to pot black, and dogs playing poker dressed as gangsters, but there was no snooker table in The Seven Stars and the greasy pack of cards behind the bar rarely had an outing. There was an upright piano with a Habitat candelabrum on top which was sometimes used for a sing-song but, since none of them ever went there in the evenings, there was no problem.

Lunchtimes were usually very quiet. They might hear shouts from the public bar occasionally as a dart found its way into the bull or the triple twenty but usually they had the saloon bar to themselves apart from the regulars.

Today, there was only Flake the hippy who had been an Open University student for the last twenty-six years and who always brought his books into the pub, opened them, and then spent the afternoon staring vacantly into space.

While Humphrey began to dilate upon his loathing of Aristotle, the cat, Secondhand Sue came in, peeled off the fur coat she was wearing despite the summer heat and revealed her tacky gold-lamé top and the purple track suit bottoms which emphasised her ample rump. She took the port and brandy which Cora poured for her and went off to see what she could add to Flake's education.

'And she slammed the door in my face,' Humphrey concluded. 'I tell you, she is the misbegotten daughter of a camel.

'And I will get that cat. Verily I say unto you: I will get that diabolical cat.'

'Amen,' said the others.

'To the ducking stool with her,' said Garth.

'Burn the witch!' said Hector.

'The Egyptians used to worship cats,' said Flake.

'That, dear boy,' said Hector, 'is because they were probably as spaced out as you are.'

'Peace out,' said Flake.

'Leave him alone, you horrible old gits,' drawled Sue. 'You've just got it in for the younger generation, haven't you?'

'Younger generation?' Hector scoffed. 'He's nearly fifty. And you should have been in a sarcophagus millennia ago.'

'Fuck off,' said Secondhand Sue.

'Don't get me on to the younger generation,' Garth grunted. 'And would you mind not snooping in on other people's private conversations, by the way, you rancid tart?'

'Fuck off,' said Sue, with equanimity.

'Children, please!' said Cora from the bar where she was browsing the local newspaper.

'Even if you get her to mend the fence, the cat will come over the top,' Norman said lugubriously.

Humphrey & Jack

Hector was camp as a row of pink tents and had a line in acidic wit; Garth was rude and bovine but he had a rich vocabulary of abuse; Humphrey was an irredeemable misanthrope, but Norman was the true miserabilist of the party. His glass was always half-empty. He could see the silver lining fade from every cloud. For Norman, what was waiting at the end of the rainbow was a crock of dung. He liked to rain on everyone's parade.

In short, Norman was the catalyst in the coterie; he inspired the others to new levels of cynicism.

'He's right you know,' said Garth. 'If a cat wants to get in, it will get in. And it looks like it's marked your territory, old trout.'

'I will get it,' said Humphrey. 'I will get a gun and shoot it. I will devise a trap and strangle it with my bare hands. I will stuff gunpowder up its arse and send it up into the stratosphere!'

'To the music of the divine Georg Frideric Handel,' Hector cried, 'your pussycat will expire and burst into a thousand stars.'

'Poison would be an even more baroque ending,' said Garth. 'Quite impersonal. You wouldn't need to get your hands dirty. Just start feeding the cat and then one day, slip some rat poison into the meat. As deadly as a Borgia breakfast. It would just slink away and die.'

'Rather horribly,' said Norman.

'But Humphrey cares not a jot about that. Do you, Humphrey?'

Humphrey shook his head dreamily.

'There is, of course, a serious chance that you might poison a passing hedgehog, or a fox, or one of the birds you are striving to protect,' said Norman.

'A price worth paying, eh, Humphrey?' said Garth.

Humphrey nodded.

'Ah, but hearken unto me, my Lily White Boys,' said Hector.

The other Evangelists leaned forward conspiratorially. 'There is an easier way: if you get rid of the owner, the cat will go too! You only need to dispose of La Bellingham et voilà!'

Humphrey & Jack

'By God, you're right!' Humphrey cried, somewhat too loudly. 'That's it! I am going to poison Mrs Bellingham! Gentlemen, I am going to poison Mrs Bellingham!'

Secondhand Sue was listening to every word.

7. Day of Wrath

What Humphrey had not told the Evangelists about was his contretemps with the obnoxious youths in the park the previous evening. It was too shaming.

At the bottom of Humphrey's garden was a rusty little gate which gave directly into Alexandra Park. He could only assume that the original owners of his Victorian house had privileged access to the park because they had somehow contributed to its foundation and upkeep. Nevertheless, it still worked though Humphrey rarely used it. Consequently, there were clusters of stinging nettles at its foot which Humphrey had to beat away with his stick.

Just beyond the gate was an ornamental pool with an ornate fountain, at the top of which three little cherubs poured water from three little urns into a series of three basins, which increased in size, overflowing into each other and then into the pool. On quiet mornings, when children were at school, Humphrey enjoyed the tranquil trickle and splash of the water.

Of course, the soothing sound was completely wiped out by the pandemonium coming from the group of youths and their diabolical machine.

Just beyond the fountain there were stone steps leading down to the Long Parade. This is where the group were sitting with their backs to Humphrey. They were mostly boys, about six of them. A couple of girls were on a lower step facing upwards, dancing to the pounding beat. Humphrey assumed it was meant to be dancing although to him it looked like vertical epileptic fits.

Humphrey & Jack

The group were shadowy and sinister. The sun had set some time ago and there was little natural light left. The group were lit only by the orange glow from the Victorian lamp by the pool.

Humphrey banged his stick on the gate. He hadn't needed it to get down the garden. He had brought it in case things turned nasty.

'Will you please turn that bloody racket off!'

The fact that he had to shout meant that a diplomatic approach was impossible.

The boys' heads turned to look at Humphrey.

'Look, this is a residential area and it's late. Just turn it off, will you?' he shouted.

Two of the boys stood up, one dark, one fair, and stared blankly at Humphrey.

'I don't know what you think gives you the right to impose your barbaric music on others. Pack it in!'

The two boys came to the top of the steps and stood just beyond the edge of the pool. They continued to stare.

'Look,' Humphrey shouted, getting a bit hoarse now. 'Stop pretending you don't understand what I'm saying.' He knew that there was a sizeable Polish community in the area below the park, but, in his experience, they all spoke perfectly good English.

'People will be trying to get babies to sleep. This is just bloody selfish.'

As he ranted, the others came up the steps. They all appeared to be a few years older than the first two boys, though these two appeared to be the leaders. They now stood in a single line staring up, their faces lit fantastically by the orange lamplight. It was most intimidating. The music thudded on.

'Right!' said Humphrey. 'We'll see about this.'

He marched up the lawn with as much dignity as his poor knees would allow, hurled the walking stick the length of the hallway in a temper, and turned back into the house. There he opened one of the two tall sash windows that looked over the park, placed an occasional table by them and heaved one of the two large speakers of his hifi equipment onto it. From his extensive record collection he selected Verdi's *Requiem* and placed it on the turntable. He switched it on, turned the volume up to full, and lowered the stylus onto the third movement.

The four great crashing chords of the opening of the *Dies Irae* belted out of the speakers. Humphrey turned up the bass and went out onto the terrace to consider the effect.

His tormentors had gone back to their places on the steps. Humphrey could see the bobbing red lights of cigarette ends. He imagined that they were probably smoking something illegal. It came with the sort of people they were.

Verdi's apocalyptic setting of the terrifying medieval hymn swirled like a very tornado of hellfire, competing with the banal thudding from below. The drums thundered and the trumpets spake. Did the bastards heed the warning about the end of days?

The bastards did not. They turned up the volume on their equipment. Humphrey was almost hopping up and down in impotent rage at the dire cacophony when suddenly it was pierced by shrill repeated blasts on a powerful whistle.

Immediately, the heavy metal stopped while the Verdi segued into the staggering trumpet fanfares of the *Tuba Mirum*.

Mrs Bellingham was standing at the fence at the other end of the terrace.

'Humphrey Icke, are you mad? or what are you?' she shouted. 'Go and turn that off this instant!'

Meekly, Humphrey went inside and did as he was told.

When he came out again, the silence was prodigious. His neighbour was still standing at the fence. He went along his terrace towards her.

'Thank you,' she said. 'Now, would you kindly tell me what in heaven or hell possessed you to make such an unholy noise? You really are the most preposterous clown at times.'

Humphrey tried to explain that he had been attempting to shame the delinquents in the park into turning off their din.

'And you thought you would do that by compounding the clamour? For a university lecturer you can be remarkably obtuse. I'm surprised you even passed the eleven plus. If you pull off a stunt like that again, I swear I'll have you sectioned.'

Humphrey heard muted laughter from the young people below. They had packed up their things and were walking down the park. Their chatter floated up, softened by distance.

'I don't know how you can be so inconsiderate. And at your age too. Aristotle was absolutely terrified.'

'Ah now…' Humphrey began.

'Ah now, what?'

'I've been meaning to have another word with you about that cat.'

'I'm not standing here half the night discussing my cat with a maniac. Good night, Mr Icke.'

'Perhaps tomorrow?'

'I shall be out.'

8. The One-Eyed Highwayman

Humphrey was not troubled by assaults on his chastity again until he was in the Upper Sixth. He was indifferent to the excitement about sex which obsessed his peers who, at times, seemed to have no other topic of conversation. Their incarceration during term time reduced their in-turned world to classroom and dormitory, chapel and refectory, and to the games fields surrounding Rowntrees, their isolated school. The nearest village, Foxet, was two miles away through thickly wooded terrain. There was a pub called The One-Eyed Highwayman, a Spar grocery, a Chemist's and a Chinese Restaurant called The Four Happies.

The village was out of bounds officially but a blind eye was turned to the occasional sixth form excursion. However, housemasters periodically reminded their charges that the pub really was strictly forbidden and that the landlord had been asked to report any transgression to the school. Besides, the beaks said, there was a perfectly good bar in the Sixth Form Common Room and boys might drink up to five pints a week, though no more than two pints in any one night.

Eric, the landlord of the Highwayman may well have promised the school that he would report any wickedness but he was a pragmatic man and was more interested in increasing the contents of his tills. Temporary escapees from Rowntrees, or 'Colditz', as the boys called it, were warmly welcomed despite their being under-aged and Eric was happy to cash cheques for them if the allowance meted out by the school ran out.

The adventurers tried often to persuade Humphrey to join them but he pleaded too much prep or a meeting of the Model Railway Club.

'Staying behind for a wank, are you, Spike?' they would say and they would walk away shaking their heads and laughing. Humphrey tried to laugh with them but it didn't work. He only ever saw Foxet on cross country runs.

The convenient laxity in applying the regulations nearly came to an end when Paul Vermont and Andrew St. Clere got lost in the woods. These two were the gods of the sixth form. They had pop star good looks; they were academically bright; they were gregarious, sporty, fashionable, generous and witty. They were popular with the masters because they had the makings of that jolly British desideratum: the all-rounder. They were idolised by the boys because they were trend-setters and trail-blazers and risk-takers. They were, of course, senior prefects.

On the night in question, Vermont and St Clere finished supervising junior prep for their house. Finding the experience spiritually depleting, they decided that only in The One-Eyed Highwayman could they be properly refreshed. Consequently they set off down the narrow snicket that led to the woods.

Once in the pub they set about getting imperially drunk: so much so that the normally indulgent Eric thought that it was time they ought to be getting back to Rowntrees. He allowed them 'one for the road' and said they would be getting no more.

The moon that had seen them arrive had deserted the sky or, more probably, been totally obscured by a congregation of blackberry-coloured clouds. The narrow tracks worn in the sandy soil were no longer visible. Worse, the woodmen had been felling swathes of trees of late and in places the track had been obliterated when the timber had been dragged over them. Certain important and long-familiar junctions had simply disappeared. The fact that they were both plastered didn't help. Nor did the rain.

They were soon slipping on tree roots, wading through chest-high bracken, slithering into gullies, stung by nettles and scratched by brambles. But the most frustrating thing of all was that they kept arriving back at the same place.

A dirty yellow glow ahead, diffused by the rain and obscured from time to time by the foliage flickering across it, turned out not to be the lamp at the end of the snicket but Foxet railway station at the far end of the village. They were even further from the school than when they started.

Three times they ended up there. It seemed that whichever way they went they ended up in the same place. They began to argue and blame each other.

They did not reach Rowntrees until four-thirty in the morning, exhausted, soaked, bedraggled and thoroughly wretched. They were not greeted by the friendly lamp they had so yearned to see but by bobbing torch-beams. It was their housemaster, with a pair of colleagues and a porter, and a few senior boys.

Over the next few days there was a terrible fuss. St. Clere and Vermont were stripped of their prefecture and gated. The rules began to be enforced with draconian rigour. The Headmaster said in chapel that the recalcitrants' loss of privilege should be a grave warning to them and to the whole school. Defiance of authority would not be tolerated and their chastisement must act as a deterrent to all who might contemplate any comparable degeneracy. Their very public shame must be a lesson to the entire school community.

He was wrong. The boys were not shamed in the eyes of the school - they were deified anew. Not since two third-formers were caned for buying cigars from the woodmen had there been such a glorious scandal.

It was true that another legendary occasion, when three boys from the Remove had run away and lived wild in the woods for a week, constituted a bigger and better outrage. This was principally because police helicopters had had to be deployed to find them and the drone of the things above and around the school had left the pupils near hysterical with excitement. They were sacked, of course, as soon as they were found, though this did not diminish their heroic status.

But this was a decade ago and, even though the tale was still told, its glamour had faded somewhat. St. Clere and Vermont, however, lived and breathed and moved among them. They had come out of the woods dishevelled and still pissed and walked into a posse of masters. Some accounts that circulated later related that the masters had sniffer dogs. One version had it that Vermont had walked up to his housemaster, Mr Darwen, he of the leonine head, and said: 'I'm knackered and I'm going straight to bed so would you kindly fuck off?'

Not even if they had retrieved the Eagle of the Ninth from the soaking woods would Vermont and St. Clere have received greater veneration.

With great sadness Humphrey idolised them too.

An all-male establishment like Rowntrees builds up sexual pressure among the boys like a steam engine, from puberty onwards. A few find furtive means of relief with each other (a matter for shame if discovered). Most have to resort to the pleasures of the palm. There were few chances to meet females at all.

There were the school secretaries and matron, of course, but the latter looked like a pantomime dame and usually the secretaries only communicated with boys through a glass panel rather like a ticket office. Glimpses had been caught of a 'tasty' blonde who, according to St. Clere, was called Denise.

Unfortunately, she only fed his fantasies for a few weeks before she was sacked. Allegedly she had twice called out the Fire Brigade on false alarms because she liked the look of the firemen in their yellow uniforms and butch helmets.

St. Clere never revealed his sources and Humphrey, despite his private adulation, was sometimes a little sceptical about his heroes' boasts.

However, despite his doubts, Vermont and St Clere were to be in the vanguard of an audacious erotic revolution at Rowntrees.

9. Generation Zee

'What I hate,' said Garth, the week after Humphrey's account of Aristotle's behaviour, 'is when you're pootling along, minding your own business and you come round a bend and there's a whole posse of them ahead of you, riding two abreast, with their Lycra-clad arses in the air, presenting at you like over-sexed simians.'

'And you can't get past them for miles,' said Norman, who was unusually animated by the topic, 'because there are bends for miles and they won't pull into single file even though they know you're behind them. And you can't pull out to give them safe clearance in case you end up facing oncoming traffic.'

'Exactly. What gets me is that they're so bleeding self-righteous about it,' said Garth, 'with their invisible carbon footprints, and their zero emissions and how buggering healthy they are. Tofu-nosed bastards.'

'They come freewheeling down behind you on Burdock Hill,' said Norman. 'And you can't hear them until they've nearly mown you down. If you just stepped sideways a pair of ripped trousers is the best you could hope for.'

Humphrey & Jack

'Correctomundo,' said Garth. 'I have often contemplated sticking my umbrella in their spokes so that they fall in the path of a passing heavy goods vehicle. I'm just working on the physics of it.'

'There was one cycling on the pavement on Shelby Road last night,' said Norman. 'Even though there's a cycle lane. About half ten. No lights.'

The provocation for this particular spate of grousing was all too apparent to the Evangelists. With a great clattering of cycling shoes on the parquet in the vestibule, a seemingly endless troupe of cyclists was filing into the pub and thronging round the bar. Some of them were still wearing their helmets.

Humphrey, who had come in behind them, was put in mind of cyborgs or very large ants with their heads on backwards. He was late because he had tried to find Mrs Bellingham. He had wanted to have a row with her about something in order to regain the moral high ground after his humiliation the previous week. The subject was irrelevant; he just felt the need for a row. Aristotle would be a suitable pretext as usual.

However, Mrs Bellingham was not in, or, as Humphrey surmised was more likely, she was refusing to answer the doorbell. It would have to wait.

Cora spotted Humphrey hovering rather pathetically behind the chattering cyclists.

'What is it, Humphrey?' she called out. 'Usual? Doom Bar?'

Humphrey gave her a thumbs up.

'Go and sit down. I'll bring it over.'

Humphrey joined the others.

'Ah, Youth of Delight, come hither,' said Hector. 'Where hast thou been? You see how we are assailed.'

'What's going on here?' asked Humphrey.

'They're practising for the *Tour de Radcestershire*,' said Garth. 'Bloody ridiculous, if you ask me. *The Tour de Yorkshire's* daft enough but at least there's hills up there. You have to have hills to get dales, you know. But there's only one hill around here - and we're on it.'

Humphrey & Jack

This was not really true. Certainly, The Seven Stars stood near the top of Burdock Hill, a fairly steep incline which led up to the cathedral and the University Parks. And it was true that on the other side of the Rad valley the terrain consisted of no more than fat folds of agricultural land. To the north, however, there was some fairly rugged country and most of the Tour took place up there. But then, Garth was never one to let facts stand in his way.

'They're probably not good enough for the Yorkshire run,' Garth resumed, 'so they go in for this Mickey Mouse version instead. As we can see, there are just about enough narcissistic herberts in Radcester to make it worthwhile.'

'What are they doing in here, though?' Humphrey asked.

'Cora's put on a lunch for them up in the function room,' said Norman. 'They'll be going up there when they've got their beers. She's put on extra staff.'

There was no sign of this happening just yet. They stood in boisterous clusters round the bar after they'd been served with drinks. They were mostly men although there were some muscular-looking women amongst them.

'No sign of Sue and Flash then?' said Humphrey.

'Must have been tipped off, said Garth. 'The idea of Sue drooling over that lot's lunchboxes is not to be borne. Just look at that clown,' he said. 'No-one should be allowed to wear shorts that close-fitting in public. The Lycra's so tight you can't just tell his gender - you can tell his religion.'

'Well now, my fellow Carpers, Detractors and Slingers of Mud,' Hector intoned. 'I think it is becoming abundantly clear what the topic for today's Two Minutes' Hate should be.'

'NO!' said Cora, as she approached with Humphrey's ale. 'Don't you dare! Or I'll bar the lot of you. If you upset my customers with your geriatric moaning and whingeing, I'll show you the door, regular customers or not. Do I make myself clear?'

Humphrey & Jack

'As clear as your beer, dear Lady,' said Hector. 'Gentlemen, we have offended the Madonna of the Pies; we have affronted Our Lady of the Mushy Peas. She must be mollified. Turn we our thoughts to other subjects for our colloquies.'

'I have no idea what you're talking about as usual, but listen up, you miserable old sods. I have made a Lancashire Hotpot for the cycling gentlemen and ladies and red cabbage to go with it. There's plenty of it and you're welcome to some on the house later on…but only if you behave yourselves. Do you hear me?'

'We hear thee, O Patroness of the Pleiades, we hear thee and obey.'

Cora's Lancashire Hotpot was legendary.

'Silly buggers,' Cora said and went to talk to the cyclists.

'What then shall be our theme?' said Hector when he judged her to be out of hearing.

'I'll give you a theme,' said Humphrey.

'Speak, mad wag,' said Hector.

'Generation Zee,' said Humphrey. 'Let's talk about Generation Zee.'

'Zed,' said Garth. 'It's Generation Zed. What are you on about, you clodpole? We're not bloody Americans, praise to the Lord, the Almighty, the King of Creation. Amen.'

'Well, that's sort of my point,' said Humphrey.

'What are you havering on about?' said Garth.

'I'm afraid you've lost me too, Humphrey,' said Hector.

'And me,' said Norman.

'I am havering on about how Generation Zed, aka, the younger generation, or The Youth, as they call themselves, are wantonly debasing our culture by adopting the most vulgar expressions, manners and cultural fads emanating from trailer-trash America.'

'Steady on,' said Hector. 'That's a bit sweeping, isn't it?'

'Is it?' said Humphrey. 'Yesterday, I was addressed in the garage as "bra". Now "dude" I am used to, much as I deplore it, but "bra" as a mode of address I haven't encountered before. Of course, I am aware of the word as denoting a female undergarment used to support the bosom, what the French call a *soutien-gorge*. I had to have recourse to the Urban Dictionary - an invaluable resource by the way. I was put onto it by a student of mine when I complained that I had no idea what he was talking about much of the time. Apparently, it is spelt "B-R-A-H" and means "brother". You will find it in expressions like: "Ho, brah, we go beach?" It comes from Hawaii, it seems, and is even cooler than "bro".'

'How perfectly revolting,' said Garth.

'Why it should be thought "cool" to imitate the patois of ill-educated beach bums defeats me,' Humphrey continued. 'I believe some historian got into trouble on the telly recently for wondering why white boys wanted to imitate black ones. That's not it, though, is it? It's why prosperous, well-educated white boys want to imitate the culture of deprivation of under-educated American blacks.'

'Don't get me on to political correctness,' said Garth.

'I wanted to say: Look here, Mr Garage Cashier,' said Humphrey, 'I am not your brah or your bro or your dude or your matey. I would prefer "Sir" as a form of address. Actually, even nothing at all would be more acceptable. But there's no point, is there?'

'And what about "we go beach?"? It's not only ignorant; it's baby talk. Generation Z doesn't only adopt seedy vocabulary but also compromised grammar.'

'Bitches be like…' muttered Garth.

'Sorry,' said Humphrey.

'It's a Facebook trope,' said Garth. 'And unacceptable on three counts, i.e. every word.'

'I've never seen it,' said Humphrey.

'If you had more than three friends, you would have.'

'Eight,' said Humphrey, rather sniffily.

'What I can't abide,' said Garth, 'is someone coming up to the bar and saying: "Can I get a packet of crisps?" No, you bloody can't, you pseudo-American oik! You can't get them; the barmaid will get them for you. It's "may I have?" not "can I get?" you vulgarian. Actually, it's even worse when you get some fifty year-old hippy with a pony-tail doing it.'

'But, surely languages evolve?' ventured Norman timidly, as if expecting, not without cause, to be shot down immediately.

'We know that, you pink poltroon. We're academics all, are we not?' said Garth, inflating himself with outrage. 'Languages also deteriorate.'

'I'm sorry,' said Norman courageously, 'but linguists argue that no one language or dialect is intrinsically superior to any other. As long as communication…'

'Balderdash!' Garth erupted. 'Hot steaming bollocks! Leftie propaganda. I'm really surprised you fall for this stuff, Norman. At your age. Oh, I grant you that maybe, just maybe, changes in words or even grammar might not matter at all. But their cultural relevance does. You mark my words, the younger generation are importing a language which is leading to a wholesale debasement of our heritage, our *mores* and our values. Whatever happened to the urbane subjunctivity of our language? Whatever happened to English politesse?'

'Politesse is French,' said Norman.

Garth ignored him.

'Do you know, brethren,' he said. 'I took myself to The Bull at Ruckland-le-Moors recently for lunch with colleagues. Given their prices, one might have expected a civilised level of service. Or one might have hoped for it. Not a bit of it. Not a bit of it, I say. A pipecleaner of a youth with a forlorn attempt at a beard approached our table and said - barely attempting to disguise his affectation of boredom, by the way - "What can I get you guys?" You will believe me when I tell you, gentlemen, that were it not for my fabled powers of restraint, (*here, Hector raised his eyebrows at Norman*) I should have smitten him between the eyebrows, yea, and that mightily!'

'It's not so much the death of deference that I lament,' said Humphrey. 'It's the demise of courtesy.'

Humphrey & Jack

'Excuse me,' said Garth, 'but I do bewail the death of deference. I had to touch my cap to schoolmasters, walk on the outside of the pavement when with a lady, stand up on the bus for women and the aged, stand at the back of the queue, know how to address a bishop, et cetera, et cetera, and what happens to us as we grow old - we have the privilege of being addressed as "you guys".'

'Well, again,' said Humphrey, 'we have young people's dismal importation of the worst in American culture to thank. It's not just their cheapened vocabulary that depresses me, it's the shrinkage. Everything is reduced to "shit" and "stuff". In fact, along with "like" as the universal filler, and "totally" as the universal adverb, we have here the aggregate of the vocabulary of American youth. "So I'm like totally down on this stuff right now and shit." And British kids think it's cool. It makes me want to weep. My students were even beginning to write like this. One of the many reasons I got out.'

'Not only have they nothing to say, they lack the patience to listen,' said Garth. 'I bought some bits and bobs from a Tesco express this morning. The girl behind the counter was wearing so much make-up, I could hardly see her. In fact, she had daubed so much mascara on her eyes, I doubt if she could see me.

'"Do you want a bag?" she said.

'"No, thank you," I said. "I always bring my own."

'"Do you want the ten pee one or the five pee one?" she said.

'I don't know where Tesco gets these people,' Garth continued. 'Just not paying attention. Away with the fairies. Or at least she would have been if they hadn't buggered off and left her behind. Brain like a sieve. Actually, no. Have you ever thought what an inappropriate simile that is? At least a sieve lets some material through.'

'I believe it's all down to their beloved smartphones,' said Humphrey.

'You've got one,' said Norman.

Humphrey & Jack

'Yes, but for me, it's a convenience, not a necessity,' said Humphrey. 'I don't have to consult it every fifteen seconds. I don't hold conversations on it while I'm being served in a shop. I don't need to know immediately if a Facebook post is getting liked. I don't photograph every morsel I eat. I use it occasionally to navigate my world. I am not enclosed in a wholly virtual bubble which is hermetically sealed from the phenomenal world. I am not a slave.'

'Exactly!' said Garth. 'And if I were you, I wouldn't acquire any more so-called friends on Facebook. I made the mistake of accepting requests from some of my students. I could unfriend them of course - by the way, what kind of word is that: "unfriend"? - but curiosity defeats me. They live in a deeply unpleasant world, you know. There's trolling for a start.'

'Which is what?' said Humphrey.

'Essentially it means getting your victims to believe something outrageous so that they make fools of themselves by continuing the thread or, even better, sharing it.'

'But that can happen in real life, can't it?' said Norman.

'In yours? Probably all the time,' said Garth.

'A friend of mine was invited to a party,' Norman said, 'and was told it was fancy dress and he spent a lot of money on an ostrich costume. You know, huge rubbery feet and a feathery backside and a beak that opened and shut by pulling a string inside the costume. And, when he arrived on the doorstep, as an ostrich, everybody else was in dinner dress. Is that trolling?'

'Certainly,' said Garth. 'Incidentally, Norman, this friend wasn't you by any chance, was it?'

'No, it was not,' said Norman. 'I have never been to a fancy dress party in my life.'

'Very wise,' said Garth. 'Anyway, as I was saying, the Facebook generation are a miserable crew. They moan and they whinge to an extent that makes us four seem like prophets of joy.'

Humphrey & Jack

'What have they to whinge about?' said Humphrey. 'There never was such a privileged generation. Look at their nutrition. Young teen boys today are several inches taller than the lads of our day. And yet this is a generation that has a troubled relationship with food.'

As if on cue, Cora and Lucja, the Polish girl who helped in the kitchen, arrived with their lunch: four generous helpings of Lancashire hotpot, the potatoes brown and crisp at the edges, the lamb glistening and savoury and with each portion there was the customary pastry crust, cooked in the steam so that it was crisp on top but soft and juicy underneath. With this came red cabbage braised with apple.

'Now then, who's hungry? On the house, boys. Not that you deserve it. What've you grouchy gits been bellyaching about today then?'

'Oddly enough,' said Garth, 'we were talking about people who have a troubled relationship with food.'

'Well, I don't imagine that that will apply to you four, will it?' said Cora.

'No,' said Humphrey. 'It definitely won't apply to us.'

10. To the Woods

Despite the Head Man's fiendish warnings about breaking bounds and consuming beer, the school soon lapsed back into its slack disciplinary ways. It was not that the masters were liberal but that they were lazy. Like overfed guard dogs they would only rouse themselves to action if it were absolutely necessary. A signing-out book had been instituted but it was kept unsupervised in the library and forgeries and creative lies were very easy. So it was barely three weeks after their public 'shaming' that Vermont and St Clere sallied out to the Highwayman again, returning this time without mishap but with fabulous news.

They had met two 'corking' girls in the pub. The very word 'girl' sent singing electric fire through the febrile and frustrated loins of the listening boys. The girls had been really 'gagging for it' according to Vermont and after a few beers they had taken them into the woods and 'done it'. The boys' peers were impressed and jealous. They clamoured for details. Humphrey was consumed with awe and a vague premonitory terror.

Of course, the two godlings went back for more, time and again, until one evening during an early summer heatwave they returned with the astounding news that there were more girls available. There was going to be a midnight party in the woods and cherries were going to pop. What is more, there would even be a girl for Humphrey.

Humphrey was aghast. Under no circumstances was he going to be involved. He loathed parties anyway and on the one occasion he had been prevailed upon to attend one, back in Radcester during the Christmas holidays, he had spent the entire evening in the kitchen getting drunk, away from the crowds, the dim lighting, the hideous music, the atavistic dancing, the snogging and groping and fumbling that he knew was going on on the piles of coats in the bedrooms. He loathed the squeezing past people in corridors whose floors were sticky with spilt booze; he loathed the impossibility of conversation without having to shout; he particularly loathed the constant invitations to 'join in' all the compulsory jubilation.

And so Humphrey stayed in the kitchen with its bright strip lights, amid the four pint cans of Double Diamond and Watneys Party 7's (almost impossible to open and tasting of tin and cold tea) and bottles of vinegary Spanish plonk, anaesthetising himself with the contents of the half-bottle of Three Barrels brandy that he had brought himself and had secreted in the inside pocket of his tweed jacket, taking swigs when no-one was there, and drinking warm Liebfraumilch from a paper cup when the snoggers and dancers surged in to top up and wandered off again.

'But it will be out in the open air, Spike,' St. Clere had said, 'and there won't be any music at all. In fact, we'll have to be pretty quiet.' They were sitting in Humphrey's dorm. His room-mate had gone into hospital with a burst appendix and Humphrey was on his own and fair game.

'But there will be booze,' said Vermont. 'And lots of it. I've just had a cheque from my dad. We might even run to some champagne.'

Humphrey & Jack

'And we have found just the girl for you, Spike,' St. Clere said. 'Haven't we, Paul?'

'Oh Spike, she is just so right for you,' said Vermont. 'She's a looker too. In fact she's so fit, Andrew was thinking of taking her on himself, weren't you, Andrew? Only he's got Millie, and you know how jealous girls get of each other.'

Humphrey didn't know but he was beginning to have just the vaguest suspicion that he was being set up. He continued to resist.

'Well. I call it pretty ungrateful, Spike,' said St. Clere, 'after all the trouble we've gone to to find you a woman. You'll end up in a monastery, you will, eaten up by guilt because you've been beating your meat in your cell after Vespers because you've got the hots for some pious little novice. Because, I think you must be queer, Spike. Do you think Spike's queer, Paul?'

'I think he must be, Andrew,' said Vermont. 'Are you queer, Spike?'

'No,' said Humphrey. 'At least, I don't think so.'

'He doesn't think so,' Vermont said, 'but I think he must be a shirt-lifter. Turning down a girl like Janet. Spike, she has beautiful…'

And he supplied the absent noun with the universal gesture of caressing with his splayed hands two imagined globes. The globes in this case were quite sizeable.

'Beautiful,' said St. Clere. 'So sad. Such a waste.'

And they went away shaking their heads in mock sorrow.

However, on the night itself, Humphrey was persuaded and this is how it happened. He had been in a kind of torment for days. He wasn't at all interested in the sexual stuff itself but, like any boy of his age, there was the urge to prove himself. Part of him writhed in fear at the twin possibilities of rejection and failure but part of him wanted to get it over with so that the teasing about his sexuality would stop. There was also the fact that he genuinely wanted to please and impress the two luminous paragons who were the idols of Roland House. And then there was the vodka.

Humphrey & Jack

Shortly before the hour appointed for the escape into the woods, the idols tapped on the door of his room. His roommate was still in hospital. There had been an infection and complications. The word 'septicaemia' had been whispered. They came bearing a bottle of vodka and a carton of orange juice.

'We thought we might just have a little drink with you before we left,' said Paul Vermont. 'Don't want you to miss out entirely on the jollifications. Of course, you'll be missing out on the main event as it were. Janet will be so disappointed.'

St. Clere took over Humphrey's only armchair while Humphrey himself sat on the edge of his bed and Vermont mixed the drinks at Humphrey's desk. He had found clean mugs on the windowsill. That was good. Humphrey would not see what he was up to. He poured moderate measures of vodka for himself and St. Clere and topped them up with juice, but in Humphrey's mug the vodka was much more concentrated.

'To Youth and the Fair Maids of Foxet!' Vermont said, and they clinked their mugs and drank.

'That's not too weak for you, is it, Spike?' he said with a wink at St. Clere which Humphrey couldn't see.

'Oh no, no, no,' said Humphrey. 'It's rather good in fact.' The first sip had made him sneeze but now he was swigging manfully. How very good of these chaps to do this for him, he thought.

'Want another?' said Vermont.

'Well, why not?' said Humphrey expansively.

'Why not indeed?'

After a third, Humphrey felt absolutely splendid and declared that he was inclined to come along to the woods after all.

'Got to go for a slash first,' he said. 'Need a clear head.'

'Mission accomplished,' said Paul Vermont when Humphrey was out of the room.

'Mission accomplished,' said Andrew St. Clere.

Humphrey & Jack

Half an hour after 'lights out', five of the upper sixth members of Roland House tiptoed along the back corridor on the ground floor. The lights were out in their housemaster's flat and he had no doubt laid his golden mane on his pillow immediately after his rounds. Exit and return entries had been forged in the signing out book in the library.

Simon Plumb, a future engineer, had disabled the fire alarms and fixed the fire exit doors so that the crash bar was noiseless and they could be opened again from the outside without being obviously propped ajar.

They slunk along the snicket silently apart from the faint tinkle of bottles in carrier bags and did not begin to whisper excitedly until they were well clear of the school's security lights.

There was a huge full moon in a clear sky crusted with stars and the sandy floor of the wood was fretted with moonlight falling through the leaves. There had been exceptionally fine and hot weather for the last fortnight and the old paths through the trees had quickly re-established themselves. It was still quite warm. Occasionally an owl would utter its screech of complaint and a bat flit past their heads. The very air seemed erotically charged.

After about a mile, they could see the red points of lighted cigarettes ahead and hear the low murmur of female voices punctuated suddenly with a scream of laughter quickly suppressed.

When they got to the junction of three paths which had been appointed as the trysting place, St. Clere and Vermont enjoyed a prolonged and theatrical smooch with their doxies whilst the others stood by lamely. Humphrey felt a recurrence of the distaste he had felt as a small boy whenever snogging had occurred on the screen at the Essoldo. It was something to do with the fact that otherwise rational people seemed to lose all control of themselves, and it was also to do with the fact that the behaviour of females was wholly imponderable under any circumstances.

In any case, when the ostentatious mating display was over, St. Clere made the introductions in a courtly sort of way.

Humphrey & Jack

'Miss Janet Dobbs, may I present Mr Spike Icke? Spike, Janet - Janet, Spike.'

Humphrey felt they ought to shake hands. He also felt it was quite absurd.

Although the moonlight was bright it was not possible to discern much of Janet's features. Her face and her glasses were large and round, her nose and her mouth were tiny, and her face was framed squarely by black hair cut in a severe fringe and cut off at the sides on a level with her chin. The effect was that of a wooden clothes peg doll. Though she wasn't pretty, she wasn't decisively ugly either. Humphrey supposed she was what used to be called homely.

Her figure was short and slender but all reports of the epic volume of her breasts fell far short of the truth. Even in the chequered penumbra of the trysting glade Humphrey could see that they were prodigious and quite disproportionate to her otherwise petite form. They looked as if they were striving to escape from her tight black jumper in order to establish independent life elsewhere. It was as though, if she were to fall forwards, she would bounce straight back up again. Humphrey felt intimidated by them.

The girls had arranged some logs to form a kind of triangular seating area and the paired group sat around as if for some sort of game. Vermont opened champagne. They passed it round drinking directly from the bottles.

When it was Humphrey's turn, the bubbly took him completely by surprise. It was warm and volatile and the first swig hit the back of his palate and went right up his nose. He sneezed all over Janet's black jumper.

In a panic, he began patting her breasts with the clean hanky his mother had said he should always carry. They moved about in a most alarming way and Humphrey was again put in mind of alien life. She can't have been wearing a bra.

'O my God! I'm sorry. I am so sorry. O my God!' he said.

'Oh, don't worry,' Janet said. 'Such things happen.'

Humphrey & Jack

Surely not, Humphrey thought. Surely her breasts were not routinely anointed with Krug? That was nonsense.

Janet kindly but firmly removed Humphrey's flailing hands.

'It's all right,' she said. 'It'll dry quickly. It's quite thin.'

There was some talk of lighting a fire but St Clere dismissed the idea.

'I don't think so,' he said. 'It's been roasting hot for ages, The wood will be bone dry. We don't want to risk a forest fire. In fact, we don't want to draw attention to ourselves at all. In any case, we aren't staying here, are we, my sweet?' He turned to the inevitably ravishing girl beside him. 'We have business elsewhere.'

He tugged her to her feet and off they went, arms around each other's waists, following a narrow trail that snaked into the undergrowth.

'Have we got anything to drink other than Champagne?' said Humphrey.

'Here!' said Paul Vermont and he threw Humphrey a bottle of vodka still about a third full and he, in turn, led his stunning paramour through the trees to their own private bower.

Humphrey took a long pull on the vodka, coughed a little and felt immediately braver. He saw that the other two couples were involved in some intensive necking and wondered how they had learnt what to do. It seemed to come naturally and unbidden. Humphrey felt that he wouldn't even know where to start.

By and by, Janet took his hand and pulled him to his feet. He took a quick final gulp of the vodka, put the bottle down, and let her lead him into the darker depths of the man-eating wood. Down into a little gully they went - she footsure - he slithering a little, but just about managing not to fall. There was a narrow gurgling stream, silver in the moonlight, and they followed it a little until they arrived at a little dell where the stream swelled into a pool before chuckling on its way down the wood further on. A little breeze had sprung up and the trees sighed deeply at what was about to happen.

Humphrey & Jack

'Isn't this spot lovely?' Janet said. 'I found it this afternoon and thought it would be just right.'

Ye gods! thought Humphrey. She has everything planned.

Humphrey now learnt the purpose of the roomy carpet bag she had been carrying and which had puzzled him somewhat. From it she pulled a large travel rug which she spread on the bank of the stream and lay down. Tenderly, she drew Humphrey down to her.

Humphrey's apprehensiveness was a little subdued by the alcohol.

As she moved in to kiss him their spectacles became entangled. Janet took hers off and put them in the bag behind her and turning back to Humphrey removed his glasses and handed them back to him. He folded them and fumbled them into a trouser pocket. It crossed Humphrey's mind that she might perhaps look more attractive without her specs, but without his, of course, she was just a pale blur, so he would probably never know.

On a second attempt their noses got in the way but on a third she locked onto his lips like a limpet. It was not at all what Humphrey thought it would be like. It wasn't like wine, or honey, or cherries; Janet's mouth tasted unaccountably of egg.

Then she thrust her tongue into Humphrey's mouth which he didn't like at all. It wasn't what he had expected. It was an invasive, writhing, reptilian, foreign object and he began to feel quite alarmed. There were the noises too, a kind of squelching. He found his mind running on suction cups and that hooked siphon thing that the dentist puts in your mouth to drain saliva.

With her mouth still glued to his she groped for Humphrey's hand and thrust it up her jumper and onto one of those remarkable breasts. Again he was surprised - it was not hot as he had imagined but quite cool. Again, images came unbidden to his mind. He thought of white blancmange, on a plate. Or of a display in a tripe shop window he had seen on a visit to an aunt in Bacup.

What made it worse was that, without disengaging their mouths, she was now breathing heavily through her nose and making noises like some kind of engine. Finally, she wriggled a little and put the palm of her hand flat on Humphrey's groin. He jumped and everything about him went rigid apart from the organ that Janet was handling. He realised he was very drunk.

He untangled himself and got to his feet, ignoring Janet's pleas and protests. He unfolded his specs and fumbled them back on. Then slipping and floundering and falling he made his way back to school.

He encountered no-one on the way.

11. Lancashire Hotpot

'By the Lord Harry, this is good!' said Garth, shovelling in the hotpot as if he expected to have it stolen from him at any moment. He put down the speed at which he ate to having been a public schoolboy. 'You can always tell a public schoolboy,' he would declare. 'Your public schoolboy will not only eat the apple; he will devour the core.'

Humphrey thought this was a poor excuse for Garth's porcine table manners. He had been to public school too but didn't remember being made to starve. In fact, because the last meal of the day in the refectory was 'tea' at five-thirty, the boys were allowed to claim 'rations' at the kitchen hatch for a snack later. Some could be seen returning to their dorms clutching whole loaves, great wedges of cheddar and jars of peanut butter.

'How do you do that?' said Humphrey.

'What?' said Garth, his mouth still full.

'Eat at that rate,' said Humphrey, who liked to savour his food. It was not the first time they had had this conversation.

'How do *you* do that?' said Garth.

'What?' said Humphrey.

'Eat so slowly. That'll be cold before you're halfway through.'

'There must be a golden mean,' said Hector wanting to avert the pointless bickering into which the topic usually turned.

Humphrey & Jack

'At least I don't eat like Generation Z,' said Garth. 'They eat with their hands, usually both hands, so that there is no physical intermediary between food and mouth. Thus was that abomination, the burger, created. Your burger is the product of greed and idleness and the root cause of childhood obesity.'

'Oh, come on,' said Norman. 'That's pushing it a bit, isn't it?'

Garth ignored him again.

'Either that or they sit, elbows on the table, dangling a fork vertically in one hand, their other hand propping up their cheek, turning the food over and over, until, after two mouthfuls, they push it away.'

'Where does it come from, this dysfunctional attitude to food?' said Humphrey. 'Why do we suddenly have so many bulimics and anorexics and vegetarians and vegans and pescatarians and so many with glucose intolerance and lactose intolerance? Where does it all come from?'

'I blame Princess Diana,' said Garth, although to be fair he blamed most of the ills of the modern world on Princess Diana. 'Her obsession with colonic irrigation went to her brain (maybe the pressure was too fierce) and thence to the nation's collective mentality.'

'That's in pretty poor taste,' said Norman and was ignored again for his pains.

'Food is bad!' Garth intoned. 'It will make you very fat if you even look at it. Shun it. You must be as thin as a stick. And ill. It is *so this week to be, like, totally ill*.'

'Exactly,' said Humphrey. 'And you must, above all, feel guilty about everything to do with food. And so must everyone else. There are now aisles in every supermarket labelled FREE FROM: free from milk, from wheat, from gluten, from eggs, free from flavour, free from nutrition, for all I know.'

'Yes but,' Norman ventured, 'there are lots of people who…'

'And do you know,' said Humphrey, 'do you know: the aisle is always just beyond the bread and the eggs? And I come to it after I have chosen my lovely crusty bloomer and my Waitrose 'very large' free range eggs, laid by British Blacktail hens, with the union jack on the box and the British Lion stamp on the eggs, and I see this anaemic food - and I feel guilty.'

'But there are people...' Norman tried again.

'And I resent feeling guilty,' said Humphrey.

'It's all about body image,' said Garth, 'the magazines and the telly bombard them with images of the ideal body and they fall for all this advertising guff. From top to toe there are commodities to make you beautiful for just a few quid. It's easy: just avoid food.

'The Internet is fizzing with it. Young girls encourage each other to starve themselves until they are wraiths, and very, very poorly.

'And not just girls. Boys are at it too. Pumping iron, living on protein shakes, competing about the number of times they repeat an activity: "How many more forced reps you doing?" "I'm getting beasted today - give me more." "Bro, do you even lift?"'

'Sorry,' said Norman, 'you've lost me now.'

'It doesn't matter' said Garth. 'It's all down to the same thing with this generation: their intolerance, their rudeness, their disaffection, their ingratitude - it all boils down to the one thing: narcissism.'

Hector, who had said nothing for a long time now, slammed his knife and fork down on the table.

'What's the matter with you?' said Garth.

'Nothing. Do carry on, please.'

'Bit touchy today, aren't you?'

'Please, please, don't mind me. Do continue.'

'Bloody hell,' said Garth, 'I was only voicing an opinion. No need to get shirty.'

He recovered after a moment's pause during which he waited for Hector to explain. Hector didn't oblige.

'As I was saying before that little tantrum...'

He waited for a reaction. There was none.

Humphrey & Jack

'As I was saying, we are talking about narcissists who are not only intolerant about nosh, but about everything. They preach freedom of speech, but they're into no-platforming. They are all shibboleths and bandwagons.

'Say "fracking" and they quiver with rage. They communicate in a hashtag world. Say "climate change", say "global warming", say "carbon footprint", say "recycling" and blame us "baby boomers" for everything that's wrong with the planet. How dare we steal their futures?'

'Exactly,' said Humphrey. 'We didn't have to pay tuition fees. We could afford a mortgage. There were jobs just waiting for us, weren't there? We had it easy and now we're in the way. Some of us have the audacity to carry on working despite huge youth unemployment. How dare we? We don't even have the decency to die on time. We're the bed-blocker generation.'

'Right,' said Garth. 'Such hatred, such envious hatred. And why? Because they have bought wholesale into the idea of entitlement. Our generation had a taste of real austerity just after the war. There were genuine shortages of basic things for a number of years.'

'I just about remember sweet rationing,' said Humphrey.

'Sweets are hardly basics,' said Norman.

'It's symbolic,' said Humphrey. 'Even kids went short.'

'It stands to reason that as the economy improved and the so-called baby-boomers began to breed they wanted their children to have everything they'd missed out on.'

'I wasn't particularly deprived,' said Humphrey. 'And neither were you.'

Garth was rather put out by the interruption.

'I'm talking generally, though the professional classes were hard hit too. You just wouldn't be aware of it as a child.'

'Apart from the sweets.'

Garth gave Humphrey a contemptuous look.

Humphrey & Jack

'Anyway,' he resumed, 'successive generations spoiled their children to the extent that by the time we get to Generation X, the teenagers of the Nineties, luxuries have become necessities. These kids look to America and its conspicuous consumption and they think: I'll have some of that. Madonna's *Material Girl* sums up the *Zeitgeist*.'

'And that's the era of The Children's Act, isn't it?' said Norman.

'Nineteen eighty-nine, I think you'll find,' said Garth. 'Oh, that was a pretty piece of work, a pretty piece of work indeed.'

'What do you mean?' said Norman.

'Oh, don't get me wrong,' Garth replied. 'Youth must be served. Children must be protected. They are the future. We must nourish our children physically, mentally and spiritually, if the human race is to survive, although sometimes, I have to say, I'm not even sure that I'm in favour of that.'

'But?...' Humphrey suggested.

'But. This was a very poorly drafted piece of legislation. I'm talking about child abuse here. Very nasty business certainly, with a very nasty history, but to presume in favour of the child in every respect was madness. Children are vindictive little buggers at the best of times. Create a situation where every brat with a grudge against a parent or teacher will be believed and you recreate the Hitler Youth, or think *1984*, where parents have no authority over their children, because they've joined the 'Spies' and Big Brother encourages them to grass up their mummies and daddies.'

'Oh, come on,' said Norman. 'You're overstating the case surely?'

'Come on yourself,' said Garth. 'Overstating the case? Am I? Am I? There's probably not a teacher in the land who's not afraid of that summons to the Head's study because some malevolent little gnome has bleated 'he touched me' just to exercise its power.'

'But what if he did?' said Norman.

'What?'

'Touch him.'

'Who?'

Humphrey & Jack

'The child.'

'What child?' said Garth exasperated. 'What are you on about now?'

'What if the teacher really did touch the child?' said Norman. 'Are you saying nothing should be done about it?'

'Of course I'm not, you witless wankpuffin,' said Garth. 'Do you think I'm some sort of pervert or something? But there has to be proportion. Too often these cases become witch hunts with the police and the press colluding. The hacks want their story and the police want their convictions and other little gnomes come crawling out of the woodwork with tales of unwanted cuddles and gropings. And why not? Lots of attention and the power to ruin a grown up? What fun!'

'Will you stop that! It's really annoying.'

This was to Hector who, for some time now, had been drumming with his fingertips on the table. Hector stopped but continued to glare at Garth who ignored him.

'Who or what are Generation Y then?' asked Norman, hoping to diffuse a growing tension in the air.

'Ah, I know that one,' said Humphrey. 'They are the millennials, the generation that came of age around the millennium.'

'Correct,' said Garth. 'And even more spoilt than their parents. They are the "rave"'generation, the "ecstasy" generation, indulged to the last degree and completely out of control. And now they're approaching forty, they haven't grown up at all. They have a hissy fit if the price of quinoa goes up. Their children are their best friends. "When people see my daughter and me together, they can't tell us apart." Of course they can, you silly mare. You're the one whose tan is from a bottle. If you want to hide that cellulite, why wear the same clothes as your daughter?'

'And the men have "man caves",' said Humphrey, 'and read *The Guardian* and worry about global 'ishoos' and they're into personal grooming and moisturiser and *Top Gear*.'

Humphrey & Jack

'Exactly!' said Garth. 'And Generation Y begat Generation Z and, do you know, Humphrey, me old fart, what is the most abysmal thing about Generation Z?'

'Go on,' said Humphrey.

'Sex!' said Garth. 'Their attitude to sex. This is a generation that sexualises everything. At it like rabbits all the time, quite indiscriminately, without responsibility or decorum or even shame. Don't you think so, Humph?'

Humphrey was suddenly as inarticulate as if someone had just asked him after the health of Schrödinger's cat. He did not want to think about this subject.

'They send each other pictures of their genitals,' said Garth. 'They watch pornography on their phones. They have "friends with benefits".'

'What's that?' said Norman.

'It means friends with whom you have casual sex but no meaningful relationship - because this lot don't know how to have a relationship. They're broken. They don't know how to connect. Sex for them is about immediate gratification. The object doesn't matter. Nor the gender very much.'

'It does all seem so very vulgar,' said Norman.

'Indeed,' said Garth, 'and it is all so very empty. They are nihilists. They have been led to believe they can have everything: sex without commitment, privilege without responsibility, degrees without work, jobs without effort, and they are doomed to disappointment.

'They toy with death, they make a cult of it: the world has let them down; they threaten to leave it.

'Utter and unbounded selfishness.'

There was a long pause. Garth looked very smug.

'Have you quite finished?' said Hector at last.

'I couldn't say,' said Garth. 'Probably not. I could go on for ages.'

'Please don't. Because I've had enough,' said Hector.

Humphrey & Jack

'Are you sure?' said Cora who had come to clear the plates and had only caught the last few words. 'There's plenty more if anyone wants seconds.'

The cyclists came clattering down the stairs and the bar was filled with their noise.

'Thank you, Cora. It was delicious,' said Humphrey, who was beginning to think it was high time someone said something positive.

12. University

Radcester University was one of the new universities created in the midtwentieth century. It had formerly been a satellite college of a much older institution but was awarded full university status in 1957. Rapid expansion began in the sixties and it was referred to in the press at the time as a 'plateglass university'. Everything about it vaunted its brash newness.

If you walk up the hill from Radcester Railway Station you will come to the cathedral which Humphrey always judged to be an architectural mess. A perfectly serviceable eighteenth-century parish church had been accorded cathedral status in 1928. No-one in Radcester had been entirely sure why. A vainglorious expansion of the building began with the addition of huge gothic transepts and a new chancel, quite out of keeping with the original building in both size and style. The old church now became the nave and the high altar was removed and a plain stone table built under the crossing, so that 'the presence of God was amidst His people and communion at the centre of things' as the leaflets in the porch proclaimed.

Worse and worse, during Humphrey's first year at university a kind of geodesic dome was built on top of the crossing. It looked as if an alien spacecraft were squatting there, to refuel perhaps. What it was supposed to represent was anybody's guess. It is true that from the inside, it was supposed to represent the celestial canopy. Each glass panel was blue and there were golden stars scattered randomly about the dome. Around the edge there was an inscription in gold lettering which read: THE HEAV-

Humphrey & Jack

ENS ARE TELLING THE GLORY OF GOD. Humphrey thought it looked like a kind of cheap and unscientific planetarium.

The university was also a hotchpotch of incongruous architectural styles. At its core was a large and handsome Georgian house which had formerly been the home of an impecunious viscount. The parish church had once stood within its grounds. The house was built of Portland stone and was of impeccable Palladian proportions. The viscount had been unable to afford its upkeep and it had been bought by an established Midlands university as a subsidiary college, specialising in teacher training and the technical and business skills associated with Radcester's principal industry, paper making.

The estate came with acres of parkland and permission was somehow obtained for the building of the university's various faculties. Administration was in the old house - admin always gets the nicest accommodation. The students' union was cunningly developed from a complex of stables, but the rest was spanking new, steel and glass and concrete.

On one side of a courtyard was the engineering faculty. The side of the building facing the court appeared to be one colossal pane of glass so that you could see all kinds of gleaming machinery on different floors. The science faculties were in a building that looked like a neat pile of Jenga bricks with each brick representing a different department, soil sciences at the bottom, astrophysics at the top. The arts faculties were in a kind of smoked-glass cube, built around another little court. Again there seemed to be a kind of hierarchy at work: archaeology and anthropology were in the basement and above that sociology. The English faculty faced into the court, modern languages was on one side, classics and theology on another, and history was at the back. History of art was in a kind of rarefied atelier perched on the top.

Because the history department faced south, the offices and seminar rooms were almost unbearably hot in summer and arctic in winter.

The most remarkable feature of all this ostentatious modernity was the university library which was underground, stretching under the principal walkways of the campus. These were set with squares of toughened glass which provided the library with natural daylight. Looking up, scholars could see the shapes of peers and colleagues walking above, and looking down, students and lecturers could see the desk lights of the scholars below. There was a legend that when it was built the glass paving was originally clear but when the designers recognised with horror that the workers in the library might be able to see right up the skirts of female students, the glass was hurriedly replaced with frosted alternatives. Humphrey thought this story must be apocryphal, generated by the over-heated fantasies of male undergraduates.

Newness was not the reason Humphrey chose Radcester as his place of tertiary education. Humphrey deplored newness. Going to university was, and is, for most young people, an important rite of passage. It is a bid for independence, a loosening of the apron strings, a flight from the nest. Humphrey wanted none of that. Radcester lay fifteen miles north of the family home in the village of Lidpole. Though he lived in halls for the entire three years of his undergraduate career, he was close enough to escape to the security (and obscurity) of home whenever the highly pressured life of university became too much.

It was not that he missed his parents or was particularly close to them. In all truth, his academic mother got on his nerves with her distrait manner and her pedantic little ways. His father was a colourless retired civil servant who always seemed confused and embarrassed about having a son and spent most of his time in a shed at the bottom of the garden writing articles about birds for *Radcestershire Life*. When he saw Humphrey about the house on one of his son's periodic retreats from Radcester, he would smile and nod and pass by, as you do with an acquaintance you haven't seen for years and whose name you can't remember, though you feel you should. His mother would talk at the supper table about the lives of cronies of hers, as if Humphrey knew them intimately, even though he had never met them and sometimes never even heard them spoken of before.

Humphrey & Jack

Even so, all this was preferable to the boisterous conviviality of life in Radclyffe Hall. There were three large Edwardian houses for males and three modern blocks for females. Humphrey was in Strachey House, an imposing Edwardian villa which once belonged to a paper manufacturing magnate back in the town's heyday. It had been divided up mostly into rooms for two or three students. Here, Humphrey had been lucky, having been allocated an attic bedroom for one student only. The garret had obviously once been occupied by a lowly servant of the household and it was poky enough.

But to Humphrey the solitude was precious. He would not have to share his time and space with any of the rugby-playing serial Lotharios who seemed to constitute the rest of the house's occupants. This was so important to him that he elected to stay in the same dingy room for the entirety of his undergraduate career.

Not that he could escape the noise. As soon as his peers returned from lectures, the racket would begin: *The Rolling Stones*, *Led Zeppelin*, *Black Sabbath* and *Deep Purple* - bands whose names intrigued him in inverse proportion to the anguish they caused him. The diabolical thumping and banging and wailing would issue from the rooms below, but not - thank God - not from above. His peers would wander from room to room leaving doors open so that *The Who* would be competing with *Judas Priest* or *The Grateful Dead*. Humphrey imagined that the dead must indeed be grateful to escape this pandemonium.

When Humphrey began his career as a lecturer at the same university, he learnt from one of his students that a band had emerged called *Def Leppard*. Humphrey liked to imagine an aged leopard extended along the bough of a tree wearing pink national health hearing aids.

The only other person in the house who liked classical music was a theology student called Nathaniel Peke and there was a short period where he would come up to Humphrey's 'sky parlour' as he called it and they would listen together to Telemann or Bach. Alas, poor Peke suffered from particularly pungent body odour which became intolerable in the confined space and Humphrey ceased his invitations.

There was an event which Humphrey came to dread. Each term each house would host a party planned by the students and sanctioned, rather grudgingly, by the warden. The houses were each paired with one of the women's blocks, so, for instance, Strachey House was paired with the Sackville-West Block. Since women's liberation had, as yet, made little impression on Radcester, the girls would prepare party food and the boys would arrange the drink.

Humphrey did not attend the parties in the other houses, of course, but when in the late October of his freshman year it was the turn of the Strachey/Sackville-West bash, there was no escaping it. A thirty-six gallon barrel of beer had been ordered from the local brewery and arrived three days before the event. It was racked on its side in the kitchen and left to settle. The day before, it was tapped and there was, of course, a certain amount of 'necessary testing' carried out. This vast quantity of beer would be supplemented, on the night, by plenty of wine and spirits. Humphrey thought that at least he would be able to get very drunk in order to numb the pain.

On the day itself, the drinking began as soon as the boys got back from lectures. The girls were not due to arrive, or rather, not permitted to arrive, until nine o'clock. They would come bearing rice salad and sausage rolls and little cubes of cheddar cheese and grapes on cocktail sticks stuck into a potato wrapped in foil to form a hedgehog. There would be several Victoria sponge cakes which no-one would eat and which would end up trodden into the carpet. Meanwhile, the time from seven to nine was for the 'lads'. Humphrey was filled with a deep sense of foreboding.

The proceedings started in the House Common Room, which had been the very grand drawing room when the building was a private residence. There was a huge mullioned window with armorial bearings in the panes at the top and a vast baronial fireplace which was now forever cold. All the cheap and functional furniture had been cleared out because this room was already designated for dancing later and disco equipment with huge speakers stood in the corner. The cheap terylene curtains were drawn and strings of fairy lights were turned on. Later there would be psychedelic disco lights.

The evening began with a series of drinking games with forfeits. The boys sat in a large circle on the floor. The standard forfeit was to down half a pint of beer in one. Later the penalties became nastier. A persistent offender against the rules had to surrender his shoe and the master of ceremonies urinated into it. Another was obliged to stand in the fireplace for fifteen minutes, stark naked, with his head up the chimney. Humphrey could not see for the life of him why this was fun but he was relieved that the only forfeits he was subjected to were of the quaffing kind.

The next entertainment had been the subject of subdued excitement amongst the young men for some time. One of them had got hold of a porn film on a trip to Amsterdam and this was to be shown in Room One. This had once been a reception room and now normally housed three students. Their beds and other furniture had been removed and stacked in an upstairs corridor and the room turned into a makeshift cinema. The sub-warden of Strachey, Dieter Lenz, a very young junior lecturer, had decided to turn a blind eye to this, knowing that the Warden would not put in an appearance until just after nine, when the event would still be relatively docile. By then, the 'cinema' would be showing Asterix films, something of a cult at the time.

As a result of his sexual apathy, Humphrey expected to be underwhelmed by this but he did not want to make himself conspicuous by opting out. What he did not expect was that the others would be disappointed too. The film was played without sound but some wag had decided to accompany it with eerie music by Philip Glass which gave the action a strange disjunctive quality.

Two blond Nordic blokes with beards and long hair copulated with two buxom girls of Mediterranean aspect in a variety of athletic positions. There would be a few thrusts and then the couples would disengage and then rather mechanically adopt a new position. After a few more thrusts, the process was repeated. Neither of the men showed the least enthusiasm for the business and the girls looked sulky and, frankly, bored. The audience quickly became bored too and, one by one, they wandered off to congregate around the beer barrel and wait for the girls. Humphrey had thought it rather odd that the flesh and blood girls had been forbidden to appear until later, so that the boys could ogle two-dimensional black and white images. A complete mystery. But then, what did Humphrey know about sex?

The girls arrived on time and the Warden came with them. He was a scholarly little Belgian with wire-rimmed spectacles and startlingly white hair who did his little round of duty as quickly as possible. He accepted a cheese straw and half a paper cup of Mateus Rosé, beamed at everyone, watched a little bit of *Astérix le Gaulois* and disappeared, leaving the real supervision to the subwardens, who were not much older than the students.

Now, the party really began to take off. Humphrey sank through strata of misery. The common room was full of heaving sweaty bodies; the pulse of the music was feverish; the swirling disco lights, bilious. You couldn't hear the film for the music: the dialogue was in French but the subtitles were in some Scandinavian language with umlauts everywhere and the exotic letter 'ø' in abundance.

Already there was rice salad all over the food table in the imposing entrance hall and cigarette ends in the potato salad. There appeared to be some kind of orgy going on in the huge cupboard under the stairs. In the kitchen, the floor was sticky with spilt beer. A girl in a kaftan with beads in her hair was sitting on the draining board crying softly.

There was no point in going up to his room to escape the deafening hubbub. The racket seemed to be shaking the building to its very foundations. Humphrey felt a desperate need to get outside. He squeezed past the necking couples in the corridor leading to the back door.

Outside, the autumn air was crisp and cold. In those days, you could see stars and among them there was mighty Orion, the hunter, wheeling about the sky. Radclyffe Hall was set in a part of the University estate which had been developed into the University Botanical Gardens. Humphrey kept on walking until the noise had abated to a numb throb. He climbed a knoll atop of which a cedar spread its majestic boughs and turned to look back at Strachey House which now lay below him, its windows pulsing with coloured light. It was good to be alone in the near darkness, or so he thought.

A woman's voice at his shoulder made him jump.

'So you hate it all too, do you?' she said.

13. Windbag

'You conceited windbag,' said Hector to Garth when Cora had cleared the plates and disappeared into the kitchen, 'you puffed up bullfrog, you arrogant dirigible, you insufferable know-all!'

'Crikey!' said Humphrey.

'I say, hold your fire,' said Norman. This was not banter. This was serious stuff. 'What brought this on?'

'He hath no children!' Hector declared, pointing theatrically at Garth.

This was true. In fact, of the Evangelists, Hector, for all his queeny affectations, was the only one who was married with children. He had two teenage daughters and there was a baby on the way.

'What's that got to do with anything?' said Garth, unmoved by the abuse. 'Just because you've sired a brood - and I'm sure they're perfectly charming and exceptions to the rule - that doesn't mean that *Homo* isn't becoming less and less *sapiens* with every passing generation. The young of the current generation is horribly solipsistic.'

'You have described a pastiche of youth,' said Hector, abandoning his high camp posturing and speaking very directly to Garth. 'You have taken every cliché from the gossip of old women in the doctor's waiting room, from old men on the bowling green and from the rancorous pages of

Humphrey & Jack

The Daily Mail and you have created a pantomime chimera and called it Youth.'

'But I thought the whole point of our meeting was to grizzle about the blemishes of the modern world?' said Humphrey.

'But not this,' said Hector. 'Not this rubbish.'

'Are you going soft in your dotage, you old fairy?' said Garth.

'Rather that than cold and brittle with hypocrisy like you. Were you never young, gentlemen?' said Hector. 'I can quite believe that *you* were not, Garth. I imagine that you were born fully inflated with your own self-righteousness. How your mother must have suffered giving birth to that swollen head.

'But Humphrey, Norman, be honest. Were you any better as teenagers? Isn't selfishness the name of the beast? Isn't it part of his becoming an individual? Isn't that what his hormones are telling him to be?'

'What do you mean?' said Humphrey.

'Well, let's take Garth's peevish little caricature apart shall we? I charge that it is hypocritical because every complaint he makes against the young was true of our generation when we were green, and might even be universally true. It's the details that are different, not the generality.'

'Tosh and flapdoodle!' said Garth.

'Are you going to give me a hearing?' said Hector. 'I listened to your catalogue of platitudes.'

'I'm not stopping you,' said Garth.

'You can't. Now, where shall I start? Ah yes, language. Of course, Norman's right. It is constantly changing. The mistake is to apply a value judgement. Every generation invents its own argot and the thing is that it's *meant* to annoy the shit out of the generation before it: parents, teachers, policemen. It's *meant* to include the tribe and exclude the trespasser. Like prison slang, like gay slang.'

'I still maintain that the current lot have invented a pretty ugly lingo,' said Garth.

'But, that's it. That's my point precisely. You're meant to hate it.'

Humphrey & Jack

Garth grunted.

'Remember how the grown-ups hated it in the days of mods and rockers and greasers and then hippies?' said Hector. 'When girls were chicks and guys were hip and you had all the gear: your Jesus boots and your embroidered flares and your grandad vest and your hessian shoulder bag with tassels. When you used to hang with your mates and things were fab or heavy or a drag or cool or funky. And you'd say: *right on* and *lay it on me, man* and *far out, dude*. And the establishment, the teacher and the preacher, loathed it because they were square. Remember that?'

'I didn't talk like that,' said Humphrey.

'No, Humphrey,' said Hector. 'I don't suppose you did.'

'What's a grandad vest?' said Humphrey.

'It's not important,' said Hector wearily, 'you're probably wearing one. Have a look when you go to the loo.'

'I had flared trousers,' said Norman. 'Just the one pair. And stacked heels. They were terrible. I kept going over on my ankle. Bright green, they were. When I was at university.'

Three pairs of eyes were trained on him in wonderstruck disbelief.

'Did you wear flowers in your hair, Norman?' said Hector.

'No,' said Norman, 'I didn't. But I did grow it quite long. When I had hair, of course. It was blond. Below the ears. It was parted down the middle and people called me "Dougal" because they said I looked like Dougal from *The Magic Roundabout*. Quite a cult programme that, when I was an undergraduate. People said it was inspired by drugs, you know.'

Garth stood up.

'Well, chaps, while we digest that fascinating, if unnerving image, I will get the beers in. It is my round, isn't it?'

'It has been for some hours,' said Hector, 'but you were so happy sounding off, nobody liked to interrupt you.'

'Same again, is it?' Garth said, ignoring Hector's jibe. The Evangelists nodded and Garth went to the bar.

Humphrey & Jack

'Make way! Make way!' he could be heard saying as he pushed through the mêlée of cyclists. 'Emergency pints! Regular coming through! Life and death! Make way!'

'You won't make him change his mind, you know,' said Humphrey.

'I thought you agreed with him,' said Hector.

'Well, yes and no,' said Humphrey.

'Humphrey, dear Humphrey,' said Hector, 'Humphrey child, if you insist on sitting on the fence all your life, you are going to get a very sore bottom. You have been arguing, along with Garth the Pachyderm, that Generation Z is degenerate.'

'Well,' Humphrey hesitated. 'I think there is something wrong, but I think maybe they're not to blame!'

'Ah,' said Hector. 'Now we're onto something.'

'Well, if you think about it,' said Humphrey.

'I hoped you would.'

'If you think about it…'

'Go ahead. Think. Think.'

'All this stuff about image…'

'Yes, yes…'

'All this stuff about body image, and clothes, and physique, and the psychosis about food, it's not really narcissism, is it?' Humphrey was thinking it through as he spoke.

'Go on.'

'Well, teenagers aren't really creating these images, are they? They might fall for them, but they don't create them, do they?'

'No, Humphrey, they don't create them. Who does, Humphrey? Who does create them?'

'We do!' Humphrey cried. 'Well, not exactly us, but adults. Adult wealth and the power of advertising.'

'Exactly!' said Hector.

Humphrey & Jack

'What are you leftards up to?' said Garth, returning with a pint in each hand. He had somehow suborned a rather confused cyclist into bringing over the other two pints. 'Conspiracy theories, is it?'

'You might call it that,' said Hector. 'I wouldn't.'

'Humphrey has been suggesting that Generation Z are manipulated by adults,' said Norman. 'Through advertising.'

'Bosh!' said Garth. 'It is young smart-arses who create the imagery that seduces them.'

'But who are their paymasters?' said Hector. 'Old gits, like us. No, not quite. Wealthy old gits. Unlike us. And, he who in one hand holds the purse strings, with the other makes the marionettes dance.'

'I say,' said Humphrey. 'That's rather fine.'

'Thank you, darling.' said Hector. 'I am an artist, you know.'

'Yes, well, that's all very well,' said Garth, 'but you don't address the principal issue in the decline of the species.'

'Which is?' said Hector.

'Which is this lot's degrading obsession with sex.'

'Oh, Garth,' said Norman. 'Oh Garth, the hypocrisy.'

'What?'

'Everyone in the faculty knows what a predator you are.'

'What are you talking about? Predator?'

'Every new girl in the office, every female lecturer and undergraduate is going to be subject to your blandishments at one time or another. Isn't that right, Humphrey?'

'Well, yes, it's true that the gossip does go that way,' said Humphrey, though he looked and felt very uncomfortable.

'Oh, come on, gentlemen,' said Garth. 'I'm only being friendly. A bit of sweet talk to make the long day pass by. A bit of social lubrication. Nothing more.'

'Well, I think you need to be more circumspect in the current climate. Your "lubrication" could so easily be misinterpreted. It could be considered inappropriate, Garth. You could be "lubricating" yourself out of a job.'

'Never,' said Garth, 'never ever, was there such a weasely word as "inappropriate". Don't give me that politically correct poppycock. I hate it. I hate it as I hate cancer, lefties and the French.

'Oh, I know what's brought this on. It's envy, that's what it is. Just because the ladies take a shine to me, despite my years, you talk about 'inappropriate' behaviour. There is such a thing as charisma, you know. Oh, sorry…maybe you don't.

'Pure envy. And no wonder. Look at you three. Barren lives. No kinetic energy in your relationships. Two of you are…spinsters…and Hector, with your cosy, bourgeois little marriage, where is the ardour in your existence?'

Humphrey thought this was very nasty, Norman looked taken back but Hector appeared unmoved.

'Now, what do you think of that, Humphrey?' said Hector.

'I don't have an opinion,' said Humphrey.

'Norman?'

'I thought it was gratuitous and disagreeable,' said Norman.

'So did I,' said Hector, 'so I shall ignore it. But I will say this: I do not find the younger generation any more narcissistic than we were. I do not find them selfish: they are idealistic with a tendency to jump on bandwagons, but so were we. They seem to care about the unfortunate and about the environment, perhaps more than we did. Their attention span might appear short to us but they inhabit a different affective world. They respond to some social stimuli more slowly but others astonishingly rapidly. If you saw my daughters multi-tasking on a lap-top and a phone at the same time, you might get an inkling. Does that make them more shallow? I really doubt it.

'I really suspect that the big differences between generations are illusory. The young always feel that they are ripe to come into their inheritance; the old stubbornly insist on living. But you know, my fossilised friends, I think that what really is different is how we see each other through the lens of the media and especially the social media where vices are amplified and virtues too. There's a thing called "virtue-signalling" and it's looked down upon but perhaps it's a form of honesty?

'So now, Humph of my Heart, come down from thy fence and tell me what you think.'

'I think you might be the real historian here, Hector,' Humphrey said. 'The question of whether human nature is universal or not is at the heart of the history of ideas.'

'Fancy that, and me but a plebby schoolmaster and dauber of mediocre canvases,' said Hector, rubbing his hands like Uriah Heep. 'And a bourgeois to boot,' he said, giving Garth another theatrical glare.

'There is, however, one area where I am not amenable to persuasion or mollification,' said Humphrey, 'Generation Z is noisy, cataclysmically noisy. They are addicted to noise. It is their element. Their noise is a stench in my ear.'

'Are you sure it's not just you,' said Garth.

'What do you mean?' said Humphrey.

'Well, you do seem to be pathologically hypersensitive,' said Garth. 'There might be a clinical reason. If I were you - which mercifully I am not - I would put my ears in a sling and trundle along to the quack.'

'What makes you think that modern kids are more addicted to noise than we were?' Hector asked.

'Maybe they aren't. I blame electronic amplification. They could screech a Concorde out of the sky. Remember Concorde? The sonic boom?'

The others nodded. Hector mimed taking off a hat and holding it to his breast.

'Goodbye Concorde, you were so beautiful. *Au revoir, Concorde. On t'aimait*,' he said.

'Listen to this,' said Humphrey, and he related the War of the Noises which had taken place recently, omitting, of course, the drubbing he had received from Mrs B.

'Bastards,' said Garth.

'Not on,' said Norman.

'Not to be endured,' Hector agreed.

'Who's for bread and butter pudding?' said Cora, suddenly appearing. 'Plenty left. With custard.'

'I couldn't eat another thing,' said Norman.

'I have to get back to school,' said Hector.

'I could probably squeeze in a moderate slab,' said Garth.

Humphrey thought he might try some too.

He also thought he might get Doctor Bell to take a look at his ears.

Nothing to lose.

14. The Party in the Park

The Annual Horror was approaching and Humphrey decided he was not going to put up with it any longer. He would up sticks and away!

It had begun four or five years ago. Humphrey was just washing up the breakfast things in the kitchen at the back of the house and wondering, not for the first time, if a dishwasher might not be the one thing that would improve the quality of his life. That and the titanic rupture in space-time that would allow him to travel back and dis-invent the electronic amplifier.

Ruefully, he concluded that the dishwasher was the more viable option, and thought that after years of dithering, he might actually get a chap in to do some measuring up.

Suddenly, he was aware of a man saying very loudly and very near:

'ONE TEEYOO.

'ONE TEEYOO.'

He threw the tea towel onto the draining board and went into his sitting room. The man wasn't in the house: he was in the park.

Humphrey & Jack

'ONE TEEYOO.
'ONE TEEYOO.'

Then a series of chords at brain-frying volume on an electric guitar followed by shrieking feedback so obscenely loud that he thought all his teeth might fall out.

He rushed out onto his terrace and beheld the ghastliness that was being prepared for him.

The lovely domed bandstand with its ornate sugar-candy pillars painted in red and green and white must have been the venue for some delightful concerts in Edwardian times. The good people of Radcester (pronounced 'Radster' by the way) would have been seated in deckchairs: ladies with parasols and gentlemen in striped blazers and boaters, and children in sailor suits. At the pavilion by the conservatory, demure young ladies with black skirts and tiny white frilly aprons would have served tea and buns and ices. And the band would have played Elgar marches and waltzes by Sousa.

That was not what today had in store.

Banks of amplifiers and other electronic nightmares were being set up in the bandstand and the old 'one-teeyoo' was repeated from time to time. Why was that affected pronunciation practically universal, he wondered.

The percussion instruments of a gamelan were being set out on the grass and small children were being allowed to play on them. Humphrey intensely disliked the music of these Javanese orchestras. Even played professionally the clanging and clattering were like applied tinnitus. However, the cacophony resulting from letting small children loose on the instruments was unimaginably hellish.

Somehow, a homunculus had acquired the mallet for the tam-tam and its odious parent was holding it up so that it could strike the enormous gong. The resounding crash made him cover his ears and howl aloud with misery. The reverberations must have travelled for miles around. Birds rose from the trees in panic. Humphrey imagined people running for cover, cars colliding, and vessels out at sea sending out distress calls. He went indoors and upstairs.

From his study window he could see stalls being set up. There would be hot dogs and burgers and the sweet reek of fried onions. There would be ice cream and candy floss (or cotton candy as young people insisted on calling it). There would be bubble machines and balloon animals. There would be stalls selling banal daubings and all sorts of tat masquerading tweely as *brocante*. The tents of the Philistines were spreading across the plain.

Some sort of rehearsal began around ten-thirty: more one-teeyoo-ing, searing shrieks from electric guitars, random bass thuds and then caterwauling from a female voice. It was a nasal whine that was accompanied by twanging, dissonant chords. It was dire. The eldritch screams of foxes mating in the night were like a Bach air compared to this.

At around eleven, the 'gig' began in earnest. Humphrey went from room to room in utter wretchedness trying to escape the din. It was impossible.

At noon, the decibels increased to an industrial and probably illegal level. This was what was known as 'heavy metal', Humphrey supposed. He wished some benign god would cause some heavy metal to fall from the sky onto the bandstand. Preferably, several thousand tons of it.

Unable to bear it any longer, Humphrey went into his throbbing bedroom, changing his carpet slippers for shoes, and went out to The Seven Stars.

Though the pub was the only refuge he could think of, Humphrey hated it on a Saturday afternoon. It was usually quite full, and full of the people he preferred to avoid. The corner normally reserved for the Evangelists was taken over by women shoppers from Primark and Poundland. They held up their purchases to bleats of admiration or shrieks of laughter which made Humphrey shudder. There were braying men wearing carnations, obviously sinking a few pints before the boring bit at the Registry Office down the road. The groom was being urged to drink more than was prudent given the solemn undertaking he was about to make. Why were people of this class incapable of conversation without shouting at each other?

Humphrey found a table near the entrance to the lavatories and tried to concentrate on *The Daily Telegraph*.

There were two dogs, a pug and a vicious little Jack Russell which snarled and bared their teeth at each other and would occasionally rush to combat. Reaching the extent of their leads, they would be jerked back to their owners making choking noises, only to resume a low growl moments afterwards.

At least there were no cats.

Soon after one o'clock, a huge throng of Radcester Rovers football supporters came in - men, women and boys. Most of them were wearing the team's strip of vertical green and black bars. Humphrey thought this the height of vulgarity. It was understandable that young boys might want to emulate their heroes but for grown men with advanced beer bellies and arms like Sunday joints to make spectacles of themselves by wearing this gear seemed to him to be silly. Vast quantities of lager were being consumed by the men while the women opted for obnoxious drinks like fruit flavoured cider and that abomination: non-alcoholic beer.

The noise level grew and grew. But even this was preferable to the Party in the Park.

For three or four years, Humphrey had endured this, but this year it was going to be different. Apprised of the annual nightmare on Twitter, he decided to escape for the entire weekend. He booked a cottage at Carlton-le-Sands, just fifteen miles from Radcester.

When he heard of it, Garth Porter was scathing.

'What is the point of going on holiday just fifteen miles away?' he sneered. They were in The Seven Stars the week before Humphrey was due to escape. 'How much is this costing you?'

'Just under two hundred pounds. And it's not a holiday. It's a retreat.'

'Bloody stupid, if you ask me,' said Garth.

'Well, I'm not asking you, so shut up about it. I wish I'd never mentioned it.'

'But, it's crazy. Look, my little tub of botulism, what is the point of spending two hundred pounds to go fifteen miles?'

'That is the point, you lardy oaf: it is bad enough that I have to fork out two hundred pounds just to avoid the crassness in the park without my having to fork out money for petrol.'

'I still think you're a damn fool,' Garth said. 'Why don't you just get some ear plugs?'

'Because concrete would not block out the racket.'

'Did you know,' said Norman Retford wistfully, 'that drummers and bass players sometimes wear special ear plugs so that they're not deafened by their own music? I saw it in a Facebook ad.'

'The utter bastards,' said Humphrey.

'Well, I think it is perfectly heroic of you, Heartface,' said Hector Podowski. 'To think of you voyaging all the way to distant Carlton-le-Sands makes me feel faint with admiration.'

'There's nothing there, you know,' said Garth. 'Just a few beach huts and a pub.'

'Exactly,' said Humphrey.

'It'll probably rain,' said Norman.

15. Gin and Jazz

Garth was right. There really wasn't very much at Carlton-le-Sands at all. There was a pub and five or six houses and that was it. Humphrey realised he must have passed along this way before on the route to Quadrant Regis, the quaint but touristy resort three miles up the coast. But Carlton was so nondescript, it hadn't even registered with him as a distinct place.

His satnav told him he had reached his destination as he approached the pub but there was nothing like the photograph of the cottage on the booking website anywhere to be seen. He pulled into the car park of the

Humphrey & Jack

Duke of Gloucester and went inside. It was totally deserted and he had to ping a bell on the counter in order to get service.

The landlord, a very young man with round gold-rimmed spectacles and a samurai topknot appeared down the stairs at the back of the bar. His black jeans were so absurdly tight they looked as if they had been painted onto his thin legs. His T-shirt bore the image of a black man with a bow-tie playing a saxophone and the legend: 'Charlie Parker'. Humphrey ordered a crab sandwich and a small glass of dry white wine and asked for directions.

There was a lane down the side of the pub, the landlord said, which would take him down to his cottage, just over a quarter of a mile away.

Humphrey finished the *Telegraph* crossword, begun that morning, as he ate his sandwich. It was quite delicious. He wondered how the owner of this place, which had obviously seen better days, could possibly make a living. He had noticed, whilst standing at the bar, that it had a phenomenal battery of different kinds of gin. Not a lot of point if nobody ever came in.

He found the cottage easily enough. The lane had high hedges on either side and descended quite steeply. He hoped very much that he was not going to meet anything coming the other way. As he drove down he encountered a thick sea mist or 'fret' which reduced visibility to just a few yards. He came quite soon to what seemed a more open space and he could distinguish a low white fence to his left. Getting out of the car, he saw that the fence had a little gate and that he had found his cottage. The mist was quite warm.

He had been lucky with the let. A late cancellation meant that he had been able to rent it at a bargain price. He had no need of its two bedrooms but he was glad of the spaciousness of the place and its tasteful furnishings. The kitchen was very well-equipped with a washing machine and dishwasher, fridge freezer and shiny black coffee machine. He would not have much use for these things. He thought ruefully that it would be pleasant to come here for a longer period of time but that the cost would probably be prohibitive.

Humphrey & Jack

As he unpacked, the sea fret began to lift and Humphrey could see the extent of his domain through the windows. The cottage was on one side of a little cove. It had a small, well-kept garden accessed through French windows, with a wooden table and chairs. In the middle of the table was a large parasol. Steps down from the concrete platform where his car was parked led through rocks onto a little beach which curved around the bay. On the far side, there were, as Garth had said, half a dozen blue and white beach huts nestling under a cliff. The tide had just turned and the gently curling waves were slowly creeping up the sand. Humphrey could see from the line of shells and drying seaweed that the high water mark nearly came up to the rocks around the little platform on which his cottage had been built.

At present, the cove was quite deserted. Perhaps the mist had deterred tourists.

Humphrey made a pot of tea and took it out to the garden along with some papers he was working on, a monograph on 'Symbolism in Medieval Royal Banquets' for the *Journal of Medieval Social History*.

This was blissful. It was quiet apart from the screaming of gulls and the gentle swish of the waves as they unfurled on the wet sand. Traffic was light on the coast road above and the occasional growl of a car did nothing to disturb Humphrey's tranquillity. The air smelt good and clean.

And it did not rain, as Norman had predicted. The last of the mist evaporated to unmask a deep blue sky.

Even when a group of boys in swimming trunks came down the coastal path on the other side of the bay and began to play with a Frisbee in front of the beach huts, their cries and laughter were attenuated by the sea breeze which made the sound seem much more distant. He watched as they rushed into the sea and began to wrestle with each other. Their bodies flashed in the sunshine as they leapt and twisted and splashed.

Normally, such a display would have made him reflect on his own aged carcass, but today he was content to watch their enjoyment without jealousy.

Humphrey & Jack

They left after a couple of hours and as they set off back up the coastal path, towels over their shoulders, one of them turned and waved at Humphrey and the others followed suit.

To his surprise, Humphrey found himself standing and waving back. A moment afterwards, he felt a little embarrassed.

He imagined he might have snoozed a little when later, judging by the position of the sun, he thought it might be time to think of preparing supper. Though no mean cook, he didn't intend to spend time in the kitchen this weekend. He had done a supermarket shop on the way out. There was cold roast chicken, a slab of Comté cheese, and plump, glossy cherries. He assembled a garlicky salad, spooning in scoops of ripe avocado and dressing it with a homemade vinaigrette which he had brought in a screw-top jar. Then he washed the cherries and tipped them in a bowl, warmed a baguette a little and sliced it into a basket, and took everything outside.

He had brought some good wine with him and decided on a Juliénas he had picked up in France in the spring. He poured a little and savoured it. This was good, so very good. He thought it must have been a very long time since he had felt so completely at ease. Overhead, gulls wheeled and squawked; much higher, parties of swifts chased about the sky at high speed in a wild career, sometimes swooping suddenly down towards the cottage and back up again. Grasshoppers churred in the gorse behind him. The sun seemed to lie on a bed of gold and purple cloud some way above the horizon.

Then suddenly:

'ONE TEEYOO.

'ONE TEEYOO.'

Humphrey nearly hurled his wine glass down the beach. What the hell was this? A line from King Lear slunk into his head: 'As flies to wanton boys are we to the gods…' The irony was indeed tragic. Had he fled the Party in the Park only to be followed by this insufferable row?

Humphrey & Jack

Several notes on a hugely amplified bass guitar boomed through the evening.

Silence.

Some twanging chords, a brief riff on the drums and brushed cymbals.

Bubbling arpeggios on an alto sax.

Silence.

'ONE TEEYOO.'

Humphrey wanted to rush into the sea and be consumed entirely by the salt deep. He held his temples in frustration.

Silence.

Then a jazz combo began to play and a husky male voice sang out: 'It don't mean a thing if you ain't got that swing...' It began at considerable volume and then, miraculously, was modified downwards until it ceased to be a torment and became...not unpleasant.

Then silence again.

As he ate the chicken salad something clicked with Humphrey. There had been roadside boards as he approached the Duke of Gloucester, and there had been posters in the pub itself. GIN AND JAZZ, they said. July 15th, nine till midnight. And there were all those varieties of gin behind the bar - and today was July 15th. He began to feel very apprehensive.

As he started on the cheese and cherries, and the sun was sinking into the sea, setting the horizon on fire, the first set began:

> *Summertime, and the livin' is easy.*
> *Fish are jumpin' and the cotton is high.*
> *Oh, your daddy's rich and your ma is good-lookin'*
> *So hush little baby, don't you cry.*

The clear soprano voice, backed by muted trumpet and a soft and lazy pulse of double bass and drums, floated out over the warm evening, and the gentle splashing of the waves seemed a natural and necessary accompaniment. Humphrey was not a great lover of jazz and so it was contrary to all expectation that he found himself rather enjoying the music, mellowed as it was by distance.

He brought out a small bottle of Calvados and poured himself a generous shot. There was silence for a little while and then the band started up again and a male voice began to sing *Night and Day*. Humphrey saw that there were bats flitting about the eaves of the cottage in the dark blue air. Inland, owls hooted in their melancholy way.

But Humphrey did not feel melancholy. For the first time in a very long time, he began to feel that it might be possible to apprehend the world other than through the eyes and ears of a miserable old git.

16. The Beach

He awoke the next morning feeling remarkably fresh considering how much alcohol he had consumed. The feeling of vague optimism following his minor epiphany the previous evening was still with him even when, on drawing the curtains, there was nothing but blank white. The sea mist was here again and visibility was down to zero.

Nevertheless, after a breakfast of buttery scrambled eggs, a croissant and good coffee, the summer sun quickly burnt off the mist and sparkled on the sea - a brilliant blue with patches of dark green further out. From time to time, far out, a wave would form half-heartedly and lazily collapse.

Humphrey took his laptop and more coffee out on to the patio.

The tide was in and the water foamed and frothed as it found channels through the rocks at Humphrey's feet and then sank back. The sea reached right into the little cove and there was no way of getting round to the other side, where he had seen the swimmers yesterday, without going up and over the cliff, a venture which he didn't think his knees would like.

He called up a map of the area on his laptop and studied the line of the coast. A couple of miles further up, with a more southerly aspect than his cove, there appeared to be a long, shallow bay, some distance still from

Humphrey & Jack

Quadrant Regis, the brash tourist resort further up the coast. Of course, there could be no guarantee that there might not be yippy dogs racing along the sand-flats, or hippies smoking pot, or poor little rich boys on quad bikes, or even cretins with boomboxes.

He had no right to expect that the beach would be quiet but it was worth a try. He wanted to walk along the sand and think. He felt a strange need to freshen up his mind, to clear it of mental detritus.

'Give that a good rinse now,' as dentists say.

That was it. He wanted to give his brain a good rinse. He had no idea what that meant but he thought he would know when he'd done it.

Later in the morning, he drove the car up the lane and turned right at the pub. After a mile or so the road turned inland for a while and then emerged into the wide bay Humphrey had seen on the map. Even sand stretched way ahead of him and, wonder upon wonder, it was almost deserted.

He was suddenly as excited as a child at this vast expanse of sand, all his. He pulled into a lay-by on the sea side of the road and got out of the car. Three steps up and then down over a low wall brought him onto a long promenade which stretched in one direction towards Quadrant Regis. He could just about make out the pier, shimmering in the sunlight. It looked pale and ephemeral, with its imitation pointed dome and minarets, like a mirage from the Arabian nights. More domes and cupolas atop the Quadrant Metropole Hotel also caught the sun and added to the exotic effect.

In the other direction lay the headland, on the other side of which lay what he had come to think of as Humphrey's Cove. The sandy promenade turned into a curving shingle path before it got there and the sandy beach turned to pebbles. Blackened wooden breakwaters reached into the water.

The tide had turned some time ago and, the beach being quite shallow, the water was already some distance out. He saw now that he didn't have the place altogether to himself; here and there, along the shore, there were figures holding buckets and poles of some kind. They appeared to be looking for something. Crabs was it? He was such a landlubber that he didn't know. But it didn't matter: they added to the picturesque aspect of the seascape.

In the distance, towards Quadrant, he could see a couple wandering along the shore arm in arm. A dog was running complex figures around them but it was not of the yippy kind. It was at quite a distance so its ecstatic barking was muted and it was, moreover, of a deep, masculine timbre. The couple caused a shadow of loneliness to pass over him momentarily but, just as quickly, it passed.

He did not know where the crowds were. It was a Sunday in high summer. The sand was yellow, the sea and the sky were as blue as they were in the railway posters of the nineteen fifties and yet here was a stretch that was quite unspoilt by the noisy moil of the vulgar with their deckchairs and windbreaks and radios, their sun lotion, their beer cans and their chicken nuggets and their burgers and their litter.

Humphrey was not a great traveller and certainly not a tourist in the conventional sense. Retirement meant that he could visit churches and cathedrals and great houses 'off peak' as it were. He hated crowds. The propinquity of others brought him out in a rash. The idea of a beach holiday was anathema to him; he could not understand why anyone would want to bake in the sun doing nothing for hours on end.

He had a sudden memory of himself on a beach somewhere, at the age of about nine. His father had erected a canvas windbreak with a great deal of fussing and pother (chocolate and mint green stripes - odd how the detail persisted). He and his mother sat now, side by side in deckchairs. His father was fully dressed in a suit and tie as was the custom at the time. He hadn't even taken his jacket off. His only concession to the hot sunshine was his battered old school boater. He sat there dozing but still upright, the pages of his newspaper lifting gently in the breeze.

His mother worked at her crochet without looking up. She could have been at home, or in Scunthorpe, or the moon, for all that she was aware of her surroundings.

Humphrey & Jack

Humphrey saw himself at the water's edge, on his hands and knees and wearing woollen bathing trunks which sagged alarmingly when wet. He was working on the moat for a very grand castle he had spent hours making. He had a spade and a bucket that could do turrets at the corners of his fortress.

His parents had taken him to Pembroke Castle the previous year and he had been overawed by its magnitude and dignity. This visit had confirmed his passion for all things medieval and he was trying to emulate the grandeur of the edifice in sand.

The idea was that the incoming tide would rush up the deep channel he had dug out towards the sea and thus fill the moat.

A boy and a girl came to watch. The boy in a green one-piece swimsuit was older than him, fourteen perhaps. The girl was about five and he held her hand protectively. The boy's swimsuit was wet and tight and Humphrey was obscurely fascinated and simultaneously embarrassed by the shape and weight of his balls. He had to look away.

'It won't work, you know,' said the boy.

The tide pulsed nearer. The boy and the girl stayed to watch. A sudden surge sent a rush of brown suds churning up the conduit but not quite to the moat. As it receded, the walls of the trench gave way, sliding into the water and sealing up Humphrey's channel.

The tide came closer, it seemed with increasing force. It came in, in long folds, which would break at a random point and then the dazzling white surf would run along, unfurling in both directions until it came seething up the sand.

And very soon the waves reached Humphrey's castle. The water rushed into the moat and it overflowed at once. One side of the castle came slithering down, turrets and all. The succeeding wave washed around it, taking with it battlements and buttresses and a barbican, of which he'd been very proud. He could see that very soon it would be just a shapeless mound and that by tomorrow it would be gone.

Humphrey & Jack

'I told you,' said the boy flatly and walked on with the girl. Humphrey could hear his mother calling and he trudged back to where she was holding out a blue towel with green fish on it.

'What have I told you about talking to children you don't know?' his mother said.

Humphrey walked towards the sea. It was not easy going at first. The sand was dry and soft and came in over the top of his shoes. He heard his mother's voice again, rebuking him for shaking sand from his sandals over the hall carpet when they got home.

'Oh, Humphrey, that was so silly. Couldn't you have done that on the step before you came in. Now Mummy will have to get the Hoover out and she's tired.'

Humphrey shut her out.

After he reached the high tide mark, it was easier underfoot. There were some footprints of shoes here and there, but not many. There were more footprints of dogs. There must have been two dogs there, chasing each other. Stretching along the bay were the deep prints of a galloping horse. Mostly, however, there were the little forked prints of sea birds, skittering about on the sand, leaving the light hieroglyphs of their busy search for food.

Further on still, there were runnels through the sand snaking out to shallow water in which a pale blue reflection of the sky rippled in a light breeze. Here and there were islets of sand. Beyond were the white lines of tumbling waves and beyond that the deeper blue of the sea. It was like looking down from a plane onto a tranquil delta.

He wanted to walk out right to the edge to see what the men with the buckets and the poles were doing. It must be crabs, or some other crustaceans, or were they just beachcombers? However, his shoes were beginning to sink quite a way into the sand and he was not inclined to ruin a perfectly good pair of brogues.

He looked closely at the sand, in a way he had never done before. It wasn't just a uniform brick red, was it? There was sand, yes, granules of sand, but there were also pebbles and smaller pebbles and minute pebbles; and there were shells and broken shells and tiny fragments of shells. And there were different colours: lots of milk-white, but also purple-black, sulphurous yellows, ochre and mauve.

Humphrey looked again at the sea, the origin of life, but also the destroyer. The sand was ground down rock and the bones of once living things. He should have been seized by a sense of a paralysing insignificance in the face of the indifferent immensity of things. It would have been so like him to feel that he was an anonymous little speck on the face of creation. But he didn't.

Humphrey felt elated. He felt expansively alive in a way he never had before.

He had a deep sense, standing on the wet sand, under a vast sky and in the face of the unrelenting sea, that his life up to this point had been a farcical waste. But he suddenly saw that he could change that by a simple act of will.

What were the current highlights of his existence? Meeting up with three other losers twice a week to grouch and gripe and bitch and beef about a world which none of them had ever done a thing to change or improve. Living within a tiny circuit of home, pub and supermarket. His relationships were limited to the Evangelists, four other Facebook 'friends', Fitzpatrick, the occasional gardener, and Mrs Price. His time was spent scribbling in a desultory way at obscure academic papers destined for obscure international journals which would be read by perhaps two dozen obscure scholars worldwide and then forgotten.

His major source of excitement was a feud with a neighbour about a cat.

Out near the horizon, spectral wind turbines rose from the sea, their blades rotating slowly but inexorably.

There must, surely to God, be more to life than standing in the same place like this - a slave to routine.

'Things are going to change around here', he thought to himself in an American accent.

He would start by taking his doctor's advice and cutting down on alcohol. In fact, he would go and see Doctor Bell and ask for advice about losing a few pounds, or even a couple of stones. He would stop eating pork pies and pasta. He might even sign up with Weight Watchers.

He would go to Venice. He had always wanted to go to Venice. He would learn origami. He would take a box at the opera. He would go to a dog track and bet. He would change his car. He would get a red one. He would join a ramblers' association. He would learn how to throw a pot. He would audition for the cathedral choral society. He would write a book. He would learn to speak Polish.

He leaned down and undid one shoelace and then took it off. Standing unsteadily on one foot, he took off his sock and put it in the shoe. Then the same with the other shoe and sock. Humphrey rolled up his trouser legs until they came halfway up his calves and then, with great determination, he walked to the water's edge and then into the little waves until they covered his feet. He squelched the sand between his toes. The sensation of the cold wavelets breaking around his ankles was delicious.

He would learn to play the tuba.

17. Minty Cresswell

'So you hate it all too, do you?'

The voice at his ear as he stood under the cedar at the top of the knoll looking down at Strachey House on the night of the party had been that of Araminta Cresswell, known as Minty, or, behind her back, Mad Minty. She was the subwarden of Sackville-West Block and a graduate student in the psychology department.

'It's diabolical,' said Humphrey.

'It's primitive,' said Minty. 'It is designed to obliterate the individual in the orgiastic frenzy of the herd.'

Humphrey & Jack

'I don't particularly want to be obliterated,' said Humphrey.

'It is Dionysian. It cancels all inhibitions. Along with the alcohol, it releases the power of the id. It is chthonic.'

'Chthonic?' Humphrey didn't know the word.

'Of the underworld.'

'Like I said, bloody diabolical.'

'Infernal,' Minty agreed.

'The worst of it is that you can't get away from it. It's not so bad up here but I can't stay here all night. It's freezing. I'll get hypothermia.'

It was true that Humphrey was only wearing a light shirt and thin trousers. It had been hot in the house.

'Do you like real music?' said Minty.

'Meaning?'

'Classical music. You know. The big B boys. Bach, Beethoven, Brahms, Bruckner, Bartók…'

'Boccherini,' said Humphrey, 'Berlioz, Britten, Barber…'

'Byrd and Buxtehude!' said Minty and they laughed.

'Would you like to come to my room and listen to something?'

'In Sackville-West?'

'Yes.'

Humphrey had never set foot in any of the women's blocks. It would be quite an adventure. Besides he was shivering. He turned to look at her for the first time.

Minty Cresswell was actually rather good-looking although she seemed to be at some pains to disguise the fact. She wore a beanie hat pulled down tightly over her ears, a pea-green duffle coat and rather formidable square spectacles.

'That would be nice,' said Humphrey, 'but aren't you supposed to be on duty?'

'Technically, yes, but Dieter won't mind. I'll just pop in and tell him where we are in case of emergencies.' Dieter Lenz was the subwarden of

Humphrey & Jack

Strachey, an affable, sporty German who was one of the 'lads' and took no interest in Humphrey, which was how Humphrey liked it.

As predicted, Dieter, who was involved in a schnapps drinking competition when they found him, had no objection and Minty and Humphrey crossed the road to the modern complex of white two-storeyed buildings called the blocks.

Minty had a compact little flat on the first floor of her block. It was functional but furnished with taste. The carpet was red, the sofa white, the curtains blue. A rug featuring a splendid peacock hung on the wall. On another wall was a very large Mondrian print. There were Habitat floor lamps in white metal and many books in a white bookcase.

'Make yourself comfortable,' said Minty. 'Who's your favourite composer?'

'Probably Mahler,' said Humphrey.

'Wow! Mine too,' said Minty. 'Shall we listen to the fifth?'

'Suits me,' said Humphrey.

Minty ran her fingers over the sleeves of a very substantial collection and placed the record on the turntable. Humphrey could only envy her impressive sound system with all its smoked glass and brushed steel.

'We don't need to worry about the volume. Everyone's at the party.'

She plonked herself down next to Humphrey on the sofa as the opening trumpet solo filled the room. The sound quality was superb. Then with a great crash on the cymbals the whole orchestra flared out into the primary theme. Humphrey was engulfed in the richness of the sombre funeral march.

'Wine?' Minty asked.

Humphrey nodded. Minty went into her little kitchen and returned with a bottle of Hungarian wine and two very large glasses.

It was all very pleasant, light years away from the barbarity on the other side of the road and Humphrey began to luxuriate in the wine and the music. During the famous *adagietto*, however, he was embarrassed to see that Minty was weeping softly. He felt he ought to say something but could only manage: 'What's the matter?'

'Oh you dear man, don't worry. It's nothing. It's just that this movement always makes me think of my ex. It's silly of me. He's not worth it. Ignore me.'

This should have been a warning to Humphrey. He felt uncomfortable and the phrase 'she wears her emotions close to the surface' came unbidden but he had no idea what he was getting into. Before she could launch into her autobiography, however, there came a knock at the door. It was one of her undergraduates with news that the party had got out of hand and that Dieter needed her to go over and take charge. Apparently there had been a water fight. It had started out with Jiffy lemons filled up with water and escalated into something much bigger, spreading to every floor in the house, including the upper floor where Humphrey's room was situated.

Apparently, Nic Latham had chased Paul Hammond up there and hurled the contents of a bucket of water at him. Paul had slipped and slid the length of the corridor which was already awash with water. An unnamed third party had opened a trapdoor in the floor at the end of the corridor and a considerable amount of water had gushed down to the floor below, taking with it the hapless Paul Hammond. It sounded like a bit of slapstick from a silent movie, except that Paul had broken his leg and Dieter had had to go with him in the ambulance. He needed Minty to go over there immediately and prevent further mayhem.

She quickly found her duffel coat and beanie hat.

'There's no need for you to come, Humphrey. Finish your wine and play what you like. I doubt if I'll be long. I think I'll shut things down. We don't want the Warden involved. Why don't you just stay here? The sofa's really comfortable. There are blankets and pillows in the cupboard in my bedroom. Through there.'

'Really, there's no need. I...' Humphrey burbled.

'Gotta go,' said Minty and she disappeared with her student.

Humphrey & Jack

Humphrey did as he was told. He played Bruch's G minor *Violin Concerto* and finished the wine. His watch told him that it was a quarter past two. He felt tired. He didn't really fancy going back to Strachey if there was still chaos going on. He was rather afraid that water may have seeped under his door and soaked the carpet.

He conquered his unease about entering a woman's bedroom in her absence. It was immaculately tidy although he felt a bit queasy about a pair of panties on the floor and a pair of tights over the back of a chair. He quickly found a blanket and a pillow and made himself a bed on the sofa, falling asleep immediately.

The next morning, he was aware of the astonishment and amusement in the air as he entered the refectory for breakfast, accompanied by Minty Cresswell. They had clearly come in from the direction of the blocks and not the houses and there seemed to be only one interpretation available.

When she joined the queue for the toast machine and Humphrey addressed his rubbery scrambled eggs and tinned tomato, Nic Latham was first in with his congratulations.

'You dirty boy, Humphrey Icke,' he said. 'Shagging a subwarden, eh. You're a dark horse, aren't you? Bet Mad Minty bangs like a shithouse door. Is that right, Humphrey, does she?'

Humphrey just grinned feebly. He could never get the hang of banter and he knew if he attempted a riposte he would make an ass of himself. He also knew that if he were to protest and say that Minty had rescued him from his angst at the party he would never hear the last of it and the teasing would be very much nastier. Part of him was pleased that he was being treated as if he were somehow 'normal'. So he let the lie stand.

As Christmas approached, Araminta Cresswell and Humphrey Icke became friends and the lie persisted. It was true that he often slept on the sofa in Minty's flat. This enabled him to escape the noise in Strachey and besides it was more comfortable in the modern building than in his chilly garret. He continued to receive amused respect from his peers and he did not disabuse them of their fanciful assumptions. Minty too gained something of a reputation, unbeknown to her, and Humphrey was used to her being referred to as a cradle-snatcher.

Minty owned a rather ancient and temperamental Morris Minor. On nights when she was not on duty they would take a ride out to the unspoilt little village of Temple Rising, three miles from the Halls of Residence. Sometimes they would take with them three or four students who would cram themselves into the tubby little car and Humphrey might find an undergraduate of either gender sitting on his knee and gossiping over his shoulder with the others in the back. Seatbelts were not yet compulsory, of course.

Their destination in the village was The Pickerel where Minty proved herself a dab hand at darts, something which impressed the otherwise dour regulars. There were also table skittles and bar billiards and they would play these rustic games for hours. They much preferred this to the sweaty press of the bars in the Halls, which were often no more than a meat market. They would drink quantities of Guinness and Minty would drive them home. The breathalyser had been introduced the previous year but the Radcestershire police seemed not very exercised about it and were not much of a presence on these country lanes.

It was fortunate that the pub sat atop a little hill because the car would often refuse to start at the end of the evening, the starter motor emitting just a sullen whine then nothing. This is where the students came in handy. They would all get out and push the car to the top of the incline and down the hill. With a bang and a roar it would fire up and clouds of smoke would belch from the exhaust as the students ran down the hill and clambered in. Minty would drive at a rash and heedless speed along the winding country lanes often with the headlights blinking on and off. This was only tolerable to Humphrey because by now he would be very drunk.

At other times there would be just the two of them. They would sit in what Minty called 'our corner'. This part of the rambling old inn contained some of the eighteenth-century box pews which had been ripped out of the pretty parish church to make way for blue plastic chairs. They afforded a measure of cosy privacy. Alarming agricultural implements with spikes hung on the wall along with pictures of placid cattle standing by brown pools. There were lamps whose shades were stained dark yellow with nicotine.

Here, Minty would oblige Humphrey to listen to stories of her tormented past. Humphrey listened out of politeness but he was dismayed by these confessionals. It was like nakedness in a public place. He felt such things should be kept to oneself or, if necessary, divulged to a professional. He did not reciprocate with tales of youthful traumas. Not that there was much to tell. He was certainly not going to tell Minty about Rupert Knight prodding his bottom with his thing in the cubicle at Pocklington Street Swimming Baths. Nor was he going to impart the trauma of Janet Dobbs' assault on his member in the moonlit dell in the woods. Such mortifying incidents were best kept locked up in a secret vault of his memory.

Minty, however, was profligate in sharing her adversities.

'You dear man,' she would say. 'I feel I can talk to you like no other man. Men have hurt me so badly, my dear, but you are gentle through and through.'

Humphrey felt that this was probably not true but hadn't the spine to say so. So he listened in muted disquiet to Minty's tales of degradation: about her bullying father, about her brother who had sexually molested her as a child, about her inappropriate and faithless boyfriends: the boxer, the scaffolder, the deputy head at her school, about her sleeping rough and about her suicide attempts. Humphrey found all this very frightening.

She kept coming back to the principal story, that of her recent ex-boyfriend, a security guard called Mick.

Mick played mind games with her, treating her like a princess one minute and a whore the next, buying her expensive presents and then destroying them during their chronic rows, going on three-day benders, sleeping with other women and expecting to be taken back, which she always did.

Humphrey & Jack

'But why?' Humphrey said. 'Why do you keep taking him back if he's so vile to you?'

'Oh, I know, Humphrey, it's so illogical, but you see, it's what happens to so many women. All they know is abuse. And the paradox is that abuse gives them a certain security. It's to do with love too. I loved Mick so much, you know. I think I still do. When he said he loved me and wanted to protect me, I so wanted to believe it that I took it all on board wholesale. And, when he turned on me like a demon, I would tell myself that it was temporary, that he could change. And he was so beautiful, Humphrey, so very beautiful.'

This cut little ice with Humphrey. For one thing he was not used to the word 'beautiful' being applied to a male. For another, he could not really grasp the illogicality. He was deeply sympathetic, but he couldn't understand.

'And even when he hit me, I would tell myself it was the booze, that it really wasn't in his nature, that he needed help and that I was the one to help him. But it only got worse. By then he knew so much about me, things I wanted kept private, and he would blackmail me with them, threatening to tell my parents or the university if I left him. And, do you know, a perverse part of me liked this because it bound me to him. You do see that, don't you?'

'Yes, yes, I do,' Humphrey lied.

'It had to end though. He beat me up more than once and I still went back but each time it was more and more violent. The last straw was when he put me in hospital. He hit me so hard that he broke my jaw and knocked out a couple of teeth. Well, the police had to be involved then, didn't they?'

'What happened?'

'He didn't come to visit me in the hospital once. Maybe the police had warned him off. But when I came out he was all over me. Flowers, chocolate, jewellery, the promise of a holiday in Santa Lucia, but I wasn't having it. Amazing how having your jaw wired up strengthens your resolve. He kept pestering me, notes, phone calls, letters. In the end, I had to take out an injunction against him.'

'Will you go back to him?'

'No. It's too late now. Anyway, he's got a new victim - more in his league - some flash blonde tart with big tits and two kids by another bloke. I pity those kids, I really do.'

And so did Humphrey.

18. Monday

Humphrey's holiday feeling of equanimity did not last long. Much of it evaporated on the journey home from the seaside cottage. He had set off early to avoid the school run which usually brought Radcester's traffic to a crawl between eight and nine-thirty.

At first all was fine. He belted along in bright sunshine with the car window open, vivified by the breeze and some very jolly Handel on the radio.

The trouble began at one of those enormous roundabouts with multiple exits and traffic lights where there's hell to pay if you're not in the correct lane. Often the arrows on the tarmac have faded under the tyres of vast continental juggernauts.

'Take the fifth exit,' said the satnav. Humphrey tried to count them. Did that unmade road count as an exit? A lorry to his left blocked his view of what might have been the third or was it the fourth exit? He was totally confused.

'Take the exit,' said the satnav urgently, as Humphrey sailed past it. 'Take the exit,' said the satnav, now that it was far too late. He would have to go round again. He switched off the Handel, the better to concentrate.

This time everything looked completely different from his first circuit and he had no starting point from which to begin counting the exits. Amid the glare and the exhaust fumes and the smell of hot asphalt, he stalled at the next traffic light just as it turned green.

Humphrey & Jack

Humphrey panicked and fumbled with the gears and by the time he had slid into neutral and started the engine again the lights turned red. There was a cacophony of horns.

What is it with these people? thought Humphrey. I didn't do it on purpose. They've been delayed for ninety seconds of their cretinous lives. So what? And he drowned them out with a prolonged blast on his own car horn.

All the same, he thought it best to get off the roundabout sharpish.

At first all seemed well. The arrow on the satnav pointed forward for a while and then suddenly reversed.

'Look, I'm sorry to interrupt,' the satnav said. Humphrey had installed the voice of Stephen Fry at a time when he rather admired him. He didn't find him particularly funny just at the moment.

'I'm really awfully sorry,' the satnav said, 'but do you think you could just turn around? When it's convenient, mind. Because it would be rather silly to turn around when it's inconvenient, now wouldn't it?'

He wants me to go back to that fucking roundabout, thought Humphrey, and then he was shocked at the swear word although he'd only thought it, not said it. In any case, it didn't look as if it would ever be convenient.

The road was straight and the speed limit was sixty but there seemed to be no sign of a lay-by or side roads or even a more humane roundabout where he could do a U-turn. Besides, there was a huge lorry in front of him and another one filling his rear window.

He lost about three-quarters of an hour in trying to get back on track which meant that when he finally reached Radcester the school run had brought traffic to the point of gridlock as usual. Humphrey cursed the precious middle-class mummies and their simpering offspring who were too pampered to walk to school. They should all be sent away to some gulag in the country - as I was, thought Humphrey.

And then he thought he could have stayed in his lovely retreat all morning, cooked a substantial breakfast, had a walk on the beach and missed out on all the angst. He had no reason to be back early. He cursed himself for a fool.

'When sorrows come, they come not single spies but in battalions.' That was Claudius in Hamlet, wasn't it? Well he was bloody well right. Humphrey carried on thinking this for most of the morning. When he went into the kitchen on arriving home there was a vile smell. He traced it to the pedal-bin and when he lifted the lid, he was appalled. It was writhing with maggots and the stench made him gag. He had forgotten to empty the bin before going away and he remembered now there had been a chicken carcass in there. He cursed himself again.

Humphrey was normally meticulous about cleanliness so this stupid omission really galled him. He pulled on his marigolds and carried the metal bin outside where he tipped a whole packet of salt over the vile things and then kettle after kettle of boiling water. The water drained out where the foot pedal was. Then he went inside and cleaned the kitchen from top to bottom. There was no reason for this other than a kind of psychological need.

By now the bin was cool enough to handle. He tipped it to release any remaining water, fastened the lid securely with gaffer tape, placed it inside a large refuse sack and then another, and drove it to the tip. He left it in the scrap metal bay. He knew that he should have emptied whatever the contents had become somewhere but 'Look on it again I dare not,' he thought. That was Macbeth.

Arriving home, he realised he had driven there and back still wearing his marigolds, so they had to go into the wheelie bin and he now felt obliged to clean the steering wheel, gear stick pommel and the car door handle.

By this time it was nearly lunchtime and the whole morning had been wasted. He felt a very large sherry was in order which he would enjoy in the garden. In the gleaming kitchen, he took out the decanter of fino sherry he kept in the fridge and placed it on a tray along with a substantial glass, a small bowl of peanuts, and *The Daily Telegraph* he had not yet had time to read. He felt a little better.

Until, that is, he noticed Aristotle crouching in his petunias. There was nothing at hand to hurl at the damned animal - the peanuts were too small and a brick would have been excessive - and besides, he was a terrible shot. He had to endure it while the cat finished its business, scratched around a little, and then stalked towards the hole in the fence turning just once to fix Humphrey with a look of feline insouciance before liquefying into the gap.

The sherry went some way toward helping Humphrey to relax and the afternoon brought some respite in the catalogue of calamities which had threatened to ruin his day. Since his retirement he rather liked Mondays. He liked to think of all the people in poorly ventilated offices or classrooms for whom the weekend's sunshine and leisure had flashed by like opening the shutter in a camera and for whom Friday evening was a far distant goal to be attained only after days of drudgery and tedium.

For Humphrey no longer had to put up with all this. His Mondays were free. He could work on his academic papers but he didn't have to. He had no commitments, no meetings, no targets, no obligations. He was answerable to no-one. And he could have a large glass of claret with his lunch and forget about his pig of a morning.

He went in and made a simple omelette, cut some slices from a baguette, poured the wine and took it outside to enjoy under the garden parasol he had bought himself as a retirement present. It was to be a kind of symbol of the leisure he intended to enjoy for the remainder of his days.

Now, it was pleasant on this Monday afternoon to sit in its shade and eat and drink. The bees were busy in the golden rod just in front of him and squirrels chased each other round the trunks of trees. The purr of traffic could be edited out and even the gardeners in the park had silenced their grass mowers for the time being. The tranquillity was delectable and Humphrey poured himself another liberal glass.

Humphrey & Jack

After lunch, he tackled the *Telegraph* crossword. He particularly liked 10 across: A million working girls return to form a plan (9). Ah, thought Humphrey, how clever and he filled in 'stratagem' which fitted perfectly. The elegance of this and two bumpers of wine put him into a mood of expansive benignity. He might even be able to regain the composure of his weekend away. Imperceptibly, Humphrey drifted into a rosy sleep.

He dreamed he was in the golden rod with the bees. Perhaps he *was* a bee. He could certainly fly and the sensation was exhilarating. He couldn't wait to tell Hector, Norman and Garth that he could fly. How jealous they would be. He watched his sister bees and imitated their movements, sipping at the tiny yellow florets. The nectar tasted like a particularly exquisite Bordeaux. He could see pollen sticking to the legs of the other bees and he looked down at his own. Though he could fly he still had but two legs and he noted with bemusement that he was still wearing his corduroy trousers. Grains of pollen were sticking to these in clusters. They were like yellow spheres with spikes and they were becoming very heavy. It was probably time he thought of getting back to the hive.

Except he didn't know the way. He began to get very anxious indeed. The pollen would drag him down and he would be grounded and die in the grass. The sky was a dirty yellow and the sun had turned an acid green. One of his co-workers suddenly took off from the flower beds and headed across the lawn. Humphrey summoned the courage to follow her strange dipping flight.

Over Mrs Bellingham's garden they flew, where Aristotle, grown gigantic, leapt up to get him, his claws raking the air and his body twisting. Humphrey escaped with little space to spare. He flew up above the clouds to escape a second attack by the cat.

As he flew on alone, weary now and increasingly agitated, day turned to night and he found himself flying towards a huge and brilliant moon. Below him was an arctic landscape of cloud with plains and mountains and gigantic dark fissures, all brilliantly illuminated in the strange moonlight.

At length, after he had been flying for what seemed like hours, the cloud thinned and he descended until he was flying over a forest. Gradually, he flew down through the tree canopy until he was hovering over a glade which he recognised. This was where Janet Dobbs had tried to steal his virginity. But Janet was not there. Instead, by the pool where she had grabbed his bits, there stood the hive, enormous and terrifying. It was silver in the moonlight but an eerie orange light leaked from within through the louvred slats around its sides. It was an angry light and angry bees hovered around the hive to deny him entry.

Far more terrifying than the light, or the hostile bees, was the noise. At first it was a crescendo of humming and buzzing. As this reached its peak, it transmuted into a different kind of noise, an industrial clanging and banging with a thunderous groundswell of noise. Squadrons of furious bees flew from the hive to attack him, alighting on his left hand. His wings fell off and he felt himself falling headlong. The bees began to sting him again and again.

When he hit the ground, Humphrey woke up with a jolt. He had fallen asleep with his head on his arm and the painful tingling in his left hand was real enough. His position had constricted his circulation and the pins and needles in his hand were the consequence. Almost immediately he realised that the noise was real too.

The scum with the boom box had returned to their station on the steps by the fountain. He looked at his watch. It was only just after three. They had never appeared this early before. Why were they not at school or college? or in hell, for all Humphrey cared?

Humphrey gathered his belongings and stomped indoors. As ever, he could hear the din throughout the house. He took a book into the guest bedroom which was upstairs on the street side of the house and thus furthest from the park. Even here, with damp cotton wool in his ears and all the doors and windows closed, he could hear the heavy thrumming of the music. He tried to be logical. Was it so very loud in here?

Objectively, no. But it was unrelenting - and that was the point. It reminded him of a frequent occurrence when he was still in post. If you are invigilating an examination and a candidate with a cold starts sniffing, that's it. You are done for. You find yourself anticipating the next sniff and because the sniffing is irregular the anticipation takes over your entire consciousness. You cannot un-hear it. And the 'music' from the park was like that. It was maddening as an earworm is. It would not leave your head.

And it went on and on, the primitive beat preventing Humphrey from concentrating on anything. After three hours of torment he decided he would go out to eat. This was not something he did often. He did not like eating amongst strangers. Their determined joviality depressed him almost as much as their table manners. But he had to get out of the house.

He discovered that the restaurant of the Blue Boar Hotel opposite the cathedral was closed on Mondays ('because we only use the freshest of ingredients'). That would have been his first choice. He would have been able to get a secluded table in some remote corner of the spacious dining room with all its Victorian pretension. The food was mediocre and the service appalling but he would have been able to keep himself to himself.

He settled instead for the Delhi Durbar which was situated in a narrow alley leading from the cathedral close. To his surprise and pleasure the place was practically empty but then, it was early and it was Monday. Humphrey wasn't complaining. He ordered onion bhajis as a starter followed by rogan gosht, with side dishes of tarka dal and bhindi bhaji. He also ordered pilau rice and a peshwari naan. He knew it would be far too much but he needed to be away from the house for as long as possible - until the bastards had gone in fact.

As it was he made a fair stab at this spread, taking his time, and washing it down with two large bottles of Cobra beer. The waiters did not badger him in the irritating American way with 'everything all right for you, sir?' every blessed minute.

It was twilight before he left and he walked home slowly relishing the cool of the evening.

They had not gone. He could hear them from the end of the road. Why had his neighbours not protested? It was practically dark. He let himself in, picked up a torch from the hall table, walked through to the garden door and out on to the terrace. He would have to confront them again.

At the little gate at the bottom of the garden he shone his torch at them.

'What the hell are you playing at? This is a residential area. That filthy racket is making it uninhabitable. Have you people no social conscience? Do you know what time it is? You've been here for hours.'

The music stopped abruptly. Once again it was the dark-haired boy who rose to his feet and came to stare at Humphrey. Only this time he came right up to the gate.

'Suck my dick,' he said.

'I beg your pardon?' Humphrey said.

'You heard, dude. You can suck my dick.'

Astounded, Humphrey held his gaze for a long moment and turned back to the house. The boy went back to his friends and the music resumed.

Humphrey went straight upstairs to his study and phoned the police.

19. Christmas

The Christmas tree went up in the oak-panelled hall of Strachey House on November 25th, 1968. Term would end on December 10th so Christmas came early at the halls of residence at the university.

Some wag had acquired phallus-shaped fairy lights on a rugby trip to Amsterdam and other decorations included condoms in gold and silver packets dangling from the branches. There were also chocolate willies and boobs. On top of the tree sat Winnie the Pooh with a tinsel halo, the topmost spike of the tree firmly rammed up his bottom.

Humphrey & Jack

Though Humphrey deplored all this, finding it crass and puerile, Minty managed to persuade him to join in the Strachey/Sackville-West 'carols around the tree' with the promise of a trip to The Pickerel afterwards. Some of the girls had put together a little wind band to accompany the singing and Nic Latham proved to be a surprisingly adept trumpet player for 'Hark the herald angels sing'. Paul Hammond sang a lyrical tenor from his wheelchair. It is true that 'O come, all ye faithful' was a little raucous but Humphrey was able to endure it because it signalled the end of the proceedings. Afterwards there were mince pies and mulled wine and, as soon as it was decent, Minty and Humphrey slipped out to the Morris Minor.

There was a real log fire near their corner in the pub, before which snoozed an aged dog called Winston Churchill, who would shudder in his dreams periodically and fart. Minty produced a deodorant spray from her handbag and squirted it in Winston's direction but he slumbered on regardless.

There were no Christmas decorations in The Pickerel as yet and Humphrey approved. Premature Christmas cheer depressed him. There was certainly nothing cheerful about tonight's instalment of *The Confessions of Araminta Cresswell* either. She told him in great detail about her suicide attempt when she learnt about Mick's new woman, the blonde with the bountiful bust.

Apparently, she had gone to Boots, to Timothy White's and finally to Chatterton's independent dispensing chemists and bought small quantities of paracetamol in each. Then in Oddbins she had bought a bottle of Bell's whisky. Back at her little flat in Lupin Street, where she lived before moving out to Radclyffe Hall, she had put on her recording of *Madame Butterfly* and drunk about three quarters of the whisky before swallowing a large handful of the pills. She had then gone to bed believing it to be for the last time.

It was the whisky that saved her. She woke up suddenly feeling very sick indeed and made it to the bathroom only just in time. She vomited in separate spasms for some time. She had eaten nothing so what came up was a colourless, viscous substance, and pills. She had probably only been asleep for a couple of minutes.

All this made Humphrey feel very queasy.

When she had finished throwing up, she rang a girlfriend who went round immediately. Minty remembered being very rude to her and saying: 'Don't think I didn't mean to kill myself; this wasn't a cry for help.' Minty's friend was not fazed by this and called her doctor. The rest, said Minty, was pretty routine. This had not been her only suicide attempt but, on the whole, she was glad she had failed.

'Aren't you glad I failed, Humphrey?' she asked.

Humphrey said he was very glad but alarm bells were ringing all the same. Why was Minty baring her soul to him unasked? It was all very one-sided. Humphrey had not invited this profound intimacy and, in truth, it embarrassed him to the core. He felt it forced him into a corner. The obligation to be polite left him no room for emotional manoeuvre since the extremity of Minty's emotional world was so alien to his usual tepidity of feeling that all he could do was listen and sympathise. And feel trapped.

And why him? Above all, why him? She was a good-looking woman when she removed her disguises. The teasing directed at him by the lads acknowledged that.

Humphrey, on the other hand, was nearly six years younger. He had not yet acquired the paunch of his later years but he considered himself unattractive. There were his telescope-strength specs, of course, which made the enlarged eyes behind them look weak and puzzled. They were too close together and appeared to bulge a little. His ears were too big and his hair was thinning already. There was a hint of a waddle in his gait. Like a 'disoriented duck' a cruel schoolmate had once said. He dressed conservatively and drably at a time when young males were imitating the peacock. His preferred hairstyle was a short back and sides.

Minty had said time and time again that what she saw in Humphrey was his charming capacity for empathy. Humphrey hadn't the heart or the stomach to tell her that though the secrets of the confessional were safe with him, he really didn't want to know. He didn't want to play either priest or shrink and when he wasn't discomfited by her revelations, he was frankly bored. He didn't want this terrible intimacy. All he had ever wanted was a companion who shared his taste for music. She had become far too clingy.

The landlord came over and gave the fire a good poke and sparks flew up the chimney.

Fortunately, this seemed to trigger a change in Minty and she began to cheer up. If Humphrey had not been quite so naive, he might have been a little wary of these mood changes too. Minty was quite a good mimic and they were soon laughing incontinently at her impressions of various inhabitants of Radclyffe Hall. Her best was of Dieter's expansive Bavarian bonhomie but she also did the Warden to a T as a shy, wool-gathering rodent.

They had both drunk a great deal of Guinness which naturally increased the hilarity. In fact, they had drunk so much that Minty, normally rather cavalier about drinking and driving, suggested they ask the landlord to ring for a cab. She could get a bus out to collect the car the next day.

Humphrey was very relieved by this. On a previous occasion, the jalopy's headlights had failed and there was nearly a head-on collision with another car which hadn't dipped its headlights, dazzling Minty who had been driving with just side lights and whose eyes had been geared to near darkness.

Back at the Halls, Minty asked him in for a night cap and some music. Despite his reservations earlier, Humphrey did not say no to alcohol and so they were soon sitting on the white sofa drinking port and listening to Ravel's *Shéhérazade*. As the bewitching movement called *Asie* was coming to an end, Minty stood, pulled Humphrey to his feet and led him into the bedroom. She undressed him perfunctorily, kneeling to remove his shoes and socks, until he stood there bemused in nothing but his Y-fronts. She undressed quickly down to bra and panties and got into bed.

'Come on, get in,' she said and Humphrey did so. Then she pulled a cord hanging above the pillows and turned off the light.

They lay side by side, facing each other in the dark. Humphrey found himself becoming aroused, physically at least. Without any kissing, or indeed any kind of foreplay, Minty reached down for his erection and began to guide him.

'But…,' spluttered Humphrey.

'Ssssh, it's all right,' she said. 'I'm on the pill.'

'Ah,' said Humphrey, as he slid inside her.

This is rather nice, he thought, as he began to move cautiously backwards and forwards.

Suddenly, she was pushing him away.

'No, no, please don't!' she said. 'Humphrey, don't.'

And she began to cry. Humphrey pulled away, swung his legs round under the covers and sat on the side of the bed in utter confusion.

'Oh, I'm sorry. It's not you,' she wept. 'It's not you, Humphrey. It's Mick. He hurt me. Inside.'

Humphrey did not really know what she meant and didn't really want to know. It sounded horrible.

'I think I'd better go,' he said.

'Please. Oh, I'm so sorry, Humphrey.'

'It's all right,' he said, though it wasn't.

He turned and groped for the light cord, dressed quickly, and for the second and final time in his life, Humphrey Icke retired from the embrace of a female.

20. Pub Quiz

Humphrey was in a stinking mood. Why had he let Hector prevail upon him to take part in a pub quiz? Had he been mad?

It was Cora who'd started it.

Humphrey & Jack

'You'll wipe the floor with them all,' she'd said, 'a bunch of professors like you. They won't stand a chance. I should think between you there's nothing you don't know. Go on, you'll enjoy it. It'll stop you moaning and whingeing and whining for an hour or so at least.'

'We like moaning and whingeing and whining,' Garth had said.

'There's a twenty-five quid prize and free beer for the winning team,' Cora said. 'And sandwiches for everybody. What's not to like? Go on, you'll love it.'

'I must say the idea of free beer is quite appealing.' This was Norman who had a reputation for being tight.

'But I don't really like the idea of coming out in the evening,' Humphrey said miserably.

'Oh, Humpy, don't,' Cora said. 'You're a long time dead, darling. Let your hair down a bit.'

Since Humphrey had very little of this commodity and since there was no point in telling Cora that he hated being called 'darling' as much as he loathed being called 'Humpy', he retreated into a morose silence.

Hector was quite taken by the idea.

'Come now, my merry men, let us attempt this gladsome thing. The Lady Cora speaketh truth. Our two historians know of all that is past or passing or yet to come, from Creation to the Last Trump. Norman has read everything that has ever been written, and I know my Bacon from my Botticelli. We shall be formidable.'

'The place will be full of chavs,' said Garth.

'It will not,' said Cora, 'you know I run a very civilised house.'

There was a cackle from across the room where Secondhand Sue was sitting with Flake.

'With certain exceptions,' Cora said to the Evangelists in a stage whisper.

'I heard that,' said Sue.

'Be silent, you grub, you maggot,' said Hector.

'Go on, have a go, you overeducated gits,' Sue retorted. 'We'll wipe the floor with you.'

'Are they in it?' Garth asked.

'League champions last year,' Sue said. 'So put that in your poncey pipe and smoke it.'

'I was not aware that you had been invited to join our conversation, you hideous writhing larval thing,' said Hector.

'Fuck off,' said Sue.

'Well,' said Cora. 'What about it?'

'I say we give it a try,' said Hector. 'What say you, my masters? Shall we try our fortunes against the world? Shall we pit our combined intellects against the Cro-Magnon crone over there?'

'I can hear you, you know,' said Sue.

'Only because you are listening, my sweet,' said Hector.

Sue raised her middle finger.

'Swivel on that,' she said.

'Well?' said Hector.

Reluctantly the others agreed.

'You'll need a name,' said Cora.

'Like what?'

'Oh anything,' Cora said. 'Usually something witty - or just silly.'

'What are they called?' asked Garth, waving airily in the direction of Secondhand Sue and Flake.

'*Knicker Elastic*,' said Cora.

'Now, why am I not surprised?' said Hector. 'What else, light of my life, fire of my loins?'

Cora did not bat an eyelid. She produced a piece of paper.

'Well, there's *Tequila Mockingbird*,' she said.

'That's an old gag,' said Norman.

'*Gadaffi Duck*?'

'I like that,' said Garth.

'*You Know Nothing Jon Snow*?'

Humphrey & Jack

'I don't get it,' said Humphrey.

Cora smiled benignly.

'*Universally Challenged*?'

'Very droll,' said Hector.

'*Ten Inches*?'

'I don't get that, either,' said Humphrey.

'Well, you should,' said Sue. 'It would do you no end of good.' And she began to cackle again.

'What?' said Humphrey.

'Ignore her, my child. She is being hideously gross, as ever,' said Hector.

'So what about you lot?' said Cora.

'Well, we are *The Four Evangelists* already,' said Garth.

'No, no, no, too dull,' said Hector.

'*The Sign of Four*?' Norman suggested.

'Too literary,' said Hector. 'We need something more…cataclysmic.'

'*Titanic*,' said Humphrey, who was feeling more and more unhappy about the whole thing.

'Tempting providence a bit, don't you think?' said Garth.

'I have it!' said Hector. 'We shall be *The Four Horsemen of the Apocalypse*!'

At the other side of the room, Sue cackled away.

***

On the appointed night, everything was much as Humphrey had feared. It was infernally noisy, for one thing. The Seven Stars was represented by *Knicker Elastic* and *The Four Horsemen of the Apocalypse* whilst the other teams came from different hostelries across the town. This was a friendly match to start the pub quiz season. Next week the tournament proper would begin.

Humphrey & Jack

A great deal of alcohol was being consumed. Humphrey thought he would go on the Guinness. It was strong stuff and he felt it might numb the pain. The others were already at their table and he joined them. It was difficult to converse above the racket.

Humphrey noted with distaste a common acoustic effect. There was a mountain of a man standing at the bar with his mates. His laterally striped polo shirt was too small to contain his belly which slopped naked out of the top of his straining waistband. His voice was harsh and grating, like a buzz saw, and his laugh was like a demented machine gun. In order to be heard above this, the people around him had to raise their voices; he increased *his* volume accordingly, and so on throughout the bar.

At last there was a hush. Cora had taken her place on a bar stool in front of the bar and after a round of applause explained that she was the Quizmistress and Referee and that she would be the sole and final arbiter of any disputes. After another round of applause accompanied by whistling, the quiz began.

It did not go well. For one thing, Cora was not the ideal questioner. Her pronunciation of proper nouns caused confusion at times. 'Afro-ditty' was easily identifiable as the goddess of love, but it took some ingenuity to decrypt her contorted pronunciation of Nebuchadnezzar.

Uncharacteristically, Norman got into a dispute with her when he pointed out that Henry Tudor *was* Henry VII and that the Battle of Bosworth field took place in 1485 not 1845 as Cora had said. She rebuffed him with: 'That's what it says here. Shut up, Norman.'

'Yeah, shut up, knobhead!' came Sue's voice from the *Knicker Elastic* table.

The Horsemen were doing abysmally.

Cora would ask a question and the groups of four on each table would go into conference briefly before writing down their answers on the score sheet. After four or five themed rounds, the sheets would be passed to another table for moderation and there was a pause so that glasses could be refilled. Humphrey was putting away the Guinness as if the Liffey might dry up, so intense was his boredom and frustration.

The trouble was that there were very few questions on their spheres of interest, such as literature, history, art, classical music, mythology and philosophy. It was all populist stuff: sport, pop music, TV programmes, 'celebrities' and fashion. Usually, they had nothing to confer about and sat there shaking their heads and muttering 'no idea'.

What was galling was that *Knicker Elastic* were doing brilliantly. Flake and Secondhand Sue had been joined by a youth with a vast blond afro and a Metallica tee shirt and a girl in a kaftan with long straight black hair parted in the middle which hung down like curtains and partially concealed her eyes. Between them they appeared to have watched every television programme since Lord Reith was around and to know about every band from *Bill Hayley and his Comets* to who topped the bill at Glastonbury that summer.

The braying mountain-man was in *Ten Inches* who were running *Knicker Elastic* close with an encyclopaedic knowledge of sport. The other members of this team were also endowed with beer bellies and bullet heads. Humphrey felt an intense and visceral dislike growing in him.

Out of boredom and because he liked attention, Hector began shouting out 'a guillemot!' in answer to any question they couldn't answer, which was most of them.

So it would go:

'Who won the FA cup in 1928?'

'A guillemot!'

'Who is the presenter of *The Great British Hoedown* on BBC1?'

'A guillemot!'

'Who won The Eurovision Song Contest in 1967 with *Puppet on a String*?'

'A guillemot!'

Humphrey & Jack

At first Hector's outbursts were met with laughter but it soon palled and the other teams began to mutter at him to shut up. At length Cora said: 'Yes, Hector, shut up. It's not funny any more.'

Garth hissed viciously: 'Pack it in. It's embarrassing.'

'What does it matter?' Hector said. 'We don't know any of this stuff. Anyway, the law of averages means that a question on guillemots must inevitably come up - and we'll get a point.'

'Bollocks,' said Garth. 'The law of averages means no such thing.'

'Anyway, I did know the last one,' said Norman.

'What?' Garth snapped.

'Sandie Shaw.'

'Sandy Shore?'

'Sandie Shaw. Won the Eurovision. 1967. In bare feet.'

The other three *Horsemen* looked at Norman in wonder and distaste.

Presently, Humphrey noticed something that appalled him. Many of their opponents were consulting their phones under the tables. This was preposterous; it made a mockery of the whole thing. It defeated the entire purpose of the game by turning it into a race to see who could Google fastest. Whatever had happened to fair play, magnanimity in victory, pride in defeat, having a go? What had happened to 'it's not the winning - it's the taking part'? This just wasn't British. It wasn't cricket. Humphrey was incensed.

The others had noticed too but didn't seem as put out as Humphrey. At the next break he went to report the cheating to Cora.

'Oh, I know,' she said, 'but what can you do? Now, don't be a grumpy Humpy. Sandwiches soon.'

It was a bitter thing to *The Four Horsemen of the Apocalypse* when after two more rounds and the totting up of the scores *Knicker Elastic* were pronounced the winners. Sue's gloating would be insufferable for weeks to come.

It was all the more galling when Cora came round to collect two pounds from each of them.

Humphrey & Jack

'You didn't say anything about that,' said Norman.

'Well, you don't think I'm going to fork out the prize money from my own pocket, do you? And it helps towards the sandwiches.'

'Bloody liberty, I call it,' Norman said. 'Anyway, you've been raking it in tonight. The place is packed.'

'Let's have less of your sour grapes, Norman. Just because you came last. I've got a business to run, lad. Now, I'm just going to put the sandwiches out. You'll do better next time, boys, now that you've got the hang of it.'

She went off to set out the food.

Humphrey was about to splutter that there would be a next time only over his cold cadaver but he was stilled by Hector patting his knee.

'Be still, child. It is a cruel injustice - let Heaven bear witness - but it is the Way of the World.'

'We'd have come last anyway,' he added.

Humphrey was feeling quite peckish by now but if he expected an orderly queue or any sort of deference to their age, he was to be seriously disappointed. It was more like a stampede.

The *Ten Inches* crew were there first and came away with paper plates piled high with beef, salmon, and prawn sandwiches, little pork pies and vol-au-vents and the others descended like harpies on the feast. *The Horsemen* were last at the spread and there were just a few forlorn curling plain cheese sandwiches left amidst a litter of cress and limp cucumber. The filling had been taken from some sandwiches leaving just the bread.

'Pigs,' said Humphrey.

***

When he got home, Humphrey was in a vile temper. Aristotle, Mrs Bellingham's cat, shot from his front doorstep where he had been licking his balls defiantly. He moved too fast for Humphrey to kick him.

Humphrey & Jack

He realised that he was quite drunk and it took him a couple of attempts to get his key in the lock. All that Guinness. He never drank anything like this much at their lunchtime meetings. His pee would probably be orange tomorrow.

All the same, he was starving now and went to the kitchen to make a proper sandwich. He cut two thick slices from a *pain rustique*, being elaborately careful with the bread knife, slathered them with butter, laid slices of cold lamb from yesterday's joint on them, topped one slice with tomato, beetroot and a couple of salad leaves, smothered the filling with Hellman's mayonnaise, put the other slice of bread on top, picked the formidable thing up with both hands, and took a huge bite.

Mayonnaise squirted out from both sides of the sandwich onto the kitchen counter and oozed down from the corners of Humphrey's mouth. Normally very fastidious, he was too drunk to care. He would tidy it up in the morning. He put the huge sandwich on a tray along with a can of chilled beer and carried it through to the garden terrace.

The air was balmy and the sky clear. It was almost quiet. There was only the uneradicable hum of traffic on Prior Ingham's Road. Humphrey tried to focus on the stars that had not been cancelled out by light pollution but they would not keep still. Down in the park, the cast iron Victorian lamps were still alight and there was a soft orange aura around each of them. However, these also danced in Humphrey's drunken view.

Gradually, as he ate his sandwich, oblivious of the mess he was making on the garden table, Humphrey's vision began to settle.

There was something very wrong.

There were lighter patches on the black expanse of lawn below him. They seemed to be more concentrated near the little postern gate at the bottom of the garden, but they stretched all along the hedge and there were even a few greyish shapes further up near the terrace.

He would have to investigate.

He nearly fell on the stone steps down to the lawn. What met his eyes on closer inspection was obscene.

Humphrey & Jack

Someone had strewn the contents of two litter bins from the park all over the grass. There was one bin in the rhubarb patch and the other had been hurled under the plum tree.

There were beer and cola cans, soggy cigarette packets, crisp packets, ready meal containers, half-eaten burgers, plastic carrier bags, apple cores, orange peel, cigarette ends everywhere, bottles, a child's sandal, and, most nauseating of all, a full disposable nappy.

Suddenly energised and single-minded, Humphrey went inside to get black bin bags and then began to clear up.

Despite his lethargy of only a few minutes ago while he was contemplating the jumping stars, he now ran hither and thither about the lawn, picking up the litter and putting it in the plastic sack. He was not systematic but scurried about at random, weeping with outrage and disgust.

He felt that someone was watching him.

He had not made much inroad on the mess when he fell to his knees. The fact that the lawn sloped had made him dizzy. He was drunk and he was suddenly exhausted and he threw up.

Then he keeled over amid the detritus and fell into a drunken sleep.

21. CCTV

When Humphrey came to, Aristotle was licking at the patch of vivid orange vomit just in front of his eyes. The cat leapt sideways as Humphrey pulled himself up onto one elbow and ran off through the hole in the fence.

Humphrey nearly retched again. He could smell the sick. All around him lay the mess, tins and bottles glinting in the early morning sunshine.

He felt bilious. Every joint ached. He was wet with dew. He lifted his hands to rub his face but they stank and he began gagging again. The mouth of the black bin bag fluttered in the morning breeze. He had not managed to collect much after all.

Humphrey & Jack

Humphrey slowly and painfully pulled himself to his feet, walked up the lawn and climbed the stone steps, his knees shrieking with pain at each jolt.

He had left the garden door open all night. What an invitation to burglars.

Do come in and help yourselves, the door said. I'm sorry Grumpy Humpy is not here to greet you but he's currently passed out on the lawn. Now, what would you like? The telly? The laptop? By all means. Chequebook? Credit cards? In the desk drawer. There's some cash in the wallet. Don't bother with a receipt.

Humphrey felt what he considered an undeserved relief when everything appeared to be intact. He locked the garden door behind him and went to run a bath as hot as he could bear. He soaked for a very long time.

Later, when he felt better (though not very much) he snapped on a pair of Marigolds and set about clearing up the filthy mess on the grass in a more systematic way.

It was wretched work and took over an hour. By the time he had finished he had two large capacity bags full of rubbish. Then, he flushed away his vomit from the lawn with the garden hose along with the yellow baby shit that had dropped out of the disposable nappy.

Now he went inside and scrubbed away at his hands, even though he'd been wearing gloves, scouring away at his nails with a nail brush. He took three paracetamol, made a pot of industrial strength coffee, and settled in his study to look at the CCTV record.

He had had the cameras installed a couple of years previously. There had been a spate of burglaries at properties around the park at the time and, though his own property had not been affected, he thought the cameras, along with the security lights, would act as a serious deterrent in the future. His apples, plums and pears had been raided for as long as he could remember but there was always much more than he could consume on his own and he was not inclined to waste time trying to trace trespassers on film.

But this was a different matter. He had a very good idea who might be responsible but he needed verification. He switched on the tape and rewound.

There he was, stumbling about the lawn like a deranged vagrant, picking up the litter with his bare hands and dropping nearly as much as he picked up. He was in the full glare of the security lights, which threw strange shadows of his lurching form. The sensors were not trained on the garden table and must only have clicked on when he went down the stone steps, although he had been too drunk to notice at the time.

This was very embarrassing. He felt himself blushing to the roots of his hair. He would have to erase all this later. He rewound at speed.

Yes, he could see a figure in blue jerking backward and forward across the lawn as if in a silent movie. There was another figure in black at the gate who appeared to pass something over to the first figure. Humphrey kept rewinding until the lawn lay pristine in the evening sunshine, the long shadows of Mrs Bellingham's cypress trees falling across the grass.

Then he played the film forward at normal speed.

It was as he had thought. The two boys involved were the ringleaders of the gang with the boom box and this defilement of his garden was clearly in retaliation for his having called the police the previous week.

The dark-haired boy, with the royal blue tee-shirt and black jeans, was the only one actually to climb the gate into the garden. Then you could see the blond boy passing over the first bin and the blue boy walked up and down, shaking the bin from side to side, strewing the rubbish about the lawn and kicking it to get a wider spread. The boy at the gate was clearly laughing.

It occurred to Humphrey that these boys must have been watching his every move. He hardly ever went out in the evenings and they had chosen their time very precisely. Humphrey found this very sinister.

Humphrey & Jack

The blond boy disappeared for a few moments and returned with the second bin which he passed over to the blue boy. He emptied it out extravagantly over the grass but this time kicking more of the refuse up the lawn towards the house. He stood looking up at Humphrey's windows for a while. Then he turned away, dropped his trousers and did a moonie at the house, waggling his backside lewdly.

Pulling his trousers up, he ran to his friend, gave him a high five, vaulted the gate and Humphrey could see their two heads, one dark, one blond, bobbing down the path until they were out of sight.

The rubbish sparkled in the slanting light.

So they knew the cameras were there, but didn't care, thought Humphrey. Well, we'll see about that.

He began making what he judged to be the clearest screen grabs and saving them on his computer. There was a very good shot of the devastation on the lawn which would be useful. There was a brilliant one of the dark-haired boy grinning up at the house. He enlarged it gradually until it began to pixillate too much and then diminished it a touch until it was as sharp as he could get it. He was pleased with this; anyone who knew the boy would be able to recognise him.

He hesitated about capturing the moonie. He didn't really want a picture of a boy's bottom on his computer and he didn't think he would use it but it might be useful evidence of ill intent at a later stage.

The blond was rather more difficult because he was further away and kept bobbing about but Humphrey managed to get a reasonable still which, again, he thought would make the boy instantly recognisable to anyone who knew him. Besides you could make out a white logo on his black teeshirt.

Humphrey took a swig at his cold coffee.

'Right, you little shits,' he said out loud. 'I have you now.'

Humphrey & Jack

22. You Did What?

'You did what?' exclaimed Garth Porter. His stout frame was infused with righteous indignation and he inflated like a bullfrog.

'I captured stills from the CCTV of the bastards fouling my garden and put them on Facebook. That's what.'

'O Lordy! Lordy!' said Hector holding up the palms of his hands in simulated despair.

'You cloth-eared, micro-brained idiot!' said Garth. 'You can't go around putting pictures of children on Facebook.'

Across the room, Secondhand Sue's ears pricked up.

'Keep your voice down,' hissed Humphrey. 'Big Ears is listening as usual…

'Anyway, that's what I did,' he continued. 'Did you not see them? They came out rather well, I thought.'

Humphrey had been on Facebook for six years. He had eight friends, three of whom were sitting with him now. Another was his cleaning lady, Mrs Price, a lugubrious Welshwoman of a humourless and puritanical disposition. The other three were colleagues from his teaching days with whom he had kept in touch in case they might prove useful for his research.

In consequence, his newsfeed was a limited affair. The daily pictures of Mrs Price's cat, David Attenborough, he could do without, but they came with the territory. Phil, one of his sometime university colleagues, posted pictures of almost every meal he prepared which was a little wearing but he was an excellent cook and he and Humphrey often exchanged recipes.

There were also the advertisements for stairlifts, hearing aids, Viking holidays and incontinence pads but they were easy to ignore.

The Evangelists never actually posted anything, apart from Norman, who would occasionally post holiday snaps which never got any likes so there wasn't really a lot of point.

Humphrey & Jack

The whole purpose of Humphrey's Facebook account was so that he could communicate quickly (and for free) with his cronies. However, on this occasion, he had changed his settings from 'friends only' to 'public' and posted all the pictures (except the one of the dark-haired boy mooning) asking if anyone out there could identify the perpetrators.

'Totally irresponsible, you muddle-headed poltroon!' Garth thundered. 'What maggot got into your brain and persuaded you to play the vigilante in your dotage?'

'It worked, didn't it?' said Humphrey.

'What do you mean, it worked?' said Garth.

'I mean once the boys' names were known, I could inform the police, and now at last they're taking action.'

'You should have left it to the police in the first place,' Garth snapped. 'Who the hell do you think you are, Judge Jeffreys?'

'Don't be ridiculous!' Humphrey was riled now. 'I contacted the police about the pagan racket in the park. Week after week, it's been going on. And what happened when I called them? Sweet Fanny Adams, that's what. Oh, they turned up eventually and moved them on, all big smiles and bonhomie, but what good was that? It was late. They'd buggered up my evening anyway.

'They rang up later to ask if the response had been satisfactory and I said yes, but told them again that it would make no difference. They just said that there was nothing much they could do because the kids were not committing an offence.'

'So you decided you would be legislator, law-enforcement officer, magistrate and executioner, did you?'

'Coming from you, that's rich, Garth Porter. You're the one who thinks his opinion is law. You have but to think it and *lex facta est*, sovereign and indisputable.'

'Children, children,' said Hector, 'you cannot conceive how your wrangling and discord vexes and grieves me. We are here to complain about the vanity of the world, not about each other.'

Humphrey & Jack

'I must admit, I cannot see what the fuss is about,' Norman said. 'Humphrey had a long-standing grievance. The police did nothing about it. So Humphrey acted. Now the police are involved. Result. Simple.'

'Not exactly, my venerable friend,' Hector said. 'These boys have been shamed publicly before any due process has taken place and before they can answer for themselves.'

'What the devil could they say in mitigation?' Humphrey said. 'The evidence of the photographs is incontrovertible. And what is more, the police have seen the CCTV record in full. They say the boys are known to them.'

'We can all understand why you have the hump, Humphrey, but these boys have friends, families, teachers. You can't know what impact your exposure of their little adventure might have on their futures.'

'Little adventure?' Humphrey spat.

'Don't you realise you might have rendered them unemployable in the future?' said Garth, 'but that won't bother Lord Justice Humphrey, will it?'

'Look,' Norman said. 'It seems to me that Humphrey has only accelerated what was going to happen anyway. These boys were being a public nuisance which progressed to trespass on private land. You could argue that Humphrey was performing a civic duty.'

Garth made a dismissive trumpeting sound.

'Don't you realise that your photographs will be there for ever?' he said. 'You've incriminated them for life.'

'No, they won't. I took them down.'

'You may have taken your post down. But you don't know how far they may have been shared.'

Hector said: 'Any judgement a court handed down - if it got to court, of course - would soon be spent. But I'm afraid trial by Facebook is a sentence for ever. Turn back, O Humph, forswear thy foolish ways.'

'So the little bastards are victims now, is that it?'

Humphrey & Jack

'It is axiomatic that you do not put pictures of children on Facebook,' said Garth.

'They're hardly children, are they?' said Norman. 'They're old enough to know the difference between right and wrong.'

'They're under sixteen, aren't they?'

'The blond one is,' said Humphrey, 'but that's not really relevant.'

'I think this has a lot to do with the fact that Garth and Humphrey are still employed in education,' said Norman. 'From what I can see from emails from my union everybody in teaching has got the willies about the Internet.'

'Quite rightly,' Garth said. 'Fanatics are making bombs out of household objects. It's Blue Peter for terrorists. "Here's one I made already" - and bang goes a bus. Infants are sending pictures of their miniature willies and perverts are drooling all over the world. Teenagers can't communicate or even copulate any more because they're only used to phone sex. No wonder educationalists are cautious. You and Norman retired in more innocent times.'

'But you can't blame the tool, only the user,' said Norman. 'Aristotle pointed out that we can use a knife to kill but also to cut bread. We can't blame the knife if the user is a murderer.'

'Oh Aristotle Finknottle!' said Garth. 'You two dotards can't see that the Internet has changed everything.'

'I'm getting fed up of this,' said Humphrey. 'Don't you want to know what happened next before you condemn me out of hand? Or have you made up your minds already?'

'The Evangelists are just,' Hector intoned. 'Be still, my brethren. Humphrey has the conch.'

'Well, when I put the pictures up, the responses came in pretty quickly.'

Garth rumbled like a volcano but was silenced by a look from Hector.

Humphrey & Jack

'I must admit there were a lot of messages of sympathy and support expressed in language I couldn't possibly condone but there were also names and they were totally consistent. There were even a couple of addresses from neighbours in their street who said that they had been running loose for years and that their parents couldn't control them.'

'Were these public too?' said Garth.

'Good God, no. I'd specifically asked for any information to be sent by private message. I wanted information not a witch hunt.'

Garth snorted but was silent.

'There was a retired primary school teacher who said that the boys had been trouble since their early years and a newsagent who said he'd reported them to the police for persistent pilfering and that they'd been cautioned.'

'So what did you do, Humphrey?' asked Hector.

'Well, I had the names now and the addresses even, so I rang the police and told them everything I told you.'

'I bet they weren't interested,' said Norman. 'Too busy with traffic offences.'

'Well no, quite the contrary. The lady on the other end of the phone thanked me for the information and said someone would be round within the next couple of days.'

'To arrest you?' said Garth.

'Give it a break, Garth,' said Humphrey. 'You're like a broken record. Do you want to know what happened or not?'

'Go on, Humphrey,' said Hector. 'Ignore Signor Windbag.'

'Actually, a PCSO arrived that same evening.'

'A what?' said Garth.

'Police Community Support Officer,' said Norman. 'One of "Blunkett's Bobbies".'

'Oh them,' said Garth. 'You see them waddling up and down the High Street in their high viz jackets. Most of them are too lardy-arsed to be proper cops.'

Humphrey & Jack

'Well, to be honest, I was pleasantly surprised. He was a very presentable and polite young man. Asked if he could come in. I said of course he could. Wiped his feet without being asked.'

They were interrupted by Cora bringing pies.

'Well, you are a dark horse and no mistake, Humphrey Icke,' she said. 'Playing the detective on Facebook, eh?'

'See what you've done,' said Garth. 'Every Tom, Dick and Harriet will have seen those photos.'

'Here,' said Cora, 'watch what you're saying, Fatty, or you'll be getting your pies elsewhere. Now, you gentlemen look as if you're ready for another drink. What's it to be? Same again?'

They nodded in turn.

'Right, I'll bring them over. I hope they catch the little bleeders, lock them up and throw away the key. What they did to Humphrey's garden is a disgrace.

'And you,' she said to Garth, 'can keep a civil tongue in your head. "Every Harriet" indeed.'

And she batted him on the head with her tin tray as she passed.

'So what did Mr Pseudo-Plod say?' said Garth. 'Gave you an ASBO did he?'

Humphrey ignored him.

'He asked if I had any objection to my showing him the photos. I said that of course I hadn't and took him up to my study. He looked through them and made some notes. Then he asked me if I had any objection to taking them down.'

Humphrey sensed Garth was about to say 'I told you so' but cut him off before he could speak.

'I asked him if I had done anything wrong in posting them and he said no, but the police would prefer it if members of the public contacted them directly instead. I pointed out that, with respect, these boys appeared to have been running amok for some time without check. And he said: "not exactly". I told him that I would be more than happy to remove the images since they'd served their purpose and that I'd taken no pleasure in exposing the boys. I just wanted something done. He sat next to me as I removed them.'

'So what's going to happen?' asked Norman.

'Well, there's not much they can do about the noise problem. The law, as it stands, is not much help. However, the consequences of their invasion of the garden mean that they can probably be persuaded that it's not a good idea to show their faces here again.

'Now the younger boy, the blond one, didn't set foot on the lawn, but apparently he might respond to a talking to and the policeman said he would be going round immediately after leaving me.'

'Just a slap on the wrist then?' said Norman.

'Wait,' Humphrey said. 'It seems the younger boy's behaviour will depend very much on what happens to the older boy.'

'Now, apparently he could be done for trespass, but that's a civil offence which could result in a fine, which the boy probably couldn't afford to pay. The littering could amount to "aggravated trespass" if it interfered with any "lawful activity" I might have been engaged in at the time but apparently "enjoying my garden" isn't an activity. It would be if I owned a golf course.

'Then there's "criminal damage" which would have a good chance of sticking though a youth court might not lean too heavily on the lad, even though he does have "form" and has been cautioned in the past.'

'No wonder there's so much vandalism and delinquency,' said Cora, bringing the beers. She had, of course, been listening to every word. 'I blame *The Guardian*.'

And she returned to her *Daily Mail*.

'Thing is,' Humphrey continued, 'the boy has a pretty wretched background. Mother died of cancer. Father went to pieces, took to drink and has had a few spells in the clink himself. So the boy was never properly looked after.'

Humphrey & Jack

'O, praise ye the Lord,' said Hector. 'Praise Him in the height. Heavenly Father, look down upon thy servant, Humphrey, in whom we perceive the stirrings of what might be described as a soul.'

'It might. Mind you, I've never really been that vindictive about it. I just wanted the bloody noise to stop.'

'Now then,' Humphrey continued. 'The officer suggested that there might be a further possibility if I were open to it. Apparently Radcestershire Constabulary run what they call a Reparation Scheme. If the victim agrees, the offender avoids court, first of all by apologising convincingly to the victim and then undergoing some kind of community service, or the victim can even suggest some kind of appropriate work, which has to be approved, of course.'

'Rehabilitation, eh?' said Norman. 'You can't quarrel with that now, can you Garth?'

Garth grunted that he could not.

'And do you have some kind of redemptive chore in mind for your juvenile miscreant, Your Benignancy?' asked Hector.

'Send him up your chimney!' said Cora, looking up from her paper.

'Send him down the mines!' said Secondhand Sue from her corner.

'Back in your hole, you secret, black and midnight hag!' said Garth.

'Boil your head,' said Sue for a change.

'Oh I have something much better in mind,' said Humphrey. 'I am going to have him build a fence between my house and Chateau Bellingham as high as the law will allow.'

'It won't keep the cat out,' said Norman.

'Maybe not,' said Humphrey, 'but it'll piss the old camel off no end.'

Humphrey & Jack

Humphrey & Jack

JACK

23. The Fence

The fence was coming along well. It was now about a third of the way up the garden. Humphrey had decided on lateral planks as it would be easier to cope with the slope. Each section would be stepped a couple of inches higher than the previous one. As Humphrey wanted the fence to be much taller than the existing one, new posts would be needed at intervals. However, there was no need to start from scratch as they could be securely attached to those that were already there.

Humphrey would not have described himself as a do-it-yourself expert, but he was quite handy about the house and had a stack of DIY magazines from a time when he had just bought the place. From these, he had gleaned what he needed to know, made a shopping list of materials and any additional tools he might need, and driven to Homebase. It had all been delivered a few days ago and stored under a tarpaulin at the bottom of the garden.

Mrs Bellingham had rung his doorbell as soon as the first posts had gone up.

'Just what is going on exactly, Mr Icke?' she said as he opened the door.

'Well now, Putin continues his sabre rattling, the ONS has its predictions wrong again, Brexit is going well or badly, depending on your point of view, and a thunderstorm is predicted later,' said Humphrey with a beatific smile.

'Don't play your silly games with me. You know perfectly well what I mean.'

'But I don't, Mrs B. Pray explain.'

'I mean the fence.'

'The fence? What fence?'

'Oh, don't be ridiculous. The fence. The garden fence.'

'Oh, the garden fence. Yes. What about it?'

'Stop wasting my time, Mr Icke. What is going on exactly? With the fence?'

'Ah, the fence. I'm repairing it. That's what you suggested, isn't it?'

'But those posts must be about eight feet high?'

'Exactly that,' said Humphrey who was enjoying himself enormously. 'Well done!'

'But why? Why so high?'

'So I can blot you out of my life, Mrs Bellingham. Now, I'm sure you could be busybodying more profitably elsewhere. Goodbye now.'

And he closed the door in her face.

Humphrey watched Jack working from the upstairs study window. He was no slacker, that was for sure. He had even told Humphrey that he'd looked at fence-building videos on YouTube and had gathered a few tips of his own. This was his third day on the job and they were still very shy of each other but Humphrey took this bit of independent research as a promising sign.

The wood still looked a little raw, Humphrey thought, but when it was finished, he would get Jack to stain it, perhaps a dark green. Then he would plant rue, pennyroyal, rosemary and more lavender. He had come across a panel in one of the DIY magazines that claimed that cats hated these plants. It would be worth a try; the fence alone would not deter Aristotle.

Humphrey & Jack

Come to think of it, he had not seen the creature recently. Perhaps Jack's presence deterred him. That might be it.

He went down to the kitchen to make coffee and carried it upstairs in a mug which had been a retirement present from one of his students, Tom Sinclair. It featured Humphrey Bogart and the caption: 'Here's looking at you, kid'. Humphrey didn't really like it but used it out of a bizarre sense of loyalty to Tom, who was one of the very few of his students he had ever taught who had shown any genuine intellectual curiosity.

When he returned to the window, he saw that Mrs Bellingham was standing at a bit of the old fence with her arms folded talking to Jack. Though he had the window wide open, for it was a very hot afternoon, he could not hear what they were saying.

He also saw that it was getting very dark. Trees were thrashing about in the garden and in the park, and a white haze was moving over the low hills opposite, gradually obliterating the neat shape of the city cemetery and crematorium. There was a faint flicker of lightning on the horizon, followed several seconds later by a low growl of thunder.

What was the interfering old camel up to now, Humphrey wondered. Suddenly, Jack turned and pointed up at the house and Humphrey stepped back abruptly from the window spilling a little coffee onto the cream carpet as he did so.

'Damn the bitch,' he said out loud.

He went to the upstairs bathroom and returned with a cloth and a bowl of soapy water. With one hand on the windowsill he lowered himself to the ground on protesting knees. He began to work on the stains from the outside in. Fortunately, he appeared to have acted quickly enough and he thought it likely that there would be no sign of the accident once the wet patch had dried.

Whilst he was down there, there was a flash of lightning which illuminated the carpet intensely for a second. A couple of seconds more and there was a loud crack of thunder. The storm was moving very quickly over the valley on which Radcester was built. Humphrey pulled himself painfully to his feet and looked out of the open window.

The sky was as dark as dusk, though it was only mid afternoon. The wind had dropped and the trees were quite still. The birds had stopped singing. Mrs Bellingham was gone and Jack had resumed work, looking up occasionally at the sky.

Humphrey had never invited Jack indoors. He had taken coffee and sandwiches out to the boy. He was more than happy to provide refreshment but to invite him in seemed inappropriate: he was there to make reparation for his anti-social behaviour, not to be rewarded.

However, the storm was about to break and he couldn't just leave him in the garden.

'Jack!' he shouted. 'Jack, you'd better come in!'

But as Jack put his tools into the canvas holdall at his feet, the first thick heavy drops began to fall and, by the time he reached the stone steps, the low-slung sky collapsed and it began to rain in sheets.

By the time Humphrey had hobbled downstairs, his knees seeming to detonate with every step, and unlocked and flung open the garden door, it was already far too late.

The boy stood there, dripping, and soaked to the very bones.

24. Jacek

'Quick, quick, come in,' said Humphrey, fussing like a mother hen. 'You're absolutely sodden. Oh dear, I'm so sorry. I should have shouted out earlier, only I spilt coffee on the carpet, and…Well, never mind that. Get those wet things off, I'll get you a towel and a bath robe.'

The boy said nothing but shook his wet hair like a dog.

Humphrey scuttled into the downstairs bathroom just off the hall where they were standing.

Humphrey & Jack

When he arrived back with a thick blue bath sheet and a towelling bathrobe that he kept for his (infrequent) guests, Jack had already pulled his wet tee shirt over his head and was fumbling with the belt of his jeans.

'No, no, no, not here,' said Humphrey, panicking at the impropriety of a boy about to strip naked in his hallway. 'In the bathroom. Here.'

He handed the boy the towel and the robe and almost pushed him into the bathroom, pulling the door closed after him.

After a couple of minutes, Jack emerged wearing the robe and holding his clothes in a bundle with his trainers perched on the top. He had draped the towel over his head like a monk's cowl.

He had still said not a word.

He handed his parcel to Humphrey who said: 'Right, I'll just pop these in the dryer. Why don't you just go upstairs? First right. I'll join you in a moment.'

Jack went up the stairs towelling his hair as he went. The bath robe was a bit long but it did the job. As the boy's bare feet turned right at the top of the stairs, Humphrey was seized with panic.

'Oh Lord above. What have I just said?' he thought. 'That boy is naked under that bathrobe. And I have just sent him upstairs. He must think I am some sort of pervert.'

The panic abated a little as he put the clothes in the washing machine and selected the fast spin. He was careful to remove the leather belt and hang it up. He propped the trainers against the skirting board. He might pop them in an old pillowcase and give them a spin a bit later. He expected them to stink but they were not malodorous at all.

He realised that if the boy had followed his instructions he would have found himself in the study, so that was all right.

No, it wasn't. What must he have been thinking as he climbed the stairs? That he was being sent to a bedroom. Without his clothes.

Humphrey felt clammy with embarrassment and confusion. This capacity to reduce any situation to its most alarming possibilities was commonplace with Humphrey.

Humphrey & Jack

He must go upstairs immediately and abuse the boy.
No! Disabuse the boy!
Christ! He was even making Freudian slips inside his own head.
When he went into the study, however, Jack was standing at the window, watching the storm which was still raging. He turned to Humphrey with an unexpected and beguiling smile.
'Do you like storms?' Humphrey asked, moving to stand beside him. Jack's hair had been roughed up into spikes by his towelling.
'Yeah. This is awesome.'
And so they stood there, man and boy, side by side, watching the tempest.

The storm was immediately overhead now with barely a moment between thunder and lightning. It was practically dark outside. The rain rattled furiously on the ivy leaves that wreathed the window and bent the branches of the trees around the lawn. Then there would be a flash and the garden would be brilliantly lit in monochrome and the thunder grumbled and cracked and banged, shaking the sash windows of the old house in their wooden frames.

Because the rain fell vertically and because the eaves of the house were deep, there was barely any water on the glass of the window where they were standing. It was open from below and they could feel that the temperature had dropped by several degrees.

Gradually the raging abated and a thin line of white began to grow on the southern horizon. The hissing of the rain diminished to a patter and then a heavy dripping.

Humphrey came to, as out of a trance, and the brightening of the sky seemed to break the strange spell between them. He felt a little embarrassed now at having this boy in his sanctum.

'I suppose I'd better get back to work,' Jack said.
'In my dressing gown? Anyway, your time for today's nearly up. I'm going to put your clothes in front of a heater in the utility room and see if I

can dry your trainers out a bit. You can't put damp clothes on. Shouldn't take long. Would you like a coffee?'

'Yeah, cool,' Jack grunted.

Downstairs, Humphrey pulled the clothes from the machine; they were nearly dry. He fished out a convector heater that he used to supplement the central heating in winter and hung Jack's clothes on a drying rack in front of it. Then he put the trainers inside a drawstring cloth bag that he used for clothes pegs and put the package inside the drum of the washing machine, choosing the fastest spin cycle. That would be better than a pillowcase. The clatter was alarming. It wouldn't dry them off, of course, but at least the boy would not be slopping about in them.

Then in the kitchen he made a cafetière of coffee and set out a packet of Jaffa Cakes on a plate.

What am I doing? he thought. Why am I waiting hand and foot on a delinquent boy? who insulted me with gross language? who trespassed on my property and desecrated my garden? who is probably even now rifling through my papers upstairs looking for what he can steal? I must be taking leave of my senses.

As he climbed the stairs with the tray his knees locked agonisingly for a few long moments and he thought he might have to spend the rest of his life halfway up the staircase.

It passed. When he reached his study, Jack was sitting at the round table in the corner absorbed in a large illustrated book.

'You've got a lot of books,' he said.

'Part of the job.'

'What do you do?'

'Well, I'm retired now, but I was a history lecturer.'

'At the uni?'

'At the uni indeed. Milk and sugar?'

'No milk. Three sugars.'

Humphrey's spoon paused momentarily as he considered the request but thought better of giving dietary advice.

Humphrey & Jack

'What have you got there?'

'*Illustrated History of Europe in the Fourteenth Century.*'

'You're interested in history then?'

Jack lifted his head and looked at him with an ironic expression which seemed to invite him to consider just how moronic the question was. Then he carried on reading. They sipped their coffee in silence as Humphrey watched him fascinated.

This felon, this trespasser with the foul mouth, was reading a chapter about the late medieval history of Poland. How easy it is to misunderstand people, he thought. He had imagined that the boy's preferred reading matter would be limited to tabloid newspapers and pornography.

Jack turned the page. There was a large illustration of a monarch in red and gold ceremonial robes with the crowned white eagle of Poland on a red badge on his shoulder. A lifetime in education had given him a facility for reading upside down.

'Ah, Casimir III, I believe,' Humphrey said.

'Casimir the Great,' Jack said, as if to correct him.

'Indeed, yes,' said Humphrey, 'he had a most impressive career. Are you Polish, Jack?'

'Why?'

Jack's expression was one of suspicion.

'Oh nothing. It's just that not many boys of your age have an interest in the medieval history of Poland. And your surname - Lis - it's a Polish name isn't it?'

'My mother was English. My father is Polish.'

'Your mother *was* English?'

'She died. Last year. Cancer.'

'I'm sorry.'

'You can't be. You didn't know her.'

He looked up and the expression was almost hostile. Humphrey was not going to be discomfited in his own home.

Humphrey & Jack

'It is a sad thing to lose a mother when you are so young. I meant that I am sorry for you.'

'There's no need to be. Can I have some more coffee?'

'Help yourself. Were you born in Poland?'

'Nah, Radcester. My father was born in Łódź.'

Humphrey was unfamiliar with the name. It sounded like 'Wudch'. The terminal consonants were soft and slushy.

'Write it down for me,' said Humphrey. 'Here.' He picked up a roller ball pen lying on the table and a corner of *The Daily Telegraph.*

The boy wrote it down in a clear round hand.

'You speak Polish then?'

'I am bilingual, yeah,' Jack said, as though it were no big deal. '"Lis" means "fox" in Polish.'

That's rather appropriate, thought Humphrey though he refrained from saying it.

'Actually, my real name is Jacek Lis,' he said. It sounded like 'Jat-sek'.

'That's a beautiful name.'

'I like it.'

'So why "Jack", then?'

'Because it's easier. Just like my friend Marek calls himself Mark. We keep a low profile. There's bullying and racism at college. They say things like: "I'd rather be a Paki than a Pole." It's not so good.'

'That's bloody disgraceful. Do the staff know that you have to put up with that?'

'Christ no. We don't want them involved. Some of the fuckers are worse than the students.'

Humphrey was taken aback by the swear word but Jack made no apology.

'We keep a low profile,' Jack said. 'But…'

'Yes?' Humphrey prompted.

'*Nie wstydzę się być Polakiem*. I am not ashamed of being Polish.'

Humphrey & Jack

'Nor should you be. The Polish are a proud and much abused people.'

'Yeah, yeah, yeah. Second World War pilots and all that. Yada yada yada,' Jack said and returned to the book.

Humphrey was stung by this rudeness but he refused to acknowledge it and merely said: 'I think your clothes should be dry by now,' and he went to check.

They were. He folded them neatly and called to Jack to come down.

'They're fine. The trainers are still a touch damp but I've done the best I can. Just hang the robe on the back of the door.'

Jack went into the downstairs bathroom and, on a whim, creaky knees notwithstanding, Humphrey went back up to his study and picked up the rather expensive book.

'This is absurd,' he muttered to himself. 'I must be losing my marbles.'

When Jack emerged fully clothed, Humphrey held out the book and said: 'Since you've taken such a shine to it, you can borrow it, if you like. Only - take care of it. It wasn't cheap.'

'Really?' said Jack. 'I can borrow it?'

'Really,' said Humphrey.

And Jack's sulky face was transformed, just for a second, by a genial smile.

'Right then,' said Humphrey, as he escorted Jack to the front door. The trees which lined Upper Bishop's Lane still dripped but the sun was out. The front garden smelt gorgeous. 'I'll see you next Tuesday. Usual time.'

Jack gave a non-committal grunt.

'Have a good weekend,' Humphrey said to the retreating back.

There was no reply.

Humphrey & Jack

25. No Show

When Jack did not turn up at nine the following Tuesday, Humphrey was surprised how much he minded. It was not just that he had gone out of his way to give the boy a chance and that, perhaps out of character, he had chosen rehabilitation over retribution. It was not just this, though, heaven knows, the decision to do the decent thing and then have your horse fall at the first fence was humiliating and frustrating enough.

It was also the very curious fact that he had enjoyed the boy's company during the afternoon of the storm. He had enjoyed fussing about drying the boy's clothes, making coffee, making conversation. He thought he had detected some small intimations that the boy was human. No-one who enjoyed thunderstorms, who was interested in the career of Casimir III of Poland, who was bilingual and who liked Jaffa cakes - no-one with these qualities could be entirely beyond redemption.

The morning wore on and Humphrey felt sad. He would leave it till Wednesday morning and then he felt he would have to report Jack's non-appearance to the CSO. Humphrey's sadness was intensified by the fact that, quite illogically, he felt he had failed.

At half-past eleven, the doorbell rang. It was Jack.

'What time do you call this?' Humphrey said, although he was privately delighted and relieved to see him.

'I've no idea,' said Jack.

'But you're very late. This isn't what we agreed.'

'Yeah, well. Things. My dad. I don't really want to talk about it. Shall I just get on with it?'

He was clearly in a very bad mood and he wouldn't look Humphrey in the eye. This made Humphrey cross but he was determined not to provoke a row.

Humphrey & Jack

'I've put the tool bag on the terrace by the garden door,' Humphrey said. 'You might as well come right through rather than going all the way round.'

'I'll make up the time,' Jack said, as he wiped his shoes rather ostentatiously.

'There's no hurry,' said Humphrey. 'Though that's not really the point.'

'Whatever.'

Humphrey hated this teen locution with intensity. Its connotations of existential indifference appalled Humphrey. It flew insolently in the face of British good manners.

But Humphrey was determined not to rise to it.

'Are you enjoying the book?' he said.

'Oh, I didn't realise you wanted it back so quickly,' said Jack. Humphrey couldn't be sure that he wasn't being sarcastic.

'No, no, no, keep it for as long as you like.'

'I'll bring it next time. Right, I'd better get on with it then.'

They were now at the door which led onto the garden terrace. Here in the light Humphrey saw that the boy's eyes were red-rimmed, as if he had been crying but he thought it prudent to say nothing.

'I'll bring you a coffee,' said Humphrey. 'No milk, three sugars, yes?'

At last, just a hint of the smile that had charmed Humphrey earlier.

Later, Humphrey went upstairs to do some reading but couldn't settle and found himself looking out into the garden. Jack was holding the coffee mug in both hands and standing back to survey his work. He had made significant progress on the fence and the coffee must be cold by now.

It was time to think about lunch. As he stood in the kitchen assembling a salad, he decided to invite Jack to join him. Previously, he had given him an hour for a lunch break and Jack had gone away and come back. But it was such a glorious day and he felt he could hardly eat outside and leave Jack working or send him off to Gregg's or something.

Humphrey & Jack

He went outside with cutlery and napkins and put up the big cream parasol over the garden table. Several ladybirds fell out and he swept them away. He called down to Jack who was fixing a new post.

'Would you care to join me for lunch, Jack? It's nothing special.'

'It's all right. I'll just go into town.'

'Where will you go?'

'I'd normally go to Subway, but…'

'But…?'

'I haven't any money.' The voice seemed to defy pity or charity.

'Then I insist. It's just pâté and cheese and some nice bread. And perhaps a glass of wine. Your father wouldn't object, would he?'

'You must be fucking joking,' Jack said. He had come up to the terrace. 'He's out of his head on Special Brew half the time. Sorry about the swearing.'

'I'm not made of glass, you know, though I wish you wouldn't,' said Humphrey. 'Well, you'd better wash your hands then. You know where it is, don't you?'

He had understated the quality of the spread. The pâté was home made and enhanced with brandy, the bread was fresh and crusty and warm and the cheeses were from an excellent *fromagerie* in the cathedral quarter run by a knowledgeable Frenchwoman. The wine was from a box but served up in a hand-painted jug. There was a homemade *tarte à l'oignon* which would normally have lasted Humphrey a week, a big green salad, and a white bowl piled with greengages.

Humphrey liked to cook though he very rarely had guests and the rather grand dining room on the ground floor of the house was almost never used. He had become quite adept at making a batch of something and freezing individual portions though he often forgot to label the boxes and bags and so he wouldn't know what he was having for supper until it defrosted.

'Wow!' said Jack when he returned from the bathroom.

Humphrey & Jack

'Come on then. Come and sit down. Don't expect me to feed you. Just help yourself to anything you'd like.'

'Got to admit…I'm starving. Didn't get any breakfast.'

They ate for a while in silence.

'Brilliant salad dressing,' said Jack at one point with his mouth full.

Humphrey nodded.

'Bloody brilliant. What's the secret?'

'Not telling,' said Humphrey and they both laughed, a little childishly, he thought, but not caring.

'What were you talking to the camel about last week?' Humphrey asked suddenly, pouring out more wine.

'The camel?'

'Mrs Bellingham. My neighbour. She of the distended nostrils and the vile temper. I saw her talking to you from upstairs.'

'She wanted to know how come I was working on the fence.'

'And what did you tell her?'

'I said I was working for the council. Something to do with health and safety. She wanted to know what that had to do with a fence. I said I didn't fucking know, did I? I just did what I was told. I said she'd have to ring the council herself if she wanted to know.'

Humphrey laughed out loud.

'Oh Jack, you gem! She'll have rung every department on the council and nagged them for hours. How wonderful.'

'She's there now,' said Jack.

'Who?'

'Mrs Bellend, or whatever. There, at her window. She's watching us.'

Humphrey turned in his seat and there she was indeed, standing at her upstairs window and holding the edge of the curtain.

'She's wondering what on earth you're doing having lunch with a council operative,' said Jack and they both burst out laughing. Humphrey gave her a wave and Jack followed suit, blowing her a ripe kiss.

Mrs Bellingham disappeared in an instant.

Humphrey & Jack

The sun was high in a hot sky with only a few whisks of cirrus to break the blue uniformity. Under the shade it was comfortable to be eating cheese and fruit. At one point, Humphrey went inside for more wine.

'This isn't getting the fence done, is it?' said Jack.

'Oh, don't worry about that,' said Humphrey. 'All in good time. I haven't enjoyed myself so much in ages, young man. Thank you for the company.'

'I could come on Saturday morning and catch up.'

'There's no need you know.'

'I don't mind. I like working on the fence. And it's only fair.'

'If you're sure…'

'Sure I'm sure. No worries.'

Whether it was the wine that relaxed them both or whether it would have happened anyway, the conversation flowed freely and Humphrey learnt that Jack was at Radcester Sixth Form College, studying History, English Literature and Polish for A level. He confessed that he'd been 'bunking off' most of the time recently.

'Why, Jack?'

'Well, to be honest, the teaching's not all that good in History. The lecturer just reads from his notes. From what I've heard he's been using the same notes for years. He left them behind in the lecture room once. Would you believe it, there were little asterisks in the margin with 'joke here' written in a different colour?

'And we have to do whatever option the lazy bastard selects. Same old stuff as GCSE. The Middle Ages never get a look in. Not relevant, I suppose.

'And I speak better Polish than the Polish guy. I'm all right in the language work but the literature is a bit tricky. We have to do a play by Gabriela Zapolska called *The Morality of Mrs Dulska*. I don't get it. I don't know whether we're supposed to laugh or cry. I get the language all right but I don't get the tone and the lecturer is all right about Poland in the Second World War, but he's shit on literature.

Humphrey & Jack

'The English teacher is good though. She cries sometimes when she reads poetry but she knows her stuff and she works hard and she treats us as individuals. And she has a sense of humour. I can talk to her.

'I mentioned the Zapolska and she asked if it was available in translation. I said it was and she said she'd be willing to try to help but that if the problem was to do with tone and culture, she might not be able to. I told her she shouldn't waste her time.'

'Aren't you a bit defeatist about all this?' Humphrey asked gently.

'Probably,' said Jack. He looked at his watch. 'Hey, look at the time. I should go.'

'Stay for a coffee at least.'

'OK. I'll just put the tools away. I'll definitely come round on Saturday to catch up. That was a lovely lunch.

'Good,' said Humphrey. 'I'll not be long.'

When he came out with the coffee, Jack had tidied up and was sitting at the table fiddling with his phone. Humphrey had brought with him a slender bottle of old Calvados which he had been saving for a special occasion, though he could not possibly imagine what that might be, unless this were it.

'What's that?' Jack asked.

'It's an apple brandy from Normandy. I like it better than grape brandy. It tastes better the older it is. Unfortunately, I can't tell you how old this is because I can't remember how long I've had it.'

'It could be really ancient then,' said Jack who suddenly realised that Humphrey might be offended. 'Shit, I'm sorry. I didn't mean…'

Humphrey laughed.

'Jack, I wouldn't be much of a historian if I thought that old age conferred either wisdom or folly of itself, or that youth was always an unconditional benefit, in and of itself, either.'

'Whoa! That's quite a sentence, man.'

'Well, I am an academic,' said Humphrey. 'Here, try it.'

Humphrey & Jack

He poured Jack a small glass and one for himself. Jack sipped at it and coughed.

'Went down the wrong way,' he spluttered, his eyes watering. He sipped again.

'Good?' asked Humphrey.

'Mmmm,' said Jack.

They sat in silence for a while. Late afternoon noise was starting up in the park but Humphrey found he didn't mind. He felt mellow.

'Jack,' he said. 'Do you think you can tell me why you were late this morning? It doesn't matter if you don't. You seemed very troubled, that's all. Maybe I can help.'

Humphrey expected to be shrugged off but the wine and spirits loosened Jack's tongue.

Apparently, he had got up in good time. He had been woken in the night around three o'clock by his father returning home drunk. This was a very common occurrence it seemed. He crashed around for a while and Jack stayed in bed knowing it was unwise to confront him when he was like this. Then he heard his father stagger up the stairs and into his own room. It was a long time before Jack could get to sleep again.

In the morning he found that his father had been sick up the hallway wallpaper, on the kitchen floor and into a sink full of dirty crockery. Glasses had been swept from a cupboard and lay smashed on the floor.

Jack had gone upstairs again and opened his father's door slightly. He had heard of drunks choking on their own vomit and Jack needed to check that he was all right - he was his father after all. He needn't have worried: he father was snoring loudly. He would stay in bed now for several days, getting up only to eat the food Jack would prepare for him or to go to the twenty-four hour convenience store on the corner for more booze. Jack had learnt to stay out of his way.

He was late because he had to clean up the vomit and broken glass and to restore the house to what order he could.

'And now, I've really got to go. Is it OK if I climb over the garden gate?'

'I'll get the key,' said Humphrey.

'No, don't bother. See you Saturday. Nine o'clock. Sharp.'

He ran down the sloping lawn and vaulted over the little gate. Humphrey watched him running down the steps by the fountain and down the curving path towards the park gates on Prior Ingham's Road.

Jack had told his story without a vestige of self-pity.

26. Casimir III

Jack and Humphrey became friends. It was not a straightforward business and there were times when Humphrey wondered whether or not he might be making a fearful mistake.

Jack arrived bang on time on the Saturday after their lunch but he seemed sullen and disinclined to talk. When Humphrey opened the door, Jack acknowledged him with a nod and walked through to the garden door without a word.

'Are you OK?' Humphrey asked.

'Sure,' said Jack.

'Everything OK at home?'

'As OK as it ever is.'

And that was it. Even when Humphrey took a mug of coffee out to him (no milk, three sugars), Jack just said: 'Put it down there, please,' pointing to a flat stone, and carried on working.

By noon, he had made good progress, and certainly made up for lost time. Humphrey checked from his study window from time to time and at one point he was amused to see Mrs Bellingham watching the boy as she hung out some washing. There was only a blouse and a couple of tea towels but she spent an age over it. When Jack spotted her, he gave her a cheerful wave. She gave him a sour smile and went indoors.

Humphrey & Jack

As he deposited the tool bag in the little vestibule behind the garden door, he said: 'That was a good lunch the other day.'

'You're welcome, Jack. Any time.'

'I wasn't fishing for an invitation.'

'I know you weren't. I mean it. Any time.'

'I can't come on Tuesday by the way.'

'Not to worry. Why not, Jack?'

'I've got to see the Director of Studies at the college. At half-nine. I don't know how long it will take. About next term. I don't think it's going to be good news.'

'Do you want to talk about it?'

'No. Not now anyway.'

'Up to you.'

'I'll come next Saturday instead. If that's all right.'

'Of course, stay to lunch if you like.'

'Sweet. I mean, yeah, I'd like that.'

'Settled then,' said Humphrey. 'See you next week. Look after yourself.'

'I don't have a lot of option, do I?' said Jack wryly. Then he laughed and ran off down the garden leaving Humphrey to try to understand how he felt.

The fence would be finished in another two or three sessions. Staining or painting it would not take long. And then what? It would be term time soon. He could perhaps offer Jack some odd jobs in the garden when his reparation contract had been worked through. For payment, of course. Or would that be too obvious?

In the end, a much more profitable way of continuing their relationship presented itself, better than an invitation to do the weeding or pruning, though that would be handy if Jack were interested.

Jack arrived on time and set to work on the fence. He had brought back the book on medieval history that Humphrey had loaned him. He was pleased to note that it had been beautifully looked after, checking it care-

Humphrey & Jack

fully while Jack was working. There was, he thought, a very special and very deep circle in Hell for those who turned down pages or scribbled in margins or who left coffee rings on the covers of books. He would have them flounder in boiling ink to the end of days.

Humphrey had gone to some trouble in preparing lunch. He had casseroled chicken thighs in cider with strips of red, yellow and green peppers and whole green peppercorns. The kitchen filled with savoury steam when he opened the oven door to check. While Jack was washing his hands, Humphrey put the finishing touches to a potato *dauphinoise*. Afterwards there would be a blueberry *clafoutis* and various cheeses. Humphrey had brought up a bottle of Vouvray which was now chilled to perfection. Its notes of fig and ginger would chime well with the cider and its briskness would interact well with the sweetness of the food.

It looked like rain so they ate in the kitchen and Jack declared it 'awesome'. Humphrey, unused to the appetites of teenage boys, was astonished by how much Jack put away, but was also very pleased.

'Do you always eat like this?' Jack asked.

'Good Lord, no,' said Humphrey. 'Normally I eat quite simply. It's nice to have someone to cook for. How's the wine?'

'Sort of zinging. I thought I didn't like white wine but this is brilliant.'

'What do you eat at home?'

'Oh, you know. Takeaways. Microwaved ready meals. That kind of shit.'

'Does your father not cook?'

'Actually, he can. He's not bad in fact. But he isn't often sober enough. In fact, he's a liability because we have a gas cooker and more than once he's turned the gas on and then forgotten about it. One of these days, he'll do that again and light a fag and we'll all be blown to fuck.'

'Jesus!'

'That's why I end up doing the food. It's safer.'

'How do you feel about him, Jack?'

Humphrey & Jack

Humphrey felt immediately that he had made a mistake. Jack's face was closed.

'I don't feel anything. He wasn't this bad before Mum died.'

It seemed best to leave him in silence for a while. Humphrey began to clear away the first course.

'Did you enjoy the book?' he said as he dished out the *clafoutis*.

'I did. Have you got anything else like that?'

'Probably. Why don't you go up and look when we've finished? Borrow what you like.'

'Cool,' he said, and then: 'O my God! This is incredible! I adore blueberries. How did you know?'

'Who doesn't?' said Humphrey, delighted that the *clafoutis* was such a hit. That word 'adore' was not, he thought, wholly commensurate with the street vocabulary that Jack affected most of the time. Most interesting.

'Tell me, Jack. What's your interest in the medieval period?' Humphrey was genuinely intrigued by the delinquent-academic paradox of this young man.

'I think it's because it's all about power, isn't it? I mean, it always is with history but in the Middle Ages it's so naked and, you know, personal, especially in the fourteenth century. You've got the aristocracy struggling for hegemony on the one hand and the king claiming divine right on the other. That is so fucking raw, man.'

Humphrey was amazed by how excited Jack was becoming. And again there was the incongruity between street vernacular and a word like 'hegemony'.

'Take Richard II, for instance,' Jack continued. 'Your favourite.'

'Why do you say that?'

'What?'

'My favourite?'

'Oh come on, you've got shed loads of books on him upstairs.'

'All right. Go on.'

Humphrey & Jack

'Well, I reckon Richard loved the mythology of chivalry his grandfather built around himself, all the Order of the Garter stuff, the new Arthurian world, the fake round table at Winchester. I think Edward III was so successful because he created this symbolism around himself to buttress the image of monarchy. But it was all realpolitik - it was as conscious as the mythos surrounding Elizabeth. She encouraged her courtiers and poets as the image of Gloriana the Faerie Queen evolved.

'Sorry. Is this rubbish?'

'No. Go on.'

'Well, I think the difference is that Richard really believed in all this iconography. Look at the Woolton Diptych. Richard is presented to the Virgin and all the angels are wearing Richard's emblem, the white hart. How's that for fucking hubris?'

Humphrey said nothing. This was wonderful. If any of his own students, when he taught at the university, had shown such enthusiasm and excitement, if they had made any such attempt to acquire a decent vocabulary, to read independently and, most importantly, to think for themselves, he would have been delighted. But no. Most of them were at 'uni' because that's what people of their age did, - like sex and drugs and cacophony.

'So, when Bolingbroke appears,' Jack went on, 'Richard is not prepared to deal with such ruthless pragmatism. Mind you, I think Shakespeare is a bit hard on Richard.'

'You've read the play?'

'I persuaded Mrs Behn to do it in English.'

'And you can't do this period in the History A level?'

'No, we have to do what The Wanker has chosen.'

'And what has The Wanker chosen?'

'Oh, *The Rise and Fall of the British Empire* is one paper. *Protest and Reform* is another - nearly the same period, and...I forget the other.'

'And there's no medieval option?'

'Oh yeah. *The Unification of Germany* - same period again. No. I mean, there are medieval papers, but you've got the Crusades on one side and The Wars of the Roses on the other. It's as if the Fourteenth Century didn't exist.'

'So where does Casimir the Great fit in?'

'Right. Get this then:

'Edward III - 1312 to 1377.

'Casimir III - 1310 to 1370.

'Nearly parallel. Both of them inherited impoverished kingdoms weakened by war and infighting. Both of them were incredibly strong. Edward regained vast territories in France; Casimir doubled the size of the kingdom of Poland. Edward made changes in government; Casimir founded a university.

'Mind you. Casimir welcomed the Jews into his Kingdom; Edward expelled them. Now, how fucking interesting is that?'

'Fascinating. Have you thought up these parallels yourself, Jack?' Humphrey asked.

'Where else would I have got them from?'

'I don't know. It's just that it's a bit difficult to square this clever and original mind with the hoodlum who vandalised my garden.'

'Why is it?' Jack's tone was quite aggressive.

'Why is it? because "thoughtless" is an adjective commonly associated with vandalism and because you are clearly capable of thinking very well indeed. Jekyll and Hyde come to mind.'

'Yeah, well. I think you might be dealing in some pretty corny stereotypes, man.' Jack's mood was getting ugly. 'Maybe I'd better go. If you knew the whole of it...'

'No, no, sit down. I'm trying to help.'

'Yeah, well. Leave the other stuff out, will you? I can deal with it. I'm doing the fence aren't I?'

There was a pause while Jack stared at the table.

'How did the interview go the other day?' Humphrey said.

'What interview?'

'With your Director of Studies?'

Humphrey & Jack

'Oh that. Not good. Pretty much as expected. I have to buck my ideas up, stop bunking off, and maybe drop History at A2 and concentrate on English and Polish.'

'But why would someone as bright as you drop a subject?'

'Well, it's about motivation, isn't it? I don't like the course or the teacher.'

'The teacher shouldn't come into it.'

'All teachers say that. They know it's not true.'

'Wouldn't that ruin your chances of getting into university? Do you want to go to university?'

'Yeah, I do. I want to go to a good uni. Not a Mickey Mouse place like Radcester.'

'I see,' said Humphrey.

'Is that where you went?' Jack laughed.

'It's not only where I went. I taught there for over thirty years.'

'Fuck, I'm sorry,' said Jack, although he was still laughing. 'I thought you were at Oxbridge or something.'

'I don't quite know how to take that. I did my doctorate at Durham and came back to Radcester to teach.'

'Oh, wow, Durham's cool.'

'Are you going to drop History then?'

'I dunno. It's even harder when I can't work at home. I never know when dad's going to go on a bender or go off on one.'

'You could work here.'

'Are you serious?'

'Of course.'

Jack stared at him.

'I don't know. I'll think about it.'

'You're not going to get into a good university with two A levels are you?'

'No. My Director of Studies wants me to do an EPQ.'

'What's that?'

'Extended Project Qualification. You research a topic of your own choosing. You're not taught the topic. You have a mentor who shows you how to go about researching it and putting it together and you produce a paper and do a presentation to your peers and the staff and they ask questions and it's a bit like a viva.'

'But Jack, Humphrey said. 'That's right up your street! You could do it on Edward and Casimir!'

'Yeah, but it's only worth half an A level. That's not going to get me into somewhere like Durham.'

Humphrey began to clear the table and put on a pair of Marigolds preparatory to doing the washing up. Suddenly, he shook his yellow hands in the air like a twenties flapper.

'Jack,' he said. 'I've had the most wonderful idea.'

And he told Jack what it was.

Later that evening, alone in his study, he received a friend request. It was from Jack. Humphrey accepted it and almost immediately he received a message.

'Welcome to my world,' it said.

27. Humphrey's Wonderful Idea

Jack's Facebook world was a revelation to Humphrey. While Humphrey had eight friends, Jack had over a thousand, a substantial percentage of whom were female.

The language of this world was remarkably candid about sex and the girls were as frank as the boys - about their desires, availability and expertise. It was a world where girls complimented each other extravagantly about their looks, with a degree of drooling hyper sincerity that Humphrey found suspect. When they were upset, they threatened suicide. They were obsessed with whatever food fad was current. They posted pictures of their experiments with make-up which Humphrey thought suited only for the circus or for Noh theatre perhaps. They wondered if they had the courage to have a tattoo. If they were injured, they published pictures of their wounds.

Boys vaunted their masculinity through their cars, their 'threads', their lifts and their bench presses. They were engaged in banter, which meant saying vicious things about each other and laughing about it. Everybody went to the gym, everybody aspired to go to Phuket, everybody was into protein shakes. Theirs was a hedonistic, misogynistic world where 'bros' came before 'hoes'. They talked of masturbation, ejaculation, genital warts and the clitoris in ways that Humphrey found depressing.

Yet despite all the vulgarity, it was a highly politicised world. These young people were mostly shouting from the left: about climate change, the destruction of the environment, about recycling, about how the older generation (Humphrey's generation) was destroying the planet and leaving a tainted legacy. As a university lecturer for so long, Humphrey found nothing new in this; it was old news. There was nothing fresh in this idealism, which Humphrey felt was bound to be disappointed in due course. Every rebellious generation became the establishment in the eyes of the next generation, after all.

What was new, at least in Humphrey's view, was the vehemence, the readiness to take offence, the extremism, and the noise, the unceasing noise.

From what Humphrey could see, after taking a quick look at Jack's timeline, was that he was a contributor to this noise and yet seemed somehow to distance himself from it it. His posts were mostly recommendations of music he liked. It was largely meaningless to Humphrey, of course, though he was very surprised to find Jack recommending Ravel's string quartet to a friend as 'psycho stuff'.

He would drop a firework into an argument, engage in it passionately for a while, and then disappear. In another thread, you would find him arguing the exact opposite with equal passion.

Humphrey & Jack

He flirted with girls incontinently, it seemed to Humphrey. And then he wondered if he was being a prude. It was not his business, after all. He thought he might be prying - but then after all, it was a very public world.

He took a slightly guilty look at the photographs in Jack's profile. There were many 'selfies' of Jack with different girls, all very pretty. One photograph was of Jack with longer hair, aged about ten, standing at the side of his seated mother. It looked like a professional portrait that had been scanned and posted. She was a stunningly beautiful woman. Jack's only caption was: 'Me and Mum, 2009'.

A moment later he decided he was being a cyber-stalker and he didn't want to be one. It was true that Jack had put a great deal of his life into the public domain, but that did not mean that Humphrey was entitled to go snooping about in it. He felt ashamed and returned to Jack's message.

'Welcome to my world,' he had said.

'It's a very alien place to me,' Humphrey replied.

Jack replied almost immediately: 'It would be. Lol.'

'Are you on here all the time?'

'Not exactly. Sporadic bursts. Don't you get addicted now.'

'Not very likely, Jack.'

'BTW…'

'BTW?'

'By the way…I've been thinking about your wonderful plan.'

'And?'

'It can't do any harm, can it?'

'I can't conceive how it could.'

'All right. Go ahead then. I reckon it's a bit of a long shot, but sure, try it.'

'I'll give them a ring tomorrow and let you know. They can only say "no".'

'Exactly.'

Humphrey & Jack

This, in summary, was the Wonderful Plan: he would telephone Jack's Director of Studies and offer to act as his mentor for an EPQ provisionally entitled *Parallels and Contrasts between the Reigns of Edward III of England and Casimir III of Poland*. As a former lecturer at the University of Radcester, he, Humphrey, would be able to recommend Jack for a reader's card at the University Library. Since Jack was fluent in Polish, it should be possible to obtain books written in Polish through the international inter-library loan service run by the British Library.

Jack had been sceptical about this at first. It seemed too good to be true. He said he would think about it.

Now that Jack had given his approval, Humphrey made the call. He got through to Jack's Director of Studies straight away and made his proposal. Mr Fairway agreed that there were interesting possibilities. Would Humphrey care to come into the college and discuss things? Would that afternoon be convenient?'

It would.

Humphrey messaged Jack with the news immediately and Jack replied about half an hour later:

'Oh well done! tbh, I'm quite excited.'

'tbh?'

'To be honest.'

'Of course,' Humphrey replied. 'So am I.' And he added 'tbh' as an afterthought.

'Lol,' Jack typed.

Fairway turned out to be an amenable sort of chap and Humphrey rather warmed to him. Naturally, he wanted to know how Humphrey had come to know Jack and Humphrey explained the reparation scheme, without going into too much detail about the offence. Fairway nodded vigorously.

'It's an excellent notion,' he said. 'It would be interesting to know what its success rate is. Do you happen to know?'

Humphrey & Jack

'I don't,' said Humphrey, 'but there are signs it might help Jack to turn his life around. I expect there's a lot of recidivism though.'

'I expect there is.'

'I must say that the boy has a good brain on him. Possibly even exceptional.'

'Oh, yes, he has. Colleagues tell me that he has tremendous potential. Unfortunately, his application and attendance have been very poor. You do know that his background is pretty grim?'

'He's told me a bit about it. And the PCSO filled in some of the details.'

'It's not hard to see why he's so defeatist. Any setback and he folds. Give him a low mark and he thinks he's useless or that it's somebody else's fault. There's a bit of a clash with his history teacher.'

'The Wanker.'

'Sorry?'

'That's what Jack calls him,' said Humphrey.

'Does he? I'm not surprised. Actually, that's really unfair. Jim has done all he can to engage the boy. Jack doesn't like the topics so he blames the teacher. A common enough scenario, though Jack plays it as if there were an Oscar available for being bolshie.'

'I'm rather hoping that if this thing takes off,' said Humphrey, 'it will boost his self-esteem enough to have a knock-on effect in his other subjects. He's quite ambitious about university, you know.'

Humphrey thought he sounded rather like a parent and was a little abashed at what he was taking on.

'I know,' said Fairway. 'There's no doubt in our minds that he has the mental capacity. Despite everything his AS results were not too bad. Mind you, he will not be able to wing it quite so easily at A2. I think I should also warn you that his attendance record has been poor this last year and his disciplinary record is pretty abysmal: coming into school drunk, sexual activity in the toilets, rudeness to staff, graffiti and so on.

Humphrey & Jack

'He has been close to exclusion more than once. We have only held on to him because of his unfortunate background. You should know that if there's the slightest infringement next year he will be out. Jack knows this but I think it's only fair that you should be aware that your work could all be in vain.'

'Thank you for being candid, Humphrey said. 'All the same, I think he's worth the risk, don't you?'

'I have to say that I'm very grateful to you for going out of your way to champion this boy. I hope he doesn't let you down.'

'It's a risk I'm prepared to take.'

'In a moment I'll get you a guidance pack for EPQ mentors, if that's not too patronising…'

'Certainly not.'

'There's just one more thing. Slightly embarrassing really. Now, you've said you'll be mentoring Jack at home and, of course, he'll be eighteen just before term starts, and so, in a sense, it's really none of our business. And, of course, you encountered Jack through the police in the first place. All the same, since you've now retired formally from teaching, we'd like you to undergo a police check. You know the sort of thing. Is that all right? Should be back shortly after the beginning of term.'

'Absolutely fine,' said Humphrey.

'Just a formality, really. But it's best to cover our backs, I think. Yours as well as ours.'

'Well exactly,' said Humphrey.

28. Library

August came to an end. Leaves seemed to have lost their lustre and Humphrey's lovely lawn began to look a little parched. The garden was not as busy with the birds' evening traffic as it had been and the swifts had already departed. Blackbirds stripped the grapes from the vine above Humphrey's garden door, furtively and with a tumble of wings in the leaves, but they did not sing. The clusters were luxuriant though the fruit was bitter to human taste and Humphrey did not begrudge the theft. At dusk now, there were often only fat pigeons waddling about stupidly, pecking at the bread Humphrey had thrown out for them.

Now as the days shortened Humphrey and Jack's friendship became an established thing.

On Jack's part, this was quite unselfconscious. The difference in age was wholly immaterial to him. He had never shown Humphrey any deference, nor any explicit gratitude, only a natural respect for what he could learn from him. He appeared to genuinely enjoy being in the house and garden.

As for Humphrey, for whom self-analysis was an enduring and sometimes toxic habit, the sixty years and more that he had spent on the planet before encountering Jack came to seem but a prelude: a second rate B-film in black and white before the main Technicolor feature.

Humphrey, who had never had a fulfilling relationship in his life, had a friend. And Humphrey, for whom a kind of subdued misery had been a constant bedfellow and waking companion, began to dare to think that this friendship was making him happy.

The fence was finished. No longer could Mrs Bellingham accost him across its stunted predecessor. She was quite shut out. And of Aristotle, miraculously, there had been little sign. Jack said an eight foot fence would not keep out a cat, though he had once spotted Aristotle crouched on top of it, his tail twitching.

They could only suppose that climbing up there, rather than coming through an established gap, was becoming a bit of a bore for Aristotle and that he had decided to establish his territory (and his lavatory) elsewhere. Humphrey prayed to every listening god that it would be on Mrs Bellingham's doorstep.

No sooner had the fence been completed than he received a letter from her solicitor threatening action because of an alleged breach of planning regulations but Humphrey had done his homework. Jack said it was 'bullshit'. Humphrey binned the letter.

Mrs Bellingham could see onto Humphrey's terrace from her upstairs window, of course, but Autumn would be upon them soon and the days of al fresco lunches were numbered. Humphrey had no doubt that she spied on Jack's arrivals and departures but decided he didn't give an ant's fart.

Humphrey declared that the fence was a thing of beauty and Jack was clearly proud of his handiwork. He had cleaned the wood and prepared the surfaces and they had driven to Homebase where they bought wood preserver and Jack had chosen a woodstain called 'Mountain Spruce'. It was very tasteful. As planned, Humphrey had Jack plant cat-repellent herbs at its base. It looked a bit stark and new despite the muted shade of green but it would soon weather. Perhaps, they could put in some climbing roses? They drank a bottle of Prosecco together to christen it.

As the fence was nearing completion, Humphrey had had to admit to himself that he felt a growing trepidation, and one which he would find it difficult to declare. He would miss Jack's visits. There was the EPQ mentoring in prospect, of course, but an hour a week was hardly the same. With the completion of the fence, the 'contract' drawn up with the PCSO would also be complete.

Humphrey had thought he might offer Jack some work in the garden or about the house but the excuse would look a bit lame since he already had a gardener and Mrs Price would not tolerate a rival indoors.

As they sipped the last of the Prosecco, Humphrey plucked up the courage to say: 'It'll be term soon.'

'I know,' said Jack glumly.

'Are you going to give it a go?'

'Yeah, if I can stain a fence, I can get into university, can't I? It's just a matter of application.'

'Quite.'

'That was a joke, Humphrey.'

'Sorry?' said Humphrey.

Humphrey & Jack

'It only needs *application*.'

Humphrey laughed.

'Oh, I say, that's really rather good,' he said.

'Pearls before swine,' Jack said and rolled his eyes.

'I'm going to miss having you around,' Humphrey said suddenly.

'There's the lessons.'

'They're not really lessons; it's just mentoring. And you'll have plenty of academic work on your plate.'

'There's the weekends. I'll still come round on Saturday. If you'll have me, that is.'

'Lunch' became the essential pretext for their Saturday meetings. Humphrey declared that the diet of fast food and takeaways on which Jack subsisted was not good for a growing teenager and that at least once a week he would get a decent meal. There would usually be a decent wine and Humphrey was careful to disguise his own over-partiality to the grape until Jack had gone.

Jack was not a fussy eater which was as well, for Humphrey was unimpressed by food fads. His only aversion was to mushrooms which was allowable if a shame. Over the coming weeks Jack devoured various casseroles, a beef curry with toasted almonds, a chicken and ham pie, tarragon salmon poached in white wine, homemade meatballs in a glossy ragù, and a cassoulet that matured eight hours in a slow oven and emerged, bubbles breaking through its breadcrumb crust. However, Jack's declared favourite was a ham risotto which was fine except that Humphrey had to stand over it much of the time as he slowly stirred in wine and stock.

Humphrey took Jack along to the University Library in person to register him for a reader's card. He seemed very impressed that Humphrey gained access to the Chief Librarian's office immediately. The office was at the side of the grand ramp which led down from the principal courtyard to the subterranean library. It was not, after all, very surprising: Humphrey had spent many years of his life working down here and he and Geoffrey Chaulker had known each other for decades. Dr Chaulker was a well-respected poet in his own right and his work was known as lean and caustic. He was, moreover, a keen medievalist and this was the grounds on which he and Humphrey had established, if not a friendship, at least an easy and affable relationship.

'Now, young man,' he said to Jack, 'Dr Icke has told me on the telephone about your interest in Casimir the Great and I must say that I'm awfully intrigued.'

'Thank you, sir,' said Jack. Humphrey suppressed a smile at the unwonted formality. Jack appeared to have been seized with awe.

'No, *thank you*, sir! It is a privilege to meet a young man with a spirit of inquiry and an independent intelligence. As you pass through the corridors of this building, you will see, not only books, more than you have probably ever seen in one place before, but many young people who think they are working but who are merely regurgitating the work of others. It has not been masticated; it has barely touched the sides of their intellectual alimentary canals; it has not been digested, and it is vomited up in unseemly gobbets in a pile of verbiage that they dare to call a dissertation.

'And the University will award them a degree notwithstanding because universities have sold their souls and become business parks rather than temples of learning. Is that not the case, Dr Icke?'

'Probably, but don't discourage the lad before he's even started, Geoffrey.'

'Indeed, Jack is not like the children of the Philistine. He stands with us at the gates of the citadel and will join us in the rearguard action against the forces of dullness.'

Humphrey found the Librarian's florid language rather embarrassing but Jack was lapping it up.

'Now, Jack, if I may call you that, I am fascinated by your proposed comparison of the reigns of Edward and Casimir. It sounds both original and potentially fruitful. You must ensure that a copy of your paper arrives on my desk when it is complete.'

Jack, obviously flattered, nodded vigorously.

Humphrey & Jack

'Now, I must confess that I am woefully ignorant of Polish medieval history. Do I not look shamefaced? I assure you that I am. I look forward to your work intensely.

'As for reading in Polish, what an advantage! I do not know offhand what we hold in the Slavic languages but I am sure Humphrey will show you how to use the catalogue and introduce you to the staff on the Inter-Library Loan desk. If you can't find what you want, ask. You are not being a nuisance. Librarians adore being asked about things - it makes them feel fulfilled - the more arcane the better.

'Now, since I sense you are eager to explore, I will approve your application for a reader's card myself which should expedite things. And if you would just sign here, Jack. Just the usual stuff about respecting the regulations and not stealing or selling on the University's property, but I'm sure you're a young man of great moral rectitude and, in any case, Dr Icke has already vouched for you. It's a privilege, Jack. Respect it and now, off you go.'

'You've vouched for me?' Jack said.

'Of course,' said Humphrey.

'Knowing what you know? About my background?'

'You won't let me down, Jack.'

'You're right. I won't.'

Jack was like a child on its first visit to a funfair. The Library filled him with wonder. As they moved along the underground walkways, he looked up and saw, through the textured glass, the figures of people moving above. When they reached the central information desk from which other walkways radiated, he could see, in a state approaching reverence, what seemed like mile upon mile of books. He gazed at the students working in carrels lining the spokes from the circular information desk and, despite everything the Librarian had said about their academic probity, privately worshipped them as superior beings, whose exalted fellowship he would one day be permitted to join.

Humphrey & Jack

Humphrey led Jack to a corridor which had offices along its length and in one of them Jack had his photograph taken. Shortly afterwards he was presented with a smart card which would not only gain him admittance but permit and monitor his borrowing and research. Then, Humphrey showed him how to use the catalogue. They traced a couple of general books on open shelves which Jack could borrow there and then and a more specialised one kept in the stacks which would be reserved for him and which he could consult at any time over the next fortnight. At the I.L.L. desk, Humphrey showed him how to put in a request for a book in Polish held by the Jagiellonian Library in Craków. Jack had discovered its existence and relevance on the Internet. The loan would cost £2.50 which Humphrey paid before Jack could protest.

And so, Jacek Lis, vandal, delinquent, disturber of the peace, despoiler of gardens, began his new career as a scholar, when only just eighteen years of age.

29. September

September advanced and the dull Midlands city shook off the dusty torpor of late summer. The undergraduates returned toting portfolios and guitars. Freshers bought pots and pans and cheap stationery in the pound shops and cheap vodka at the discount supermarkets.

At certain times of day, there was no point in Humphrey attempting to take the car to Waitrose. The city's traffic would be in gridlock because of the school run and the commuters coming in from outlying villages where, at the weekends, businessmen rode to hounds.

Jack returned to college and, Humphrey noted, began to attend all his classes regularly. His timetable left an opening for him to visit Humphrey on Friday mornings for his EPQ tutorial, but he continued to visit on Saturdays too and would stay for lunch and most of the day.

From the start, the project seemed a terrific success. Jack was keen to the point of obsession. His ambition was to go beyond attaining a distinc-

Humphrey & Jack

tion and to astonish his teachers and Humphrey assured him that this kind of enterprise was exactly what university admissions officers were looking for.

Not everything went smoothly, of course, neither with Jack's work, nor with their cautiously developing friendship. There were disappointments and setbacks: inevitable really, given the scale of Jack's ambitions.

He had been waiting with childlike impatience for the books in Polish to arrive and was so beside himself with excitement when they did that it was a joy for Humphrey to behold. What for him was a commonplace transaction had generated such a delirium in Jack that Humphrey felt an ominous twinge.

Sure enough, on the Saturday when next they met, Jack was very down.

'God!' he said about one of the books, 'I stayed up all night reading it - and for what. It's as dry as dust. The language is really pompous and intellectual. What's that word about ordering words and ideas?'

'Syntax?'

'Yeah, that. I mean, it's all tangled and endless and he uses important sounding words and when you look them up the meaning doesn't fit the context and it's like he's making himself look important by being obscure. Either that, or I'm too thick to understand it.'

Humphrey found that this was typical of Jack. If he encountered a reversal he would put it down to personal shortcomings and he would sulk.

'You're not thick, Jack. I'm afraid that stylistic obfuscation has been a feature of academic writing for too long. It came in with post-modernism.'

'Stylistic what?'

'Obfuscation - the business of making something unclear. The opposite of clarification or illumination. And I'm afraid you're right, Jack. Too many academic writers, who ought to know better, succumb to this ghastly fashion, in order, as you say, to sound important or original.'

Humphrey & Jack

'All fucking night, all fucking night, and I doubt if I got more than two or three marginal ideas out of it. Waste of frigging time. Might as well jack it all in.'

'Hey now, don't give in at the first setback. I'm afraid you'll have to get used to that. Research is rarely about epiphanies and eureka moments. Most of the time, it's what you're experiencing now. It's like looking for something in a vast cluttered house equipped only with a torch with failing batteries - something that might not even be there.'

Jack gave a grunt which might mean anything.

'One day, those three little ideas might just gel with lots of other little ideas you've collected and there'll be a reaction and a spark and you'll be on your way to something fresh. But it won't just happen. Persistence is the name of the game.'

'Hey, you're good, you are,' said Jack.

'Where do you get that from?' said Humphrey. He wasn't entirely sure whether Jack were being sarcastic or not.

'Ex-students of yours on Facebook.'

'What do they say?'

'You'll get big-headed.'

'Me? Hardly likely.'

'Well, they do reckon your lectures were a bit boring.'

Ouch. This was Jack all over. He was quite incapable of a little white lie. Humphrey supposed he ought to admire Jack's intellectual honesty but it stung all the same. And it stung the more because Humphrey had to accept the justice of it.

He had worked hard at writing his lectures and he knew that their substance was what his students needed. However, he had always been aware that the delivery was rather dull. He didn't go in for slides and videos and role-play like some of his younger colleagues. Besides, he truly thought that public lectures were the worst imaginable way of conveying information.

Humphrey & Jack

'On the other hand,' Jack said, seeming to enjoy the discomfiture which Humphrey had found it impossible to hide, 'loads of people thought that your tutorials rocked.'

'Does that mean they approved?'

'Of course it does, you muppet. I told you you'd get big-headed. There you go. Fishing for compliments.'

'Yes, but why did they rock? I mean why did they approve?'

'Because you treated them as people. You know your stuff inside out. You tailored your teaching to the kids as individuals. You were strict but fair. Oh, and you've got a sense of humour. That's what they said.'

Humphrey barely recognised himself.

'A sense of humour?'

'Well, to be honest, some people reckon your jokes bombed a lot? But, you know, a way with words? Turn of phrase? Sarky put-downs?'

'Try not to use that rising inflexion, will you, Jack?'

'Yeah, sorry. I will. But anyway, people like that kind of thing. Apart from the tossers who claim they've been abused if you even look at them.'

'Sarcasm? Me? Oh dear. I'm afraid the authorities rather frown on that kind of thing.'

'Fuck the authorities,' said Jack.

'Do you know, Jack, I'm constrained to agree.'

'There you go,' said Jack.

'Where?'

'Sarcasm.'

'Oh no, Jack,' said Humphrey. 'If you only knew how much I mean it.'

'You're weird,' said Jack. 'I can't get the measure of you.'

'Neither can I,' said Humphrey and they both laughed.

'What's post-modernism?' Jack asked.

'Big question. Ask me again on Tuesday. Come on, let's have lunch.'

'So that's what people talk about on Facebook,' Humphrey said as they were eating. 'In your vast circle of acquaintance, I mean?'

Humphrey & Jack

'What?'
'My tutorials?'
'Oh, definitely. All the time. Amongst other things.'
'Such as?'
'Sex,' said Jack.
'Ah,' said Humphrey. 'That.'

30. Keys

'My tutorial' is how Jack referred to their Tuesday meetings. He made it clear from the start that he did not want any help whatsoever with the content and conclusions of his paper. He insisted that it must be entirely his own work. Even though he knew, from his own limited observation and experience, that second-rate and even plagiarised submissions could be passed by over-stretched examiners, he wanted his work to be seen to be exclusively his own.

'Just don't interfere is all,' Jack said and Humphrey meekly swallowed the rudeness.

In one respect, Humphrey could not help even if he wanted to. He did not speak Polish and knew little about the troubled history of the state. As far as the reign of Edward III was concerned, however, he itched to assist. After all, his own field was the reign of his grandson, Richard, and he was an acknowledged world expert on the Plantagenets in general.

In reality Jack accepted help because Humphrey was cunning about it, posing questions which Jack would follow up in his own time, so that he would be able to claim the outcome as his own. He also accepted, without demur, any suggestion that he might be off track or making unsupported assertions and he welcomed bibliographical advice.

That apart, Humphrey's role was more general. He gave advice about form and structure and about the difficult art of comparison, valid and invalid correspondences, forced similitudes, disparities in scale. He taught Jack about historiology and how its principles weren't fixed; he explained

Humphrey & Jack

the significance of historicity. Jack lapped up the more philosophical aspects of the subject and he said that it was making the modern history A level more interesting for him and that it was also really helpful in English too. The topic was *The Literature of Love through the Ages* and historicity was a core element.

Humphrey's principal job was as a proof-reader and editor. Commenting on the coherence (or lack of it) in Jack's work was permitted, as was Humphrey's meticulous copy editing. Actually, Jack could write both fluently and accurately. His work would already disgrace that of many an undergraduate. Any errors were usually typos and Jack acknowledged this as soon as they were pointed out.

One Friday morning, Humphrey was late for Jack's tutorial. He had always been a stickler for punctuality and this was unprecedented. He had nipped to Waitrose in the car for some bits and pieces that he'd run out of. He had left plenty of time but a set of roadworks with temporary traffic lights had delayed him. They took so long to change that he thought at first that the operator must have gone into a coma. After a while, he realised that there were no workmen to be seen anywhere which made the delay even more insufferable. The wretched lights must be on a timer. But for how long? A decade?

The old ill-temper began to rise in him again.

When he finally reached the store, there were further frustrations. Though Christmas was still nearly two whole months away, the stock layout had been changed to make way for an aisle given over to Christmas stuff. The result was that he had trouble finding the things he wanted.

Then at the checkout the queue was much longer than usual at this time of day, even for a Friday. When he got within sight of the till, the woman before him unloaded enough food to have withstood the siege of Troy for the whole ten years, all the while regaling the checkout girl with her family history. Her Waitrose card was not in her purse and then she remembered it was in another purse which was somewhere in the bottom of an enormous handbag. When she found it, after much rummaging, she

Humphrey & Jack

announced that she wanted to pay in cash. She handed over the notes but then began scrabbling about in a tiny compartment for the exact coinage.

When she discovered that she was 35p short, she began looking for a credit card. Humphrey only just managed not to scream. The checkout girl gave him a look of anguished apology. Behind him people in the growing queue tutted and shuffled. Unbelievably the credit card was rejected and in looking for another the woman found a little wad of discount vouchers which the cashier had to sort, discovering some of them had passed their validity date. All the time the woman was talking about how her sister was coming over from Sussex and how her little nephew was such a fussy eater.

At last, her debit card was accepted and she sailed away still talking - to herself apparently.

Humphrey's few items were bagged and paid for in moments.

On the way back, he was held up at the traffic lights again, for several millennia this time. There were still no workmen to be seen.

The final irritation was to discover, on arriving home at last, and fifteen minutes late for his appointment, that he had not brought his house key with him. There was no sign of Jack. He must have been and gone. Humphrey was a little surprised at how very sad that made him. Damn and blast that woman at the checkout. He would have liked to suffocate her under a pile of her own shopping.

Fortunately, he was not locked out. He always kept a key for the garden door on his car key ring. He retrieved his shopping from the boot of the car and went down the narrow passage at the side of the house and round into the garden.

There, at the end of the terrace, was Jack, in a pea coat and scarf, sitting at the garden table despite the chilly wind, correcting a document with a pencil. He had placed a stone on the paper to stop it blowing away and with his left hand he was absent-mindedly stroking Aristotle, who lay, with an air of bland insouciance, on the table beside him.

'Oh Jack, I'm so sorry!' he said.

Humphrey & Jack

'Hey, no worries, man,' Jack said. 'It's cool.'

At another time Humphrey would have told Jack how much he hated this pseudo-hippy talk but he was so relieved to see him that he sat at the garden table with him and told him all about the reasons for his delay. It was only when he had finished that Humphrey realised that he had been stroking Aristotle too.

'But you must be freezing, Jack,' he said. 'What would you say to some hot chocolate?'

'I would say: "Hello, hot chocolate, I think we were made for each other."'

'Come in then, come in. What've you got there?' said Humphrey, pointing at the paper.

'It's about the coronation ceremonies of the two kings. You'll like it. I'm quite proud of it.'

'Excellent. Excellent. Chocolate first, then history.'

They went into the house and Aristotle came with them. As Humphrey was pouring milk into a saucepan, the cat rubbed himself against his leg, back arched and tail high. Humphrey poured some milk into a saucer. Aristotle sniffed at it rather disdainfully and looked up at him.

'Not good enough for you, eh?' Humphrey said. He looked into the fridge and found some peeled prawns. He put a few on another saucer and put them down. These were much more to Aristotle's taste.

'I thought you hated that cat,' Jack said. 'You won't get rid of him now. He'll be round here all the time.'

'Any friend of yours is a friend of mine,' Humphrey said, thinking smugly of how outraged Mrs Bellingham would be if she knew they had kidnapped her cat. He gave Aristotle a few more prawns.

Evidently he was not allergic to cats at all.

Presently they sat at the kitchen table with mugs of chocolate and Humphrey began to look through Jack's work. After a moment or two, he looked up and said:

Humphrey & Jack

'We can't have you waiting about like that again. I must see about getting you some keys.'

31. Games

Soon the leaves yellowed and became thin and limp and at length they began to drift down. Windy days tugged away more and more. Humphrey's gardener, Mr Kirkpatrick, raked them up regularly lest they rot and damage the roots of his grass. Humphrey would not allow him to use a leaf blower. He said the insufferable things had been designed in Hell to blot out the trump of doom and postpone the apocalypse. Mr Kirkpatrick didn't know what he was talking about but Humphrey paid him well so he got on with the raking, though he grumbled all the time.

However, Humphrey could not prevent the use of leaf blowers in the park beyond his garden.

'What's the bloody point?' he moaned to Mrs Price. He had a habit of following her about as she waxed and polished the dining room table, dusted bookshelves or washed down doors, even though she'd told him that this annoyed her intensely. 'They just blow them up into a pile and then the wind whips them all over the buggering place again. All that racket for nothing.'

When Mrs Price could no longer bear his whingeing and wanted him out from under her feet, she would produce the Hoover, forcing Humphrey to seek sanctuary in his study from the odious din.

Keys had been cut for Jack and Mrs Price had been told that he had been granted access at any time. She looked rather sniffy about it and went away muttering to herself in Welsh but she made no direct protest. In any event, Humphrey was always at home when Jack came round so the keys came to have a merely symbolic significance.

Jack stayed longer and longer after their Saturday lunch.

One day he asked if Humphrey had a chess set. Humphrey found one in the cupboard under the stairs, dusted it down and they went into the din-

Humphrey & Jack

ing room to play. Humphrey said he was rusty and it was true. He hadn't played for years and Jack beat him swiftly in their first game. Humphrey's mundane and plodding manoeuvres were no match for Jack's sharp logic, guileful seductions, and capacity to anticipate several moves ahead. Humphrey found himself sacrificing pieces needlessly, blundering into traps, and foolishly losing his undefended queen. Checkmate followed with Jack's next move.

Despite the humiliation - and Jack's gloating was insufferable - Humphrey was up for a game the following Saturday. He lost again, but this time without the mortification. You could even say he lost honourably. It was coming back to him. There were even some quite imaginative moves, though he played more circumspectly and Jack complained that he took so long to make a move that Edward III had thrashed the Scots in a shorter campaign.

The next time, Humphrey won and thereafter victory and defeat more or less alternated. Jack was a sore loser. He would go very quiet and just sit at the table analysing where he had gone wrong. When the score reached 6:7 in Jack's favour he declared that he did not want to play again. And they never did. As far as Jack was concerned, that was the final score.

Their last game was memorable. Humphrey had felt himself on form. He drew white and established a command of the board from the beginning, deploying his knights to devastating effect, creating no-go areas for Jack's pieces. His queen licked up Jack's pawns and there was crossfire from his rooks. The black king already had limited room for manoeuvre and then Humphrey took his queen. When he sacrificed his bishops in order to crown a white pawn as a new queen, it looked as if it were all over. With two queens, how could he lose?

Checkmate was a move away. Or so he thought. A distant black bishop came flying across the board, cope and mitre ribbons flying, and created a new lethal diagonal. A forgotten black knight trapped his king in a corner. It was a brilliant checkmate. The bishop and knight stood on the only two squares not covered by the might of Humphrey's pieces as Jack could not resist pointing out.

Jack did not gloat too much this time but he would not play again. So they turned to Scrabble. Despite Humphrey's immense vocabulary, Jack always won. He was a much better tactical player and he was not averse to cheating. After a few challenges, Humphrey found that his adversary was very good at inventing plausible high-scoring words. Humphrey said they needed a referee and produced the *Chambers Twentieth Century Dictionary* which he used for crosswords.

'Why can't we use the *Twenty-First Century Dictionary*? Is there one?' Jack asked.

'Because I don't have a copy. And because it's inferior. Yes, it exists,' said Humphrey.

'How can it be inferior? Surely it's more up to date?'

'It's inferior because it's full of neologisms and rarefied technical terms.'

'What's a neologism?'

'A newly coined word.'

'What's wrong with that? Language is evolving all the time.'

'I know that. But a new word ought to earn quite a wide usage before it deserves to be in a reputable dictionary. It ought to be bedded in, gain its credentials. The *Twenty-First Century Chambers* is too gimmicky.'

'Who says?'

'Academics. Cruciverbalists.'

'Cruci- what?'

'Cruciverbalists.'

'What is it? You made that up!'

'I did not. A cruciverbalist is a solver of crossword puzzles. Look it up.'

'Fair enough,' said Jack and they agreed to use the *Chambers Twentieth Century Dictionary*.

Humphrey & Jack

All went well enough for a while though Humphrey continued to manage very meagre scores despite some very fancy words which Jack challenged unsuccessfully.

One day Jack put down CONIINES.

'Challenge!' Humphrey shouted immediately.

'Look it up,' said Jack and Humphrey did.

'Is it there?'

'Yes, but there's only one 'i' - look!'

'OK,' Jack said, 'but look at this.'

Jack did a search on his phone with that dexterity with two thumbs that all young people seem to have in common but which was beyond Humphrey though it impressed him.

Humphrey read on the screen: 'Coniines: Alkaloid that makes up the poisonous part of hemlock.'

'What dictionary is that?' Humphrey asked.

'*The Official Scrabble Dictionary*,' said Jack.

'But we agreed on the Chambers.'

'Yeah, but we are playing Scrabble so it stands to reason that we should use *The Official Scrabble Dictionary*.'

'But you can't change the rules in the middle of the game.'

'Why not if it makes sense?'

They continued to squabble until Humphrey managed to lose with a more pitiful score than ever before. Normally he didn't mind but today he was genuinely irritated.

'Another game?' said Jack.

'I don't think so,' said Humphrey.

'Are you sulking?' said Jack, which made Humphrey sulk the more.

The following week, Humphrey agreed to abide by the *Scrabble Dictionary*.

'Is that agreed?'

'Yes,' said Jack.

Humphrey & Jack

'This dictionary will be the one and only absolute and final arbiter of any challenges?'

'Yes,' said Jack.

'Let's play,' said Humphrey.

Jack thrashed him. It was clear that in the intervening week Jack had been busy looking up the most arcane words he could find and learning them.

Humphrey felt that somehow the principles of fair play, magnanimity in victory and cheerfulness in defeat that had been instilled in him as a child were being flouted. He said as much to Jack.

'Is it victory at all costs with you?' he asked.

'Yes,' said Jack. '*Vae victis*! Woe to the vanquished!'

'Very clever, Jack, but what about the Geneva convention?'

'I never signed it,' said Jack.

But still, Humphrey felt that in their games an element of trust had been corroded. During the chess era, if Jack needed to use the lavatory mid-game, he would photograph the state of play on his phone so that Humphrey could not cheat. He would do the same with the Scrabble board and, what is more, being a head taller than Humphrey, he would place the bag containing tiles on top of the dresser where he knew Humphrey could not reach it.

The paradox, of course, was that Humphrey would never dream of cheating. For him, it would defeat the point of the game.

Before long, Humphrey decided he was sick of Scrabble.

'Is it because you always lose?' Jack said.

'Probably,' Humphrey said, though it wasn't the whole truth.

'Have you got a pack of cards?'

'Somewhere,' Humphrey said.

'Shall we play poker?'

'I don't know how.'

'I'll teach you.'

'I'm not playing for money.'

Humphrey & Jack

'That's fine. I haven't got any. But we'll need some kind of chips.'

'Hang on. We can use Monopoly money.'

'Perfect.'

Humphrey found the cards and notes and they began, but first Jack said: 'We need to swap places.'

'Why?' said Humphrey who couldn't see what difference it could possibly make.

'You'll see,' said Jack airily.

At first, Humphrey did brilliantly, raking in hundreds of 'pounds'. And then the tide turned and Humphrey began to lose every hand. At first he was stoical about it but as his luck got worse and worse and he was approaching insolvency, he burst out with:

'What the hell is going on here? You let me win at the beginning, didn't you?'

'Might have done,' said Jack.

And then he explained that Humphrey had been conned. Jack had been reading his cards in the reflection in Humphrey's specs.

'So that's why you wanted to swap places?'

'Exactly.'

'So you could get the light right?'

'Yes.'

Humphrey was not amused.

'I think you'd better go,' he said.

Jack was laughing.

'Don't take it so seriously,' he said.

'I've been good to you, Jack. I don't deserve this.'

'It was only a bit of fun.'

'For you, maybe. I'm not laughing.'

'Shall I still come round next Friday?'

'Yes, yes, of course. Don't be silly. But I've had enough of you for now. That was cruel, Jack. Come on. Pack up your things.'

Humphrey & Jack

When the street door had closed after the lad, Humphrey found that he was actually shaking with anger and humiliation. He went to the kitchen and fixed himself a very strong Martini.

Gradually, (and after two more Martinis) he began to unwind and wonder if perhaps he hadn't been a little too harsh. The scam had been pretty clever after all and, with hindsight, it probably was quite amusing. He could see how a third party might find it so.

And he began to feel rather embarrassed about the 'I don't deserve this' stuff. It was a bit melodramatic, wasn't it? Anger turned to embarrassment and a fear that their friendship had been jeopardised by his grandstanding.

At around half-past eight the doorbell rang. Who could it be? He never had visitors at this hour. Unless it was that blasted Bellingham woman with some complaint.

Aristotle had been a frequent visitor of late. He seemed to know when Jack would be arriving and came in with him. They both indulged him with tidbits and attention. That would be it.

Right. He would send her away with a flea in her ear.

But when he flung the door open with an exuberance fuelled by alcohol, it was Jack who stood on the threshold.

He had been beaten up. There was a deep cut on his lower lip which was badly swollen. There was another nasty cut on his right eyebrow and the eye was almost closed. There was a trail where blood had run from his nose. It had dried and caked. He was covered with dirt.

'I didn't know where else to go,' he said.

32. First Aid

'Dear God, what's happened, Jack? Of course, you were right to come here. Come in, come in.'

As he ushered the boy in, he thought he caught a glimpse of Mrs Bellingham withdrawing into her porch.

Humphrey & Jack

Once inside, he drew Jack into the kitchen and perched him on a high stool he hardly ever used nowadays, because clambering down from it was tough on his knees.

'Let's have a look,' he said, gently drawing Jack's hands away from his face and brushing back his hair. 'OK, first thing is to clean this up. Move the stool nearer the sink - that's better. Hang on.'

In the downstairs bathroom he found his first aid box and a pile of hand towels and returned to Jack. I must not behave like a panicking hen, he told himself. What was needed was the calm, impersonal professionalism of a nurse or doctor.

Considering how much he'd drunk earlier, he was amazed, as he got to work, at his self-possession and steady hands.

Leaving the tap running, he soaked a corner of one of the towels and dabbed away at the surface dirt and grit. Then from the first aid box he took a sterile gauze pad from its packet and began to clean out the cuts. Jack winced from time to time.

'Your lip is not as bad as it looked but your eyebrow is still bleeding.' He took another sterile swab from its packet. 'Here. Put your head back. Hold it tight against the cut. We need to stop the bleeding, if we can. It looks quite deep. Who did this to you, Jack?'

'I fell.'

'Rubbish. Were you mugged?'

'No.'

'Who was it then? People from college?'

'No, just leave it. It doesn't matter.'

'Of course it matters.'

It suddenly came to Humphrey who Jack's assailant was.

'It was your father, wasn't it?'

Jack was silent.

'It was, wasn't it?'

Jack nodded and his eyes filled, though he didn't cry.

Humphrey & Jack

'Right,' said Humphrey, 'when we are finished here, I am going to ring the police.'

'No!' Jack cried, attempting to stand up.

Humphrey kept his hand firmly on the boy's shoulder.

'Keep still, please. Keep your head back.' Reluctantly, Jack settled. 'Why not, Jack? He can't be allowed to get away with this.'

'Just don't. You don't know what he's like. He'll just make my life an even bigger misery.'

'The man is clearly dangerous. He needs to be…'

Jack took the swab away from his eye and looked at it.

'If you ring the police, you won't see me here again,' he said quietly and sadly.

Humphrey was shocked. That was impossible. He couldn't allow that to happen.

'Okay, okay, relax. I won't ring the police.'

'You've got to promise. I don't want you ringing them behind my back.'

'I promise. Now, keep the pressure on that eyebrow. I'll dress it in a minute.'

Jack did as he was told.

'At least tell me why he attacked you.'

'He doesn't need a reason. He was drunk. He often flies off the handle when he's drunk.'

'You mean it's happened before?'

'Loads of times.'

'And you still don't want to report it?'

'Leave it will you. I can't do that to him. I've told you before: he's my dad.'

'I'm still baffled.'

'Tough.'

'Let's look at that eye.'

Jack lifted the swab away.

Humphrey & Jack

'All right. I'll put a dressing on it, but you ought to have it looked at. I'd drive you to A and E but I've had a few drinks.'

'It's all right.'

'I could ring for a taxi. It could probably do with a couple of stitches.'

'I said it's all right. They'll be all over me with questions. Probably drag the police into it anyhow.'

'There'll be a scar,' said Humphrey.

'Good,' said Jack. 'It'll make me look sexier than ever.'

They stared blankly at each other for a suspended moment and then Jack burst out laughing and it was so infectious that Humphrey joined in too.

'Right, now keep still,' said Humphrey. 'This is going to sting.' And he applied a drop of antiseptic cream over which he placed a small piece of gauze. 'It's stopped bleeding but don't mess with it when I've finished. I'm going to have to put a bandage round your head so that it covers your eye.'

'Can't you use a plaster?'

'Not unless you want to rip out the hairs on your eyebrow when you take it off.'

'No, thank you.'

'Thought not. Tell me then, what sparked this particular attack off? There must have been some sort of flashpoint. What was it?'

'You.'

'Me? I don't know him from Adam.'

'He said I was spending too much time up here and he was going to come up and sort you out.'

'Jesus!'

'Oh, don't worry. He's a complete coward. He'll happily beat up a teenager but he'd never face up to an adult. Not even you, Humphrey.'

'Thank you very much.'

Humphrey & Jack

'Well, you're not exactly a cage fighter, are you? Anyway, I told him I'd do what the hell I liked and you'd done more for me in a couple of weeks than he'd ever done in a lifetime. He said I wasn't to come here again and I told him to go and fuck himself with a bog brush. So he beat me up and threw me out into the street.'

'Literally?'

'Literally. Hence all the dirt. He threw my bag after me and called me a pervert and said I didn't live there any more. Well, fuck him.'

'And you don't think he'll come up here?'

'Nah! He'll have thrown up everywhere and passed out. Nobody will see him for days.'

'There, I think we're done,' said Humphrey, tying off the bandage.

'I want to see,' said Jack and he went off to look in the mirror in the hall.

'O my God!' he said. 'I look like Pudsey the Bear from Children in Need.'

'You do,' said Humphrey. 'Stop fiddling with the bandage. Is it not secure?'

'Yeah, it's fine. Just a minute. I've got an idea,' and he fiddled in his bag which had been dumped in the hall and produced a sweatband. He put it on over the top of the bandage. 'There you go. Keeps the bandage in place. Stops me fiddling with it. Genius or what?'

'Thou art wise as thou art beautiful.'

'What?' said Jack, following Humphrey back into the kitchen.

'*A Midsummer Night's Dream*. Never mind.'

Jack looked at the bloodied towels on the floor.

'I've ruined your towels.'

'Not really. I'll put them into soak in cold water. Then they'll go in the wash. They'll be fine.'

'Where did you learn all this stuff?'

'What stuff?'

'First aid?'

Humphrey & Jack

'Oh, I did a course at school. Probably to avoid something else. I've never really needed it before.'

'I'm glad you did.'

'So am I, Jack,' said Humphrey.

There was a pause while Jack watched Humphrey busying himself with towels and the first aid box. Then he said:

'I can't go home, Humphrey.'

'No, Jack. You can't.'

'Can I stay here? Just for tonight.'

'Of course you can. You must. There are two guest bedrooms upstairs. I sleep down here. You can have the room above mine opposite my study. It has a view of the park and its own bathroom. We shan't be in each other's way. Come and look.'

They went up. The room was spacious and tasteful if a little chilly. Humphrey clicked on a supplementary heater.

'You'll be snug in no time. Here's the bathroom. Now, let me get you some clean towels. I think there's a new toothbrush in the cabinet. Yes. Here it is.

'And Jack.'

'Yes, Humphrey.'

'Stay as long as you like. You can think of this place as a refuge if ever you need to.'

'Thank you. I appreciate it.'

Humphrey checked the hot water. It was fine.

'Right, I'll leave you to it. I suggest you clean yourself up a bit. Have a bath if you like but I wouldn't get your head wet for the time being. There's a robe behind the bathroom door. Bring your clothes down and I'll put them in the wash.'

'Again,' said Jack.

'Again,' said Humphrey. 'I'm turning into your valet. Then we'll think about food and perhaps a drink. How does that sound?'

'It sounds like a plan.'

Humphrey & Jack

'Is that good?' asked Humphrey, pretending to be unfamiliar with the idiom.

'It sounds awesome,' said Jack.

Down in the kitchen, Humphrey found nothing in the fridge that might appeal to Jack and thought he might ring out for something, pizza perhaps. He rarely did this himself and regarded pizza with a degree of suspicion but he knew it was popular with kids.

He thought a sunny, robust Costières de Nîmes would go well with it and opened a bottle. He was sniffing the cork when the doorbell rang. He went into the hall and opened the door just as Jack appeared at the top of the stairs in a towelling robe with pink and black stripes, holding his clothes in a bundle.

It was Mrs Bellingham.

'I was just wondering if Aristotle was in here,' she said, craning over Humphrey's shoulder to get a better view of Jack who had come down three or four steps but stayed on the staircase.

'Do you know what time it is?' Humphrey said.

'Yes, but I haven't seen him for hours and I fret.'

'It's after eleven o'clock. I don't want strange women on my doorstep after eleven o'clock at night. What'll the neighbours think?'

'I wish you wouldn't let Aristotle into your house. You used to hate him.'

'You were perfectly happy to let him march around my garden.'

'Oh, don't start that again, Mr Icke. You really are most provoking. Have you got him?'

'No, I haven't got him. I am not an abductor of cats.'

'That young man doesn't work for the council,' she said suddenly pointing at Jack. 'He lied to me.'

'Mrs Bellingham,' said Humphrey with exaggerated politeness. 'I wonder if there might possibly be somebody else's business you could mind, or if it's not too much to ask - maybe even your own? Now, fly away, Ladybird, your house is on fire. Goodnight.'

Humphrey & Jack

And he closed the door and switched off the porch light.

He heard her feet crunching on the gravel as Jack came downstairs. At the very moment he reached the hall, Aristotle slunk round the open sitting room door, where presumably he had been sleeping, rubbed himself against Jack's ankles and sauntered toward the kitchen with his tail in the air. At the door, he turned to look at them. Humphrey had no idea he'd even been there.

They both burst out laughing.

'I was so very tempted to flash at her,' said Jack.

'I'm so very glad you didn't,' said Humphrey.

33. Pizza

Jack was very much in favour of pizza so Humphrey installed him in the sitting room with a glass of wine. He hardly ever watched television himself but they checked through the programmes that he had recorded and found that *University Challenge*, followed by *Endeavour*, would appeal to both of them so he left Jack on the sofa while he went to phone from the kitchen.

They had found the site for Domino's on Jack's phone and he had opted for a large Mighty Meaty while Humphrey decided on a 'personal' Meateor. This apparently meant four slices, which would be more than enough for Humphrey, whilst 'large' meant eight.

Jack asked if he could also have some twisted dough balls with a cheese and herb sauce and Humphrey, though he curled his lip in disdain, could deny him nothing.

In the kitchen, Humphrey put the order through and took Jack's clothes into the utility room and popped them in the washing machine.

When the food arrived, Humphrey took it through to the dining room in between the kitchen and the sitting room and then thought better of it. They would eat in the kitchen as usual. But when he went through to the sitting room Jack was sitting on the floor with his back against the sofa, totally engrossed in the episode of *Endeavour*. Humphrey knew that if you took your eye off the ball in any episode in *Morse*, *Lewis* or *Endeavour*, you would lose the plot for good. Though he was utterly disdainful of so-called TV dinners he thought he would make an exception this once and went back to the kitchen for trays.

Jack laughed at him for producing cutlery and linen napkins.

'We could have eaten them from the box.' he said. 'Save washing up.'

'Not in this house,' said Humphrey.

He sat perched on the edge of an armchair eating his pizza with a knife and fork from a tray on an occasional table. It felt uncomfortable but the pizza was surprisingly good. Jack half-sat, half-lay on the carpet eating his first slice of pizza with one hand and the other under his chin to catch any crumbs or slivers of molten cheese that might dribble down his chin. He did not take his eye off the screen for a second.

'Jack. No! Freeze!' Humphrey said suddenly.

'What?'

'I don't want you putting your greasy hands on the carpet.'

'I won't.'

'Never mind.'

And Humphrey shot into the downstairs bathroom, returning with a huge bathsheet which he asked a grumbling Jack to spread under him.

'And watch the wine too,' said Humphrey. The carpet was cream, and expensive.

'Stop fussing,' said Jack. 'You're like an old woman.'

'Yes, well…' said Humphrey.

They continued to eat and to watch in silence until Humphrey said: 'What's happened so far?'

'Ssssh!' said Jack.

Later, Humphrey and Jack finished the wine in the kitchen while Humphrey loaded the new dishwasher and went through to put Jack's clothes on the spin cycle again.

Humphrey & Jack

'I'll have to go back to the house sometime,' said Jack. 'Probably sooner rather than later.'

'But not tonight?'

'Not tonight, no. But for one thing I need to get clothes.'

'I can't really help you there,' said Humphrey. 'Nothing of mine will fit you and you wouldn't like it if it did. You're welcome to socks.'

'Might take you up on that,' said Jack. 'Mine are getting pretty threadbare. The other thing is my books and stuff. I wouldn't put it past my dad to trash them out of spite once he knows I'm gone. There are library books in my room as well. Christ! I'd better go round there first thing tomorrow.'

'Won't he be there?'

'If he is, he'll have crashed out. Even if he's not, he's never up before ten. It'll be fine.'

'Do you want me to wake you?'

'No, don't bother. I'll use my phone. I've got my keys to get back in.'

'What time will you go?'

'About half six.'

'I'll have breakfast ready when you get back.'

'No, don't put yourself out. You've been really kind already. Have a lie in or something. Don't fuss.'

'But what if I like to fuss? And, in any case, I won't feel happy until you're back safely. You can have breakfast and relax and even go back to bed if you like.'

'I might just do that.'

'Tired?'

'Absolutely knackered,' said Jack, and he yawned and stretched like a big cat.

'Go on up then,' said Humphrey. 'I'm going to turn in shortly. See you tomorrow.'

In bed, shortly afterwards, Humphrey thought again about how he felt. He ought to have exercised his responsibility as an adult to report the assault. If Jack's father attacked him again, it would be partly his fault. He ought to have insisted that Jack go to Accident and Emergency. It was perhaps naive of him to let Jack stay overnight given that the boy had a criminal record. But what then?

If he had reported it, what would have happened? Jack was eighteen now. He might not necessarily have been given shelter. It might have been regarded as a 'domestic' and warnings issued. He thought he had read somewhere that domestic violence was so common that police rarely acted upon it. And after all, Jack had been thrown out of the house. What would reporting the case have done about that? Did a father have a legal obligation to house his son once he had reached the age of majority? Humphrey simply didn't know.

And again. Jack had refused to go to the hospital. As a legal adult that was his right. If he had a scar or the wound turned septic, that was also his own responsibility. Humphrey had no duty of care.

In the strange interface between sleep and waking, when the shades of unknown faces rise up behind your tired eyelids, Humphrey continued to hear the whispers of contrary voices. It was a little like the angel and the devil at your shoulders which cartoonists are so fond of.

Except that sometimes the devil wore the halo and the angel had the horns. And sometimes the devil had the face of Mrs Bellingham and the angel the face of Jack - and sometimes it was the other way round.

He woke just before seven. He was aware that his 'conscience' had finally given his subconscious mind a rest for, as he turned the bedside lamp on and stretched himself properly awake, he remembered that he had dreamt of a special way to stop sheep and ducks from interbreeding. It involved extruding the stuff of which seaside rock is made into railings. The birds and mammals were told not to cross the barrier. He had woken up just as the ducks were planning a concerted attack.

'And now, *Herr Professor Doktor Freud*,' thought Humphrey, 'just what do you make of that?'

He must remember to tell Jack.

Humphrey & Jack

He wanted to check that Jack had left early as he had said he would but he didn't want to invade his privacy. Jack must feel that his space was sacrosanct.

In the end, anxiety and curiosity got the better of him and he went upstairs and tapped softly on the door. Receiving no answer, he pushed it open. There was no sign of Jack and the bed had been neatly made. For a moment, the thought flashed into Humphrey's mind that he might have dreamt everything that had happened the previous night and that Jack had never been there at all. Then he noticed a few coins on the bedside table and, propped beside it, Jack's shoulder bag. He had forgotten to turn off the light in the bathroom and there was a thin line of bright yellow under the door.

Humphrey closed the door as softly as if Jack had been in there.

Downstairs he set about preparing breakfast. Outside, it was still dark and quiet. There was the occasional car whose lights raked the kitchen window - there would be little more until eight when motorists would begin using the lane as a shortcut between two major roads. He heard the whine of the electric motor that drove the buggy with brushes which swept the pavements two or three times a week. It would stop soon so that the driver could have a fag break. Humphrey wondered if the council knew that its operative stopped for a fag every hundred yards or so.

Humphrey looked in the fridge. There was bacon, there were sausages, eggs, tomatoes, mushrooms - Jack didn't like mushrooms - how could you not like mushrooms? - there was bread in the crock, and there were hash browns in the freezer. He preferred tea, at least in the mornings; Jack liked coffee. He would make both.

He laid out the ingredients and was setting the table when he heard crunching on the gravel and saw Jack coming up the drive carrying a sports bag and with a large rucksack on his back.

While Humphrey was cooking breakfast, Jack told his tale.

When he'd got to the house on Bagot Street, he saw that the front door was wide open. He thought at first that that meant his father was still in there and then realised that that didn't make a great deal of sense. He crept into the house cautiously and found that it was indeed empty. The keys were on the inside of the door.

Inside, there wasn't the mess Jack had expected. Up in his room, which had not been ransacked as he had feared, he retrieved his laptop, which he always kept hidden, clothes, books and papers, and stuffed everything into a rucksack and a holdall. He thought of leaving a note but then thought, why should he?

Finally, he took the keys from the front door and left them on the cluttered kitchen table. Then he let himself out into the street locking the door after him with his own key.

'When he gets home, he won't be able to get in!' Jack said with a broad grin.

'Don't you think he'll come up here to find you and give you another leathering?'

'No, I don't think so. Sure, he might put two and two together and assume I'm here, but to be honest, thinking about it, I'm not even sure that he knows where you live.'

'Where do you think he is?'

'I reckon he must have stormed off after beating me up. Off his head. I mean it's pretty stupid of him to throw me out and leave the front door open to the street. He'll have gone off to find his cronies.

'You know, I don't think he was just drunk. He's used drugs before, barbiturates I'd guess. His mates are definitely druggies. They used to come round the house and take the piss. Gross bastards.'

'Well, you're here now. Take your stuff upstairs and wash your hands,' Humphrey said. 'Breakfast in ten minutes.'

Jack did as he was told.

Breakfast in ten minutes? Humphrey thought. Wash your hands? I sound like a toddler's mummy.

When he came down, Jack wolfed down the enormous fry-up in no time.

Humphrey & Jack

'Awesome,' he said. 'Any more sausages?'

Humphrey put two more sausages in the frying pan and made more toast.

'I like having you here, Jack,' Humphrey said.

'Yeah, it's cool,' said Jack, still eating, 'but it can't be permanent.'

'Nothing is,' said Humphrey.

34. Noise

Humphrey sat in Dr Bell's waiting room, tense and cross, and wondering what had caused him to make an appointment at this time of year. There had been a freezing mist on his way to the surgery and he had had to pull up short at a pelican crossing when a cyclist with no lights shot across before the lights had changed. This had shaken him rather and he found himself reverting to a crabby pre-Jack mood.

He looked at his watch. His appointment was for 8.45 and it was now 8.55. What was the point of an appointments system if no-one stuck to it? He looked around at the other waiting patients, half of them malingerers no doubt. Were any of them for Dr Bell? Were some of them before him?'

Dr Bell appeared at a side door.

'Mrs Carter, please,' he said.

A heavily pregnant woman lifted a toddler out of a baby buggy and moved towards the door which James was holding open for them. They disappeared.

Ever living God, thought Humphrey, they'll be hours.

He looked around again. He counted the other patients. Seventeen. There were four GPs in the practice. That's four patients each, plus one.

Mind you, one of the doctors might be off duty. So that would be five patients each plus one. Some of them might have appointments after Humphrey. Some of them might be couples, one of whom might be there just for support.

Humphrey & Jack

Mind you, he was willing to bet that that wasted looking girl, with the sunken eyes and a complexion like raw pastry, was before him. She would be in there for centuries.

After what seemed like an hour, Humphrey looked at his watch again. Four minutes had passed.

The fug in here is intolerable, he thought. He understood that it was cold outside and that it was important for the elderly, who, after all, constituted a majority in here, to keep warm. But this was unnecessarily tropical. What's more, the room must be acting as an incubator.

These people were ill or they wouldn't be here. Who was to say what germs were multiplying, what nasty microbes were pullulating, what vile diseases were being nourished in this hothouse? He was certain that he was, even now, contracting a strain of influenza which would see him die in shivering agony over several days.

He looked at his watch again. 9.05. Jack would be in his first lesson and here he was in the House of the Imminently Dead.

Some of them were sniffing. He could not endure sniffing. After the first sniff, the sniffing could not be unheard. It was torture.

But worse than the sniffing, worse than the waiting, worse than the prospect of a slow and agonising death, was the noise - and the noise was that of Radio 2.

It was not that it was loud particularly, though the volume was higher than it need be in this Hall of Silent Sufferers. It was its inescapability.

The presenter was gabbling at breakneck speed about absolutely nothing. His interviewee got barely a word in edgeways. The 'News' comprised four or five soundbites. The weather and traffic news were delivered at such a velocity that it made little sense. Then the presenter, whose ego drowned out everything else, announced *Highway to Hell* by AC/DC. This racket involved a monotonous drumbeat, howling guitars and vocal screaming.

'Hey, Momma, look at me!' howled the dervish, and the presenter joined in.

Humphrey & Jack

Just as Humphrey could bear no more and was about to go, the side door opened and the pregnant woman emerged, beaming. James Bell was behind her, also beaming. He looked around, saw Humphrey and nodded. Humphrey stood up and James retreated behind the door again.

'The bastard,' thought Humphrey. 'Did he do that on purpose?'

A few moments later, he reappeared and Humphrey realised a bit sheepishly that James would have had to write up his notes on the previous patient and check up on Humphrey's notes.

Once inside the surgery, James said, as expected: 'Excellent. Excellent. Take a seat. Good to see you. Now, Humphrey, what can we do for you today?'

'Well, there are a couple of things actually, and I don't want to waste your time but the first one has been troubling me for years and I think it's getting worse.'

'OK, if it's troubling you, you're not wasting my time. Out with it.'

'It's my ears, James.'

Doctor Bell looked at his ears and Humphrey felt uncomfortable. He knew that they were very large and that they stuck out of his head at right angles. He had had to endure a lot of gyp about this at school.

Other boys would call him 'Radar' and walk behind him going 'bip bip bip' and saying 'frigate north north east ten miles' or 'any news from Mars today, Spike?'.

Humphrey frowned.

'Well, Humphrey,' said Dr Bell, 'I have to say that this is a problem that is usually addressed in childhood, typically after the age of five or so. There are no physiological problems, of course, but one appreciates that when a kiddie starts school there can be bullying which will cause short term misery and sometimes long term psychological issues. Which is not the case with you, is it, Humphrey?'

'I don't really have a clue what you're talking about,' said Humphrey.

Humphrey & Jack

'So, I have to say again,' Doctor Bell continued, 'that I'm a little surprised that you've come to see me about it at your stage in life.'

'I'm only a year older than you,' said Humphrey.

'Well, exactly. Now, not to worry. Something can be done. The surgery is usually available to children on the NHS but most adults have to go privately, except in cases of extreme psychological distress, which is not your case, is it?'

'What on earth are you on about?' said Humphrey.

'Now, I can refer you to the Ear, Nose and Throat Department at Radcester General, or directly to a plastic surgeon. What do you think?'

'Plastic surgeon?' said Humphrey. 'What for?'

'To correct your...' (It began to dawn on James Bell that he might have been barking up the wrong tree) '...protruding ears,' he almost whispered.

'I'm not here about sticky-out ears, James.'

Humphrey assumed the slightly superior tone he usually employed to his junior.

'I've lived my life with the blasted things up to now and any "psychological distress" evaporated long ago. It's not about my not-very-shell-likes: it's about my hearing.'

'Ah, experiencing some impairment are we? Only to be expected. *Anno domini*, you know.' Dr Bell was clearly pleased to be on exclusively clinical grounds.

'I'm not going deaf - if that's what you're saying,' Humphrey said. 'Quite the contrary. I seem to be abnormally sensitive to noise.'

Humphrey went on to describe his symptoms along with some examples: leaf blowers, screaming children, car alarms, not excluding the obnoxious breakfast presenter of Radio 2.

'Why you want to have that bilious crap blaring out when people only want to suffer in silence is quite beyond my comprehension,' he said.

'I don't think it would be my choice either,' Dr Bell said, 'but we did a survey of our patients and they opted overwhelmingly for Radio 2.'

'No-one contacted me.'

'It was by email. You must have missed it. It wouldn't have made any difference though.'

'Was silence one of the options?'

'No. Now, let's have a look inside your ears.'

He produced a black instrument like a spike on a stick.

'What's that?' said Humphrey, who was suspicious of all medical instruments, especially the blood pressure thing.

'It's called an otoscope. It lets me look inside your outer and middle ear. There's a light inside it. You won't feel anything.'

'It's not an x-ray thing, is it? I don't fancy having my ears irradiated.'

'It's a simple mechanical gadget, Humphrey. Keep still, please.'

And he crouched over Humphrey and examined each ear in turn.

'Hmm,' he said, sitting down again, 'I can't see anything physically wrong. I can refer you to an auditory specialist, of course. It may be that you're suffering from hyperacusis.'

'Which is?'

'Which is a collapsed tolerance to environmental sound. You would be tested for tolerance to volume levels first of all. Tell me, is it just loudness that disturbs you?'

'I don't think so. I particularly dislike heavy metal, Radio 2, muzak, announcements on trains, stations, airports and supermarkets, and buskers. I curse and damn to the lowest circle of hell whatever deviant who invented the portable amplifier.'

'But isn't all that partly a question of taste?' said Dr Bell.

'No it bloody isn't,' said Humphrey. 'Having good taste shouldn't reduce you to existential despair.'

Dr Bell decided to ignore this.

'Of course, it may well be,' he said, 'that what is distressing you is a collapsed tolerance to certain frequencies, or it may even be a combination of frequency and volume.'

'But, is it treatable?' said Humphrey.

'Well, as far as I understand, and to a degree, yes.'

'And what's that supposed to mean?'

'You'd have to ask an expert, Humphrey. I believe that one approach is to use broadband pink noise to alleviate symptoms and restore a level of tolerance over time. It's used in the treatment of tinnitus and insomnia too. You could be fitted with a special hearing aid which generates the noise. You can try out what it sounds like yourself. Just type 'pink noise' into Google and it will take you to YouTube examples. Now, would you like me to refer you?'

'Sounds like a plan,' Humphrey said, realising immediately that he had picked up the idiom from Jack.

'Fine. OK. I'll write to the appropriate consultant and you'll hear directly from the hospital. Now what was the other thing?'

'The other thing? Oh, the other thing? Oh no, it's all right. The other thing isn't important.'

He had planned to ask Dr Bell about asexuality. Was it, as Jack would say, 'a thing'?

His absence of libido had been, at least since the days of poor mad Minty, something he had taken for granted. Of late, however, he had become quite curious about it.

He had found a questionnaire online and answered the questions honestly. It went like this:

THE ASEXUALITY METER

Are you asexual? Take back control of your life with this clinically approved quiz.

Q. Do you think about sex at all?
A. No (at least I try not to)
Q. Do you think you perceive sex differently from other people?

A. Yes (I have no real idea how other people perceive things. They do talk about sex a lot though)
Q. Would you say that you think about sex in a very clinical way without experiencing erotic feelings?
A. Yes (spot on - jolly good)
Q. Is it true that you don't know whether you're straight, gay, lesbian or bisexual?
A. Yes (It would be truer to say that these terms don't really mean a great deal to me. I'm pretty sure that I'm not a lesbian)
Q. When you see naked bodies are you sexually aroused?
A. No (although it's probably fair to say I don't tend to see many naked bodies around on a day to day basis)
Q. You don't like masturbating, and if you do, you don't fantasise about naked bodies while you're doing it
A. (I'd rather not talk about this but -) Yes (- masturbating is a kind of physical hygiene with me. I get it over as quickly as I can and hope it will be a long time before I have to do it again. And yes, you're right. I don't summon up any images whatsoever. Just a blank)
Q. You never initiate sex
A. (How well you know me.) Yes, I never initiate sex
Q. Do you find sex in films and books boring?
A.   Yes (And unnecessary)
Q. Have you ever had to fake an interest in sex?
A. (Oh, very clever!) Yes

He had pressed the button that said: **GET THE RESULT** and an icon with coloured dots on it went round and round and then:

You are **95% asexual**. You are an **aromantic**.
Studies show that **1%** of the population identify as **asexual**. More and more psychologists and other clinicians are recognising that asexuality is an **autonomous sexual identity**. **Asexuality is not a dysfunction**.

Humphrey & Jack

We can show you how to **embrace** your asexuality and **liberate** yourself from society's limited preconceptions. Read your very own **asexuality manual**:

'Walking back to Happiness'

which contains physical and spiritual **exercises** that will help you reach a plane of self-awareness and self-regard which will, in turn, **enrich your life**.

Humphrey had, at first, read the book's title as: 'Wanking Back to Happiness'.

There followed a list of 'Famous Asexuals' which included Emily Brontë and T.E. Lawrence. Oh, this really won't do, Humphrey thought. *Wuthering Heights*, that coded kettle of boiling lusts? And Lawrence, who rogered Arab boys in the dunes? Come on.

This 'clinically approved' guff was clearly cobblers, a con to sell a crummy book. There was even a button labelled: 'Not the result you wanted?' The author was a manifest mountebank.

Humphrey would need to talk to a proper doctor if he really wanted to know.

But, when it came to it, he bottled out. He just couldn't discuss this stuff with James. And anyway, what did it matter? It was all too late.

'If you're sure,' said Doctor Bell.

'Sure about what?' said Humphrey.

'That there's nothing else.'

'Oh yes, quite sure. I've already forgotten what it was,' Humphrey lied.

'OK, well, we might as well check your blood pressure while you're here.'

'If you must.'

'Just take off your jacket, if you will.'

Humphrey did as he was told and the nasty cuff went on.

'Relax your hand, Humphrey.'

Discomfort and then relief as the thing deflated. There was a pause.

'110 over 70,' said Dr Bell.

'Is that very bad?' said Humphrey.

'No, it's very good. Have you been taking my advice? Cutting down on the booze?'

Not on your nelly, thought Humphrey.

'Yes,' he said.

'Good man.'

'And do you know, James - booze and noise apart - I feel so much more relaxed these days, so much more purposeful?'

'And do you know why that is?'

'I couldn't possibly say,' said Humphrey.

35. Cohabitation

Jack stayed at Humphrey's for just over a week.

Humphrey was well aware of the stereotypes of teenage boys as noisy, untidy and even malodorous but Jack was none of these things. If anything, he was quite fastidious about personal hygiene.

He was quiet too and spent a lot of time at his studies. Of course, he couldn't live without the hideous music that had precipitated their first clash. However, he listened through noise-cancelling headphones, and with his bedroom door firmly closed, the racket was hermetically sealed.

Who would have thought, given that confrontation in the early summer, that by Christmas they would be living under the same roof and that a boy who had been on the brink of following his father into a career of petty crime would end up swotting for entrance to a distinguished university?

Humphrey & Jack

There was, however, the question of the socks. When Jack had said that his socks were threadbare, it had been an understatement. All the socks that he had brought from Bagot Street had holes in them. Humphrey showed Jack where his sock drawer was and told him to help himself. He wasn't to know that Jack would do so daily and that given Jack's idiosyncratic habit of wearing odd socks, he would end up with a drawer containing a good many unwedded socks too. When he joshed Jack about it and called him a sock pilferer, Jack just laughed, but the next day, on his return from college, he handed Humphrey a small parcel.

'What's this?' said Humphrey.

'Present,' said Jack.

Humphrey opened the packet. It contained a pair of socks with a neat design of interlocking leaves, red ones alternating with green, like a jigsaw.

'Thank you, Jack. There was no need, you know.'

Jack smiled and shrugged.

'Summer and autumn,' Humphrey said.

'I don't think they're meant to be symbolic,' Jack laughed.

'What are they, do you think? Sycamore? Maple?'

'*Cannabis sativa*,' said Jack and laughed even harder at the expression on Humphrey's face.

They did not get in each other's way. Jack was at college on most days. Humphrey thought he might write a book. It would be different from the academic stuff he had produced in the past. For now it was just the germ of an idea but he began to spend a lot of time in his study researching it.

When Jack got home they would have a cup of tea and Jack would tell Humphrey about his progress. Humphrey was quietly delighted when Jack brought home a formal academic report to show him.

He was doing remarkably well. Humphrey noted phrases like 'genuine intellectual curiosity'; 'individual spirit of inquiry'; 'original flair' and 'powerfully motivated'. His tutor had written: 'what a delight it is to see someone who was threatening to come off the rails coursing toward success. He must aim high.'

As Humphrey looked through these accolades, he was moved to see Jack's face flushed with a sense of fulfilment at last.

'Thanks for showing me this, Jack,' Humphrey said.

'You've got to sign it. Or at least, someone has to. To show it's gone home and not been thrown in the bin. It should be my dad really but (here he grinned broadly), I guess you'll do.'

'It'll be an honour. And we'll talk about 'aiming high' at dinner.'

'Sure. Right, see you later. I've got an English essay to write.'

'On?'

Jack consulted a notebook.

'"*The only true love is unrequited love* - Discuss with reference to one example from the courtly tradition and one example post 1900." Awesome title,' Jack said.

'It is,' said Humphrey. 'Dinner at seven-thirty?'

'Cool,' Jack said, and went upstairs to work.

It was all most extraordinary, thought Humphrey as he chopped onions. Here he was cohabiting with an eighteen year old wastrel who appeared to have reformed himself. And not just cohabiting either but washing his clothes, cooking his meals, caring for him, attending to his needs, like a…like a what?

He knew perfectly well that there were censorious people out there all too ready to question their friendship. There were no doubt some who would even be keen to put a lewd interpretation on it. Well, a hippo's fart to their imputations.

Could it be, he thought, as onion tears streamed down his face, that asexual Humphrey, celibate Humphrey, sterile Humphrey, eremitical Humphrey, Humphrey the Lonely, Humphrey the Outcast - could it be that Humphrey was happy? The emotion was quite new to him so he couldn't be entirely certain.

Humphrey & Jack

The tears, at any rate, did not stem from emotion. They were caused by a chemical irritant in the onions and he was a sentimental old fool. A happy fool though.

Jack always came down long before dinner was ready. He would sit at the table, not exactly holding his cutlery upright in his fists, but with that sort of expression.

'It'll be half an hour yet,' Humphrey would say.

''s all right,' Jack would reply.

'I can't do it any faster.'

''s all right.'

And he would sit there in a kind of pre-feeding trance. At first it was a bit irritating but Humphrey had learned to live with it.

This evening it was Jack's favourite, a ham risotto. Humphrey had to serve up Jack's portion first and then add some pre-soaked porcini mushrooms for himself.

'How are the university applications going,' he asked. 'Are you aiming high?'

'Nearly there. Will you have a look at my personal statement with me?'

'Of course,' Humphrey said, 'where are you applying? What's your first choice?'

'I was thinking Durham.'

'Why not Oxbridge?'

'Because I'm not good enough?' said Jack with that rising inflexion that so annoyed Humphrey.

'How can you be so sure?' he said.

'Well, let's just say that I didn't want to waste an option. Anyhow, it's immaterial now. The deadline was in October. Durham's cool though, isn't it? Isn't that where you did your doctorate?'

'How do you know that?'

'I Googled you,' Jack said with a crooked grin.

Humphrey laughed.

'I didn't know I was on Google,' he said.

'Everybody is. It's just that if you have a pretty common name you won't be near the top. There aren't that many Humphrey Icke's in the world. In fact, you may be the only one.'

'In which case, the world is blessed that there has only ever been one woman as heartless as my mother when she chose my handle. What else appeals about Durham?'

'Well, it's partly that it's not Oxbridge. I can't explain it but I don't need the shit around it. You come across somebody who went there and they get it into the conversation within the first minute. And then it's: "Oh, what college?" Boring, man.'

'Durham has colleges.'

'Yeah, but there's not the same crap about it. I want to get into University College. That's the Castle, isn't it?'

'It is, but you've got to remember that lots of applicants will go for it and if you don't get in you'll be allocated to another college without appeal.'

'How do they decide?'

'I don't know. A sorting hat. Casting runes. Some arcane algorithm. I don't know. But you might think about looking at the other colleges too. You might find one that fits your interests closely and where the chances of a match are higher. Do you want some more risotto?'

'I can't now, can I?'

'Why not?'

'You've put your slimy fungus in it.'

'Have some cheese then.'

'Sure.'

'Which college did you go to?'

'Did not the God Google tell you?'

'It was a devastating moment when I discovered that the God is not omniscient but it didn't, no.'

Humphrey & Jack

'I was originally down for Ustinov which is just for graduates. It has a large proportion of international students and has a reputation for being intense. I didn't fancy intense. Anyway, a chance to get a room in Hatfield came up. It's attractive, opposite the east end of the cathedral. The food is excellent, so I leapt at it. I reckoned it would be easier to live a secluded life in an undergraduate college. And I was right.'

'You're weird,' said Jack pleasantly.

'I came to that selfsame conclusion a very long time ago,' said Humphrey.

They ate in silence for a while and then Humphrey said:

'I have an idea.'

'Go on.'

'What if I were to take you up to Durham to have a look around?'

'O wicked! That would be awesome.'

'When do you have to decide? What's the deadline?'

'Middle of January. The fifteenth, I think.'

'Hmm, a bit tight. It'll have to be after Christmas. I'll make a couple of calls tomorrow. It might just be possible to get a couple of guest rooms in Hatfield before the Epiphany Term starts.'

'Is that what it's called? Epiphany Term?'

'Michaelmas, Epiphany, Easter.'

'O wow! I just have to go somewhere that has an Epiphany Term.'

'Talking of Christmas, would you like to come here, Jack?'

'Not really.'

Humphrey had made the invitation on the spur of the moment. His disappointment was sudden and visceral.

'Where will you go? It won't be much fun with your father, will it?' he said, trying to hide his feelings. There was a slight catch in his voice that Jack didn't notice.

'O, to hell with him. No, it's all sorted. I'm going to my friend Marek's. His mother does an incredible *wijilijna zupa migdalowa* - almond soup. We fast on Christmas Eve until the first star appears - and then we feast, starting with the soup.'

'It sounds delightful,' said Humphrey.

'What are you doing for Christmas, Humphrey?' Jack asked.

'Oh, expect I shall be on my own,' Humphrey said.

36. Custody

After breakfast the next morning, Jack set off for college. The day was dank and bleak but Jack never grumbled. Humphrey felt guilty as he made more tea in the warm house and went upstairs to his study.

Soon after nine o'clock, he phoned Hatfield at the University of Durham. Bed and breakfast accommodation was indeed available during vacations but only at Easter and throughout the summer. He was in luck, however. The college was hosting a conference from the eighth to the tenth of January and two undergraduate rooms could be made available, especially for an alumnus.

Jack would be thrilled. They could have stayed at a hotel, of course, but Hatfield would be a little foretaste of university life for him, while Humphrey, who liked his creature comforts, would have to endure the straitened confines of an undergraduate room for the lad's sake. Mind you, breakfast would be good.

He thought they would go by rail. This had several advantages. Firstly, if the weather were bad the roads might be treacherous. Secondly, he could relax and enjoy the journey. Thirdly, and most importantly: as the train takes its last, prolonged bend, the sudden striking view of the castle and the ancient cathedral high on the promontory above the loop of the River Wear would be bound to captivate Jack.

Humphrey couldn't wait to tell his news; the day was long and tedious as a result. He couldn't seem to settle to anything and just fannied about unprofitably most of the morning.

Humphrey & Jack

It being Thursday, he pottered along to The Seven Stars at lunchtime to meet the Evangelists for a curry and a pint and a most satisfactory griping session about the Secretary of State for Education.

Garth was on excellent derogatory form, referring to the Minister as the Archshit, the Sphincter, The Plague Sore, Clinkermouth and Turd Laureate and the others applauded the epithets and were, for once, all on the same side.

Over their lunch, once the high tide of outrage had ebbed somewhat, Humphrey could not help telling the others how well Jack was doing and about the projected visit to Durham.

'Good for him,' said Hector, 'and good for you. You've helped that boy to a chance in life.'

'Oh, I wouldn't say that,' said Humphrey.

'Neither would I,' said Garth. 'A leopard doesn't change his spots nor a tiger his stripes. Once he's tired of you and your treats (which will be sooner rather than later) you won't see him for dust. Humphrey boy, you haven't got the brains of a rocking horse, have you? I think you're making a soppy fool of yourself, if you want to know.'

'I don't think I do,' said Humphrey.

'You want to think about how other people see this friendship and step out of your rainbow-hued bubble for a moment. A sexagenarian like you and a schoolboy! How do you think that looks?' said Garth.

'Only if you have a dirty mind,' Humphrey said.

'And he has,' said Hector.

'My mind is not relevant,' Garth said.

'Thank God for that,' said Hector.

'It's what other people think,' Garth said. 'There you are holed up in that big house and you have this, this adolescent coming and going, and, and living with you. What are people going to think?'

'And people talk,' said Norman.

'They do. And everywhere you go, Humphrey, it's "Jack this" and "Jack that". Are you in love with this boy, Humphrey? Are you?'

Humphrey & Jack

Humphrey did not deign to reply.

'By Isis and Osiris, Garth Porter, you are a nasty piece of work,' Hector said.

Humphrey left soon afterwards, claiming some spurious appointment. Garth had cut him deep but he would not be bowed. He was not so naive as to have failed to recognise that there would be detractors who, through prurience or a failure of imagination or both, might want to misread their friendship. Until now he just thought: well let them. But Garth's unpleasantness had cast a shadow of fear.

He didn't for a moment doubt Jack's loyalty - but those people, those other people. The thought rankled all afternoon.

It vanished as he heard a key in the door (Jack had been trained to use it at last) and the boy came bounding up the stairs.

Humphrey couldn't wait to tell him about Durham but Jack had hotter news.

His father was going to prison. After throwing Jack out he had indeed joined up with his mates. They'd got high, or even higher than they already were, and then launched a devastatingly incompetent attack on a chemist's on the High Street, probably looking for drugs.

Jack's father had form. He'd been in prison before and had a string of offences to his name. He had always whined that he needed to look after Jack and had therefore managed to wheedle himself out of a custodial sentence, until he was caught yet again after a bungled burglary at a house, oddly enough, further along on Upper Bishop's Lane. For this he had been given a two year suspended sentence.

The farcical raid on the chemist's shop meant that the sentence would now have to come into force. In addition this latest offence would be taken into consideration. There were no mitigating circumstances this time as Jack was now over eighteen. On the other hand, there were plenty of aggravating factors: he had failed to comply with court orders; he had committed this most recent offence while under the influence of drugs; worst of all, when apprehended, he was found to be carrying an offensive

Humphrey & Jack

weapon, a long kitchen knife. He was currently in custody and there would be no bail. He would be facing a long stretch.

All this had been relayed to Jack by the Pastoral Officer at college. They were concerned about where Jack was going to live. He had no living relatives in Britain. He had explained where he was living at present but that he wanted to go home. The Pastoral Officer saw no objection to this. She would find out what support and benefits might be available under the circumstances. There would be a meeting the following afternoon, Friday.

'But Jack, you would have been perfectly welcome to stay here for as long as need be, till you go to university even,' Humphrey said.

'That's kind of you and don't think I don't appreciate it but I don't want to impose on you,' Jack said.

'You're not imposing on me.'

'Humphrey, I want to go home.'

'Don't you like it here?'

'I do. Now back off will you, man. You're giving me a hard time. You don't get it, do you? A guy of my age needs his independence.'

'Of course you do,' said Humphrey quietly. 'Sorry.'

'Oh, man, said Jack. 'Don't look like that. It's just that…'

'No, no,' said Humphrey recovering. 'It's fine. I understand. Let's just see how it goes, shall we? You're not going immediately, are you?'

'No, no. Stuff to sort out. Anyway, we've got the tutorial tomorrow. There's the meeting tomorrow afternoon. And I'd like to stay for lunch on Saturday, if you'll still have me.'

'Of course.'

'I may go back on Sunday. We'll see.'

The next morning, Humphrey was startled out of dreams of nomadic tribes setting up yurts in Alexandra Park by a very loud high-pitched whine like a dentist's drill. He and Jack had stayed up late drinking whisky. Humphrey had proposed the date and time of the excursion to Durham and Jack was wildly enthusiastic. When he had calmed down a

Humphrey & Jack

little, Humphrey taught him how to play backgammon, perhaps against his better judgement given his experiences with chess, Scrabble and poker. They had decided by mutual consent that, since Jack did not need to go to college until the afternoon and the tutorial was usually at ten, there would be no need to get up in the dark and they could have a bit of a lie-in.

Humphrey pulled on his dressing gown and went upstairs to his study to get a better view of whatever it was that was going on. There were tree surgeons at work in the park. Jack had heard the study door and came in in his bathrobe. He joined Humphrey at the window.

'Did it wake you too?' Humphrey said.

'Not half,' said Jack.

Though it was cosy in the house, the sunlight outside looked cold and brittle. There were two great ash trees on the avenue which ran parallel to the wall at the bottom of Humphrey's garden. They were always the last of the trees to come into leaf in spring and in recent years one of them had seemed to push out its foliage a little later each time.

Humphrey had read somewhere about a fungal infection that was attacking British ash trees. He thought the article had said that mature trees stood a better chance of withstanding the blight but he couldn't be sure.

They had to admire the agility of the young man moving about the lower boughs of the smaller tree. He was roped up somewhere above and swung with something approaching grace from bough to bough, the saw swinging from his waist. Then he took it up and began to remove the lighter branches first.

Now he sawed off boughs at the sides and finally turned to three branches growing upright, their leafless limbs looking feathery and frail as they waved over the pollarded stumps below. He took the screaming saw to these, one by one, cutting first at one side, then working at the other. Even at a distance they could see the sawdust spewing out of the cut and sparkling in the crisp winter sunshine.

Would it come crashing into his garden, thought Humphrey. But no, the young man knew what he was doing. The bough leaned sideways, as if in slow motion, appeared to be suspended for an instant, and then went crashing down into the avenue. And so for the other two branches.

Humphrey looked at Jack who stood there transfixed.

'Come on,' he said. 'Breakfast.'

Later, when he had bathed and dressed, Humphrey went up to his study and was immediately astounded at the blankness in the window. The tree had gone! It was very sad. No doubt the woodmen had their reasons but there was a sense of absence. The larger tree still stood and there would still be green shadows rippling on his study walls in the summer. On the other hand, where the diseased tree had been, the prospect had opened up. He could now see clearly down into the valley and across to the moorland beyond. He could see the cemetery down by the farther riverbank and he shuddered.

Of course, the felling of the tree exposed the house too. The owners of the yippy dogs in the park had only to look up and, if he could see them, they could see him standing at the window.

What had Garth said? That he and Jack were 'holed up in the big house' and what would people think? Well, there was considerably less privacy now. Humphrey had not been conscious of being secretive where Jack was concerned but he resolved that henceforth he would be as open as the vista before him. Whatever the outcome of the pastoral meeting later, he would take Jack out to dinner that evening.

When Jack knocked on the door for his tutorial a while later, Humphrey said 'Come!' and heard Jack laughing as he came in.

'What's funny? Humphrey said.

'Are you pretending to be a Cambridge don?' Jack said.

'Not especially. Are you pretending to be a Durham student?'

'No, why?'

'You don't usually knock.'

'I am a very polite person,' Jack said.

'Strange boy,' said Humphrey.

'Wow!' Jack said suddenly. 'It's gone! It's only just registered. Aw, what a shame!'

'There'll be good reason.'

'Sure. Quite a view though. Oh look!' he said pointing. 'You can see my house down there in the slums.'

'Come on,' Humphrey said, not wanting to be reminded that their ménage was coming to an end.

The EPQ was coming along brilliantly and was nearly ready. Jack had more material than he could use and Humphrey gave him advice on editing down the current draft.

'God, it'll be like auto-amputation,' Jack said.

Afterwards, he told Humphrey, he would have to prepare a presentation.

'I'd like you to come,' he said.

'I should be honoured,' Humphrey said, 'if the college will let me.'

'Of course they will,' Jack said, 'the more the merrier.'

Afterwards, Humphrey asked Jack if he could take a look at his wireless printer which was malfunctioning. Jack checked the connexions at the back and then got down on his knees to look at plugs and sockets and the router connexion.

'If I got down there, I'd never get back up again,' Humphrey said.

He supposed he had never been as lithe and flexible as Jack but all the same - how the body betrays. Physically, age has nothing to recommend it, he thought. He admired the arch of the lad's back and found himself studying the nape of his neck where the short dark brown hair came to a point.

He was instantaneously flooded with a strange and singular feeling of tenderness. Nonsensical in a way because he was the one who was heading for the final frailty and Jack was fit and strong. It wasn't even as if Humphrey was in a position to protect him from life's buffetings. The lad had already had more than enough hard knocks, while it was Humphrey who had led a sequestered, congenial, even gracious existence, in a house bought with inherited money, with no personal liaisons to tie him down or to vex him.

'I can't find anything wrong with it. Have you tried turning your computer and your printer off and then turning them both on again?'

'Not at the same time.'

A few minutes later all was resolved and Jack set off for college.

That evening, true to his resolution, Humphrey took him out to dinner. Jack's advisors had assured him that it would be financially viable for him to return home, especially since Jack had said he intended to get a job. He would lose benefits if he worked more than fifteen hours a week but that was fine. More than that and there would be a detrimental effect on his studies and Jack wasn't going to let that happen.

Humphrey put a brave face on it and said they would go out to celebrate. He gave Jack a choice between the Blue Boar and the Delhi Durbar and Jack chose the latter without hesitation. As Humphrey led the way in, he thought everyone must assume that he was some kind of pervert and Jack a rent boy but, it being Friday evening, it was very busy and nobody paid them a blind bit of notice, apart from the waiters who were very attentive.

'Have you been here before?' Humphrey asked as they scanned the menu.

'I haven't even been into a restaurant since Mum died,' Jack said.

'No, I suppose not,' Humphrey said. 'Sorry.'

'No need,' Jack said.

The waiter came up to take the order.

'Is this your son?' he said, beaming.

'I'd be very proud if he were,' Humphrey said.

'Indeed yes,' the waiter said.

'Oh dear,' said Jack when the waiter had gone.

'What?' Humphrey said.

'Nothing.'

'Is it because the waiter thought you were my son?'

'No. Forget about it.'
'What then?'
'What you said. Don't worry about it. It doesn't matter.'
But it did.

37. Marek

The trip to Durham was an unmitigated success and they returned with Jack totally fired up. The standard offer of A*AA was daunting but Jack's ambition had been boosted. He thought he could get the A* in Polish and was aiming for the star in the other two subjects too. He had found an article from *The Sunday Times* on the Internet that claimed that nearly one in five successful applicants to Durham had completed the Extended Project Qualification. Jack wanted not only to complete it but to excel.

Privately, Humphrey wished that Jack had applied to Cambridge. He would have been assured an interview and would have been able to demonstrate his unique qualities. Jack argued that the EPQ would be his ticket to distinction. There was also the fact that Durham had a reputation for giving fair access to disadvantaged students to an extent that some schools found unfair.

Soon, the EPQ was submitted. Humphrey had pronounced it exceptional. A public presentation was part of the assessment procedure and Humphrey was invited.

'I don't know why I want you to come,' Jack said. 'Submitting it on paper is one thing but standing up there and having people shoot questions at you is another. I'll probably dry and make a complete dick of myself.'

This was typical of Jack. In the face of any significant enterprise he would predict failure. It was a kind of insurance policy. If he succeeded, he would say: 'yeah well, had a bit of luck there, man'; if he failed, he could come back with: 'I told you I'd cock it up'.

Whether or not Jack believed his own auguries of doom, Humphrey couldn't be sure.

Humphrey & Jack

There were three projects scheduled before Jack's. Appearing first was David, a very tall youth who delivered his talk on something to do with quarks without any modulation whatsoever. Jack had told him that it was brilliant but Humphrey couldn't understand any of it, though he was sure Jack was right.

A pretty girl called Fanny (not her real name, surely?) with tattoos and a nineties grunge outfit did a satirical talk on 'Rebranding the Tories'. She was funny, original and pertinent and received vigorous applause. Humphrey noticed Jack clapping energetically.

Next was Bernadette, a slender girl with braided hair and a folk-singer's smock, who was down on the photocopied programme to talk about 'The Real Life of Sylvia Plath'. She began by relating how Plath was found dead of carbon monoxide poisoning with her head in the oven. She had sealed the rooms between her and her sleeping children with tape, towels and cloths. Here Bernadette immediately burst into anguished tears and couldn't go on. She was taken off to the college infirmary and a member of staff, after huddled discussion with colleagues, announced that another date would be found and that Bernadette would be allowed to deliver her paper *in camera*.

Jack was next and Humphrey could have burst with pride. He was as smooth and as polished as the best TV presenters. Jack delivered his tour de force wholly without notes. It was well-paced, nicely pointed and modulated, illustrated with powerful images and some animated maps. Humphrey looked around him in the penumbra of the lecture hall. Every face was rapt. He noticed that a very high proportion of the audience was made up of girls.

When he finished, Jack was greeted with an ecstatic ovation which included screaming and whistling as if he were a pop star. The panel of lecturers on the podium beamed at each other. Humphrey's protégé was on his way.

In the succeeding weeks, Humphrey began to see a little less of Jack. The EPQ 'tutorials' were no longer necessary, of course, but there were still their Saturday lunches. Once or twice, Jack excused himself, pleading pressure of work. In compensation, as it were, there were a couple of occasions where he agreed to join Humphrey for a restaurant meal in the evening where he would 'stay over' in the guest room which Humphrey now always thought of as Jack's room.

He was becoming more and more conscious of Time's wingèd chariot and so these occasions were precious. In a few months, Jack would be off to university, whether to Durham or not, and Humphrey would not see him for over two months at a time.

Now that was all well and good and it would be the escape from Radcester that Jack so passionately wanted but it would leave Humphrey washed up on the shore of his own loneliness again, like a crab in a rock pool.

One bright April day, when the daffodils along Jack's fence were looking tired with dried orange fringes to their trumpets and stems leaning toward the ground, Jack said he wouldn't be coming round the following Saturday.

'Oh, that's a shame,' Humphrey said. 'It's Easter Saturday.'

'I know,' said Jack.

'I was going to do you the full Paschal Feast. You know, roast lamb with all the trimmings.'

'I promised I would hang out with Marek. We're going fishing really early on the Roman Canal and then we're going to the cinema in the afternoon.'

'That's not a problem,' Humphrey cried, seeing his chance. 'Bring him!'

The moment he said it he had reservations. He was the other boy, the blond one, the accessory to the fouling of his garden. The fact that he was a friend of Jack's was no assurance of anything. True, there had been no sign of him since the incident and none of the rest of the gang had come anywhere near his garden. All the same, there was no guarantee that the boy was not still feral.

Humphrey & Jack

However, there was no going back on it now.

'Are you serious?' Jack said.

'Why not?'

'Well, he helped me trash your garden,' Jack said with an impudent grin.

'But you turned out all right, didn't you?'

'Allegedly.'

And so it was decided.

The following Saturday the boys arrived bearing rods, nets and other paraphernalia which Humphrey asked them to leave in the porch.

Inevitably, Mrs Bellingham appeared briefly at hers.

'Hello, Mrs B!' Jack shouted, waving extravagantly and she disappeared.

'Hush, Jack,' Humphrey said.

'This is Marek,' Jack said. 'You can call him Mark. And this is Humphrey.'

The boy who was fiddling in his haversack did not look up.

'Hello, Mark,' Humphrey said.

The boy didn't reply. Instead he offered Humphrey two shiny fish with dark stripes and fierce dorsal fins.

'Whoa,' said Humphrey, who did not want to handle them there and then, 'bring them through.'

The boys followed him into the kitchen where Humphrey found a colander into which Mark placed them and Humphrey set them under a running tap.

'What are they?' he asked the boy.

'Perch,' Jack said. 'Really good fried in butter. Mark's mum does them a treat, doesn't she, Mark?'

The boy nodded, head still down.

'Who caught them?' Humphrey was still addressing the boy.

'He did,' said Jack.

'Does he talk?' Humphrey said.

Humphrey & Jack

'Not a lot. He threw a couple of dace and a chubb back. The dace were a bit small and chubb tastes a bit muddy. Well, I think so anyway. You do too, don't you?'

Mark nodded.

Humphrey looked at him. There were a number of reasons Humphrey felt uncomfortable about him. There was his deplorable past record of impudence and vandalism. There was this silence. There was this bizarre gift of fish. Most of all there was the fact that he looked much younger than he did in the CCTV image. He could only be thirteen at a guess. And he was exceptionally pretty: straw-coloured blond hair, almond-shaped deep grey eyes, flawless blue-white skin and very high cheek bones. What was Jack doing hanging about with someone five years younger than himself?

Then Humphrey had to shake himself out of his own hypocrisy. He was more than forty years Jack's elder, for heaven's sake. The age gap between Jack and Mark might have put a taboo on their friendship at Humphrey's school but in the real world, and perhaps especially in the tight-knit Polish community, it was unremarkable.

Turning to Jack, he said: 'Did you catch anything?'

'Nothing. Zero. Diddly squat. Jack shit. Zilch. *Nul points*!' Jack said and both boys burst out laughing.

'Right,' Humphrey said. 'I think I'm going to freeze these chaps. I'm going to descale and gut them before we eat, then it's done.'

'I'll do it,' said Mark. Humphrey was right about his age. His voice hadn't yet broken.

'Are you sure?' Humphrey said.

'Let him,' said Jack, 'he knows what he's doing.'

A little warily, Humphrey handed him the filleting knife.

'Salt?' Mark said.

Humphrey took a drum of table salt from a cupboard and pushed it to Mark who took it, and poured a little onto the fingertips of his left hand. Picking up the first fish by the tail, he used the back of the knife to scrape the scales from the fish with downward strokes. Then, deftly, he slit the belly, gutted the fish and cut off the head, tail and fins. He ran it under the tap then patted it dry with kitchen paper and laid it on the counter. And so for the second fish. Seeing foil on a roller above the counter he made a parcel. It was all done in a trice.

'See,' said Jack. 'He's not just a pretty face.'

'I am impressed,' said Humphrey. 'Thank you for the fish, Mark.'

The boy just shrugged.

'He does catering,' Jack said.

'Ah,' said Humphrey.

'I need to wash my hands,' said Mark.

'Ah yes,' said Humphrey. 'Of course. Sorry. Jack, show him where the downstairs bathroom is.'

When Jack returned, Humphrey was popping the fish parcel into the freezer. Then, as he opened the oven door the savoury aroma of roast lamb with garlic and rosemary pervaded the kitchen.

'We're in the dining room, Jack,' he said. 'Would you set the table, please?'

Soon they were making short work of the lamb which was sweet and succulent. As expected, his decision to provide a huge mound of roast potatoes had been wise and there were generous portions of parsnips, carrots, and peas. There was a gravy made in the roasting tin with a splash of wine stirred in and some redcurrant jelly.

Humphrey had chosen a seven-year-old St. Amour and poured for himself and Jack.

'Would you like a coke or something, Mark?' Humphrey asked.

'Give him some wine. He drinks it at home. And vodka.'

'Does your mother know you're having lunch here, by the way?' Humphrey asked.

'Course she does,' Jack said. 'She's well laid-back your mum, isn't she, Marek?'

Mark smiled slyly.

Humphrey & Jack

'Perhaps just a glass, then. All right, Mark?'

'Whatever,' said the boy.

Humphrey had to restrain himself from coming over all pedagogical. He had learnt from Jack that this non-committal grunt was not to his generation the grotesque piece of rudeness it was to Humphrey's. He said nothing and poured Mark a glass.

Jack and he chatted animatedly throughout the meal but any attempt to draw Mark into the conversation was met with monosyllables. Perhaps the boy was just shy so Humphrey didn't press him. Actually, he had been quite touched by the gift of the fish and its preparation. Perhaps his apprehensions had been unfair; perhaps the boy was not a good-for-nothing after all.

After the lamb, there was a bread and butter pudding. Humphrey had used hot cross buns instead of white bread and there was cream laced with a little Calvados to go with it. Both boys declared it to be 'awesome'.

'Thank you, Humphrey,' Mark said, taking Humphrey by surprise. The use of his first name was premature to say the least but he was rather charmed by it.

'It's been a pleasure, Mark,' he said. 'You must come again.'

'Oh my God! Look at the time!' Jack cried, checking his phone. 'Sorry Humphrey, we've got to run or we'll miss the start of the film. Come on, Marek.'

'What is it?' Humphrey asked.

'New Bond film.'

'Not my cup of tea,' said Humphrey.

'No, I wouldn't think so. Can we leave the rods and stuff here? I'll pick them up next time. We'll just take the bags.'

'Of course, I'll put them in the utility room.'

'Wicked. See you next week!'

Humphrey stood in the front porch and watched them racing along Upper Bishop's Lane. Then he gathered their rods and things and turned into the hallway.

Humphrey & Jack

The silver-framed clock which normally stood on the hall table was gone.

38. Summer

The clock itself didn't matter much. It had been one of the presents he received when he retired from the History Faculty at Radcester University. It was in the art deco style with a white rectangular face and the Roman numerals and hands were in black. The frame was silver plated. In one corner was the Harrods logo. It would have been expensive but not valuable, in the sense that the antique claret jug, which had been his principal present, was valuable. But that was not the point.

It wasn't even the point that it had been a gift. What mattered was the feeling that he had been an utter fool letting that boy into the house.

He must have snaffled the clock and moved it to his bag in the porch when he went to wash his hands. Had he offered to gut the fish as part of a strategy? No, that was fanciful, Humphrey decided, it was just an opportunistic theft. The boy was probably a kleptomaniac.

For a sickening moment Humphrey wondered if Jack could have been in on it. But then, why would he? For a paltry clock which cost a hundred quid at most and was probably worth much less to a receiver? Besides, Jack had had the run of the house for months now and nothing had disappeared.

Would the boy tell Jack what he'd done? Humphrey doubted it. Jack probably knew that the little bastard was a thief but would have expected him to be on his best behaviour. No, Jack wasn't complicit. Humphrey wouldn't believe it.

But what was to be done? He couldn't go to the police. There would be too many questions. Not that he'd done anything wrong. The boy's mother had known he'd been at Humphrey's, after all, but it was - awkward.

Humphrey & Jack

In any case, if it were referred to the police, Jack would find out and Humphrey didn't want that. It would become complicated. There would be emotional 'noise' and it would be intolerable.

Best then, Humphrey thought, to do absolutely nothing - though the little shit would never cross his threshold again. That was for certain.

Jack's A level exams were approaching and he committed himself to a programme of revision which meant that he and Humphrey saw little of each other though they communicated several times a day through Facebook Messenger. Sometimes it would be simply a matter of 'Good morning, Humphrey,' or 'Sleep tight, Jack.'

Humphrey was learning banter. He had to learn not to take offence at Jack's put-downs but equally not to be afraid to go on the offensive himself. Jack was wildly amused when Humphrey typed 'pwned' on an occasion when he believed he had got the better of Jack and even more so when he typed 'fml' when Jack had made a palpable hit. All the same, Humphrey made no attempt to increase the number of his online friends, though he did agree to include a profile picture Jack had taken with his phone. Though 'flattering' was not exactly the word, a combination of angle and lighting had contrived an image which managed to prevent him looking like Mr Potato Head and even succeeded in disguising his jug ears.

Summer, meanwhile, had brought birdsong back to Humphrey's garden. Late May brought a heatwave and it was good to be able to sit in the garden again in the shade of the parasol and watch the young squirrels chasing each other across the grass, leaping onto the bark of a tree and pausing, tail twitching, before spiralling round the trunk onto a branch. He was amused one morning to see a squirrel teasing Aristotle. It was at the very end of a springy branch and bouncing up and down. As Aristotle crouched, the squirrel bounced to within an inch of his nose; as he leapt up, paws clawing the air, the branch and the squirrel whipped up and away out of reach. A dangerous game, Humphrey thought - he could sense Aristotle getting more and more cross.

Humphrey & Jack

Humphrey took most of his meals outdoors on these halcyon days. Each morning he stepped out to breakfast under skies of hot blue. It was mostly quiet apart from the birds' melodies. The grass and the leaves were still fresh and green, and the flowerbeds bright with soft colours, blue cornflowers, pink roses and, best of all, beautiful purple peonies. He would read or write or just watch the birds hopping close to Aristotle, snoozing in the sunshine.

He had grown quite fond of the cat now he was sure that his 'allergy' had been an illusion. It adored Jack, which was good enough for Humphrey, and there was, of course, the fact that Mrs Bellingham was hugely put out by every second that Aristotle spent *chez Humphrey*. He had started to buy cat treats from the supermarket in order to tempt Aristotle to stay even longer and intensify her vexation.

Lapped in the simple pleasures of his pastoral world, he didn't forget to think of Jack poring over his exam papers in some ugly exam room where dust hung in the air and a dropped pencil was an echoing event. Jack had messaged his exam timetable so Humphrey knew exactly what he was sitting and when.

Years of invigilation made it easy for him to imagine the scene - probably a vast sports hall with high windows through which the hot sun has already been blazing for some hours. There is a smell of leather and stale sweat. The mood is anxious and jittery as the victims file in. Jack's mind is taut and focused. Nervous tension crackles in the air until the invigilator says: 'You may begin' and a sacramental hush descends on the initiates, each in his private world in the silence and the humidity.

In the evenings when Jack had had an exam Humphrey would message him and ask how things had gone. The reply would be non-committal at best and once, quite alarming.

'It was a right balls-up. I'll be lucky to get in anywhere now,' he'd typed. Humphrey was used to Jack taking a pessimistic stance as insurance against disappointment but this was genuinely alarming. If Jack were to fail in his aspirations the ramifications could be grave. He could easily revert to the nihilism of not so many months ago, with the anger and anti-social behaviour that that entailed. Humphrey made soothing noises but was inwardly fretful.

It was not until much later that he found that what Jack meant by not finishing the paper was that there was not time to write down a final sentence that he had wanted to include. Humphrey's angst had probably been redundant.

At last, one Thursday in mid-June the ordeal was over and Jack invited himself round.

'Does it have to be a Saturday?' he asked on Messenger.

'Of course not. Whenever you like,' Humphrey said, and he allowed himself to say, 'I've missed you.'

'Yeah, yeah. I know,' Jack said.

'When do you want to come?'

'Now?'

'Okay.'

'Is that all right?'

Humphrey had been about to set out for The Seven Stars for a curry with the Evangelists but that would just have to go by the board. Besides, he had begun to find these meetings tedious and jejune and could not see himself turning up for them much longer.

'Of course it's all right. Where are you now? In town?'

'Yeah.'

'Okay. Meet me at the Market Cross at half twelve. We'll have a pub lunch.'

'Sounds cool. But can we make it two? I said I'd play squash with a mate.'

'Sure.'

A little later they were installed in the beer garden of The Swan with Two Necks. Jack ordered a 'Swanburger' which did not of course contain swan but was a multi-storey thing which only remained upright thanks to a wooden skewer.

Humphrey & Jack

'You'll never get that in your mouth,' Humphrey said.

'Watch me,' said Jack.

Humphrey had opted for a Caesar salad.

'That won't keep body and soul together,' Jack said. 'You'll waste away, Humphrey. You'll become a wraith.'

The likelihood of this happening was remote, to say the least. There had been a time when Humphrey would have been hurt by this reference to his girth but he now knew that taking offence at a jibe was against the rules of banter.

Besides, he was fat. What was the point of denying it?

A riposte was called for.

'See that goat?' he said.

The pub had a pet goat tethered to a post in the middle of the garden. It was reputed to eat anything the punters fed it.

'That's you, that is,' Humphrey said.

'Nice one, Humphrey,' Jack laughed. 'Do you want those fries?'

Humphrey had been served unbidden with a portion of those horrible spiky chips in a miniature chip basket.

'No, take them.'

Jack ate about half of them, despite having demolished the monstrous burger and his own portion, and went to feed the rest to the goat which devoured them in a trice.

'Humphrey, watch!' Jack called.

Jack held out an empty crisp packet which he had found on a nearby table and the goat ate it. And another. And another.

'Jack, don't, you'll make it ill.'

'Rubbish, they've got industrial strength digestive juices.'

'Like you.'

'Like me.'

Later they strolled along the River Rad where other liberated students were sprawled along the banks, sun-worshipping in various states of undress or playing ball games on Pentecost Common. Some of the girls had taken off their bras and made no attempt to hide their breasts. Humphrey averted his eyes.

He had half-expected Jack to be downbeat and even depressed. If his diagnosis of his own position were correct, his chances of getting into Durham were now minimal and Jack had put so much emotional investment into his ambition. To his surprise, Jack seemed remarkably buoyant. When Humphrey mentioned it, Jack said:

'Ah, the rewards of pessimism, Humphrey.'

Odd how his name never sounded quite so ridiculous when Jack said it.

'Your optimist,' Jack went on, 'is doomed to serial disappointment. Fate holds out her hand to him. He is full of hope. She closes it.

'Now your pessimist knows Fate is a fickle mistress and turns his back on her. When she scourges him, he says to himself: "I expected that" but when she taps him on the shoulder and offers unexpected gifts, it's a bonus. So, I go into an examination full of ambition, drive and purpose and I come out knowing I've fucked up. If the results are atrocious, it's only what I expected; if they're okay it's a pleasant surprise. The other way around and reality smacks you hard in the face.'

'Blimey,' said Humphrey, 'you've become a poet.'

'Nothing so shallow, Humphrey. I am going through my philosophical phase. There is nothing I can do about it now. So why worry. I intend to enjoy my summer. My ambition is to attain a state of *ataraxia*.'

'What's that?'

'Holy shit! A word not in the Humphreyean vocabulary? *Ataraxia* is a state of serene calm, a tranquil disengagement from the world.'

And he suddenly broke into a run, sprinting about a hundred yards along the path and looping back over the grass of the common until he fell back into step again with Humphrey, his breathing rapidly returning to normal.

Jack was hailed by several people as they walked along and just before the Rainbow Bridge a girl ran up to them. The bridge was so called because during Radcester Pride coloured ribbons had been tied to the railings of the otherwise nondescript bridge - red at one end and violet at the other, with green at the central arch, and so on, so that the display covered the spectrum. It was rather jolly, Humphrey thought. He marvelled at the number of ribbons and was surprised that they had not been removed or spoilt. There could have been no such spectacle 'back in the day' - an expression he had picked up from Jack. Its perpetrators wouldn't have got as far as orange without being hounded as degenerates.

There was no doubt about the girl's sexuality. She kissed Jack on the mouth, put both arms around his waist and gazed up into his eyes. She appeared to be trying to persuade him to take her to some 'gig' and Jack, smiling, seemed to be holding out.

Humphrey was embarrassed. Jack didn't introduce him - though he had no wish to be introduced, and therefore, according to the etiquette instilled in him by his mother, he could not address the girl. She didn't even acknowledge his existence apart from one hostile and suspicious glance. He stood there like a lemon for a few moments and then edged away out of earshot and pretended to be seriously interested in a small flotilla of ducks who were quarrelling noisily just by the near bank.

At last, the girl, who was wearing the tightest of very short shorts in shocking pink and a navy blue cheesecloth shirt tied just under her breasts, kissed Jack long and sumptuously and ran off, calling 'think about it!' She was very beautiful.

'Is that your girlfriend?' Humphrey asked as they resumed their stroll.

'God no,' said Jack.

By and by, they came to The Swallows' Return just by the weir and Jack said: 'Shall we have another drink?'

And Humphrey said: 'Is a frog's arse watertight?'

'Humphrey!' said Jack, feigning shock.

Humphrey & Jack

39. London

The weather that summer was glorious and Humphrey and Jack spent a good deal of time together. They took meals in the garden though once or twice they had to withdraw indoors because it was too hot or because wasps were troublesome. Jack said they would give up if you just ignored them but they didn't give up. Humphrey hated the way one would hover about six inches from the end of your nose and whichever way you turned your head, and no matter how quickly, there it would be, exactly the same distance from your face.

Once they went to London.

Jack had only ever been there a couple of times as a child with his mother and his memories were vague. Humphrey knew his way around quite well, partly because of academic conferences, but also because he had taken several vacations there. He would attend concerts and plays and find anonymity in the crowds.

Jack adored it. He was excited by the Tube which Humphrey found tiresome. Jack said he particularly liked the twang of electricity along the rails and the rush of cool air which announced the approach of a train and its thunderous arrival into the station.

They took the Docklands Light Railway to Greenwich and sat at the front of the driverless train. Jack wanted to know if Humphrey always sat at the front of the carriage.

'When it's free,' he said.

'And, in your head, do you pretend you're driving?'

'Doesn't everybody?'

'I'll just ask them,' Jack said, making to get up to interrogate the other passengers.

'You'll do no such thing,' Humphrey said, pulling him back down.

At Greenwich, Jack was overawed by the formal beauty of the Old Royal Naval College and said he might think about going through a neo-

Humphrey & Jack

classical phase. The Painted Hall struck him dumb. Humphrey was gratified by this; it had always been a favourite with him and there is a particular pleasure in introducing a friend to places in which you have taken especial delight.

From Greenwich, they took a river cruise to Westminster. As the boat left the pier and made a broad loop to face up river, they saw the Naval College as it was meant to be seen - from the Thames. Jack said it was the most beautiful building in the world.

As they looped they also had an excellent view of the O_2 Arena. Humphrey said that it had originally been built as the Millennium Dome and that he had been invited by an academic colleague from UCL to visit it on the first of January, 2000. They had had VIP tickets because Dorothy, as she was called, was a councillor in the Borough of Greenwich. He had only gone because, out of an exaggerated sense of courtesy, he hadn't the heart to refuse her and also because, as a historian, he was intensely curious. Even though, as mathematicians at the university insisted, the real first day of the new millennium would not be until 2001, Humphrey wished to see how the event would be celebrated.

'You were just a toddler at the time,' he said to Jack.

'How was it?' Jack said.

'It was atrocious, Jack. You can't imagine. Kitsch and cheap and nasty. It was like being inside a dirty washing-up bowl. There were zones, if I remember rightly, with names like Mind, Body and Faith, but the exhibits inside were shallow and patronising. It was supposed to be a monument to the achievements of man over a thousand years but it was as synthetic as a Kinder Egg. And the noise - the noise was brutish and abominable. The whole thing was a testament to a single-use throwaway culture.'

'You didn't like it then?' said Jack.

Humphrey missed the sarcasm.

'No. We got a taxi to The Prospect of Whitby. You'll see it in a minute, coming up on the north bank. Yes, look, there it is!'

'Is that how you navigate London? By pubs?'

Humphrey & Jack

'Perhaps I should write "The Annals of a Solitary Boozer",' said Humphrey lugubriously, remembering his exploration of the capital armed with *The Good Beer Guide* on those lonely holidays long, long ago.

Jack fell silent as he always did if the atmosphere showed signs of becoming charged with feeling. He spoke only to ask Humphrey to identify various landmarks which came into view: the Shard, even while they were a long way away, and Canary Wharf. Soon they were in the Pool of London approaching Tower Bridge. Humphrey explained that many tourists thought that this was London Bridge but Jack already knew that.

Once under the bridge, the landmarks came thick and fast. The Tower of London on the right and City Hall, otherwise known as 'The Testicle', on the left. Humphrey asked Jack what, as a medieval historian, he thought of the two buildings but Jack just shushed him. He was on his feet, like many of the other tourists on the boat, taking photographs with his phone.

Humphrey knew what he thought himself. The Tower was a royal palace, a treasury, a prison, a place of execution. The Tower was a statement of power going back to the Romans - and the 'Testicle' was a temporary eyesore which would probably have to be demolished while the Tower still stood and would still stand for another millennium or more.

Other modern monstrosities came into view: the Gherkin, the Walkie Talkie and the Cheese Grater. Jack said they were rather amusing while Humphrey merely grunted.

Just then there was a sudden shower of rain. It was brief but quite heavy. With much shrieking, teenage girls rushed for the covered part of the upper deck or the gangways to the steps leading to the body of the boat. Others followed apart from a number of Chinese tourists who pulled on plastic raincoats and carried on snapping or filming. Many were using selfie-sticks which Humphrey had initially mistaken for golf clubs until Jack had put him right.

Jack and Humphrey stayed put.

'It'll pass,' said Humphrey, scanning the sky.

Humphrey & Jack

Jack pulled up his hood.

'You should get a hoodie, Humphrey,' he said.

'As if...' said Humphrey, another idiom picked up from the boy.

As they passed, the golden ball on top of the Monument was hit by a sunbeam which had leaked from somewhere in the livid sky and seemed to burn in its own light. As they reached St. Paul's, a rainbow arced across the river.

A pleasure craft passed them going in the opposite direction. It had once been a paddle steamer and was very picturesque with its twin funnels and great wheel, although the wheel did not turn and no smoke issued from the chimneys. Humphrey supposed it ran on diesel.

Leaning on the rail of the walkway on the upper deck were some jolly young men wearing striped blazers and bow ties who greeted the tourist boat by waving champagne glasses about with raucous cries of 'ahoy there, me hearties' and the like.

Jack waved back and Humphrey grunted again.

Would Jack become a Hooray-Henry like this, Humphrey wondered. He would almost certainly gravitate towards London eventually as ambitious young men do. A shadow of the impending parting passed over him as they slid under the ugliness of London Bridge but he would fight it, Humphrey thought, as the sodden rain clouds began to clear to the east. Under Cannon Street Railway Bridge they passed and under Southwark Bridge. Already the white magnificence of St. Paul's shone in clear sunlight and the Millennium Bridge sparkled and now the great red-black finger of Tate Modern pointed at a sky of unmitigated blue.

Occasionally, Jack would mutter 'Wow!' or 'Fuck me!' and Humphrey was powerfully aware that the wonders of the imperial city were quite new to his friend. Humphrey felt rather jaded by comparison and envious of Jack's youth. However, this ran in the background only.

Sometimes even, Jack would point out things that Humphrey had not taken in before, such as the waterman's steps by Southwark Bridge or the massive piers which had once supported an earlier bridge and now rose strangely out of the water between Blackfriars Railway Bridge and the Road Bridge. Jack noted their durable paint in terra cotta red and their elaborate Corinthian capitals.

'They look really robust as if they're denying that the bridge has gone,' said Jack. 'As if it's still there but we can't see it any more. Weird.'

'This one is all too visible,' Humphrey said, as they came in sight of the Jubilee Walkway alongside the Hungerford Bridge. 'What do you think of that?'

'The suspension bridge?'

'Yes.'

'It's very elegant,' Jack said. 'The trouble with you, Humphrey, is that you think of architecture as one thing and engineering as another. That bridge serves both purposes, doesn't it? Functional and pleasing to the eye. There you go. Modernity.'

'All right, what do you think of that then?' Humphrey pointed out the Royal Festival Hall.

'What the hell is it?' Jack said.

'That was modern in its time. It was built as part of the Festival of Britain, a massive cheering-up exercise to celebrate British talent and expertise. It's a concert hall - the Royal Festival Hall.'

'Jesus,' said Jack, 'the Radcester Tesco is more inspiring.'

'Well, if you like the Jubilee walkway so much,' Humphrey said as they passed under it, 'there's one on the other side - turn around.'

And so there was, but now, ahead of them, there was a clear view at last of the Palace of Westminster, of the former City Hall, the London Eye and Westminster Bridge in all its busy beauty. Red London buses in the scene were supplied as standard.

Despite the familiarity of the vista from TV and from countless films, Jack was agog at Pugin's masterpiece. All about them tourists were on their feet, selfie sticks extended, freezing their cheesy smiles for posterity and for future admiration in Hong Kong, in Beijing, in Tokyo, in Queens-

Humphrey & Jack

land, Australia, in Little Rock, Arkansas and, for all Humphrey knew, Big Rock, Candy Mountain, all with the mother of parliaments as a backdrop.

The pleasure boat swung about ready to dock at Westminster Pier and impatient passengers began to crowd towards the exit. Humphrey and Jack stayed where they were the better to enjoy the moment. Just as the vessel bumped along the quay, the Westminster chimes began to ring out followed by Big Ben announcing twelve noon, each boom reverberating above the dirty roar of London traffic.

A couple of hundred cameras caught the hands of the clock face standing vertically and there was some ragged applause.

'How clever of you to time that just for me,' said Jack.

'I suspect the timetable is geared to please tourists in general,' said Humphrey, 'not just your lordship.'

'But it can't arrive at noon every day,' Jack said. 'What about tides and things?'

'No idea. Ready for lunch?'

'Isn't it a bit early? But yes.'

'I want to be sure we get a table.'

'Where are we going?'

'You'll see.'

They let the 'tourists' off first, then climbed the stone steps to the bridge, past the statue of Boudicca in her chariot. They turned right into Whitehall and at the first corner they came to a pub called St Stephen's Tavern with hanging baskets outside.

'Here we are,' said Humphrey.

'So you do navigate around London by pubs?' Jack said.

Humphrey laughed.

'I'll let you into a secret,' Humphrey said. 'I was a bit of a real ale fan when I was a postgrad. I used to look up interesting pubs in the Good Beer Guide and go and find them.'

'Did you have a beard and sandals?'

'No, I did not have a beard and sandals.'

Humphrey & Jack

Inside it was already very busy. The décor was that of many a Victorian London pub: lots of dark oak panelling; carved arches; globe lamps on fluted brass pillars or hanging from brass brackets; etched mirrors behind the bar, frosted windows in front of which the shadowy forms of Londoners went about their urgent business like so many giant ants. Around the walls of the bar were green banquettes.

'Like the House of Commons?' Jack said.

'Yes,' said Humphrey, 'whether by design or not, I don't know. But look!'

Humphrey pointed to the corner window. Neatly framed was the Elizabeth Tower, commonly known as Big Ben.

'Wowser!' said Jack.

They ordered Badger Beer and bangers and mash and managed to find a table.

'Do you see that little wooden box behind the bar?'

Jack followed where Humphrey's finger was pointing.

'Yeah. What is it?'

'A division bell. That one's electric but there are other pubs around here with an actual bell. When there's a division, or a vote, in the Commons, any Members in the pub will rush across the road to vote. When the House is sitting you'll sometimes see quite famous faces abandoning their ale and hurtling out. Churchill and Baldwin came here quite a lot.'

'Remember that do you?'

'Very funny. Apparently, sometimes tourists think it's a fire alarm and pile out too.'

'Now, that I would like to see,' said Jack.

After lunch, they walked up Whitehall to Trafalgar Square and into the National Gallery where Jack spent a long time gazing at the Woolton Diptych. Thence, at Jack's request, to the British Museum.

'I'm going through a Japanese phase just at the moment,' he declared and after a brief look at the Elgin marbles - 'Give 'em back' was Jack's peremptory judgement - they went up in the lift to the Japanese rooms.

Humphrey & Jack

Here, their tastes differed hugely: Jack was excited by the samurai weapons and uniforms, and by a display of manga comic books at which Humphrey snorted in derision; meanwhile Humphrey was very much taken by two tiny porcelain elephants with golden tusks and exotically painted blue motifs and by the netsuke, exquisitely carved button-like ornaments in ivory or wood, formerly worn to suspend articles from the sash of a kimono but nowadays prized as objects in their own right. There were minute rabbits and monkeys and birds and an octopus, a skeleton, wrestlers, a piper, a washerwoman, a snake charmer and a glossy penis from which Humphrey recoiled in alarm and blushed furiously as if afraid and even guilty that Jack might have seen his reaction.

Later they had dinner upstairs at The Swan where Humphrey had calves' liver and onions with polenta, at which Jack pulled a sour face, and Jack had chicken chasseur which he pronounced 'divine'.

Opposite, across the Thames, the floodlit dome of St. Paul's glowed against a rose-grey dusk.

'Don't you think it's just a little too majestic?' Jack said. 'I'd rather get married somewhere gothic and mysterious.'

'You have plans for a royal wedding, do you?' Humphrey asked.

'Not in the immediate future,' Jack said. 'The only available princesses are grotesque. I might have to wait for years.'

In the train home, Jack fell asleep with his head on Humphrey's shoulder, like a little boy after a tiring day in town.

The elderly lady opposite looked up from her crochet and beamed at them as the train sliced through England in the dark at 125 miles per hour.

40. Parting

Two days before Jack was due to leave for Durham, they got drunk together. The day had been hot and oppressive and the cool of the evening was welcome. They had strolled to the Delhi Durbar, where these days they were treated as regulars ('Ah, Dr Icke, sir, and Mr Jack, sir, welcome gentlemen, usual table?') and they were pleasantly full and mellow after two bottles of a quite tolerable Merlot. Two bottles in honour of the impending parting.

Back at Upper Bishop's Lane, Humphrey proposed they sit in the garden and drink some fine port he had been saving for the occasion. Jack thought it an excellent idea.

Humphrey brought out some citronella candles to repel insect life and lit them. There were also champagne truffle chocolates. The Dow's port was sweet with black fruit and an acidic tang. Humphrey suggested there was a nutty hint of marzipan and perhaps black pepper and Jack said he was a pretentious twat, but approved the port.

They sat in silence for a long while looking out over the pinpoints of light in the lower city. The garden breathed sweetness. Occasionally the headlights of a car would appear on Crookback Hill on the opposite side of the valley, search the sky for a moment, and then descend towards the city centre.

As they sat in the little pool of candlelight, Jack said: 'Are you gay, Humphrey?'

Humphrey was completely taken aback.

'Why, are you?'

'Christ, no, I'm as straight as they come.'

'That's what I thought,' said Humphrey, blushing in the dark.

'Well, are you?' Jack said. 'It doesn't matter, you know.'

'I don't think so,' Humphrey managed to say.

'You don't think so? Don't you know?'

'It's not a subject I'm very comfortable with, to be honest.'

'Have you ever been in love?' Jack persisted.

'No, definitely not. I'm sure about that,' said Humphrey.

'What do you think love is?' Jack asked. 'I mean, two years studying *The Literature of Love* for English and I'm none the wiser.'

'You're asking the wrong person. I think it might be a delusion. A posh word for sexual attraction. Why the catechism? Are *you* in love?'

Humphrey & Jack

'Sometimes I think I might be. But I'm not sure. If I'm not sure, I can't be, can I? You might be right. It might be a delusion.'

'I think friendship is more important,' Humphrey said.

There was a long pause.

'You've been very good to me,' Jack said. This was quite out of character. It must be the port, Humphrey thought.

'Yeah, well…' was all Humphrey could manage.

They sat in silence as a brilliant moon arose behind the house and began to cast strange shadows.

'What's that?' whispered Jack.

'What?'

'On the lawn. Under that tree.'

Sure enough there was an indistinct fuzzy patch.

'Mushrooms? Toadstools? Quite common at this time of year,' Humphrey said.

'Moving about?'

'There's a torch on the hall table,' said Humphrey.

Jack went to get it and then cautiously they crept down the steps to inspect the moving fungus.

It was a sizeable hedgehog, which froze in the torchlight but didn't curl up.

'Have you seen him before,' Jack whispered.

'No, never, but then I'm not usually out here in the middle of the night.'

'Well, there you are then. You have a new friend to keep you company when I'm gone.'

'I'll call him Jacek, if that's all right.'

'I think that's an excellent idea.'

Jacek began to move rather tentatively towards the hedge.

'He might be a girl, of course,' Jack said.

'Couldn't be,' said Humphrey without explantation.

'No, I suppose not,' Jack said.

Humphrey & Jack

'Looks a bit like you.'
'A handsome beast. Yes. I quite agree.'
'Are you drunk, Jack Lis?'
'I believe I might be, Dr Icke.'
'Well then, another glass will make no difference.'

And they returned to the table. Humphrey popped inside for his iPad and they listened for a while to Chopin nocturnes.

'Do you like this?' Humphrey asked after a while with the precise enunciation of someone who is very drunk.

'Very much,' said Jack.

'Bit melancholy,' said Humphrey.

'Bit,' said Jack.

'What about this then?' Humphrey said. He found Berlioz' *Les Nuits d'Été* and put it on at high volume. 'It's luxuriant, resplendent, opulent!'

And soon the mellow soprano of Kiri Te Kanawa and the gorgeous orchestration filled the garden and the night.

'Whoops,' said Jack.

'What?'

'Look,' he pointed to Mrs Bellingham's house where a light had snapped on in an upstairs window.

'The evil Queen of the Night has arisen,' said Humphrey and he ramped up the music to full volume. Even on an iPad the effect in the quiet of the night was prodigious.

Humphrey and Jack cackled like mad things.

It was Jack who came to his senses first and turned the volume right down.

'We don't want her coming round do we?'

Humphrey shook his head like a naughty child.

'No.'

'Or ringing the police?'

'Christ no.'

A thin line of light limned the eastern horizon.

Humphrey & Jack

'What time is it anyway?' Jack asked.

Humphrey looked at his watch.

'Good Lord, it's nearly half-past five. And there's no port left. Time for bed?'

'Definitely.'

'We are going to have a bitch of a hangover in the morning, or the afternoon, or whenever we emerge. Don't bother getting up until you want to.'

'I don't get hangovers,' said Jack.

'That's probably because you've never drunk as much as this before,' said Humphrey.

As he undressed, he could hear Jack banging about in the bedroom above his own and then there was silence, apart from the weird cries of screech owls down in the park. He climbed into bed and, rather than drifting gently into sleep, he pitched into a sudden coma.

Moments later, or so it seemed, the room was full of light. The curtains, though lined, could not keep out the full power of the noonday sun. A gap between them allowed a brilliant streak of light to slice across his face like a laser. It was this that had awoken him. He moved his face out of the way but it was no use.

He lurched into a sitting position on the edge of the bed. He would have to get up. This would be the last time he would see Jack for many weeks and he could not waste the time. Moreover, he could not be lying in bed when Jack got up. The very idea offended his sense of decorum and responsibility.

But, by God, he felt bad. He had endured many a hangover but none so life-threatening as this. His body was a dead-weight, his brain felt too big for his skull, his eye balls were on fire, his teeth felt loose, and some kind of acrid crud had been painted on his tongue overnight. A savage indigestion churned behind his sternum. He itched everywhere. The pattern on the carpet rippled insolently.

Humphrey & Jack

He staggered to the bathroom where his face in the bathroom mirror terrified him. He had turned into a ghoul. What hair he had at the sides of his head stood upright and his grey skin looked as if it were sliding off his face. Bloodshot eyes stared out of the mask.

This would never do. He could not let Jack see him like this.

He shaved with extreme caution and managed not to nick himself though there was a slight tremor in his hands. He cleaned his teeth with manic vigour, first with a manual brush and then with his electric toothbrush, until his gums tingled. Then he took the manual brush again and scrubbed at his hard palate and his tongue. This made him gag but he persevered. He swilled mouthwash around several times until the nearly full bottle was half-empty.

Cupping his right hand by his chin he breathed out and tried to determine whether he could smell spearmint or a sepulchre and, smelling nothing, decided that that was probably a good thing.

Now he took three paracetamol and turned the bath taps on. Almost immediately, he turned them off again. Given how fragile he felt, he could not be certain that he would ever be able to get out of the bath again without assistance. He took a shower instead - as hot as he could bear it. This made him feel marginally better.

However, as he was towelling himself dry, he saw that the itching sensation he had felt had been nothing to do with his hangover. He had been eaten alive by midges or possibly even mosquitoes. The fountain at the bottom of the garden had been out of order for some days now and the stagnating pond around it would have been a perfect breeding habitat in the recent sultry weather.

The hot water had brought out angry red lumps which itched like hell. They were concentrated on his wrists and ankles, though there was a maddening one on a knuckle, one on his left temple, and one of the bastards had got his left earlobe.

Humphrey & Jack

Back in his bedroom, he unearthed from the bottom of the wardrobe the biscuit tin in which he kept his meds and found a tube of antihistamine cream which he slapped liberally on the lumps.

The relief would probably be temporary, he thought. To take his mind off the returning itch and his pulsing hangover, he must keep busy. He dressed and made the bed. Then he went out into the garden, where the sunshine hurt him terribly, and retrieved the empty port bottle and the glasses which he took into the kitchen to wash. There he made coffee as thick as treacle and drank two mugs of it hot. There was no discernible improvement in his fettle; on the contrary, he felt decidedly jittery.

Systematically, he began to assemble the ingredients for a full English breakfast so that he could rustle it up in no time when Jack should emerge. He moved deliberately and quietly. Jack had a habit of getting up as soon as he heard Humphrey stirring and, today, Humphrey wanted him to lie in as long as possible, especially if Jack felt anything like he did.

He dropped an egg on the floor and felt like weeping with anguish and despair. His knees grated as he got down to deal with the viscous mess. He wanted to throw up at the sight of the little red dot in the yolk and bits of shell stuck to his fingertips and everywhere until he finally got the tiles clean.

As he was down there, Jack came in, rubbing his eyes.

'What are you doing, Humphrey?' he said.

'Preparing your breakfast,' Humphrey said.

'What, on the floor?'

'Yes.'

He pulled himself upright by leaning on the table and the edge of the counter.

'God, I feel shit,' Jack said.

'Told you.'

'And you're all right are you?'

'Now more than ever seems it rich to die,' said Humphrey.

'What?' said Jack.

Humphrey & Jack

'Keats.'

'Ah yeah. Morbid git.'

Jack was sitting at the kitchen table with his knees up and his feet on the edge of the chair. He was scratching at the red lumps all over his calves. He had been wearing shorts the previous evening.

'You been bitten too?'

'Poxy mozzies,' Jack muttered.

'Don't scratch them…'

'…you'll only make it worse,' Jack finished in a nannyish sing-song. 'What are you supposed to do? Grin and bear it? Stiff upper lip? It's like when you're having a coughing fit or a sneezing fit and people say "Are you all right?" and you want to say: "Of course, I'm not all right. I'm coughing my guts up or sneezing my brains out," but you can't say anything because you're having a coughing fit or a sneezing fit and can hardly breathe, let alone talk.'

'I can offer you paracetamol and antihistamine cream - silently, if you like,' Humphrey said.

'Yes, please,' Jack said.

'Would you like some breakfast?'

'Yes, please,' said Jack, somewhat mollified. 'Is it all right if I have a quick shower while you're making it?'

'Of course it is. Come on. I'll get you the cream and paracetamol.'

He handed Jack the stuff at the bottom of the stairs.

'Have you got hash browns?' Jack said on his way up.

'None left. I can do you fried bread?'

'Awesome.'

Humphrey returned to the kitchen and made a start on the meal. He still felt very strange. It was as if some alien being had taken possession of his body and it didn't quite fit. He would have liked to have curled up in a pile of leaves under a bush somewhere and died quietly and obscurely as animals do.

Humphrey & Jack

On the other hand, very soon now, Jack would walk out of his life and he wouldn't see him for some months to come. So it had better be an 'awesome' breakfast. He laid the table for one and set to.

By the time Jack appeared, looking spruce and smelling fresh, there were only the eggs to fry.

'Feeling better?' Humphrey asked.

'A bit, yeah,' Jack said. 'Aren't you having any?'

'The very thought makes me feel bilious.'

He watched in wonder as Jack devoured bacon, sausage, black pudding, tomatoes, two eggs, fried bread, orange juice, and then asked for more tea and some toast and the lime marmalade he liked which Humphrey got in especially for him and which would now probably go to waste.

As he was eating Humphrey said: 'Are you sure you don't want me to drive you up to Durham tomorrow? It's not as if I have anything else to do.'

'Oh not again, Humphrey. Leave it, will you? I'd much rather go by train. I'm no good at goodbyes. Anyway, I've got my ticket.'

'I just thought I could help with the luggage and things.'

'I won't have any luggage, will I? Just one suitcase.'

'Ah, true,' said Humphrey wistfully.

He had suggested himself that Jack send bulky luggage on ahead and arranged and paid for the carriage.

'Would you like to stay over tonight and I can drive you to the station at least?'

'Humphrey, the station is ten minutes away. And anyway, I have to shut the house up. The kitchen needs cleaning and all sorts of other stuff. I need to do that myself. In fact, I need to be going pretty soon.'

'Ah, yes, of course.'

Radcester College had arranged for social security to pay his rent up to his departure for university. Henceforth, his address would be Durham

Castle. What would happen in the holidays had yet to be sorted but he had promised Humphrey that he would spend the Christmas vacation with him.

'Anyway, I said I'd say goodbye to Mark this evening.'

'Right,' said Humphrey, and thought for a moment that he might tell Jack that his friend was a common thief, and then thought better of it.

Jack swallowed the last of his tea and stood up, brushing crumbs off his trousers.

'Thank you, that was sick,' Jack said. 'I feel better already. Right. I'd better be off.'

He collected his sports bag and Humphrey accompanied him to the gate.

'So,' said Jack. 'This is it.'

'This is it,' Humphrey echoed.

They shook hands.

'Hey, cheer up,' Jack said. 'It will be Christmas in no time.'

'That's not true and you know it.'

'You can come up and see me sometime then.'

'I can. And I will. I'm sorry, Jack. I'm being silly and sentimental.' He took Jack's hand and shook it again. 'Have a great term. Blow their socks off. Now off you go.'

'You look after yourself, Humphrey. Thanks for everything.'

Humphrey watched him until he disappeared at the bend in the lane and then went inside to mix the mother of all Martinis, though it was only three in the afternoon.

41. Art

Humphrey was mature enough not to go into a decline. He was not going to droop about like a teenage girl seized with the greensickness. And yet the days seemed long and the house empty.

Humphrey & Jack

Aristotle seemed to feel it too. He still visited often and would range the rooms looking for Jack, or he would sit on the kitchen floor gazing at Humphrey as if in accusation. Jacek the hedgehog failed to appear.

Humphrey's life had been empty before but in a different way. There had been a kind of numbness, of accidie - a mental and spiritual sloth. Now he knew what was missing and it gave him a sharp pang when he thought of it. Jack had made his existence meaningful and his friendship had been rejuvenating. He thought he must not let that go to waste. He must take control. He must busy himself.

Normally the idea of private tuition would have had him mentally retching with distaste, but when Radcester College phoned him to say that they had a very bright Oxbridge aspirant in their Lower Sixth and would Humphrey consider coaching him in medieval history, much to his surprise, he found himself agreeing. The subject was engaging; it would not be a case of trying to squeeze a duffer through A level, and it would occupy his mind. He didn't need the money but it would be profitable in other ways.

Not that he expected to encounter another Jack - which was just as well. Mr Fairway from the college said that Oliver was bright and so he was, very much so: he mastered the material quickly, had a keen eye for detail, and was possessed of a very logical mind. He didn't have Jack's oblique originality of perception, however, and he certainly didn't look anything like him. Oliver Gothland was unnecessarily tall for one thing; he had a tiny mouth and his brown eyes looked huge behind massive spectacles in circular black frames. His drab brown hair was plastered flat on the top of his round head with some kind of 'product'.

Humphrey began to enjoy his weekly visits to the college and, despite early misgivings, soon became on speaking terms with a number of members of the staff who seemed more cordial than many of his colleagues when he was at the university. Oliver was courteous and pleasant and the lessons became quite enjoyable, even stimulating.

Humphrey & Jack

It was on one of his weekly visits to the college that he saw a poster in a corridor advertising extra-curricular art classes - 'All Welcome!' Actually, the poster said 'co-curricula classes' but Humphrey mentally corrected it. They were held on the same afternoon as Oliver's lessons but a little later. He could perhaps have a cup of tea in the staffroom and take a look.

The reason for Humphrey's strange interest had to do with his secret project. For months now he had been researching this venture. He had already published on the rituals of feasting in the England of Richard II. Now he wanted to produce a plush companion volume of medieval recipes. He wanted it to be a working text, not just a dry historical account. By that he meant that he wanted people to be able to cook from it. He would suggest modern equivalents to medieval ingredients or even find stockists. He would arbitrate on whether a food processor might furnish a legitimate shortcut or whether only a good mortar and pestle would do. And he would like to illustrate it himself.

He had said nothing to Jack about this. He wanted to have it well advanced and meant to try out all the recipes himself and feed them to Jack for quality control. He imagined the illustrations in ink and water colour and wanted to have some ready before he approached his publisher about the viability of the proposal.

Humphrey was sipping ghastly tea that he thought might be made from floor sweepings when Fairway came into the staffroom. Humphrey wanted to know if the art classes were for pupils only.

'Heavens no. "All welcome" is what it says on the tin and that's what it means. In any case, we have quite a few mature students in the college. I think there are a few in Althea's class. Would you like me to introduce you to her?'

'That would be excellent, yes,' Humphrey said. He had a near-pathological fear of meeting new people so the offer of an intro was appreciated.

'There's no hurry though. Do finish your tea.'

'I think I'll give it a miss, thanks. Do you have to drink this stuff every day?'

Humphrey & Jack

'Bilgewater, isn't it?' said Fairway. 'Come on then.'

Althea Hemmings proved to be very amenable, especially when Humphrey confessed to being rather shy.

'Oh, don't worry about that, darling. We're a mixed bunch here with talents ranging from Rubens to rubbish.'

'I should think I'll be at the rubbish end of the spectrum,' said Humphrey.

'That won't matter one bit. It'll be a starting point and you'll never get worse. That's the way to look at it, innit, darling? And you needn't worry, 'cos everybody just gets along with their own thing and I just go round giving advice. Sometimes the punters don't say a word to anybody until the end and then we all go down the Quarryman's Arms. How does that sound, darling?'

Humphrey thought it sounded ideal, though he didn't really appreciate being addressed as 'darling' on first meeting - or ever, for that matter. On the other hand, Althea's enthusiasm was charming so Humphrey would give it a go, starting the following week.

'There's a life class on Friday evenings as well, darling. That interest you at all?'

'Well, let's not run before we can walk, shall we?' said Humphrey without hesitation. 'I was never any good at people. Still life's more my thing.'

In the event, Humphrey proved to have a modest talent - more than modest, according to Althea. On his first lesson she gave him a great deal of friendly attention and she had been quite right: the others were absorbed in their own projects and not inclined to communicate much. The atmosphere was peacefully industrious and Humphrey loved the quiet. He had chosen a still life as his first project and they spent a while assembling it on a small table by the easel that had been set up for him.

Like art teachers everywhere, Althea had a collection of objects and *trouvailles* for this very purpose. Humphrey rejected the various animal skulls and bits of wrought iron that were lying about and was very uncomfortable about a stuffed woodcock. Instead they found a square bottle of thick uneven glass, which Humphrey rather liked. There was a large basket of fruit and vegetables on Althea's desk and she asked him to make a selection. He chose some apples, a banana and an orange.

'A bit ordinary, don't you think, darling?'

'Well, perhaps we could cut the orange in half?' said Humphrey.

'You could,' said Althea. 'You could do that. You could definitely do that if you wanted to set yourself the advanced problem of trying to catch the light on each tiny glistening cell of cut fruit. A bit advanced that. Look, let's try this.'

She lightly ruffled up a sheet of cartridge paper and placed it over the table, placing a couple of bricks under the paper in one corner to add an extra level. She put the rustic bottle on the table, and arranged around it some old potatoes that had begun to sprout, a fat leek, a head of purple garlic, and then she took a packet of green lentils from her shopping basket, cut it down one side and placed it on the raised level, letting the lentils spill into the design.

'Lesson number one: there is a difference between making images of beautiful things and making beautiful images of things. You will have brought in with you clichéd preconceptions of what apples and oranges look like but I want you to really look at those potatoes. I suggest you start with a pencil sketch and then we can experiment with other media until you find your "voice".'

'I don't really know where to start,' Humphrey said.

'Anywhere. Here, let's set the ball rolling.'

Deftly, she drafted the outline of one of the potatoes and part of the top of the leek, where she outlined three of the leaves, including one of them that had been bent back and broken and the ragged edge of another that had been torn. She caught the thick ribbed texture of the upper leaves with a hint of shading and already this little fragment was acquiring the illusion of three dimensions.

Humphrey & Jack

'Don't rush it but work briskly. Work on your outlines first. Look and draw. Don't think.'

Althea went off to give advice and support to the others, returning from time to time during the two hour session to encourage Humphrey. She showed him how to soften a line by gentle smudging with the edge of the thumb and how to create roundness with cross-hatching. Towards the end of the lesson, she helped him begin to create the transparency of the bottle by removing shading with an eraser to create highlights.

At intervals, the others would take a break to collect a coffee from the machine in the corridor outside and they would have a wander round the studio appraising each other's work. This was always positive and gentle. Humphrey felt this gave him licence to do the same, especially as he had been given some very warm comments along the lines of: 'Hey, man, that's really taking shape,' or, 'Wow! have you had lessons before? That's mega.'

Humphrey would make self-deprecating noises about beginner's luck but he had to admit, it really wasn't bad.

They were a very mixed bunch. Most were in their late teens. Their projects were pretty eclectic too. Elspeth, a very pale, thin girl was creating an enormous doll's house based on the board game Cluedo. There was a study, a library, a dining room, a ballroom, a beautiful conservatory, and so on. The difference was that there had been a murder in every room. Mrs Peacock could be seen hanging from the ballroom chandelier. Colonel Mustard was slumped over a desk in the study with an axe in his back. And Miss Scarlet had been beheaded in the lounge and lay in a welter of blood. Humphrey said it was 'disturbing' which appeared to make her very happy.

Stuart, who wore a paisley silk scarf over a ripped white tee shirt and tight red trousers, had been making casts of his own hands. These had been affixed to a plank which had been painted black, and each hand had been painted evenly in acrylic in the colours of the rainbow, so that there was a red hand, an orange hand, a yellow one, a green one and so on to violet.

Humphrey & Jack

Stuart told Humphrey that his installation was called 'Handjob'. He wanted to make a statement, he said.

Humphrey said that he had certainly done that.

There had been a time, not very long ago, before Jack perhaps, when Humphrey would have sneered at the very word 'installation' but here he felt humbled and disinclined to criticise.

The other youngsters' work was less traumatic than the murder house and Stuart's striking fantasy but there was still an element of the gothic about much of it and Humphrey wondered when youth had learned to be so sad.

There were three other mature students. Two of them, Hamish and Lucy, were into landscapes done from photographs and both of them were quite accomplished, one in oils and the other in water colours. Loretta, however, was something else.

She had insisted on working on a vast canvas. Althea had pointed out that her budget wouldn't run to it but Loretta said that was immaterial she was happy to pay for it herself. Humphrey later learnt that when it had been stretched and framed and delivered, there had been a bit of a row. Althea said that if it were erected where Loretta wanted it, it would block off half the light in the studio, and eventually she had prevailed despite sulking from her pupil.

Today, Loretta was working at it halfway up a tall stepladder. It was certainly monumental. Humphrey had no idea what it was supposed to represent, if anything. Perhaps it was just an abstract. He didn't like to ask in case he caused offence but Loretta was so absorbed that the question didn't arise.

It was in oils, applied with a palette knife and thick brushes. There were tormented expanses of dark chocolate brown with purple patches and flecks of yellow.

When Althea next came round to his easel, Humphrey asked about it.

'It's god-awful, isn't it?' she said. 'It's supposed to be the cathedral.'

'Well, that's god-awful in the first place,' Humphrey said.

Humphrey & Jack

Althea laughed.

'You and I are going to get on famously,' she said. 'We humour her, you see. She has absolutely no talent whatsoever but did you notice the look of ecstasy on her face? I don't think I have the right to deny her that. It would be like telling a nun that she's missing out on sex.'

Humphrey felt himself blushing but said: 'Would you talk about my work behind my back?'

'Good God, no!' Althea said. 'Loretta is quite different. Besides, your piece is very promising. That potato is a little flat, though. Do you want to take it home and finish it or do you want to come back to it next week? You are coming back next week, aren't you?'

'Yes, definitely. I'll leave it here, I think.'

'Excellent. Time's nearly up, darling. You'll join us at The Quarryman's, won't you?'

'Well, actually, I don't think…'

'Rubbish, I'll buy you a drink.'

Humphrey felt it would be unchivalrous to refuse and began to pack up his things. Althea labelled the arrangement:

Ingredients for Lentil Soup
Humphrey Icke
DO NOT TOUCH!

Humphrey continued to attend the classes. The next week he attempted the same still life in poster paint, even though the vegetables had become a little faded. Subsequently, he worked on fabrics and drapery, sketching first, then trying acrylics and then oils, which he didn't like at all. He felt he was clumsy and deplored the mess.

Then he tried pastels and there was an epiphany. This was his medium. He felt the softness of the pastel sticks enabled him to render more exactly the texture of the materials. He was particularly pleased with a joint piece of work. Althea sketched a figure of a Roman Emperor for him and

Humphrey & Jack

Humphrey did the robes in pastel. It was striking. The pencil figure was left as it was, classically austere, but the deep burgundy robe with a border of golden oak leaves was richly worked and the way the soft light was blended into the folds gave it substance.

The others admired it hugely and Althea said she would buy it. Humphrey tried to demur but Althea wouldn't have it. She thrust three tenners at him and said he could buy a round at the Quarryman's later.

When he arrived the following week, Althea had framed it tastefully and it was on display in the studio for a month or so before she took it home. After his success, Humphrey went to Campion and Herrick's stationery shop in town and bought the most expensive box of oil pastels they had in stock and quantities of paper in different colours and calibres.

One day, in between Oliver's lesson and his art class, Humphrey went to the coffee machine in the corridor to get something more palatable than staffroom tea. Someone was already there. As the machine was doing its impression of someone choking, he realised that the someone was Mark, or Marek, Jack's friend and the prime suspect in the purloining of Humphrey's clock. Humphrey was about to do an about turn but was too late. He had been seen.

'All right, mate?' Mark said.

Humphrey winced internally but only replied:

'Yes, and you?'

'I'm good. What are you doing here?'

'I do a little teaching and I also go to an art class.'

'With Miss Hemmings? She's fit she is.'

Humphrey's distaste for this boy increased. He thought he might mention the clock and then he thought he wouldn't. He didn't want a scene. Mark lingered. Humphrey chose hot chocolate.

'What about you? Are you a student here?'

'Yeah. Catering. Mum says I should get a trade.'

Larceny not paying enough, Humphrey thought.

'Well, she's right, you know.'

He picked up his cup and made to leave.

'Heard from Jack?' Mark said.

'Yes, from time to time. You?'

'Not much. Seems to be enjoying himself.'

'Yes. Yes, he is.'

'Right then. See you!' Mark said.

I do hope not, thought Humphrey.

Much later, after his art class, and after three pints at the Quarryman's, Humphrey was in his study reading with a tumbler of whisky to hand when there was a ping on his computer and moments later on his phone.

It was a friend request from Mark.

Humphrey accepted it.

42. Aristotle

Humphrey need not have been apprehensive about joining the others at The Quarryman's Arms. For one thing, it was a very agreeable venue. Humphrey was surprised he had never even encountered it before. It was down a side street near the river. On their first visit, it was quite busy and a little noisy. Humphrey's heart sank.

However, Althea showed them through to a back room which, on the days of her art classes, was apparently reserved for her group. There was a sign above the door which said 'The Library'. The walls were lined with books. There was a notice which said that customers could borrow a book for as long as they liked so long as they put a replacement book on the shelves in the meantime. This was an arrangement that appealed to Humphrey's sense of decency and fair play. It was true that many of the books were cheap thrillers and bodice rippers but Humphrey noticed the complete works of Walter Scott, that stalwart of secondhand bookshops, and there was also a row of Kingsley Amis novels, an author whom Humphrey admired for his bad temper and his portrayal of grumpy old men. A beautiful eight volume Folio Society edition of *The Decline and Fall of the Roman Empire* in a white and gold binding looked unread - which it probably was.

In the middle of the room was a large oval table, ancient and battered and kept stable by little piles of grubby beer mats under the legs. There was a banquette along one side and various ill-assorted chairs around the other. Althea took their orders and returned with a tray full of drinks along with a pint of Humphrey's favoured Doom Bar ale.

They talked mostly about aspirations. Stuart had a grant to study fine art in Paris, Elspeth wanted to be a stage set designer, Hamish and Lucy said they were going up to the Lakes together to paint landscapes (and there was some ribbing here about them becoming an 'item').

Loretta told them that through her husband's business contacts in Italy, she had been commissioned to paint the interior of the apse of a church in Tuscany.

'And it will depict the Wrath of God,' Althea whispered to Humphrey, who was sitting next to her at the other end of the table, and he nearly choked on his beer.

Humphrey, further relaxed by the alcohol, told them about his Plantagenet cookbook project. They were very enthusiastic and, in an extraordinary moment of largesse, Humphrey said he would invite them all for dinner if it ever got off the ground. Althea told hilarious and entirely unprofessional tales about her colleagues.

'Can't I persuade you to come to life class on Fridays?' Althea said to Humphrey. 'There's live folk music in here afterwards.'

'Not my cup of tea,' said Humphrey whose expression would have curdled milk and whose loathing of folk music equalled his fear of naked bodies. 'I'm very happy with things just as they are.'

Things just as they were included an unexpected relish for this weekly conviviality. He was surprised at being accepted so readily just as he was and he was surprised to be treated as an equal member of the crew even though he was new to them. And he was surprised and delighted by how positive they all were and how much that pleased him.

By comparison, the meetings of the Evangelists came to seem arid. The reactionary carping no longer seemed amusing but diseased and he began to dislike Garth more and more.

It was not that he had experienced a Pauline conversion or something. Pointless noise continued to depress him; the prodigious number of cretins on the planet, especially on the roads, still made him irritable; the shallowness of the media, the death of good manners, the bleating of interest groups - all this made him itch with frustration, but rather than bang his head against the wall, he chose, as Voltaire recommends in *Candide*, to *cultiver son jardin*.

And so he ceased to attend the twice-weekly meetings at The Seven Stars on anything like a regular basis. All the same, one Tuesday in late October, he thought he would look in for old time's sake. He was due to visit Jack the coming weekend and was consequently in high spirits and, so he thought, immune to any toxicity in the atmosphere.

'By the pricking of my thumbs, something wicked this way comes,' said Hector as he came through the door.

'Returning to the scene of the crime, eh?' said Norman.

'Like a dog to its vomit,' said Garth.

'What's it to be, gentlemen?' said Humphrey.

'Lo, he comes with clouds descending,' Hector sang in a high tenor.

'Shut the fuck up with that fucking racket!' Secondhand Sue squawked from the hinterland.

'Ignore her, she's having trouble with her haemorrhoids,' said Cora from the bar.

'And you can shut it an' all,' Sue said. 'Or I'll bar meself.'

'That'll be the day!' said Cora. 'Nice to see you, stranger,' she said to Humphrey.

Garth and Norman asked for Speckled Hen. Humphrey ordered just a half of Doom Bar for himself. He carried the beers over to their table.

Humphrey & Jack

'What's that?' said Garth, pointing at the half as if it were a turd.

'I've got the car with me and besides, I may not stay long,' Humphrey said. Garth rolled his eyes.

'Now, you gladsome thing, let me fill you in on today's topic for disapprobation,' said Hector. 'We have been fulminating against the evils of social media. We were going to talk about Brexit but Garth began foaming at the mouth and had to be sedated and so Norman and I decided it was too dangerous and changed the tune.

'So. Humphrey. Do you receive daily requests to post naked selfies of yourself on Snapchat? Or do you regard social media merely as a faster version of Her Majesty's Royal Mail?'

'For a start, I have no idea what Snapchat is,' said Humphrey, 'although I will confess that I receive frequent email requests from someone called Olga offering to send me photographs of mature Russian women.'

'Ah, I can see you now, Humphrey,' said Hector, 'serenading a roly-poly babushka with your balalaika.'

'Oh, very likely,' said Humphrey. 'Just a minute, haven't we done this topic before?'

'Not as such,' said Norman, and Humphrey stared at him because he had always found the expression uniquely vacuous and couldn't understand how an educated man could bring himself to use it.

'Perhaps,' said Garth, 'Humphrey doesn't want to discuss the expansion of his activities on Facebook?'

'What do you mean?' said Humphrey.

'You seem to be gathering quite a little academy of young men sitting at your virtual feet.'

'What do you mean?' said Norman.

'Humphrey has been engaging in late night conversations on Facebook about Nietzsche and Wittgenstein and the meaning of life, the universe and everything.'

'Oh that, they're just Facebook friends of Jack's at Durham and other universities,' said Humphrey, failing to catch the malice in Garth's tone.

Humphrey & Jack

'And Humphrey, our Humphrey, presides over these discussions as if he were Socrates or Gandhi…'

'Steady on, Garth,' said Hector, who had caught his tone precisely.

'Or Jesus, with his disciples…'

'Oh, I wouldn't go that far,' said Humphrey. 'Most of them are far brighter than I am. Better-read, anyway. I find it quite stimulating.'

'Or Oscar Wilde…'

'Leave it, Garth. Ignore him, Humphrey. He's had a head start with the beer.'

'Yes, or Oscar Wilde. Remember that flowery speech from the dock at his trial. About how intellectual the love of an older man for a younger is. The love that dare not speak its name. And all the time he had been buggering rent boys. How is Jack, by the way, Humphrey? How is your catamite?'

'My what?' said Humphrey.

'Your botty boy. Your bum chum.'

Humphrey rose to his feet, spilling all the beer, his chair falling down behind him.

Garth stood up to face him.

'Just repeat that, if you dare!' Humphrey said.

Several things occurred to Humphrey all at once. One: what he had just said was ineffably stupid. Two: Garth was a Goliath of a man. Three: Humphrey wasn't. Four: Humphrey was no use at fighting. Five: Garth probably was. Six: there was now no way he could really get out of this.

Despite all these things, he threw a punch at Garth's head, which missed.

Garth hit out at Humphrey and did not miss. In fact he cracked him right in the eye. Humphrey's shattered specs fell to the ground. Humphrey joined them, smashing a chair.

'Seconds out. Round two,' said Flake, showing more animation than he had done in years. He had grabbed a bar towel and was waving it in Humphrey's face.

Humphrey & Jack

'Fight! Fight!' said Secondhand Sue, hopping from foot to foot and shaking invisible maracas.

'Never mind "fight".' Cora was on the spot instantly.

'Right, you four, out! And don't come back until you've grown up. You'll be paying for these glasses too. And that chair. I've never seen the like.'

'Ought to know better at their age,' said Sue.

'And you can stop stirring, madam. Come on. Move it!' said Cora.

Hector helped Humphrey to his feet and picked up what he could of the ruined spectacles. Cora herded the four Evangelists to the exit and slammed the street door behind them.

'Now look what you've done!' said Garth.

'Just shut up, Garth. Just shut up for once in your life,' said Hector. 'Humphrey, go home. Don't argue, go home.' He pushed him in the direction of Upper Bishop's Lane.

'I've got the car,' said Humphrey. The car park was on the other side of the pub.

'Oh dear,' said Hector. 'You can't drive without these, can you?' He handed Humphrey the mangled remains of his spectacles.

'It's all right. I've got prescription sunglasses in the glove compartment.'

'OK, drive carefully then. And put something on that eye. It looks a mess.'

Humphrey thought, as he found the sunglasses and put the car into gear, that he probably shouldn't be driving at all. He was still shaking with rage and humiliation.

At the traffic lights at the top of Burdock Hill, he was going to go through on amber but changed his mind at the last minute, causing the car behind to screech to a halt. The driver hit his horn repeatedly until the lights turned green and Humphrey could see him in his rear view mirror gesticulating furiously.

Humphrey & Jack

As he pulled into his drive he swung into his usual parking space and saw Aristotle lying there, basking in the late autumn sunshine. He braked sharply and Aristotle tried to leap out of the way but they were both too late. There was a slight thud and that was that.

Hoping desperately that he had only stunned the animal, Humphrey got out of the car. It was no good. The cat lay there, its eyes wide open, as if in shock.

Humphrey went indoors and into the kitchen. He took a bottle of gin from the fridge and poured a tumblerful of neat spirit which he drained in one. Then he found the first aid tin in the downstairs bathroom and began to bathe his eye. Upstairs, in his study, he found an old pair of reading glasses which would have to do until he could have new prescription glasses made. Then he returned to the kitchen and drank another tumblerful of gin to steel himself for what needed to be done. He felt very strange.

Humphrey knew that if you ran over a cat you did not need to report it. He toyed with the idea of disposing of the body and saying nothing but knew that it would not do. He would have to do the honest and honourable thing.

He pulled on a pair of marigolds and found a shallow box in the pantry containing tins of chopped tomatoes. He unpacked them and left them on the floor. Then he lined the bottom of the box with a swing bin liner and took it outside.

As he lifted Aristotle into the box the intestines popped out. Humphrey pushed them back in as best he could. He closed the cat's eyes and went back inside for a tea towel. He found one with pictures of Radcester Cathedral on it (where had he acquired that?) and laid it over the corpse.

Still wearing his marigolds Humphrey carried the makeshift coffin to Mrs Bellingham's front door and rang the bell.

When she appeared he held out the box.

'I'm afraid there's been an accident,' he said.

Mrs Bellingham lifted the tea towel and then looked Humphrey in the eye.

'You unspeakable shit,' she said.

Humphrey & Jack

Humphrey & Jack

MARK

43. Humphrey has a Visitor

When Humphrey told Mark that Jack had been in touch from time to time, he was being a little disingenuous. Jack was proving to be a poor correspondent. There had been a time, whilst Jack was working on what he called 'Project Casimir' when they would chat on Messenger three or four times a day. Now there might be a brief exchange once or twice a week. Or it might be days before Jack replied to a message.

Humphrey had been brought up to believe that one should reply to correspondence as soon as possible. However, he had to recognise that things had changed. Jack would say he was 'insanely busy' and Humphrey would look back to his own university days. He had worked exceptionally hard and yet there had been blank acres of time when he had been bored and lonely. The difference was, of course, that Jack had friends.

The divergence in their attitudes to electronic communication had led to the point where there was nothing from Jack for a fortnight. Humphrey had bombarded Jack with enquiries from: 'Are you all right?' and 'Have I offended you?' to: 'Just what is going on, Jack?'

Eventually, Jack replied with: 'The more you pester me, the less likely it is that I will reply.'

Humphrey was angry at first, then hurt, then amused.

Humphrey & Jack

He must be suffering from 'empty nest syndrome'. This must be what parents felt when their children left to live their own lives. The wrench was well-documented and Humphrey knew that the advice of a thousand agony aunts (read in tattered magazines in doctors' and dentists' waiting rooms) was true: 'you must learn to let go.'

To the extent to which he had been a sort of surrogate father to Jack the scenario certainly applied. And yet, he had been close to Jack for little over a year, not the whole of his young lifetime. What right had he to arrogate to himself the sadness of a parent? In fact, he supposed that he would have been a dreadful dad. Just think: the nappies, the tantrums, the noise…

And after all, wasn't he being melodramatic?

All the same, he found he was checking Facebook more frequently than was healthy or dignified. Jack posted less on his timeline than he used to do though his old habit of starting an argument and then arguing with all comers on all sides with great and equal conviction was sometimes still in evidence. Just once in a while Humphrey would join in and, just once in a while, one of Jack's friends would send him a friend request which he always accepted. Occasionally there were fragments of social chitchat about a lecture, a movie or a gig.

One day Humphrey noticed a thread between Jack and Mark about plans to go to a concert in the summer and whether they could afford to buy tickets. By concert they meant, of course, one of those occasions where a stand is erected in a field somewhere and a throng of, perhaps otherwise sensible, young people stand or lie in the mud, listening to diabolically loud 'music' and talk in pseudo-American English whilst smoking weed.

At the end of the thread, Mark had written: 'btw saw your old man in college a couple of weeks ago.' There was no response from Jack.

'Old man'? 'Your old man'? Humphrey supposed that this was not a vulgarism for 'father'. It meant just what it said. That was how everyone saw him and why they looked askance at his relationship with Jack.

Humphrey & Jack

On the morning after the altercation in The Seven Stars and the death of Aristotle, Humphrey received a message from Mark. It said: 'Hi, how ya doing?'

Humphrey couldn't have told you why he had accepted Mark's friend request. He didn't know himself. Perhaps, obscurely, he imagined it would give him an emergency channel for communicating with Jack. Perhaps - he felt shame at the very thought - he wanted to spy on his friend. In any case, the familiar tone of Mark's message was outrageous.

He went to look at his damaged eye in the bathroom mirror. It looked very much as Jack's had on the day his father had beaten him up. He couldn't go out until it had settled down.

Back in his study he went to his friends list and deleted Mark.

Just then, the doorbell rang.

Unjust gods! he thought. It must be Mrs Bellingham. He had been unnerved by her anguished face the previous day when he had delivered the corpse of Aristotle. He had been shocked by the word 'shit' coming from such a woman.

'You can keep the tea towel,' he had shouted at the door which had been slammed in his face, immediately realising how stupid and inept and callous that must have sounded. He hoped she hadn't heard it. That cat meant everything in the world to her.

The doorbell rang again.

He couldn't face her. He knew it was cowardly but he couldn't. What could he say? He turned off the radio. Perhaps, if he kept very quiet she would assume he was out and go away. He couldn't postpone it for ever and, in any case, part of him wanted a chance to apologise and commiserate, even though it wasn't his fault.

But the bell ringing was persistent and Humphrey went downstairs. He could see immediately that his visitor couldn't possibly be Mrs Bellingham. The shadowy figure beyond the leaded lights of his front door was much too tall for that. Was it the police?

For killing a cat? Surely not? He opened the door gingerly.

Humphrey & Jack

It was not the police. It was Hector Podowski.

'My dear, you look frightful. I was beginning to think you must be out. Promise me you won't hit me, won't you?'

'Come in, come in,' said Humphrey, looking about the garden in case Mrs Bellingham might be hiding behind a shrub with a poisoned dart. 'Come into the kitchen. Coffee?' he said.

'Mandatory,' said Hector. 'I thought I would drop by to see how you are. I told the Head that I had to visit a sick friend who had not many days left him on this earth. I hope that is not the case with you, my pugilistic friend. I say, are these yours?'

He picked up some charcoal sketches of a box of eggs and a pastel sketch of aubergines in a basket that Humphrey had been working on earlier. He had not told the Evangelists about his art classes for fear of mockery. He explained to Hector now, as he filled the cafetière and set out mugs.

'But these are really very good, sweet wag. You have been hiding your light under a bushel. But tell me now. How are you really? I mean really?'

'Well, physically,' Humphrey said. 'What you see is pretty much the whole story. It's not particularly painful. I do have a bad headache though. And my coccyx is rather sore. I won't be going to The Seven Stars again any time soon.'

'Well, you don't need to worry about that. We're all barred.'

'What? You and Norman as well? You didn't do anything.'

'Felons by association, me old squire.'

'Oh, that's not fair. I'm so sorry.'

'Do not worry your pretty head, child. Norman and I are only barred for a week. You and Fatty Arbuckle are barred pending apologies and payment for breakages.'

'That'll be the end of the Evangelists then?'

'Well, Garth will never apologise and will say that you threw the first punch.'

Humphrey & Jack

'Which I did. Would you find out from Cora what I owe? I'll send her a cheque and apology by post. But I'm afraid I won't be coming back. You'll have to be the Holy Trinity or something.'

Hector burst into song:

> *Seven for the seven stars in the sky,*
> *Six for the six proud walkers,*
> *Five for the symbols at your door…*

Here, Humphrey joined in:

> *…Four for the Gospel makers,*
> *Three, three, the rivals,*
> *Two, two, the lily-white boys,*
> *Dressed up all in green, ho ho,*
> *One is one and all alone*
> *And ever more shall be so.*

And they laughed and banged on the table like children, for a moment or two.

'I wonder what it means,' Humphrey said.

'I have no idea,' said Hector. 'I feel inspired to go away and paint it. But yes, I fear the Gospel Makers are no more. And it may be that it's just as well. It won't survive as a threesome either. These things have a limited life - like religions and book clubs. What began as a diverting little game has turned into something increasingly unpleasant.'

'Well, if I ever see Garth Porter again, it will be a day too soon.'

'I quite understand. He has become increasingly hard to stomach. I learn incidentally that some floozie he has been pursuing threw him over just recently. That might go some way towards explaining his vile temper yesterday. I will name no names, of course. You wouldn't expect it of me but it is rumoured that the said floozie might just be the wife of the Chair of Astrophysics.

'He was quite outrageously out of order yesterday, you know. I shouldn't take anything he said to heart.'

'It's a little late for that,' said Humphrey.

'For myself, I don't think I shall be twinkling much in The Seven Stars from now on. Let us amuse ourselves with the thought of Garth and Norman grousing fruitlessly about us, which is what will happen for certain.'

'There is some comfort in that, yes,' Humphrey said.

'Well then, put away these dumps and dolours. Put on a cheerful countenance. You're going to see Jack soon aren't you?'

'Yes, it isn't that, though I'm a little apprehensive that our relationship will have changed.'

'Well, that's inevitable, isn't it? But I'm sure that your friendship will prove solid at the core.'

'Maybe, but that's not it. You see there was another disaster yesterday.'

'Pray tell.'

And Humphrey told Hector about the sudden and tragic demise of Aristotle, Mrs Bellingham's cat.

'*Requiem eternam dona ei, et lux perpetua luceat eo,*' Hector intoned nasally. '*Eheu! Eheu! Felis infelix!* Alas! Alas! Unfortunate cat!'

'It's not funny,' Humphrey said.

'I thought you hated that cat,' said Hector.

'I did, but it took a shine to Jack and was always round here following him about and I tolerated it at first and then grew quite fond of it… him.'

'Ah. But you haven't warmed to Mrs Bellingham, have you?'

'No, not really. But I feel dreadfully sorry for her. And I feel terribly guilty though I know that logically it wasn't my fault. I'm too much of a coward to face her. I thought that was her at the door. That's why it took ages for me to answer.'

'Write to her then. There'll have been vet's fees for the disposal. Offer to pay them. Offer to pay a decent sum to a cat charity. Do it today.'

'Excellent,' Humphrey said.

'Well, I must be going. Mustn't let the Head man panic. Thanks for the coffee.' Hector had picked up Humphrey's sketches. 'These are impressive. Perhaps you might let me give you some tips one day?'

'I'd like that. Look, we always go to The Quarryman's after art class. Why don't you join us sometime?'

'Maybe I will.'

That evening Humphrey wrote his penitential letter and then on a whim he sent Hector a message inviting him to dinner the following week.

As he was locking up before going to bed, he peered round the door into the silent garden for a moment, fearful lest Mrs Bellingham be out there beyond the pear tree with a crossbow or under the hedgerow with a harpoon.

44. **Durham**

The car journey to Durham was tedious in the extreme. Huge juggernauts tried to overtake each other but hadn't the traction to do it quickly, causing long tailbacks. Heavy rain swam across the windscreen and the beat of the wipers was scarcely enough to cope with it. Besides, the lorries threw up filth and small stones and Humphrey feared that the glass would be shattered. When he could pass, the hiss and roar of the beasts was unnerving and he had to keep a firm grip on the steering wheel for, when he emerged from the lee of the lorries, he could feel the buffet of a heavy cross wind.

He wished he had caught the train. He was sustained by the fact that, if he lived through this, he would see Jack on the morrow. He had told Humphrey that he had a formal dinner that evening and Humphrey had said that he was coming up early so that he would not be travel weary when they did meet. They would lunch together the next day.

He had booked a room in the Royal City Hotel, on Old Elvet just over the bridge, insisting on a view of the cathedral and castle. It would be expensive but this was a special occasion. The hotel also offered parking, absolutely essential given the vile weather. Of course, when he reached his room there was no view at all, just the relentless rain streaming down the windows.

Still the room was cosy. He tried out all the lamps, as one does, and was about to ring down to tell reception that they didn't work when they began to glow. Of course, it was because they had these wretched long-life bulbs that took a while to come on. He tried all the cupboards and drawers and checked that the shower did not have a temperature regulator that required a degree in engineering to operate. Then he read for most of the afternoon.

Later, he went down to the bar, where he drank two Martinis. Though he gave the obliging barman, who was called George, the precise proportions of gin to vermouth that he required and though he requested a couple of cocktail onions rather than a twist of lemon, the drink tasted insipid compared to the near-mortal preparation he was used to at home, so he had a third.

Now he felt better and remembered that he had read somewhere that the trouble with Martinis is that they seem to be having no effect whatsoever and then you suddenly find you're having a conversation with a chair. Humphrey had a conversation with the barman instead. He felt inspired to recite a little ditty by Dorothy Parker. It went:

> *I like to have a Martini,*
> *Two at the very most.*
> *After three I'm under the table,*
> *After four I'm under the host.*

Humphrey & Jack

Humphrey and George laughed uproariously though Humphrey wasn't quite sure whether the barman was laughing genuinely or professionally.

'Better not have a fourth then, sir,' said George and they fell about again.

Humphrey had a sudden suspicion that George might be taking the piss and decided it was time he went off in search of dinner. He mustn't have a hangover when he saw Jack tomorrow. That would spoil everything after all this time.

He borrowed an umbrella from reception and stood in the vestibule for a few moments peering out into the night. The deluge had abated somewhat, as had the wind. There was now just a fine drizzle falling in thin clouds under the street lamps. He crossed Elvet Bridge and on to the North Bailey and an Italian restaurant that had been there since his days as a research student.

It was little changed. It was not very busy on this foul-weathered week night. What clientele there was were all locals, middle-aged or older. As he examined the menu (also little changed) Humphrey listened with pleasure to the familiar Durham accent, softer and more intelligible than the full-on Geordie.

He had a lasagne with a good Barolo followed by a panna cotta. He did not drink coffee in the evenings since it prevented him from sleeping but he could not resist a generous shot of Strega.

Then, feeling very mellow, he went back to his hotel. The rain had stopped, the wind had dropped and the late autumn evening felt mellow too. He went straight to bed and slept immediately.

The next morning, he woke early. There was still no view of the cathedral and castle as both were shrouded in a dense mist. Actually, as he looked closer, he could see the outlines of the two ancient sandstone structures as if they had been sketched with red-brown chalk on heavily textured white paper. The effect was curiously two dimensional.

After a light continental breakfast, he wandered across the bridge to the Market Place. It was not yet eight-thirty. The mist was burning off and a timid sun shone on the yellow-grey of the imposing buildings around the square. It was as he had remembered it, familiar and yet strangely alien. There was the church of St Nicholas in the corner with its spire. Here in the centre was the equestrian statue of the Earl of Londonderry. And there was Boots the Chemist whose white frontage looked quite out of place amid this antique stone.

Humphrey went inside and bought some Ibuprofen. He didn't have a hangover but there was the ghost of a headache at the back of his skull and he didn't want it to develop.

Back in the square, he sat on a bench for a while and watched undergraduates hurrying to lectures. That was what was alien, he thought. They seemed like impostors. The university which had belonged to him and his peers had been occupied by a new generation. They did not carry brief cases, or parcels of books under their arms, nor as Humphrey had, did they carry their study materials in a Marks and Spencer carrier bag. Instead, they sported brightly coloured rucksacks. In their hands they carried plastic bottles of water or coffee in cardboard containers.

There were many more girls, of course.

He sat on for a while, thinking he might see Jack but there was no sign. They had arranged to meet at twelve-fifteen outside the cathedral and there were over three hours to kill.

Humphrey strolled over to the little quasi-ecclesiastical arcade which led into the indoor market. Little had changed here: the same stalls with their red-and-white or green-and-white awnings under the steel and glass roof; the same echoing noise of chatter and laughter; the same smells of warm bread, of fruit and vegetables, of leather, of coffee and bacon from the café, and the sickly smell of joss sticks from the oriental stall. In one corner the salty reek of fish overwhelmed everything else.

'Ten quid the lot!' cried a stall owner with the better part of a dinner service spread expertly up his arm.

'Any less and I'd be robbing meself, pet,' he heard the butcher say to a pensioner.

Humphrey & Jack

Humphrey loved it. There was once a similar market in Radcester but it was torn down when Humphrey was in his teens and replaced with a covered market with a curved concrete roof which dripped rusty water onto the stalls, and through which a chilly wind rushed even in summer. That, in its turn, had been demolished and a modern mall had grown up in its place. It was known locally as 'The Precinct' for some obscure reason and was mostly empty since the rents were too high and some of the retail outlets were boarded up because the businesses had gone bust or because they had never been leased in the first place. It was quite soulless.

But this bustling place had a human face. Humphrey remembered that there had once been a barber's stall here. He found it quite quickly in a side booth. There was no queue and Humphrey asked for a short back and sides from the barber who sported a green waistcoat and a red bow tie.

Humphrey wished he could export this chap to Radcester. He got on with it without talking about football or the weather or Humphrey's line of employment. In fact, he didn't talk very much at all, except to ask for instructions. He provided what Humphrey asked for, unlike his barber at home who never cut it short enough and always attempted a quiff which Humphrey would claw out as soon as he was on the doorstep. Humphrey couldn't be bothered to complain about it but had told him in no uncertain terms that he had no interest whatsoever in football. Thereafter, the infuriating prat had started watching football on his iPad whilst cutting Humphrey's hair. Inertia had stopped him going elsewhere.

This chap, however, was totally professional. Without being asked he trimmed the irritating growth of hair inside and on the outside of Humphrey's ears and also trimmed his eyebrows. Humphrey tipped him generously and went to have a closer look at the stalls.

He bought a Victorian butter knife for himself at a bric-à-brac stall and a handsome copy of Shakespeare's *Sonnets* for Jack at an antiquarian bookshop. As an afterthought, he bought him a pomegranate. By now, he was pleased to see that it was just after half past ten.

Humphrey & Jack

Humphrey sauntered up the quaint curve of Sadler Street and on to Palace Green where he had a coffee and some carrot cake. Then he spent a pleasant hour in the cathedral. It was chilly but it was pleasant to wallow in nostalgia. He revisited the vaulted nave supported by drum columns with bold geometrical designs that always made him think of thick sticks of candy; he revisited the Chapel of the Nine Altars; he marvelled anew at Prior Castell's Clock and the Sanctuary knocker. The flood of bittersweet feelings was something of a surprise since Humphrey had spent his three years at the university in a kind of emotional no-man's-land, neither particularly happy nor particularly sad.

But now it was time to meet Jack and, as Humphrey emerged into the cool sunlight, there he was. You could say this for Jack: he was almost always punctual. He was wearing a mauve track suit and carrying a squash racket in its press. He looked rather impatient.

'There you are,' he said.

'I'm not late,' Humphrey said.

'Come on then. We've only got just over an hour.'

Humphrey was indignant.

'You mean I've come all this way in driving rain for an hour?'

'Don't lose your blob,' Jack said laughing. 'I've got a squash match this afternoon and I need to loosen up a bit in the court beforehand. I'm playing for the university already, Humphrey. Aren't you impressed?'

'I am. Well done. But Jack - an hour?'

'For now. We'll meet up for dinner later and you can have my undivided attention. Come on, pick your feet up.'

'Where are we going?'

'St Nicholas' Tavern. Pub lunch.'

'I've just come from Market Square.'

'So? Don't be difficult, Humphrey. Sharp haircut by the way.'

'I've missed you, you know.'

'I know. Come on!'

Humphrey & Jack

He pressed ahead. The words TEAM DURHAM in white on the back of Jack's tracksuit top filled Humphrey with pride. The despoiler of his garden had come a long way.

The pub was a disappointment. It was a sports bar and full of loud and hearty young men. Jack appeared to know a number of them. Television screens were playing footage of a game somewhere in eastern Europe which was being relayed at near live volume. The only free table was squashed in a corner near the lavatories. Jack ordered 'BBQ' chicken wings and a mineral water and Humphrey Steak and Ale Pie and a pint of Greene King IPA.

The excellent beer was the only consolation. Jack ought to have known that Humphrey would find a place like this anathema. Humphrey realised with disgust that there was a juke box and that there was loud music playing *in addition* to the racket from the television screens. The food arrived late and, though it was palatable, Humphrey felt obliged to rush it - something he hated doing. From time to time, one of Jack's chums came over and chatted to Jack about lectures, sports and gigs. Jack made no attempt to introduce them and Humphrey felt wholly out of place. He was the oldest person in here by decades.

Worst of all, Humphrey and Jack had no real opportunity to talk. Any conversation had to be shouted and Humphrey had no wish to add to the din. This was certainly not the place to hand over his gifts. And to crown it all, he was paying.

They parted outside on the pavement. Humphrey felt cheated. He had had to mark time all morning and now he would have to fill the afternoon somehow.

'Sorry Humphrey,' Jack said. 'I guess that was not your sort of place, was it?'

'Hardly,' said Humphrey, with a face as lugubrious as a bloodhound.

'I wasn't thinking,' Jack said. 'Still, what do you expect in a university town?'

'We're not going there tonight, are we? Because I couldn't bear a second more of that imbecilic racket.'

'God no,' said Jack. 'We're going to Shaheen's. The food is brilliant, even better than the Delhi Durbar. Can you pick up some wine? It's better to take your own. I've booked for seven. It'll be fairly quiet on a week night if we go earlyish. Gotta go. See you there!'

And he sprinted off across the square.

'Where is it?' Humphrey shouted after him, exasperated.

Jack ran backwards for a few steps and shouted back: 'Google it!' And then he disappeared around a corner.

Humphrey bought two bottles of Rosé d'Anjou at the Tesco Metro in the square and took them back to his hotel, popping them in the fridge in his room for later. He didn't feel like any more tourism and tried to read but felt an unaccustomed drowsiness. Though he had never really been able to sleep in the afternoon, he thought he might try. Setting the alarm for four-thirty, he climbed into bed and was off in a trice.

Waking with the alarm, he felt refreshed and in a much better humour. He showered again, changed into fresh clothes and went down to the bar where George showed him where the restaurant was on the North Bailey. Humphrey had probably passed it the previous evening but he hadn't noticed. He had a couple of dry Martinis and was pleased to note that George was getting the hang of it. Then he set off with his carrier bag of wine.

Jack was already there, talking to a waiter.

45. Changing Course

It was as if they had never been apart. They slipped immediately into their old intimacy and Humphrey began to feel relieved and relaxed. Jack had chosen a large table in the middle of the restaurant. Other cutlery had been cleared away and there were just the two settings with plenty of room for

Humphrey & Jack

the dishes when they ordered. The only other people were a pair of middle-aged gentlemen who might conceivably be lecturers. Humphrey approved.

The waiters were cheerful and solicitous without being a nuisance. They opened one of the bottles of wine and took one away to keep chilled. As usual, Humphrey and Jack ordered a variety of dishes, more than they could possibly eat. Over poppadoms and pickles, Humphrey told Jack about his art classes and about their gatherings at The Quarryman's.

'That's Miss Hemmings, isn't it? I remember her. You're a dark horse, Humphrey. What are you up to? Dangerous Liaisons, is it?'

'Certainly not!' said Humphrey, colouring. Taking off his spectacles he began to clean them vigorously on his table napkin. He had forgotten that the marks of the fracas with Garth Porter were still upon him. Although the contusion had faded from ripe aubergine to a shiny yellow on his cheekbone, his eye was still bloodshot.

'Christ!' Jack said. 'Been fighting over her, have you?'

'Walked into a door,' he said, replacing his glasses promptly. He certainly wasn't going to tell Jack about the humiliating little scrap, nor what it was about.

'They all say that,' said Jack and then, seeing Humphrey's intense discomfiture, relented and said. 'I'd like to see some of your work when I get back.'

'As it happens...' said Humphrey.

'As it happens,' said Jack. 'You happen to have some examples about you.'

'They'll bore you,' said Humphrey.

'No, they won't,' said Jack.

Shyly, Humphrey produced from his shoulder bag some still life pastels and a water colour of the bottom of the garden in autumn with the fountain and the steps in Alexandra Park.

'That's where we first met,' said Jack.

'It was and I can remember your first words to me at the time.'

'I can't,' said Jack. 'What did I say?'

Humphrey & Jack

'I believe you said: "Suck my dick!"' Humphrey whispered, blushing.

Jack laughed.

'Oh my god! I didn't, did I? Sorry.'

'No need. Best forgotten.'

'But you won't forget, will you? I've scarred you for life,' said Jack. 'I am so so sorry.'

But he was still laughing.

'Hey, Humphrey,' said Jack, 'these are seriously good.'

'Really?'

'I mean really. I'm glad you've found something to occupy you.'

'Oh, I have a much bigger project in mind, in fact it's quite well advanced.'

'Yeah? Go on.'

'I'll tell you at Christmas.'

He wasn't going to tell Jack about The Plantagenet Cook Book just yet. It was coming along well. His collection of recipes was nearly complete and had been sorted into sections, and his publisher had been delighted by his illustration for the chapter entitled: *Of Custards, Sweete Jellies, Flummeries and Fooles.*

When their food arrived it was immediately obvious that it was made from fresh ingredients. There were no lurid dyes and the complex and differentiated flavours burst richly on the tongue. The peshwari naan was, as Jack had promised, to die for.

'But what about you?' said Humphrey. 'That's what we're here for. How's the course?'

'Ah,' said Jack, suddenly cagey and helping himself to more brinjal bhaji, his favourite side dish. 'I meant to tell you. I changed. Quite early on in fact. I hope you don't mind.'

'Mind? Why should I mind? It's your career not mine.'

There was, he had to admit, a slight tinge of regret, though he kept it to himself.

Humphrey & Jack

'What have you changed to?' Humphrey asked.

'Polish Studies,' said Jack.

'Why did you change then? Do you mind me asking? You had a flair for history.'

'That's just it,' said Jack. 'I don't want to sound supercilious but it was too easy. I was streaks ahead of the others - that's partly down to you - and I was beginning to find most of the lectures boring. Is that arrogant?'

'Not at all. Better to be honest. And what does Polish Studies entail?'

'Literature, Language, History and Culture. You see, I've already got a head start, haven't I? And get this: second best of all - the class sizes are really small, especially compared with History.'

Humphrey winced at the clumsy Americanism but only said: 'And best of all?'

'Best of all is that I spend my second year in Poland.'

Humphrey's heart took a lurch though he took pains to hide it. A whole year's absence - and so soon. He hated himself for his own selfishness and hoped he was giving nothing away.

'Well, that sounds ideal, Jack,' Humphrey managed to say. 'The best of all possible worlds. Are you enjoying it?'

'Yeah, it's a big improvement. There's a real sense of community in the Department. History was so anonymous and the contact time was pathetic. And there was less vodka.'

Jack laughed merrily.

'And can you afford the year out?' Humphrey said. 'I'll help if you need it.'

'No, I should be fine, thanks. There's a bursary already sorted. And I'm saving up. I've got a job in Morrison's part time.'

'That won't interfere with your studies, will it?'

'Nah. I won't lie. I get knackered a bit sometimes, what with lectures, essays, work and squash. But it's fine.'

'You would say? If you needed money, I mean?'

'Yeah, yeah, yeah. Don't worry about it, Humphrey. It's all good.'

Humphrey & Jack

Humphrey felt this as a slight rebuff but was not going to let it spoil his evening. He tried to put the future aside. There would be time to brood when he was alone.

Jack sat back in his chair and spread the fingers of both hands across his belly.

'That was incredible,' he said. 'I feel as if I've eaten a medicine ball.'

'I know what you mean,' Humphrey said, still eating, though beginning to fade a little. 'You were right. This really is first rate.'

When he finally put his fork down, the waiter was with them in a moment, asking if they would like to see the dessert menu.

'Oh, thank you,' Humphrey said, 'that was perfectly delicious but I couldn't possibly eat another thing - probably not for a fortnight at least.'

'Ah, but you must try the kulfi,' said Jack. 'You must. It's the house speciality and it is delectable. Can you come back in about twenty minutes, Adam?'

'Of course,' said the waiter.

Jack was growing up, thought Humphrey. Here he was effortlessly at ease, taking charge of the situation like the young gentleman he was becoming.

'You know what kulfi is?' he said to Humphrey with a paternalistic air Humphrey found amusing.

'Yes, of course,' he said. 'Indian ice cream. Made with condensed milk and cardamom.'

'Ah, that's the cheat's way,' said Jack smugly. 'They make it on the premises here. The milk is simmered until it's reduced by two thirds - takes about four hours. Incredibly labour intensive, but authentic. Adam told me all about it.'

Later, Jack ordered pistachio and saffron flavour and Humphrey thought he could manage pistachio and rosewater. It was indeed sublime, the subtle fragrance of nuts and roses on a caramelised base. The second bottle was brought out at Humphrey's request. He felt, for the moment, at one with the world.

'Can I take a look at your rooms afterwards?' he said.

'Room, singular,' Jack said. 'Oh, you don't want to do that. It's a complete tip and it's nothing.'

'But you were so desperate to get into the Castle,' Humphrey said.

'Yeah, I know, and dinner in the hall is pretty magical and all that, but the room's a bit disappointing. It's got the top half of a gothic window in one wall but it's all boarded up where the glass was. Otherwise, it's like any generic student room. The window looks out over the kitchens and the bins and it's a bit chilly, to be honest.'

'Oh dear.'

'It's fine. In any case, I'm not staying there after this year. I'm going back-packing in Europe with some mates this summer. Then, it's Poland. And then, in my third year, I'm going to share a house with these guys and perhaps a couple of girls.'

Humphrey's heart lurched again and with it the spasm of guilt. This sense of freedom, of the fullness and freshness of youth, and of the future as an unopened treasury was exactly what he wished for Jack. And yet, when it came to it, there was the sour taint of a shameful jealousy. He felt as if he was being left behind.

The memory came to him, quite unbidden, of the time he had been made to run in the 1500 metres on sports day at school. He had come in last, almost a whole lap behind everyone else, hot with humiliation and self-loathing. The polite crackle of applause for being a 'good sport' that greeted him when he crossed the line had been intensely mortifying.

'You are still coming for Christmas?' he said.

'Yes, of course,' Jack said. 'Why wouldn't I? Is there a problem?'

'No, no, of course not. It's just that you seem to have everything mapped out.'

'Well, to be honest, I'll be technically homeless in the holidays this year. We get turfed out because there are conferences and weddings and all manner of horrible covens and conclaves. Bagot Street has been re-let and

Humphrey & Jack

I couldn't afford it anyway so I shall be beholden to your charity, Humphrey.'

'Charity! Phooey!' said Humphrey. 'You have a home in Radcester whenever you need one. Let's have no talk of charity.'

When Humphrey had paid the bill, with a handsome tip for Adam, Jack said: 'What would you like to do now? We could go to the JCR bar?'

Humphrey remembered the Undercroft from his time in Durham.

'Won't it be full of hearties and rugger buggers?' he said.

'Probably.'

'Well, I'll give it a miss then, if you don't mind,' Humphrey said. 'I'd feel horribly out of place. They would look on me as the spectre at the feast.'

Jack laughed. There was nothing spectral about Humphrey's shape.

'We could go to the hotel bar?' Humphrey ventured.

'Yes, that's a good idea,' Jack said. 'Paupers like me don't often get the chance of a look at the inside of a five star hotel.'

'Four,' said Humphrey.

'Whatever,' said Jack.

It was probably a mistake. The bar was beige, bland and boring. Vanilla, Jack would have said. There was no-one in there at this hour, not even any bar staff, apparently. A Chopin mazurka tinkled softly away through sub-standard speakers. A telephone rang unanswered in the distance. They waited for a long time.

'Assert yourself, Humphrey,' Jack said.

'Hello!' Humphrey said. 'Are you there, George?'

'He won't hear that,' Jack said.

'HELLO! GEORGE!' Humphrey bellowed, embarrassed.

A mousey girl who looked about fourteen emerged from behind the scenes, wiping her hands on her apron.

'I'm sorry. I was loading the glass-washer. We were very busy earlier. George has finished his shift. What can I get you gentlemen?'

Her eyes were fixed on Jack.

Humphrey & Jack

'What was that stuff we had in the garden the first time we had lunch outside, you know, when I was doing the fence?' Jack asked Humphrey.

'I can't remember. Was it red?'

'Not with the meal. Afterwards. With the coffee?'

'Ah, Calvados. What a good idea!' He asked the barmaid for two large glasses.

'I don't think we have it, sir,' she said without looking.

'Yes, you do. There. Second shelf up, third bottle along. Double measures, please. No, not in wine glasses. Those brandy glasses there would be better. Yes, those.'

'Ice?'

'God, no. Jack?'

'No, thanks.'

'Oh, sorry. I'm new, you see. I don't suppose we have a lot of call for it,' said the girl.

This was belied by the fact that the bottle was now nearly empty.

They went to sit down.

'You needn't have been so hard on her,' Jack said.

'Oh, was I? I didn't mean to be. They shouldn't have put her on the bar on her own before she was properly trained. She couldn't take her eyes off you. I thought she was going to spill it.'

'Par for the course,' Jack said and hurled himself onto a caramel-coloured leather sofa where he reclined like a river god. Humphrey lowered himself gingerly onto the opposing sofa and was alarmed to find that it was so soft that it felt as if he had sunk through almost to the floor.

Whether it was the suffocating dullness of the place, or whether Jack was tired, they found they had nothing much to say to each other. Not even the Calva could kick-start the evening again.

Fairly soon, Jack said: 'I'd better be going.'

'It's early,' said Humphrey.

'I know, but I've got to go to the gym first thing, lectures all morning and a shift at Morrison's in the afternoon.'

'I see,' said Humphrey, failing to hide his disappointment and embarrassing Jack.

They shook hands.

'Have a safe journey back,' Jack said. 'And I'll see you at Christmas.'

And he was gone.

46. Sunshine and Showers

Humphrey travelled back the next morning through sunshine and showers. As he was travelling south most of the way, the sun was troublesome, especially since he had forgotten his sunglasses. When the sun was reflected from wet tarmac, the glare was alarming: he would be temporarily blinded and he had to hope the road would still be there when he could see again. It was a relief when, somewhere near Leeds, a bank of thick cloud began to cover the whole sky and a steady drizzle began to fall.

He had plenty of time to think about his visit. Had it been a success? On the whole, he thought so. Their friendship had been resumed where it had been left off and apart from a few thoughtless moments their easy amicability was quite intact. It was the future that gnawed at him. Certainly there was Christmas and probably the Easter vacation too. But then what? There seemed to be what the weathermen called 'an occluded front'.

There would be no repetition of last summer's idyll. In the coming long vacation Jack would be travelling around Europe with friends and then there was a whole year in Poland. And then what? Humphrey saw their encounters becoming shorter and more infrequent. There would be less and less to say to each other. Jack would marry and Humphrey would be relegated to a pew at the back of a church crowded with Jack's friends. Jack would cease to be a Don Juan and find 'the one'; he would shut out the world as lovers do. There would be children and Humphrey would be asked to be godfather despite his being what he had once described to Jack as 'a high Anglican atheist'. Humphrey would visit once a year with gifts.

Humphrey & Jack

What was there to bring Jack back to Radcester either? It had little to recommend it. His mother was dead and his father in prison for the foreseeable future. With its featureless town centre, its squat cathedral and its second-rate university, it was hopelessly dull and provincial, like Humphrey himself, he thought. It was dreary and banal, nowhere in itself - merely on the way to other places. Jack would want to move to London, he was sure of it.

What made everything so very much worse was that Humphrey despised himself for thinking like this. The boy was growing up. It had to be this way. This is the way the world wags. He should want Jack to be enterprising and to spread his wings. It was churlish - and childish - to resent it. But the sense of impending loss was there all the same.

He made good time and was home earlier than he had expected. As he turned into his drive - always with extreme caution these days - he noticed a large and garish estate agent's sign in Mrs Bellingham's front garden. Her house was up for sale. Come to think of it, he hadn't seen her around for a very long time. Was she still living there? Despite their past warfare, he didn't like to think he might be the cause of her moving out. She had never replied to his letter offering to pay for Aristotle's obsequies. He had stopped short of offering to commission King's College Choir to sing a requiem but his offer had been very generous. It met with nothing but drawn curtains.

He kept himself busy during the next six weeks until Jack was due to come 'home' for the Christmas Vacation. He worked hard on his book and even invited Hector to dinner, the week after his return from Durham, where Humphrey brought to the table a large venison pie with a rich gravy scented with nutmeg and juniper berries. The pie lid featured a trellis with pastry leaves intertwined. Hector declared it the eighth wonder of the world.

'And where, thou Fanny Craddock of my riper years, didst thou find the recipe?'

Humphrey & Jack

'I can't remember exactly, to tell you the truth, but I'm using it in *The Plantagenet Cookbook*. I'll show you after dinner.'

After a pomegranate and rosewater sorbet, Humphrey cleared the dining room table and laid out his camera-ready manuscript along with the pastel illustrations, preserved from smudging with fixative, and further protected with tissue paper. He had abandoned his earlier idea of watercolours, finding that he could achieve greater depth and toothsomeness with pastel.

And now Humphrey turned a page and here was the pie they had just eaten, the shortcrust pastry glossy and golden with its egg glaze. It was for the title page of a chapter called: *Of Savoury Pies and Pasties, Sweet Tarts, Tartlettes, along with Sundry Other Honied Délices*.

'Nearly finished,' Humphrey said. 'Just a chapter on cheese to go.'

'Phenomenal!' Hector said. 'It must be rather wonderful to discover a talent you never knew you had.'

'You're very kind. I hope you don't think me maudlin, but if I had never met Jack I would still be in the same wretched rut in which I've spent most of my life.'

'Not impossible. Speaking of ruts, have you been to The Seven Stars recently?'

'No, have you?'

'Just a couple of times. Garth is permanently barred because he won't apologise and Norman just sits on his own reading *The Guardian*. By the way, Cora says thank you for the cheque but she's not going to cash it. Reckons you were provoked.'

'True. But how did she work that out?'

'I told her you were goaded beyond measure.'

'Well, thank you,' Humphrey said, 'but I won't be going back, you know.'

'I know,' said Hector.

Shortly after the evening of the dinner, the last illustration was completed. Madame Roussel who owned the *fromagerie* near the cathedral had kindly let him into her storeroom to take photographs for the illustration to the penultimate chapter: *Of Cheeses, both Englisshe and Frensshe and of Spicie Jams and Chutnies*. Humphrey promised her a copy of the book when it came out.

He worked on the illustration all that evening. There were great wheels and rounds of cheese, truckles and tranches, chalk-white, cream, yellow and orange, veined with blue or mottled red, washed in wine or rolled in ash. Humphrey was so pleased with the result that he thought he might use it on the cover of the book as well as at the beginning of the chapter.

The next day, he packed everything up with meticulous care and drove to Leicester where he delivered the package to his publishers.

Back home he continued with his art classes. His student, Oliver Gothland, was invited to Corpus Christi, Cambridge for interview right at the end of term and everyone had their fingers crossed.

Occasionally, Humphrey would bump into Mark Kapel in the corridor. The boy was always effusively cordial but Humphrey tried to make any conversations as short as possible although this didn't seem to put Mark off. Humphrey was deeply suspicious of his air of camaraderie but felt he managed to hide it.

He also kept up his convivial visits to The Quarryman's. On one occasion, he introduced Hector to the group where he was an instant success, as Humphrey somehow knew he would be. His flamboyance and baroque turn of phrase suited the eccentricities of the little group. Althea was most amused by his capacity to wind up Loretta without her realising. His lavish praise of her ideas for her Tuscan commission goaded her to ever more extravagant plans. The fact that Hector had never seen so much as a brush stroke of her work did nothing to depreciate her admiration of his judgement.

Christmas came and with it Jack.

Humphrey had never been one for Christmas decorations. Normally, he would receive no more than half a dozen cards which went straight into the bin and he had certainly never sent any. This year the cards from the art group shamed him into buying some quite expensive ones since the cheap ones in the shops were excruciatingly sentimental and because his friends and colleagues had gone to some trouble to select tasteful ones. There was also a card from Cora saying he would be welcome back at The Seven Stars anytime. Humphrey didn't see himself as complying with her wish, though he sent a card in return.

He had sent one to Jack but hadn't received one back. Humphrey didn't suppose Jack had ever bought a postage stamp in his life. However, he did send Humphrey an animated electronic card by email. It featured the three wise men performing a slavonic kick dance, elbows out, in front of the crib. The greeting was in Polish.

In the past, he had always received a small card from Mrs Bellingham but not this year. It had been quite clear that she had moved out. The estate agent's sign was still there and Humphrey had not seen any lights on in the house for ages. Moreover, the huge Christmas tree with its multicoloured winking lights, which used to appear in the bay window on the street side of her house in the last week of November, had not appeared.

Now that he had enough Christmas cards to put on his mantelpiece without them looking forlorn and ridiculous, he thought he would go in for a little festive decoration. Not a tree, which would drop pine needles on his cream carpet and not tinsel which he thought vulgar. Just some strings of lights - white - not coloured - which he would drape around the pictures in the sitting room. They came with electronic chase effects which Humphrey played with for hours.

Jack didn't even notice. Or at least he didn't say anything. He didn't even notice that Humphrey had installed a Georgian rosewood writing table in his room. Humphrey had seen it in 'Stuff for Sale in Radcester'. The asking price was reasonable and it was in remarkably good nick. Jack had said that he had a lot of work to catch up on, so Humphrey had splashed out. He had set the elegant little desk in the window of the room so that Jack would have a view of the garden and Alexandra Park beyond.

Humphrey & Jack

Piqued at Jack's failure to acknowledge the addition, Humphrey pointed it out.

'Wasn't it there before?' Jack said.

'No. I've just bought it. I thought it might be handy for your academic work.'

'Oh. Yeah. It's nice,' was all the reply Humphrey got.

What Jack did notice, however, was the absence of Aristotle. Humphrey had no option but to come clean.

'Oh, Humphrey,' Jack said. 'How could you?'

'It's not as if I did it on purpose.'

'Are you sure, Humphrey? Are you really sure?'

'Of course I'm sure!'

'I loved that cat,' said Jack.

'It was mutual,' said Humphrey.

'And that poor woman…Oh, Humphrey,' Jack said in a funereal voice.

'I think she's moved out anyway.'

'I saw the sign. I'll have a look later.'

'Don't you go trespassing now. Steak and chips do you for supper?'

'Sweet. Oh, I'm going out later,' Jack said. 'If that's all right?'

'Of course it is,' Humphrey said. 'But Jack…your first night back? I haven't seen you for weeks.'

'Well, I won't if you don't want me to, but remember, I haven't seen some of my friends for much longer than that. I haven't seen Mark since the beginning of term, for instance.'

'Jack, you must come and go as you please. You're not a prisoner. This is your home while you're here. That's why I gave you the keys.'

'Ah, well, now…that's just the thing…'

'What is?'

'You see, I've left them in my desk at Durham. They'll be safe enough till I go back. And in any case there's nothing on the ring to identify them.'

Humphrey & Jack

'You cloth-head,' said Humphrey. 'Luckily for you I think I have a spare set but for God's sake don't lose these. I'd better have another set cut when I go into town.'

'Thanks for that. We can't have you sitting up with your knitting ready to rolling-pin me when I fall through the door at four in the morning out of my tree on drink and drugs.'

'Don't even think about it,' said Humphrey, 'or you'll be banished to the shed.'

'We haven't got a shed,' said Jack.

'Exactly,' said Humphrey, though he was tickled by Jack's use of 'we'.

Nevertheless, he felt very dejected when Jack left after supper. Jack had told him that he would be going to Mark's on Christmas Eve, at his mother's invitation, and staying till Boxing Day. He would be sharing a new double bed with Mark.

Humphrey had put on a Frankie Howerd expression but felt very silly when Jack said:

'There's no need to pull faces, Humphrey. I'm quite comfortable with my sexuality.'

'It's just that I've got everything in for Christmas dinner. I was so looking forward to it. You might have said.'

'Well, to be fair, you've only just said I can come and go as I please.'

It was undeniable, though Humphrey didn't think it fair at all.

'I did mean to tell you, but somehow it slipped my mind,' Jack said. 'Anyway, we can postpone it, can't we? I mean, it's not as if you're a Christian, is it? And the date's a fiction anyway. We'll have our own winter festival and invent our own traditions. Right, I am going upstairs to get ready.'

Humphrey smiled bravely but his forced courage was pretty transparent.

'Shall we go for the twenty-eighth?'

'Holy Innocents? Excellent. I might invite some friends.'

Humphrey & Jack

'Cool. Can I invite Mark?'

'I'll have to think about that,' said Humphrey, meaning he would have to think up a viable excuse for saying 'no'.

Jack looked into the kitchen later as Humphrey was loading the dishwasher.

'I think you should get yourself a kitten,' he said. 'See you when I see you!' And he was off. The front door banged.

When he'd finished, Humphrey poured himself a bountiful measure of scotch and watched a couple of ancient Morecambe and Wise retreads in the sitting room. Why were they not as funny as they used to be?

The cards on the mantelpiece and the sparkling fairy lights around his pictures seemed to mock him.

47. Port

Humphrey slept better than he thought he would. All the same, he was awoken in the night by the front door being opened and then a muttered 'fuck!' as Jack collided with the stack of umbrellas just by the street door. The glowing red digits of Humphrey's alarm clock flicked to 02:18. Jack must have crept up the stairs very cautiously but when he turned on the taps the old house's plumbing began to clank and when he flushed the lavatory the roaring avalanche was followed by distant moans and gargling in the pipes. Then there was a bit of thudding for a few moments and finally, deep silence. Humphrey slipped back into sleep.

If Jack had been drunk the night before, there was no sign of it the following morning. He was up before Humphrey and bright as a button. What's more, he was making breakfast. Coffee was ready, butter and apricot jam were on the table, and rolls and croissants were warming in the oven.

'Where did you get all this?' Humphrey asked.

'Late night Tesco. Hope I didn't wake you last night. I tripped over the umbrellas.'

Humphrey & Jack

'You did, but I got straight back to sleep again. Were you drunk?'

'Sorry. No, not particularly. Bloody silly place to stack them, if you ask me. Anyway, breakfast is served, my Lord.'

This was a first and very gratifying.

'Is this the shape of things to come?' Humphrey said.

'I wouldn't bank on it,' Jack said.

Nevertheless, the gesture put Humphrey in an excellent mood which was enhanced when the postman brought a parcel for him which had to be signed for.

He realised that here were the proofs of *The Plantagenet Cookbook*. He was dying to open the parcel and show Jack his handiwork but he managed to contain himself until breakfast was cleared and the table was as clean as an operating table. Only then did he open the parcel and lay out the proofs. Jack was enthusiastic in his praise.

'You dark horse, Humphrey,' he said. 'You secret, black and midnight horse. This is incredible. I love it.'

Humphrey glowed like an eight year old who has brought home an excellent school report to show his parents.

'So what happens next?' said Jack.

'I proof-read it.'

'You won't have made any errors. Not Doctor Humphrey Icke.'

'You would be surprised. You are so close to your work, you see what you think you wrote, rather than what is actually there. My editor flushed out masses of silly mistakes in the first draft. This is my last chance to weed out anything that remains. It's a bit tricky. I've given the chapter titles quaint period spelling but the recipes and commentary have to be in modern English or it wouldn't be fair to anyone trying to cook from it.'

'I'll proof-read it for you,' Jack said.

'Are you serious?' Humphrey said. 'That would be wonderful! I will cite you in the acknowledgements. And a quid for every mistake you find.'

'Are you serious?' said Jack in his turn.

Humphrey & Jack

'Never more so,' said Humphrey.

The next few days passed comfortably. It was just like the easy cohabitation of last summer with the added bonus of Jack's work on the proofs confirming that they were of use to each other. His attention was meticulous, not just because of the prospect of earning money, but because he got a malign kick out of catching Humphrey out in solecisms and typos. In the end, Jack earned £37 which Humphrey rounded up to £50.

Since Jack was going to be away on Christmas Day, Humphrey gave him his Christmas present early, a brand new copy of *The Illustrated History of Europe in the Fourteenth Century*, the book which had in a way helped to germinate their friendship.

'Wow!' said Jack. 'That is amazing. I'll treasure this. Just a minute.'

He bounded upstairs and returned with a bottle of Graham's 1977 Port loosely wrapped in newspaper. He handed it to Humphrey, looking uncharacteristically shy.

'I don't do Christmas wrapping, I'm afraid.'

'Dear God, Jack! How could you afford this?'

'It's older than I am,' Jack said. 'Are you pleased?'

'Pleased? I'm thrilled. But I'm not sure if I can accept it. It must have cost a hundred pounds or more…'

'Well, it's on the market for £119. I looked it up. But don't worry. I didn't pay anything like that. There was an end of term sale in the JCR bar. I think it must have been a mistake - probably destined for the Master's cellar or something. I just snapped it up without saying anything.'

'Well, we'll have it after dinner on Wednesday. I'll have to decant it carefully.'

When the time came for Jack's departure for his traditional Polish Christmas, Humphrey had schooled himself not to mind too much. He had invited Hector and Althea for his own feast later in the week and he directed his energies toward that. Hector said he would be relieved to get away from his family by then and Althea was never tied down by convention anyway so they would be a comfortable four at table.

Humphrey & Jack

Humphrey was intensely relieved that Jack seemed to have forgotten the idea of inviting Mark. Humphrey had thought up a number of excuses - that Mark was too young, that five was a strange number, that he wouldn't like the food Humphrey had planned, that he would be bored in adult company - but they sounded a bit hollow and Humphrey was glad he would not have to use them. Mention of the clock would have been wholly convincing but it would only stir up trouble.

Humphrey had spent so many Christmases on his own that his solitary festival was no hardship. On Christmas Eve he drank three high-octane Martinis whilst watching Carols from King's and joined in with *O come, all ye faithful* with great gusto. It was most enjoyable and he took note merrily that he would not have been able to do that if Jack had been around.

On Christmas Day he got up late and had a mound of bacon and tomato sandwiches with champagne for breakfast. Dinner began with devilled mushrooms, followed by pheasant with red cabbage and game chips - foods which he thought Jack would not have liked. *Madame Butterfly* was on the TV in the evening and Humphrey scoffed too many chocolates and too much brandy but was not discontented on the whole.

He managed his Boxing Day hangover by not getting up until he had to, remaining in his dressing gown, reclining on the sofa like some sybaritic potentate, and grazing on cold pheasant and endive salad, honey roast ham, cold potatoes and sundry cold saucissons and salamis with assorted pickles. He didn't even touch any alcohol until eight in the evening and by bedtime he was much restored.

Jack returned the following day and spent much of it working in his room upstairs, which suited Humphrey very well as he wanted to make preparations for the morrow.

By the time Althea and Hector arrived the next day, the table looked splendid. Normally Humphrey couldn't do with tablecloths - they always acquired indelible turmeric or beetroot stains on first use and could never be brought out again. However, for this special occasion he had bought a beautiful white and gold linen one and there were napkins to match. He had never bought Christmas crackers before - one could hardly pull a cracker with oneself, after all - but here they were, also white and gold (and ludicrously expensive). Tall white candles from the cathedral shop stood in the four branch candelabrum in the centre of the table and crystal glasses at each setting sparkled in the candlelight.

Althea and Jack knew each other already, by sight at least. Humphrey had been a little concerned about whether Hector and Jack would get on with each other but he needn't have feared. Jack was much amused by Hector's theatrics and Hector seemed much taken, as Humphrey had been himself, by the easy way Jack conversed with people much older than himself. There was no deference and yet there was respect.

Humphrey served champagne and home-made canapés before taking Althea up to his study to see his corrected proofs. He was really gratified by her approval and she also said that she thought it charming that Jack had done the proof-reading for him.

'He is clearly a gifted boy, darling,' she said.

'I think so,' said Humphrey.

When they came downstairs, Hector and Jack were getting on famously and conversing in Polish.

Of course, thought Humphrey. He had simply never made the connexion that they were of the same nationality.

'You can stop that right now!' said Althea.

'What's the matter?' said Hector.

'Jabbering away in a foreign tongue,' she said. 'How rude! You could have been talking about Humphrey and me for all we know.'

Hector looked quite taken aback but Jack had seen straight through Althea's mock outrage.

'Well, what do you expect?' he said, with a cheeky grin. 'You've hardly arrived and you disappear upstairs with Humphrey. What were we to think? I hope he didn't ravish you.'

'Well, that's for us to know,' said Althea archly, 'and you to find out.'

Humphrey & Jack

'I told you he was a dark horse,' said Jack to Hector.
'Known for it,' said Hector.
Dinner was a triumph. There was smoked salmon with water melon. Then Humphrey produced a beautiful topside of beef. It had been smothered in a mixture of flour and mustard so that it had a gorgeous crust and it was very pink inside. It was accompanied by golden cumulo-nimbus Yorkshire puddings, puffed up to perfection; home-made horseradish sauce; peas, carrots, parsnips and a mound of roasted potatoes, crisp on the outside and fluffy within, and there was a sumptuous gravy, made in the roasting tin. To drink, Humphrey had opened a couple of bottles of Nuits-St Georges. He had surpassed himself. To follow, there were peaches in Grand Marnier and a mini-truckle of Stilton.

Later, with Jack's help, Humphrey cleared the table and withdrew the cloth. He placed fruit and walnuts on the table and then produced the port Jack had given him, decanted ever so slowly into a clear modern decanter.

'Crimson nectar,' said Hector.
'Sublime,' said Althea.
'It has the vivacity of a can-can dancer,' said Jack, savouring it with a profound expression.
'What?' Humphrey cried.
'I know. Wicked, isn't it?' said Jack. 'It actually says that in a review on the net for this very vintage. Look it up if you don't believe me.'

Hector proposed a discussion about who was the most pretentious: the art critic, the music critic, the literary critic or the wine critic. Hector and Althea opted for art critics, Humphrey for literary critics, while Jack, opting for the wine critic, looked up various wine reviews on his phone and came up with example after florid example.

'Oh wait!' he cried. 'This is the dog's ballocks! Listen: "The smooth introduction of an accomplished lover, deeply sensual with a long, multi-orgasmic finish like the coda of a Brahms symphony."'

The others applauded and declared it the winner.

Humphrey & Jack

Humphrey poured himself another glass of the 'crimson nectar' and passed the decanter on. He leaned back and watched his laughing friends.

Not long ago - eighteen months or so - this would have been unthinkable. Back then he had no friends. He had given the occasional dinner for members of the faculty when he was still in post. He had hosted dinners for visiting lecturers and even put them up at the house for a term or so. But he regarded all that as business and he had enjoyed the cooking more than the eating. He had offered studied politeness rather than conviviality.

This was quite different. He felt so proud of Jack and so grateful to him. Not long ago, he would have derided his own feelings as sentimental. Even now, he kept them to himself. This was enough: the glow of the logs in the rarely-lit fire, the sheen of the highly polished table, the chiaroscuro of faces in the candlelight, faces young and old, but all, smiling or laughing, flushed with good wine.

The room, with its heavy brocaded curtains drawn against the December night might be hanging in a boundless void, turning slowly on a meaningless axis. It might have been all there was. It was, for now, all that mattered.

The spell was broken by Althea.

'Christ on a bike! Have you seen the time? I know I try to play at being a Bohemian but it's a quarter to three and my brother's family is descending on us tomorrow at daybreak. Jee-sus! Hector, come and see us at the Quarryman's sometime soon. Humphrey, it has been fabuloso - and Jack, you are an utter darling. I could eat you up.'

Hector rang for a taxi and was promised one in ten minutes. He and Althea lived quite close to each other so it was all convenient. There was the bustle of gathering up belongings and putting on coats and scarves and gloves. Jack moved to start clearing up.

'No. Don't bother,' Humphrey said. 'Leave it. It can all wait until tomorrow. Come and say goodbye to our guests.'

Humphrey & Jack

They stood in the doorway, like a more conventional couple, as their guests walked up the drive, still waving, towards the lights of the taxi.

Humphrey thought perhaps that it ought to be snowing softly.

But life is not like a Dickens novel.

48. Snow

January was a bore. Colour seemed to have ebbed from the world and grey days followed each other monotonously. The remaining great ash at the bottom of the garden stretched out the black tracery of its boughs and branches against flat slate-grey skies. The birds were silent. Jack, back in Durham, was almost silent too.

'Sorry, insanely busy,' was the usual curt message which met Humphrey's enquiries. He tried not to be hurt but he was frustrated nonetheless. Having been rebuked once before for flooding Jack's inbox, he was chary of doing so again.

There was some good news. Humphrey was delighted to hear that his student, Oliver Gothland, had been made a generous offer by Corpus Christi and he took him for a lunch at The Swan with Two Necks by the river, though it made him nostalgic for his visit there with Jack last June. News came too from his publishers that *The Plantagenet Cookbook* would be launched in the summer and they made enquiries about a follow-up. What did they want? *Medieval Household Management? Plantagenet Knitting Patterns?* Humphrey wrote back to say that an Elizabethan cookery book could be possible but he thought that it might have been done already. Really, he just wanted to concentrate on his drawing and painting.

He decided that he ought to give painting in oils another try although as a novice he had deplored the mess. He attempted some small still life paintings and found that he rather liked the mess so long as he could walk away from it and leave it behind in Althea's studio.

Now that Oliver had been offered his place, Humphrey was no longer a member of the college staff and visited only for his evening classes. He rather missed the tutorials but it did occur to him one evening as he was setting up his easel that there was now less chance of his bumping into Mark Kapel. He had taken a visceral dislike to him quite out of proportion to the fact that he was minus a Harrods clock. He thought it might be something to do with jealousy on account of Jack's affection for the younger boy and the thought made him feel somehow dirty.

He had planned to visit Jack again in Durham midway through the Epiphany Term and it was the thought of this excursion that had kept Humphrey going through these bleak, disheartening months. However, at the beginning of the second week in February it began to snow. And it did not stop snowing.

At first, it was beautiful. It began just as Humphrey was going to bed and he sat awhile at his desk watching the huge white flakes falling ceaselessly and silently against the black backdrop of the sky. The next morning the landscape was transformed into a world of dazzling white. The virgin snow lay thick along his terrace and down the lawn and across the open spaces of Alexandra Park. It lay eight inches deep on the garden table as if someone had laid a white mattress there in the night. The garden chairs had acquired white cushions. The sundial stuck out of the snow, its base hidden, and it looked very much like a cake stand, for on it stood an eight-inch-high cake of snow with perfectly perpendicular sides. And still the snow kept falling.

He bathed and dressed and went down to the kitchen for breakfast. From the window, here on the north side of the house, he could see that the vista was much the same. The drive was pristine snow. There was another mattress on top of his car. Nothing moved on Upper Bishop's Lane.

Out of curiosity, he went to the front door and opened it a little: not for long for the air was cruelly cold, but the silence! - the silence was a thing of wonderment. It was so lovely that Humphrey thought he could endure frostbite in order to drink in more of it, but the warmth was leaking out of the house. Humphrey recovered his natural prudence and closed the door.

Humphrey & Jack

Later, looking out through the sitting room window and the park again, Humphrey thought that Nature had framed the view of the garden - the table and the sundial and the fountain down in the park - with such artistry that he had to fetch his sketchbook and do some studies for a landscape in oils which he would work on in the college studio next week.

In the afternoon, the silence and the chastity of the snow were compromised by children. They were down in the park, tobogganing down the slopes or throwing snowballs at each other. It was like a scene from Bruegel. Humphrey couldn't begrudge them their glee though, not too long ago, he might have done. The noise filtered into the house only very faintly. He had no memories of such abandoned rapture, he thought sadly - only of being bullied at Rowntrees, rolled down a steep slope in the woods until accretions of the stuff had turned him into a sort of human snowball. He vaguely remembered sitting on a radiator later, still damp and steaming a little in the fug.

His plan to turn his sketches into a painting had to be delayed. It was to be more than three weeks and the beginning of March before he could get down to the college. It continued to snow for the whole of that first day but more thinly towards evening. The following day it stopped but the temperature fell. It would sink towards minus ten over the next couple of days, the BBC forecast said. The prospect made Humphrey begin to feel rather trapped.

Gradually, Radcester tried to resume its normal business. Gritters were out each night and traffic resumed fairly quickly on Prior Ingham's Road below the park, and even on Burdock Hill. Humphrey was not inclined to go out at all, however. There were reports on the local television news of pile-ups on the major roads around Radcester and Humphrey felt he was in no need of any such adventures. He decided to order supplies online and let the Waitrose driver face the peril of negotiating icy roads.

The one occasion he decided to go out on foot was aborted immediately. He thought he might just try to get to The Seven Stars. It was the nearest boozer and Garth Porter would not be there. It might be tolerable to sit by Cora's open fire with a book and a pint. He managed his own front drive without difficulty and there was a reassuring crunch of snow under foot. The road was a different matter. The snow had been trodden down and was very slippery indeed. Humphrey turned back.

A few days later, the sun shone on Radcester for a whole afternoon and the trees began to drip but it was a false hope. The overnight frost was bitter and the next morning it began to snow again so thickly that the trees at the bottom of the garden were barely visible. The wind rose too and the snow began to drift. It was all too depressing.

The dreariest part of it was that his visit to Jack was out of the question. County Durham was suffering even worse disruption than Radcester. Communities up there had had their electricity cut off and blizzards had completely isolated many households. Stretches of the A1 had been closed off and there were pictures on the news of stranded motorists being dug out of their cars by the emergency services. Some trains were getting through but timetables were haphazard and some journeys were terminating at York.

Upper Bishop's Lane must have been one of the most treacherous streets in town. The villas at the top of the park, Humphrey's and Mrs Bellingham's included, shut off the sun from the south side of the street so that when the thaw eventually came the snow here was the last to melt.

When, after three weeks, there were just a couple of patches of grubby snow left near the top of the lawn, Humphrey suggested to Jack that he might now think of coming up to Durham. It was two days before Jack replied and when he did he simply wrote: 'Probably not worth it. Only three weeks to the end of term. Incredibly busy.'

Once again Humphrey's heart plunged into his socks. Why did he allow himself to get his hopes up so high? What did he expect of a relationship when there was such a disparity in age? There's no fool like an old fool, he told himself.

Humphrey & Jack

All the same, he could not help writing: 'I wish you would reply more promptly, Jack. I do understand that your life is packed but it makes it difficult for me to make any plans of my own if you leave me in limbo.'

His finger hesitated over the return key which would send the message. He didn't want it to seem as though he were whining. He knew that Jack had a tendency to clam up if pushed. But press the key he did.

It was, of course, utter tosh. He didn't have any plans. The art classes and sessions at the Quarryman's had resumed but there was nothing Humphrey couldn't drop in an instant. He was surprised that Jack replied immediately.

'Sorry - but Humphrey, don't get stroppy. I want to get a first. I want to get a blue in squash. I've got a girlfriend. I'm busy. What don't you get? Besides, I don't look at Facebook much any more. It's been taken over by old people. Lol.'

'Like me, I suppose,' Humphrey wrote. 'But, Jack, it's the only means of communication I have with you when you're away.'

'I know. That's why I check it out from time to time.' (That was something at least). 'Anyway, cheer up. I'll be back in Radcester at some point over Easter.'

'At some point?'

'Yeah, I've got an international squash tournament in Rotterdam just after the end of term and then I'm staying with a college friend in Edinburgh. They have this incredible Georgian house in Charlotte Square. Can't wait. I'll be back for a few days though.'

'Is that all?'

'Probably. Hey, what's the urgency? There'll be plenty of other times.'

Will there? Humphrey thought but did not write: Jack, you do not know how the decades shrink to years and months and sometime soon all that will be left will be hours and minutes and then the dark and the incinerator. But all he wrote was:

'OK, just let me know when.'

'Sure.'

Humphrey went downstairs to the kitchen and mixed a strong Martini, though it was only three o'clock in the afternoon. His disappointment was acute. He thought he might be jealous. Not of the girlfriend. That would be despicable. Not even of the anonymous friend. Humphrey was jealous of Time.

Once upon a time Jack had needed his attention and had almost wooed him. He had been of use. Now the balance of power, which had never been very much in Humphrey's favour, was entirely in Jack's. Humphrey found he didn't like this dependency. It was inevitable, of course; he had always known it, he supposed. But he didn't like it.

Besides, he hadn't been feeling well of late. There had been days when he felt nauseous and he lost his, normally very healthy, appetite. He thought that there was a bit of swelling in his legs, though he couldn't be sure. One morning he had caught his hip on the corner of his desk. He took off his belt and pulled down the top of his trousers to inspect the bruise in the full length mirror in 'Jack's' bathroom. It was huge and angry and seemed out of proportion to the slight knock he had sustained.

He ought perhaps to go and see Doctor Bell, he thought. On the other hand, if it was nothing, he would feel embarrassed. If it was serious, he didn't want to know. It would sort itself out.

In April, Jack came to stay for three days.

49. Mark

The three days flashed by like a view seen from a train: a sunlit landscape - then a rush of dark shrubs and a tunnel. Jack was full of Edinburgh: the dour, brooding castle; the Royal Mile; Holyrood Palace (where he had particularly enjoyed the private apartments where Mary Queen of Scots had been forced to watch the murder of her friend, David Rizzio); Calton Hill; Jenners Department store; the trams; the Scott Memorial and Princes

Humphrey & Jack

Street, and the elegant Georgian New Town which had been his home for the last few weeks.

'Rizzio was stabbed fifty-six times, you know,' Jack said with relish. 'My God, it was cold up there. Then we went to Leith and saw the Royal Yacht, Britannia. It's tiny. You'd never believe it. And we came back on an open-topped bus. That was bloody silly. I thought my nose and fingers would fall off, it was so bloody cold. And one night, Archie's dad treated us to dinner at the Café Royale. It was amazing. It had dazzling white tablecloths and those globe lights that make you think of Paris. Well, I've never been to Paris, but you know, like that Manet painting of a barmaid. Have you ever had Cullen skink, Humphrey? It's incredible. It's just a soup made from smoked haddock and potatoes but it's sublime.

'Oh, and Archie's house. My God, have they got some money. His dad's a hedge fund manager or something. Room after room full of antiques. They have a real Holbein and a couple of Picassos and a grand piano and a grand staircase and a grand dining room and grand everything. And I once thought your house was posh...'

Despite the slight pang at Jack's customary lack of tact, Humphrey was rather pleased. Any feeling of estrangement he had felt during the term evaporated all of a sudden. Here was Jack spilling out his excitement in a jumble, like a small boy reporting his adventures to his dad. That's what it was. Humphrey was someone to return to, a base, a hub. It didn't matter for how long, nor how briefly, nor about the spaces in between. Hector had been right: the friendship was solidly grounded.

'And I got you this,' Jack said, holding up a carrier bag and snatching it back as Humphrey reached for it. 'I was going to get you a tartan tie. There are gift shops all along Princes Street claiming to identify your family tartan but they didn't even have Icke on their lists. Anyway, here you are.'

In the bag were a jar of Scottish heather honey and a tartan scarf.

'I was going to buy you some Edinburgh rock,' Jack said. 'But I thought your teeth might not be up to it.'

Humphrey & Jack

Humphrey feigned a blow at him and Jack ducked.

'Anyway, I know you like honey,' Jack said.

'I do,' Humphrey said. 'Jack, this scarf is beautiful. It must have cost a bomb. It's cashmere, isn't it?'

'Certainly is. Black Watch tartan. I thought it was the coolest.'

'It's incredibly soft. Thank you.'

'Yeah well…'

They made the most of the three days. They had pancakes with honey. They went to the Delhi Durbar where Jack was greeted like an old friend. They even went to the cinema to see a film Jack wanted to see. Humphrey hadn't been to the pictures since he was in his first year at university. He had been on his own to see *The Prime of Miss Jean Brodie* at the Roxy. He had been enjoying it immensely when a man put his hand on his knee. Humphrey moved along the row, leaving a vacant seat between them. He wasn't traumatised by this assault because he didn't really know why the man had wanted to touch his leg, but he didn't like it.

When he told Jack about it, Jack just laughed.

'Don't you worry,' Jack said. 'You'll be safe enough with me.'

Apart from Jack's company it was not at all an agreeable experience. The film was some spy caper, not a genre Humphrey particularly liked: it was full of chases, violence, fast cars, gadgets and well-endowed young women. Of course, Humphrey had never encountered surround-sound in the cinema before and he found it very alarming. More than once he was tempted to look behind him to see what was going on. The volume was an agony to him.

Deplorable too were the giant buckets of popcorn being wolfed down by teenagers and adults and the huge beakers of sticky drinks. Crisp packets crackled everywhere. Worst of all was the fact that the youngsters talked and laughed quite loudly throughout the film. It was as if everything had to have a commentary, no matter how obvious or trite.

'Did you enjoy that?' Jack asked.

'Yes, very exciting,' Humphrey lied.

Humphrey & Jack

When the time came, Humphrey offered to drive him back and once again Jack refused. He had little luggage as his room had not been required during the vacation. Humphrey said he would see him off and, despite Jack's protests, he drove him down to Radcester Central Station.

It had been raining and now the sun had come out. The rails gleamed but water dripped lugubriously from gaps in the steel and glass canopy of the Victorian booking hall.

'I'll see you before too long, I hope,' Humphrey said.

'Yeah, sure,' Jack said. 'Definitely. But about this term…'

'I know what you're going to say,' Humphrey said. 'This term is exam term and if I came up to visit halfway through, I would be a nuisance and a distraction.'

'Well, yes, I wouldn't have put it like that but that's about it.'

'But I will see you in the summer? I mean, I know you're going back-packing and all that but you will come and stay for part of the vacation at least?'

'Ah, I was going to ask you about that? Have you got somewhere I can store my stuff? I'll have to clear everything out of my room for the long vacation and then there's the summer and next year I'm in Poland, aren't I?'

'Well, yes, of course,' Humphrey said. 'There's the loft. Bags of room up there. Only we'll need help to get it up there. I doubt if I can manage the ladder any more.'

'Why not?'

'Knees.'

'Oh yeah. Right.'

'And you want me to come and pick you up with your gear at the end of term, yes?'

'If it's not too much trouble.'

'Of course, it's no trouble,' said Humphrey. 'And you'll stay for a bit?'

Humphrey & Jack

'Well, we're off almost immediately,' Jack said, 'but we get back about three weeks before I'm due to fly to Kraków. I'll come and stay then. Promise.'

'Excellent. Here's your train. Do try and keep in touch.'

'I'll try.'

Jack went aboard without turning back and the train slid out of the station with a doleful blast on the horn before entering the tunnel at the end.

After this visit, Humphrey felt better equipped to deal with the long absence. He was perfectly sure that Jack would make little effort to be a better correspondent but Humphrey felt he would now find it easier to bear it. He also had the beginnings of a new project in mind.

He knew that there were plenty of books on *courtoisie* written in the late medieval period, codes of etiquette, precedence and even table manners. Would there perhaps be a market for a scholarly compendium, illustrated by the author? It would be the third in his series. He began his research with a thirteenth-century Latin verse manual called *Urbanus Magnus*, or *The Civilised Man*, by one Daniel Beccles.

There he learnt that if you felt like belching at table - and there appeared to be no interdiction against this - you should remember to look at the ceiling. If you wished to keep something secret, you would be unwise to tell your wife. It was considered rude to mount your horse in the hall and the most frightful bad manners to attack your enemy whilst he was squatting to defecate. There was much more of this kind of thing at the populist end, right up to more sophisticated and comprehensive manuals such as Castiglione's *Book of the Courtier* at the beginning of the Sixteenth Century. He couldn't help thinking that Jack might be amused by this at some time in the future.

There might be a bit of a problem with the illustrations, Humphrey thought. He didn't see how he could avoid having human figures in them. When he mentioned this to Althea in the Quarryman's she again extended an invitation to Humphrey to attend her Friday evening life classes.

Humphrey & Jack

'I don't think there is much call for nudity in medieval art, is there?' said Humphrey, panicked by the idea of naked models into being obtuse.

'Well, there's Adam and Eve, of course,' she said.

'And the damned,' said Hector. 'The damned are always naked.'

And thus, accidentally, Hector gave Humphrey a clue to a fitting style. The figures of medieval manuscripts were flat and two-dimensional. Very often they were quite disproportionate. If he were to use this kind of idiom, he needn't worry about anatomy and the distracting curves of human flesh. It was Hector too who suggested that Humphrey put away his oils - with which he had never been entirely happy - and his beloved pastels and chalk, and use poster paints. With these he could emulate the intense colours of medieval drapery, especially blue, and he could also employ gold.

So Humphrey began to spend hours underground in the University Library researching old books of manners and devouring medieval iconography. Later, though it was still a little chilly, he would have lunch in the garden, wearing two jumpers, and then spend the afternoon co-ordinating notes, making drafts and attempting preliminary sketches.

This year, it was as if he could see spring happening. First the hawthorn came into leaf and then a silver birch at the bottom of the garden. Next sycamores and maples. Then there was plum and pear blossom. A tree that was quite naked in the morning would be covered with tiny leaves in the afternoon. Now the oaks, and last of all, the mighty ash at the bottom of the garden. The trees sported different shades of green, not the uniform green of late summer, and these greens themselves shifted in shade as the breeze lifted the branches and the strengthening spring sunshine threaded through them.

His blackbird of two years before returned and a cheeky robin would sometimes land on the very table where Humphrey was working. He would watch, his head cocked to one side, as if to say: 'What are you up to now, Humphrey?'

Humphrey & Jack

There was no cat to disturb the birds now, he thought, and Aristotle's shadowy ghost padded across his conscience stirring up remorse, though he knew he was not guilty.

Mrs Bellingham had definitely gone too. Jack had reconnoitred the house one night on his latest visit and said that the rooms were quite empty of furniture. Humphrey was afraid that her house might be turned into flats for young families with squalling children, or worse, be occupied by squatters. No-one could afford these town villas any more.

But, apart from that, everything in the garden truly was lovely again. Humphrey made progress with his etiquette project with great enjoyment and, this time, did not pine for Jack.

'I'm growing up at last,' he said to himself.

Early June was dull and windy and drove him indoors for a couple of weeks but just before the summer solstice there was a heatwave. Days of flawless blue skies succeeded each other and the huge hypericum bush by the stone steps to the lawn blazed into blossom, its clustering flowers like a dense constellation of yellow stars. It was time to collect Jack.

It took several journeys from Jack's room to load the car and though the Volvo was capacious, Humphrey began to worry about the suspension. Jack had acquired a great many books and even though most of them were paperbacks the back of the car, from which Humphrey had removed the seats, was sitting pretty low. In addition, Jack had taken up weight-lifting and was full of the jargon of the pursuit. On his rare appearances on Facebook these days, he was given to putting down or 'owning' a friend with the comment: 'Bro, do you even lift?'

So Humphrey found himself coming down the steps to the car carrying a bell weight and a large jar of protein shake. Jack's packing had been haphazard and inefficient so they had to make more journeys than was probably necessary, especially since Jack would only trust Humphrey with random individual items.

'Sorry about this,' Jack said. 'Archie was supposed to help but he went back to Edinburgh this morning. Are you sure you can store all this?'

Humphrey & Jack

'Easily,' Humphrey said. 'The loft is vast. Mind you I haven't been up there in years, but don't worry.'

'Crazy that I've got all this stuff and yet I'll be travelling with just one backpack.'

'We'll see about shipping what you need on to Poland.'

'That'll cost the earth,' Jack said.

'Probably,' Humphrey said. 'Now what about a late lunch before we hit the road?'

Back in Radcester they first unloaded Jack's stuff into the hallway.

'I told you that you would need to get some help to get this up into the loft,' said Humphrey. 'Let me show you.' He led Jack up to the first floor, pulled a cord hanging from the ceiling which released the trapdoor downwards. Built into the trap door was a telescopic ladder. 'I haven't been able to get up there for two or three years now. Go up and have a look.'

Jack pulled down the ladder, climbed up and merely said: 'Wow! There's masses of room. Right, I'm off to recruit some help. I'll only be about half an hour.'

Humphrey occupied himself in the kitchen, little thinking what the results of the recruitment might be, when, more than an hour and a half later, he heard the key in the front door and animated conversation. Only then did it fall into place that Jack's companion was Mark.

Humphrey could scarcely disguise his indignation though he found it impossible to say anything about it.

'Sorry to be so long,' said Jack. 'I needed to have a chat with Mark's mum. She's been very good to me. Right, let's start with the heavy stuff first.'

They began by carrying the luggage bit by bit from the hallway to the first floor landing where eventually Mark began to pass bags and parcels up the ladder to Jack in the loft.

Humphrey & Jack

Humphrey decided that he wanted to absent himself from all this and took a book into the garden where he simmered in silence and could not concentrate.

After about an hour Jack appeared at the garden door with Mark at his shoulder.

'We're done,' he said.

'Did you work out how to close the hatch?' Humphrey said without looking up from his book.

'Sure,' said Jack, 'easy-peasy, lemon-squeezy.'

'Splendid!' said Humphrey. 'Thanks for your help, Mark. I suppose you'll be off now, will you?'

'Yes, sure,' said Mark, sounding a little confused.

'Jack will show you out,' said Humphrey.

He could hear them chatting on the doorstep. Minutes later Jack came back into the garden and sat down at the table where Humphrey was reading.

'What was that about?' he said.

'What was what about?' said Humphrey.

'That was rude. It was good of him to do that. Could you not at least have offered him some coffee or some fruit juice or something instead of just dismissing him like that?'

'Whatever,' said Humphrey to Jack's astonishment. 'I don't need to explain myself in my own house, Jack.'

'You don't like him very much do you?'

'I'm afraid I don't,' said Humphrey.

'Why not?'

Because he was an aider and abettor in the despoliation of my garden and because he is a purloiner of clocks, Humphrey thought, but wasn't going to explain.

'Oh, just because…' was all he would say.

Humphrey & Jack

50. Missing

Humphrey said no more and Jack did not raise the matter again. Jack's stay was going to be very brief and this was no time for friction. He planned to meet Archie at Heathrow in two day's time. Later they would take a cheap flight to Amsterdam and from there would continue on a tour of Europe. They had bought Interrail student passes but had not planned their journey in any detail.

Humphrey, who rarely took a holiday, preferred to have everything planned in advance down to the last rail ticket and restaurant reservation. All the same he could see the excitement in tracking across a continent without a route map. Jack thought that they might take in Prague and Budapest and certainly Rome and maybe Avignon - it would depend on how long the money held out - but beyond that everything was purposely vague.

One thing was certain, however. Jack stipulated very precisely the date of their return and would spend three weeks with Humphrey as promised, before setting off for Poland.

In the end Humphrey drove Jack to Heathrow, setting off very early in the morning. At the airport they met Archie, whom Humphrey found to be pleasantly urbane, and he bought the two boys lunch before they were called to their gate.

Humphrey booked into a functional hotel in Hounslow and travelled back to Radcester the next morning. The previous day he had sent Jack up into the loft to mark carefully any luggage that he wanted forwarded to Poland during the summer holiday. Humphrey would contact a baggage shipping firm and and have it sent on to the address in Kraków that Jack had given him. It was indeed extremely expensive but Humphrey did not want to see Jack begin his studies with only the contents of a rucksack as his worldly goods.

Humphrey & Jack

The long summer stretched ahead and Humphrey decided that the only way to deal with it was to be stoical and to get on with his book of etiquette. The time wasn't without its entertainments. He was invited to dinner at Hector's home where he found himself, to his total bewilderment, to be monopolised by Hector's two young daughters. There was also a delightful alfresco dinner in Althea's garden where the food and wine were delicious but the wasps a torment.

During the Easter term, Jack's correspondence via Facebook Messenger had been rare and brief. Humphrey was quite happy to put this down to the exigencies of revision and examinations. Jack had warned him that it would probably not be possible to make much contact over the summer either. It would either be expensive or impossible. Humphrey wasn't entirely convinced but resigned himself to what Jack called 'radio silence for the duration.'

So it was that he was surprised to receive not one but three glossy postcards from different European venues. The first was of Cologne Cathedral and said, in Jack's round handwriting: 'Drinking Kölsch in front of this awesome cathedral. When does your book come out?' Humphrey smiled at the unthinking pointlessness of a question he had no practical means of answering. Underneath, in a bold masculine hand, Humphrey read: 'Thanks for the lunch - Jack is behaving himself (up to a point) - Archie.' Now, that explains things, thought Humphrey. Jack had never been known to use snail mail and the idea of his buying stamps in a foreign country was out of the question. Archie must have encouraged Jack to write whilst buying his own stamps and cards. Blessings on the youth!

The second card showed the winged lion of St Mark on his granite pillar by the Doge's Palace in Venice. Jack had somehow managed to get it wet and the writing had run. It was a miracle that the Italian and British post offices had managed to get it to its destination. All Humphrey could read was: 'See the lion on a stick. Jack loves his lion. His lion is called Ro…' and '…rich gits in Florian's…'

Humphrey & Jack

The third card was rather crumpled but legible. It was of the papal palace in Avignon and read: 'Have you been here Humphrey? Every medievalist should. It is amazeballs!!! Went to a *son et lumière* inside on Sunday. Totally blew my tiny mind. Like a really good acid trip. Wish you'd seen it. Picnic by the Rhône later. Returning via Tours and Paris. See you soon. J.'

The reference to drugs alarmed Humphrey for a second until he reassured himself that, the only time the subject had come up, Jack had been very snooty about people who needed 'synthetic substitutes for an imagination.' Humphrey hoped this was still true.

As for his book, his publishers had set his launch date during the second week of August when, by happy accident, Jack was due to return. Humphrey, quite out of character (which made it all the more fun) began hatching plans for a garden party to celebrate the two events. He would invite Althea and Hector and the students from his art class and colleagues from the college and Radcester University. He would invite Cora from The Seven Stars - he had no grudge with her - and Norman Retford - who would not come. He would not, of course, invite Garth Porter. He would ask Jack to invite Archie, even though it was quite a distance to travel from Edinburgh, and any other friends he might choose to invite, but not Mark.

He began to become quite excited about it. He would have Mr Fitzwilliam manicure the lawn to cricket square perfection. He would let Mrs Price loose with her vacuum cleaner to persecute every last atom of dust in the house. He would have Waitrose do the catering so that he was free to talk to his guests. He bought three cases of Taittinger champagne and a case of Chinon for anyone who might prefer a red. There would also be Pimms, for those who liked that sort of thing - Humphrey didn't - and iced tea for teetotallers and recovering alcoholics, should there be any such among Humphrey's acquaintance.

He went to collect Jack, this time at Manchester Airport. Archie had taken a different flight, from Charles de Gaulle directly to Edinburgh. Jack was shattered and a bit grubby and slept in the car most of the way back to Radcester but by the evening he was his sprightly self.

Humphrey made sure the following days were filled with entertainments. Jack was free to come and go as ever but they spent a good deal of time together. Humphrey was only too aware that these were the End Times before a year's separation. What Jack thought was, as ever, inaccessible.

The weather was so wonderful that they were able to eat alfresco most evenings. They spent a couple of hysterically boozy nights in the Quarryman's. They took a trip in *The Radcester Queen*, a two-tier pleasure boat. Alighting at The Water-Pipit, two miles downriver, they had lunch.

One hot day, they took a day trip to Lincoln. The gothic towers of the cathedral were visible from twenty miles away as they came in from the north. It was cool inside and Jack declared it breathtaking. He sat on the floor of the nave taking photographs with his phone. Later, in the beautiful decagonal chapter house, they tagged on to a guided group for a while and overheard that in 1327 Edward III had held a parliament there.

'Whoa! that's badass. My main man, Eddie!' said Jack rather too loudly as heads turned and Humphrey winced. 'Respect!'

They even made a visit to The Seven Stars, which, in the end, was to prove rather ill-advised. Ostensibly, this was to invite Cora, and Norman, if he were there, to the book launch party in his garden.

Norman was indeed there, reading a newspaper.

'I'll have to see,' he said when Humphrey issued his invitation. He stood up, folded his paper and finished his pint.

'I was just leaving anyway,' he said, and left.

'He won't come,' Cora said.

They stood at the bar and ordered beers.

'But I will,' Cora said.

They helped her with her crossword. Secondhand Sue and Flake watched them and muttered conspiratorially.

'So this is Jack, is it?' said Cora. 'We've heard a lot about you.'

Humphrey & Jack

'Oh, dear,' said Jack.

'All very complimentary,' Cora said.

'Oh, dear,' said Jack.

Together they finished the crossword very rapidly.

'Blimey, that would normally take me all afternoon. Well, you are clever boys and no mistake,' Cora said.

The garden party was a *succès fou*. A large box arrived some days beforehand containing copies of *The Plantagenet Cookbook*. It was beautifully done and Humphrey was very proud of himself and especially so since Jack declared the illustrations mouthwatering. The author and illustrator sat under his sunshade with piles of his books before him and signed copies for his guests, who formed a queue along the terrace. It made Humphrey feel like 'the real thing'.

Jack, meanwhile, played the host beautifully, topping up glasses and directing people to the buffet which the caterers had set up under the deep shade of a sycamore. He was totally at ease amongst these people, many of whom he had never met before. Cora, looking very elegant in a cherry coloured dress and a broad white hat, monopolised him a little.

'I built that fence, you know,' he overheard Jack saying to her.

'And it is the most beautiful fence I have ever seen, dear,' she replied.

Good God, Humphrey thought, she's flirting with him.

Shortly afterwards, he saw him talking animatedly to Mrs Price. She was dressed in a rather unbecoming lilac, like Victorian half-mourning, and she was laughing.

Later, when the signing was done and the shadows were lengthening across the lawn, Humphrey moved from group to group, chatting to his guests and inwardly marvelling at himself. An evening like this would have been unthinkable before he met Jack. I have no small talk, he would have said. And little wonder. His life had been so bloodless that he had had nothing to talk about.

Humphrey & Jack

Although the invitation had read six-thirty to eight-thirty, many guests still wanted to linger. As the trees were darkening and the sky turned a deepening violet, Humphrey brought out a couple of bottles of port. Mindful of a previous occasion, Humphrey whispered to Jack that he should pop into the downstairs bathroom, where Humphrey had left out a bottle of insect repellent.

It was not until midnight, under a vast shining moon, that the last stragglers left. Among them was a rather tiddly Mrs Price.

'Don't bother about tidying up the plates and glasses and everything now,' she said. 'I'll do it tomorrow, isn't it? Goodnight, Dr Icke. Goodnight, Jack.'

'Goodnight, Myfanwy,'

'I don't believe it,' he said to Jack when all were gone. 'Old Mrs Grouch has a soul. You've charmed her, you devil!'

'I have that effect on women,' Jack said.

'I'd noticed.'

'Mrs Price is a cougar at heart.'

'How do you mean?'

'A cougar is an older woman who preys on handsome young boys.'

Humphrey spluttered with laughter.

As they were going in, he said: 'She's not really called Myfanwy, is she?'

'I dunno,' Jack said.

***

But there was no help for it. The idyll was soon over and summer's lease all too quickly spent. The time came for Jack to leave. The language department at Durham had arranged a KLM flight from Leeds to Kraków and Humphrey drove him there to catch it.

Humphrey & Jack

'Just don't say anything,' Jack said at the terminal. 'It's not even for a full year. I'll be back before you know it. Just go now. It's easier. And thanks for everything.'

Awkwardly they shook hands and Humphrey nodded dumbly, not risking speech. He watched Jack walk towards security and then couldn't help blurting out: 'Stay in touch!'

Jack didn't turn but just raised his hand.

And, of course, he didn't stay in touch. There was the occasional message, usually when he wanted Humphrey to do something for him back home. And at Christmas, there was an electronic greetings card in Humphrey's inbox. It said: *Wesołych Świąt i Szczęśliwego Nowego Roku* which was not difficult to translate given that it featured dancing reindeer choreographed by Santa himself, although it was odd to see him in a mitre rather than a bobble hat. Jack had simply written: 'Love it here. Won't want to come home, but don't worry, I will.'

Humphrey managed to sustain his stoicism to a degree. He had much to occupy him. The cookbook was doing well and Humphrey was invited to do readings and signings in July at prestigious bookshops in London and York. He found the prospect rather alarming though he rather enjoyed an appearance in a Saturday morning chat show on BBC Radio Radcester. For much of the time his friend's absence was little more than a dull ache.

In March, Jack sent a message to say that he would be returning to the UK in mid June and that he would be backpacking around Poland during the Easter holiday. 'I might be a good way away from any good wifi signal so don't expect a running commentary.' Humphrey could have laughed out loud. The six or so messages he had received since Christmas could hardly be described as a commentary. But it was good to know roughly when he would return.

A week or so after Easter Humphrey noticed an image on Facebook which registered instantly. He recognised the blond hair and almond shaped eyes of Jack's friend, Mark. The post was being shared widely. It read:

Humphrey & Jack

Boy, 15, missing for five days

Police are appealing for help tracing a Radcester teenager who has been missing for five days.

Marek Kapel (also known as Mark) was last seen near Radcester Station on April 11 at around 8 am.

Radcestershire Police say they are worried for his welfare.

They said in a statement: 'He has had contact with his mother over the phone on one occasion since, and there was an unconfirmed sighting of him at St Pancras Station in London later on the same day, but we want to know he is safe.

'Marek is white, around five foot five with blond hair. He was last seen wearing grey jeans, a green and white tracksuit top, and white Converse trainers. He was carrying a large navy blue rucksack.'

There followed a number and log reference for contacting the police.

51. Police

Humphrey's first, and overwhelming, response was one of guilt. He knew perfectly well that he was innocent of anything to do with this boy's disappearance and yet he could not escape that kind of creeping guilt that seizes you whenever you see a police car in the rear view mirror or when you're going through customs, even though you know that your bags contain nothing untoward. You are very conscious of the expression on your face, feeling that it would be fatal to look worried and equally fatal to look cheerful.

The advertisement kept cropping up on Facebook and also on Twitter to which Humphrey had recently subscribed. Humphrey genuinely felt for the boy's mother. Neither Mark nor Jack had ever mentioned a father and Humphrey had randomly assumed that Mark had been brought up by a single mother. It must be the most devastating thing imaginable to have your child reported missing, Humphrey thought.

The police narrative was mysterious. The boy had phoned his mother to say what? - that he was safe and that she shouldn't worry? - or was it to say that he had been kidnapped and that his safety was at risk if she did not pay up a specified amount of money?

But that didn't stack up really, did it? It would make no sense to kidnap a boy from a background of relative poverty. And what about the sightings? They suggested that the boy had taken a train to London. The worst possible scenario was that he had fallen into the hands of drug dealers or even sexual abusers. Much as he actively disliked the boy, Humphrey couldn't bear to imagine how he would feel if Jack were reported missing in the same way. That intolerable thought prompted him to share the post both on Facebook and on Twitter. It might do some good.

He could not help thinking that Jack might have some inkling of what was happening. He and Mark were very close after all and Jack might have some idea how his mind worked. But Humphrey had not heard a word from Jack for well over a fortnight now.

That evening, Mark's mother appeared on the local television news appealing for information about her missing son. She was obviously going through mental torture but carried herself with great dignity. Humphrey was surprised at how very young she looked. After she had spoken a senior officer from the force said that officers had been drafted in from neighbouring forces and that the search would be relentless. He said that the police were pursuing several lines of enquiry and that the St Pancras sighting was only one of them. He said that there was some evidence to suggest that the boy might still be in the local area and that anyone with any information whatsoever should come forward, no matter how trivial it might seem. Door-to-door enquiries were taking place in the area around the boy's home and elsewhere.

Again Humphrey had the insidious feeling of guilt. Was there anything he knew that he ought to be telling the police? He rehearsed in his mind the two occasions on which Mark had visited the house; there was the occasion when he had cleaned and gutted the fish and then stayed for lunch and there was the occasion when he had helped Jack to put his baggage in the loft. There was nothing there that could possibly be of any help to the inquiry and yet he still felt vaguely responsible somehow. There was the question of the stolen clock, of course, but that would have been of no interest to the police in the current perturbing circumstances.

On the morning following the television interview, Humphrey was not unduly alarmed to find two police officers on his doorstep. The one who seemed to be taking the lead was male and appeared to be of southeast Asian background. Humphrey thought at first he was a little plump until he realised that it was the yellow quilted jacket whose pockets were stuffed with gadgets which gave him his deceptive contours. His companion was a female officer who had a sharp pointed nose and high coloured cheeks which made her look rather horsey.

'Good morning, sir. Sorry to disturb you. I am Constable Michael Tuan and this is Constable Jenny Veitch. We are conducting door-to-door enquiries about a missing person.'

He held out a copy of the photograph that had appeared in the media.

'Can I ask you if you've seen this boy?'

'No I haven't,' said Humphrey. 'Not recently at any rate - but I do know him.'

Humphrey noted a brief flicker of eye contact between the two officers.

'Can I ask how you come to know him?' said Constable Veitch.

Humphrey & Jack

'Well, he's been here a couple of times. He's a friend of another young friend of mine. Well, I say friend…he's a friend now. I suppose he started off as more of a protégé.'

'A prodigy?' said Constable Tuan.

'No, protégé. I first got to know him through the police reparation scheme and subsequently he became a kind of student of mine and later a friend.'

'This is Marek Kapel we're talking about is it?' said Constable Tuan.

'Oh no, no, no,' said Humphrey. 'No, I'm talking about Jack Lis, Mark's friend. Look, I'm just confusing everything, aren't I? Why don't you come in and I'll try to make it clearer. Would you like a coffee, perhaps?'

The two officers followed Humphrey to the kitchen, having wiped their boots very thoroughly on the doormat. Humphrey made coffee and explained in detail his relationship with Jack and the two occasions on which Mark had infiltrated the house. He still saw no reason to mention the theft of the clock.

The officers took notes and once or twice Humphrey caught them exchanging a look.

'So you're a teacher then, are you?' said Constable Tuan.

'I taught at the university for many years,' Humphrey said, 'but I am now thankfully retired. As I said, I did give Jack some academic encouragement and a little help in finding his university place. I also did a little teaching down at the college.'

'But you didn't teach Marek Kapel?' said Constable Veitch.

'No. I saw him about the college occasionally but I didn't teach him. He was only ever here as a guest of Jack's. I can't honestly say that I liked him very much, to be honest.'

'And why was that then?' said Constable Tuan.

'Oh, I don't know - just an instinctive feeling, I suppose.'

'And when he was here, is this where you had lunch, in the kitchen?'

'Yes,' said Humphrey.

Humphrey & Jack

'Did he go into any other rooms, that you can remember?'

'No, I don't think so. I can't think why he would. He went to the downstairs loo to wash his hands after dealing with the fish but I don't think he went anywhere else. I can show you round if you like.'

Much later Humphrey would consider this invitation to have been naive. But, for the moment, feeling that he had nothing to hide, Humphrey considered that he was doing all he possibly could to help the police with their enquiries.

'That would be very helpful, sir,' said Constable Veitch.

Humphrey showed them the downstairs rooms, including the sitting-room and his own bedroom.

'And you're sure Marek never had cause to go upstairs?' said Constable Tuan.

'No, why would he?' said Humphrey. 'As you see, there's a bathroom down here.'

'So, when he helped your friend - Jack was it? - with his luggage, they didn't go upstairs?' said Constable Tuan.

'Oh yes, of course they did,' said Humphrey. 'Sorry about that. I wasn't thinking. Come up. I'll show you,' and he led the way upstairs.

He showed them his study.

'Lovely view,' said Constable Veitch. They crossed the landing.

'And this is Jack's room, or at least it is when he stays. It's got the same view as the study and there is an ensuite bathroom here which also connects with another guest room beyond.'

'Can we see?'

'Yes, yes, of course. Just go through the bathroom.'

'Any reason the bed's been stripped? Anyone sleep here recently?' said Constable Veitch.

Humphrey laughed a little nervously.

'No, not at all. In fact, the room's been unused so long, I thought it was time the bedding went into the wash and the room was aired.'

'And where is the bedding now?'

Humphrey & Jack

'I couldn't say. You would have to ask my cleaning lady, Mrs Price.'

'We might have to do that,' said Veitch. 'If you could let us have her details.'

And I really thought you were the good cop, Humphrey thought.

'If you come back to the study I'll write them down for you.'

'And does Jack often stay?' said Constable Tuan as Humphrey wrote Mrs Price's address and phone number on a card.

'Well it varies,' said Humphrey. 'His father is in prison, you see, and his mother is dead, so this has become a kind of second home for him, whenever he needs it. He's at university in Poland this year though.'

'And has Marek ever stayed here overnight?' said ConstableTuan.

'No,' said Humphrey, 'certainly not! I've already told you. And on the second occasion I didn't even want him here. Jack said he would find a friend to help. I didn't realise that he would bring Mark around.'

Humphrey was beginning to feel less at ease.

'What's in the other room? said Constable Veitch.

'Nothing really. I don't have a use for it except for lumber. I had plans of turning it into a library, and I might yet do that. I still have books in storage from my time as a lecturer.'

The police officers had a quick look around and the three of them came back out onto the landing.

'And what's up there? said Constable Tuan pointing up to the loft hatch.

'Just the loft,' said Humphrey.

'Do you mind if we have a look?'

'Not at all. If you just pull that cord…that's it!'

The hatch opened and the telescopic steps appeared. Constable Tuan began to climb up.

'There's a light switch on the floor to your right,' said Humphrey as Constable Tuan disappeared.

It was quite a while before he came down again.

'Very roomy,' he said with a rather longer look at his colleague. 'Well, I think that will be all for now... unless?'

Constable Veitch shook her head.

'You've been very helpful,' she said.

When they were gone Humphrey began to feel very uncomfortable. They were obviously suspicious. Humphrey particularly disliked Tuan's question about whether Mark had ever stayed the night. Humphrey had not said anything to suggest that that might be the case. It was as if they were trying to catch him out.

It was the customs business again. Humphrey knew that he had broken no law but that didn't make him feel any better. As usual when under pressure he had recourse to his drinks cupboard. A very large scotch helped steady his metabolism.

That evening he turned on the local television news to see if there had been any developments. The missing boy had become big news and his story was at the top of the bulletin. Clips from his mother's appeal of the previous day were shown again and a police spokesman said that it was now believed that the theory of the boy's absconding to London had been a false lead. Enquiries were now focusing on the area around Alexandra Park and on the estate which led down to the River Rad. Police divers had been at work searching the river since early light. The story ended with the usual appeal for further information.

As he was breakfasting the following morning, the same two officers were at Humphrey's door.

'Are we addressing Mr Humphrey Icke?' said Tuan.

'Well yes, I believe I am indeed the same person I was yesterday,' said Humphrey, immediately feeling that sarcasm was probably not apposite. 'Actually, it's *Doctor* Icke.'

'We've come to ask you a couple of quick further questions, if you don't mind,' said the male officer. 'Can you confirm that you are the owner of these premises.'

'I can,' said Humphrey.

Humphrey & Jack

'We've been taking statements from your neighbours,' the officer continued, 'but there appears to be no one living next door to the left. Can you give us any information as to where the owner might be?'

'I can't,' said Humphrey. 'She's called Mrs Bellingham and the house became vacant some time ago when the estate agents' notices first appeared. I imagine the estate agents could track her down for you.'

'Thank you. We've already actioned that. Can you tell me if she was still in residence on the occasions when Marek Kapel stayed at your house?'

'On the first occasion when he came to stay for lunch, yes, I'm almost certain that she was. On the second occasion definitely not. She was gone by then. But just a minute. I have already told you that the boy never stayed here. Please don't put words into my mouth.'

Constable Veitch said: 'Dr Icke, have you seen Marek Kapel since the occasion when he helped with the luggage?'

'I have not,' said Humphrey.

'How would you describe his character?' Constable Veitch continued.

'Well, I wouldn't,' said Humphrey. 'Or rather I couldn't. I've spent very little time in his company, you understand, and he never said very much. He was polite and affable enough when he did speak but I must say I felt that there was something untrustworthy about him.'

'Why do you say that?'

'Oh, I don't know. Just something about him. I couldn't put my finger on it. Just instinct, really. I'm afraid that's not much use to you is it?'

'Not really.'

'Just on instinct,' said Tuan, 'would you say that he was the sort of boy to just disappear?'

'I couldn't possibly say.'

'Not even on instinct ?'

'No,' said Humphrey. 'How long has he been missing now?'

'Seven days,' said Constable Veitch.

Humphrey & Jack

Tuan handed Humphrey a sheet of paper.

'Would you just give this a quick look over for review,' he said, 'and sign it if you agree.'

Humphrey gave it a quick scan read. The handwriting was atrocious. He scribbled his signature. Veitch handed Humphrey a card and said: 'You can reach us on this number if you think of anything else.' They left him in a state of some agitation.

Once again Humphrey reached for the scotch.

52. The Gentlemen of the Press

Humphrey told no one about these unwelcome visitations, not even Hector. The thing was that he felt obscurely humiliated. He didn't feel he could bear Hector's kindness just yet. He did, however, leave a message for Jack which said: 'URGENT! please get in touch'. Humphrey knew that Jack objected to capital letters in text messages. He said that it was just like shouting and very bad manners. Humphrey just hoped that, on this occasion at least, capital letters would jolt Jack into replying. Wherever he was.

The afternoon would bring Humphrey further cause for upset. To calm himself he thought he would make some bread. Kneading it would be therapeutic. In fact he would not just knead the dough; he would belt the living daylights out of it. When he checked his pantry, he found that he had no yeast and was low on strong flour. There were other things he needed to stock up on too, so it seemed a trip to Waitrose was in order. But when he went to the car, he found that there was a gang of journalists standing at his gate.

'Mr Icke, this way!' one of them called and as Humphrey turned, a flash went off in his face, followed by further rapid flashes.

'What do you know about the missing boy, Mr Icke?' another voice called out.

'Do you know where Marek Kapel is?' cried another.

'Have you got something to hide, Mr Icke?'

Humphrey & Jack

Humphrey tried to remain composed although his heart was beating fast. He walked up to the gate and said:

'Gentlemen, I don't know who or what your source is, but you have been misinformed. Your questions suggest that you have been fed a deliberate distortion of what I may or may not have said to the police. Now, whether the police are responsible for that distortion or whether you are, I have nothing more to say. And that is that.'

Humphrey returned to his car and drove out into Upper Bishop's Lane to a barrage of flashlights. He lingered in the supermarket for much longer than it took to buy ingredients he needed for the bread. He also bought some good beef and some brown ale and other ingredients he would need for a *Boeuf Flammande*. Cooking would keep his mind off things.

The gaggle of hacks was still there when he returned and one of them had the audacity to come through the gate as he was parking and take a flash picture of him through the car window.

'This is intolerable,' said Humphrey. 'You are trespassing. Get off my property immediately or you will find out very soon that I still have rights. And I am Doctor Icke, not Mister.'

When he got inside Humphrey found that he was trembling. Whilst he unpacked his shopping he could see that the pack of journalists was still there. He pulled down the blind and turned on the work light over the kitchen counter, poured himself a large glass of red wine and set about mixing the bread dough.

It was hard not to worry. He felt, not that the police were trying to trap him, but that they were inviting him to misrepresent himself. He began to feel that the best thing that he could do would be to omit nothing. And though he couldn't for the life of him think what relevance the theft of his clock might have on the case, he thought he had better let the police know about this lest it come back to bite him later.

After he had subjected the dough to violent kneading and set it to prove, he poured another glass of wine and rang the number on the card he had been given. He was told he would probably receive another visit and he said that was absolutely fine except that he was now sure that he had nothing to add to what he had said already.

That evening, he served up his beef in beer along with the bread, which had turned out excellently. Though it was delicious, he pushed the plate away after finishing just half of the serving. His appetite had been poor of late, no doubt a result of stress. He watched the television news.

The story had gone beyond the regional bulletin and was now featured in the national news. There was an interview with the Chief Constable where it was clear that the press were piling on the pressure. One of the rat pack asked why, after more than a week, no progress had been made. The Chief Constable said that, on the contrary, a great deal of progress had been made and that an arrest, or arrests, were imminent. This led to a fusillade of questions but the Chief Constable gathered his papers and said that he had no further comments 'at this moment in time', but that he would 'report on further developments going forward in due course'. And he left the platform.

Humphrey snorted. 'At this moment in time' - what a silly piece of jargon. What else would a moment appear in other than time? Soup? And what about 'further developments going forward in due course'? What a hideous cluster of semantic redundancy. Still he was glad that the investigation was making progress. He thought of the continuing agony which Mark's mother must be suffering. He imagined her dreading an announcement which began with: 'The body of a white male, aged around 15 years has been found, etc...' Under the circumstances, his account of the stolen clock must seem pretty small beer to the police.

Humphrey listened to the last act of *Der fliegende Holländer* and then washed up. When he went outside to take some rubbish to the bins, he was pleased to see that the parasitical reporters and cameramen had gone. The whole business had been very unsettling and Humphrey felt tired and a little bloated. He went to bed early but had some difficulty in getting to sleep because his skin felt itchy, especially in those places he couldn't reach to scratch. He tossed and turned until the digital clock flicked to 2:07 and soon after that he must have drifted off.

He woke from a terrifying dream where he was being washed out to sea by a tsunami. He was being thrown about by gigantic waves in which he could discern smashed-up articles of his furniture. Books whirled by close enough for him to read their spines. Several times, his stolen clock rushed past his line of vision.

He awoke suddenly and realised that the crashing of the waves was actually a banging at the street door. A voice was shouting:

'Dr Icke! Dr Icke! It's the police. We need your help.'

His eyes gummy with sleep and his hair all over the place, Humphrey pulled on a robe and stumbled to the door. When he opened it two plainclothes officers were standing there holding out their warrants.

'Dr Humphrey Icke?'

'Yes.'

'You are under arrest on suspicion of the abduction of Marek Kapel. We also have a warrant to search the property.'

There followed the statutory caution, familiar to Humphrey from episodes of the Morse dramas.

Humphrey felt a sense of vulnerability and bewilderment which had characterised much of his childhood. One of the men pushed past him and began examining the hallway and the rooms off it. The other said brusquely: 'Get dressed.'

Humphrey stood and gawped as others invaded his house: there were uniformed officers and officers in what looked like white boiler suits. There was a sniffer dog with his handler.

'I'm sorry,' said Humphrey. 'Can you please tell me what is going on here?'

'Everything will be explained to you at the station. Now will you please get dressed?'

'May I just make a phone call?'

'No, sir, you can do that at the station.'

Humphrey & Jack

A little later, dressed and handcuffed, as he was bundled into the waiting police car he could see that the press were back. Flashlights flared in the chilly dark. It occurred to him to think that at least Mrs Bellingham wasn't around to witness his mortification. Only when the car was speeding through the empty streets did Humphrey look at his watch. It was still only four in the morning.

At the police station, the desk sergeant took his watch from him along with the contents of his pockets which were itemised and Humphrey was made to sign a docket. His belongings were placed in plastic bags and labelled. He was taken to an adjoining room.

'Right, Humphrey, first off we are going to take your picture,' said a cheerful uniformed officer. 'Now, if you just sit there and face straight ahead. That's right.'

And full-face and profile mugshots were taken. This was humiliating enough although Humphrey wasn't entirely certain whether the unwarranted use of his Christian name wasn't an even bigger affront.

Next he was led to another tiny room where his fingerprints were taken. He expected a rather messy job with an ink pad but instead, starting with his thumb, his digits were scanned by a kind of miniature photocopier.

In yet another room a man in a white coat wearing disposable medical gloves was waiting for him.

'You're not going to do an intimate probe on me, are you?' said Humphrey.

Humphrey saw a brief smile hover on the man's lips. He did not look unkind.

'No, no, no, I'm just going to take a DNA sample. It's just a question of taking a little swab from the inside of your cheek.'

'I wish someone could tell me why all this is necessary,' Humphrey muttered to himself. 'I've told the police everything I know more than once.'

Humphrey & Jack

'No use complaining to me, mate,' said the DNA man. 'I'm only doing me job.'

Humphrey was now allowed to make his phone call. The handset was on a wall and it was difficult to hear since the station was such a noisy place. He had to cup the mouthpiece and hold the receiver very close to his ear. A uniformed officer stood close by. The only people he could think of to call were Althea and Hector. Althea, he calculated, would be high on the emotional support, whilst Hector would be more likely to have some idea as to what he might actually do. His instinct was correct.

When Humphrey had outlined his predicament, Hector said: 'Hang on in there, old scout, they can't start interviewing you until you have a solicitor, unless you waive the right, of course. Don't do that and don't accept a police solicitor. I'll find you one and get him or her there before you can say Oswaldtwistle. Leave it to me.'

In a bleak interview room Humphrey was cautioned again.

'You do not have to say anything,' said one of the two detectives, 'but it may harm your defence if you do not mention, when questioned, something you later rely on in court. Do you understand?'

Humphrey said he did but that he would prefer not to say anything until his solicitor arrived.

Humphrey was now led to a cell. It was stark and bare and smelt vile. There was a bed which was little more than a shelf with a filthy stained mattress and a single blanket rolled up at one end.

A uniformed officer offered him a choice of cottage pie or fish pie.

'Why?' said Humphrey who had lost all sense of time.

'Late breakfast? Early lunch? Whatever,' said the officer.

'But I'm not really hungry,' said Humphrey.

'I'd go for it if I were you. Once your solicitor arrives and the interview starts, it might be a good while before you get a chance to eat again.'

'I see,' said Humphrey. 'I'll have the cottage pie then.'

'Good choice,' said the constable. 'The fish pie's terrible.'

Humphrey & Jack

A quarter of an hour later, the microwaved meal appeared. It had been slopped onto a paper plate and there was a plastic fork to eat it with. It was insipid but Humphrey found he was hungry after all and finished it greedily.

When the officer came to take away his plate, he said: 'Your brief's coming up from London apparently.'

'How long will he be?' said Humphrey.

'I've no idea, have I?' said the constable. 'How long is a piece of string?'

The cell doors banged shut and Humphrey was left to his own devices. The time passed agonisingly slowly. He had no watch and there was no clock in the cell. There was only a long thin rectangle of light in the window high in the cell. The day was overcast and Humphrey could get no inkling of the time through changes in the light. Although the invasion of his house had taken place so early in the morning and although he felt exhausted, there was no question of him sleeping on that narrow bench. He had the absurd feeling that if he allowed himself to sleep at all he would wake up as a beetle.

The noise was not conducive to sleep either. There was boorish shouting everywhere, the occasional female scream, a clanging of metal doors and the constant cacophony of telephones ringing. Someone very close to his cell, probably high on alcohol or drugs, was singing tunelessly at the top of his voice. Other voices, in surround-sound, as it were, were yelling at him to stop.

There was nothing to read and he tried to pass the time by thinking about his book on medieval etiquette and by mentally composing a letter to Jack telling him about his travails and misfortunes in a light-hearted way.

At last there was a jangling of keys and the door was opened. A well-groomed young man in a striped charcoal suit came in and shook Humphrey by the hand. No introductions were needed. Humphrey recognised his star pupil at the university from long ago, the one who had

Humphrey & Jack

bought him the Humphrey Bogart mug. Tom Sinclair had taken a first, and gone on to study law in London. He had clearly made a great success of it.

'My dear Humphrey,' he said. 'I'm so sorry to see you like this. I came as quickly as I could. I saw you on the television and I was already about to pack a bag when Hector telephoned. He has given me an outline of what is going on from what you told him. I also come armed with the jabbering speculation of the gentlemen of the press which I look forward to rubbishing.

'Take heart, Humphrey. I am itching for a fight. It seems to me that the case, such as it is, is preposterous. There is a strict limit to the time that they can keep you here without charging you, but don't worry. They will try to unnerve you but keep your cool. Answer directly and keep your answers simple.

'And just keep your chin up.

'The bottom line is that I am not going anywhere until we get you out of this place.'

53. Interview 1

'Oh dear, I'm not in the papers, am I?' said Humphrey.

'I'm afraid you are, old boy, and on the telly too. You are an ogre and a weirdo and public enemy number one. But let's not worry about the media morons just now, shall we? I have plans for them. But all in due course, Humphrey. All in due course.'

Tom rapped on the inside of the door and when it was opened he said: 'We are ready, I believe.'

They were escorted to an interview room which, though spartan in appearance, felt over-heated. The walls had been painted an institutionalised mushroom colour till halfway up and then a kind of dirty cream. There was an industrial carpet underfoot which had seen long service. There was a table in the middle of the room with some kind of recording device at one end. A wall light was angled on to the table. Humphrey and

Humphrey & Jack

Tom were directed to sit on one side of the table and two detectives sat on the other.

One of the detectives switched on the recording machine and said: 'Interview commencing at 17:09 hours, April 20. I am Detective Sergeant David Bennett of the Major Crime Investigation Unit and I am accompanied by Detective Constable Jeffrey Amis, who is also attached to the unit. Facing me is Dr Humphrey Icke. How would you like us to address you, as Dr Icke or as Humphrey?'

'I am quite indifferent,' said Humphrey.

'Very well, I shall call you Humphrey,' said DS Bennett. 'It makes life easier, especially as I may have to ask you some fairly intimate questions later.'

DS Bennett continued to address the recording machine: 'With Dr Icke is his solicitor. Could I ask you to identify yourself?'

Tom, who had been making notes from the start on a yellow legal notepad with a very expensive-looking fountain pen, said: 'Certainly. My name is Tom Sinclair of Galloway Sinclair Kent, West Hampstead, London.'

DS Bennett turned now to Humphrey.

DS Bennett: Do you know Marek Kapel?
Humphrey: I do.
DS Bennett: I would like you to tell us how you came to know Marek?
Humphrey: He was brought to my house by my protégé, Jack Lis.
DS Bennett: Would you explain, please, what you mean by the term protégé?
Humphrey: You know what a mentor is?
DS Bennett: Of course.
Humphrey: Well, a mentor is to a protégé as a teacher is to a pupil.
DC Amis: Why did Jack bring Marek to your house?

Humphrey & Jack

Humphrey: Well, Jack was in the habit of coming to my house on Saturday lunchtimes. On this particular Saturday, he said that he wouldn't be coming because he had planned to go fishing with Mark, or Marek, if you prefer. I said that this was not a problem and that he should bring Mark along with him if he wished.

DC Amis: And when was this?

Humphrey: I couldn't be sure exactly without consulting my diary but I would say it was just under two years ago. Will that do?

DC Amis: For the moment, thank you. And what was your first impression of Marek?

Humphrey: I was rather shocked at how young he was, to be honest. I'd imagined him to be the same age as Jack.

DC Amis: And how old did he seem to you?

Humphrey: I'd say about thirteen.

DC Amis: What else?

Humphrey: Well, nothing very much at first because he was almost completely mute. He seemed pleasant enough but when he did speak it was only in monosyllables. And then he did something very strange. He thrust a couple of fish at me, much as a very small child will offer a gift. You know, at arm's length. He'd caught them – I can't remember what kind they were – and I said I would descale them and gut them and pop them in the freezer. I'd already prepared lunch for the boys, you see.

DC Amis: I see. Go on.

Humphrey: Well, then he said he would do it himself. And jolly good he was at it too. I think Jack told me he was doing catering at college.

DC Amis: Then what happened?

Humphrey: And then we had lunch. I can't remember what it was. Jack and I chatted away as usual but again Mark said next to nothing. I didn't pay much attention. Oh I forgot. Before we sat down to eat, the boys went off to wash their hands. Jack came back first and Mark a little later.

DS Bennett: And what did Marek look like? Can you remember?

Humphrey & Jack

Humphrey: What was he wearing, do you mean? I can't remember. Jeans and some sort of top, I suppose. Like any kid his age.

DS Bennett: No, I mean what did he look like?

Humphrey: I remember thinking that he was a very good-looking boy.

DS Bennett: Attractive?

Humphrey: That's not what I said. I said that he was a very good-looking boy. There's a difference.

[Humphrey turned to look at Tom but he was taking notes.]

DC Amis: So, tell me, what did you do after you'd eaten?

Humphrey: Nothing. The boys were keen to get off to the cinema. They asked if they could leave their fishing things at my house but they would keep their bags with them. Jack said he would pick up the rods later. I said that was fine. It was only when they'd gone that I noticed the clock was missing.

DC Amis: What clock was this?

Humphrey: It was a present from my colleagues at the University when I retired. It had a certain amount of sentimental value. It was from Harrods and it had a silver gilt frame and black hands. Art Deco style. I noticed it wasn't on the hall table just after the boys had left. I can only surmise that when Mark had washed his hands, he purloined the clock and stashed it away in his bag in the porch.

DS Bennett: Did you report this to the police at the time?

Humphrey: No, I did not.

DS Bennett: Can you tell us why not?

Humphrey: I didn't want to trouble the police with such a minor incident.

DS Bennett: But it wasn't such a minor matter to you, was it, surely?

Humphrey: I've already said that the clock was of sentimental value but I don't think it was very valuable in itself.

Humphrey & Jack

DS Bennett: The fact is that you wanted to protect the boy. Is that it?

Humphrey: No, it's probably more likely that I wanted to spare Jack any fuss. Mark was his friend after all.

DS Bennett: Did it not cross your mind that Jack might be involved himself?

Humphrey: Yes, it did. But then I thought that it would be completely out of character. And I still think that. Look, I told the police all this when I telephoned. Why do I have to keep repeating things? Why are things not joined up?

DC Amis: We need to make sure, in everybody's interests, that we have the facts right.

DS Bennett: Why did you leave it so long before telling us about this clock?

Humphrey: I've told you I didn't want any fuss.

DS Bennett: Isn't it the case that you're trying to protect the boy? Aren't you trying to keep him out of trouble? You took a shine to him. That's the fact of the matter, isn't it, Humphrey?

Tom Sinclair: You don't have to answer that.

Humphrey: But I want to answer that. No, that isn't the fact of the matter, DS Bennett. The fact of the matter is that I was very angry. I felt that I had been used. The fact of the matter is that I took a profound dislike to the boy.

DS Bennett: Enough to want to hurt him?

Humphrey: Certainly not enough to want to hurt him. I am not a violent man.

DC Amis: You say you don't remember what you cooked for lunch?

Humphrey: That is correct.

DC Amis: Can you remember whether you served alcohol during this meal?

Humphrey: Yes, I can. I opened a 2009 St Amour.

DC Amis: It was good, was it?

Humphrey: I'd say it was exceptional.

DC Amis: Did you buy it locally?

Humphrey: No, I brought it back from France.

DC Amis: It must have been good for you to remember it nearly two years later. The sort of wine you'd save for a special occasion, would you say?

Humphrey: Possibly. What are you trying to suggest, Detective Constable?

DS Bennett: Did you regard your lunch with this boy as a special occasion?

Humphrey: Which boy?

DS Bennett: Either boy.

Humphrey: I am trying to educate Jack in all sorts of things, good food and wine included.

DC Amis: Did you give Marek any wine on that occasion?

Humphrey: Just a very small glass. But it was okay. His mother knew that he was at my house and Jack said that he was allowed alcohol at home.

DC Amis: Jack said?

Humphrey: Yes. Jack said…

DC Amis: Jack said? Not Marek? Are you sure about that?

Humphrey: That's what I said, yes.

DC Amis: So you're saying you gave an underage boy alcohol believing, on Jack's say-so, that Marek's mother knew where he was and had given permission?

Humphrey: Effectively, yes.

DS Bennett: But you see, Humphrey, I have a problem with that. My problem is this: Marek's mother didn't know where he was that lunchtime.

Humphrey: But how can you possibly know that? Who told you that?

DS Bennett: Marek's mother did.

[Pause]

Humphrey & Jack

Humphrey: I see.

DC Amis: Tell me, why did you give a thirteen-year-old boy alcohol, Humphrey? Was it to butter him up? Get him to like you? Make him want to come back sometime?

Humphrey: Certainly not.

DS Bennett: I want us to move on now to Marek's second visit to your house. Are you happy to talk to us about that?

Humphrey: I am.

DS Bennett: This was on June the eighteenth. Is that correct?

Humphrey: Yes.

DS Bennett: Can you be sure?

Humphrey: I can because Jack was due to depart on holiday two days later and we had been making arrangements for some time.

DS Bennett: I understand you invited Marek to help you move some baggage from the hall up to the loft. Is that correct?

Humphrey: You understand incorrectly. I did not invite Mark to help with the removal. Jack did. It was clear that he would need some assistance. I could not be of much help because of arthritis in my knees and it is painful for me to go up and down the stairs, let alone up into the loft. Jack said that he would enlist the help of a friend. I little thought it would be Mark.

DS Bennett: You were pleased when he arrived, weren't you?

Humphrey: I was pleased that Jack had found some assistance. I was not pleased that it was Mark.

DC Amis: Did you watch the boys whilst they carried out the removal?

Humphrey: I did not. I thought it best to keep completely out of the way. In fact, if I remember rightly, I sat in the garden and read.

DC Amis: Did you encourage the boys to stay afterwards? Did you offer them a meal or any other refreshment?

Humphrey: I did not. Or rather not to Mark. I was anxious that he leave the house as soon as possible.

Humphrey & Jack

DS Bennett: Which of the boys actually went up into the loft?

Humphrey: I believe it was Mark.

DS Bennett: You believe it was Mark?

Humphrey: It was Mark.

DS Bennett: How do you know that if you were out in the garden?

Humphrey: Because the doors were open and I could hear them shouting to each other. Besides, it was the more sensible modus operandi. Jack was the stronger of the two. Jack went up later at my insistence to make sure that everything was stowed away neatly.

DS Bennett: How long would you say Marek was up there?

Humphrey: I couldn't possibly say. About an hour perhaps?

DS Bennett: And Marek was in the loft the whole time?

Humphrey: I really don't know. As I said, I was in the garden.

DS Bennett: Would you say the job took longer or less time than you thought it would? Or would you say the time was about right?

Humphrey: Good heavens, I don't know! I'm not a professor of ergonomics. It took longer than I'd hoped, shall we say?

DC Amis: Were you aware that Marek had a really good look around while he was up there? His fingerprints were everywhere.

Humphrey: Well, I suppose he was exploring. Young boys like exploring. Especially attics and cellars and caves and tunnels.

DC Amis: You know that from experience of young boys, do you?

Humphrey: I do not have any experience of young boys. But you've only got to read Enid Blyton's *Famous Five* books to corroborate my point.

DC Amis: Read a lot of Enid Blyton, have you?

Tom Sinclair: Can we get on?

Humphrey: I hope your search of my house has not left a mess.

DS Bennett: Of course another explanation as to why there were so many of Marek's fingerprints in your attic is that he had been there before.

Humphrey: Certainly not.

DS Bennett: Or since?

Humphrey: No.

Humphrey & Jack

DS Bennett: We have had reports of a constant stream of young boys entering your house.

Humphrey: I can't imagine who told you this. It is not true.

DS Bennett: Are you in the habit of inviting young boys to your house?

Humphrey: Quite categorically, no.

DC Amis: Was Marek Kapel a frequent visitor to your house?

Humphrey: I have already told you, no.

DC Amis: Was Jack Lis a frequent visitor to your house?

Humphrey: Yes.

DC Amis: Did he come and go as he pleased?

Humphrey: Yes, and with my blessing.

DC Amis: Does Jack possess keys to your property?

Humphrey: Indeed he does. I had them cut for him.

DC Amis: Jack could have introduced Marek into your property without your being aware, could he not?

Humphrey: Well, yes, he could have, I suppose, but why would he? I'm sorry, gentlemen. I'm trying to be cooperative but I'm very tired. I don't really see what you want of me.

Tom Sinclair: I'm inclined to agree. I really can't see where this line of inquiry is going.

DS Bennett: Very well. I'm going to be very precise. Humphrey, you abducted Marek Kapel, didn't you?

Humphrey: I did not.

DS Bennett: You know where Marek is, don't you?

Humphrey: No.

DS Bennett: Why don't you just tell us where he is, Humphrey. Just think of his mother. You're capable of compassion, aren't you? You let him make a phone call on the first day, didn't you? That showed some good in you. There's no point in holding him now, Humphrey. Help us put that poor woman's mind at rest. Tell us where he is.

Humphrey & Jack

> Humphrey: I've told you and I've told you and I've told you: I don't know anything about this business. I have no idea where he is. I would help you if I could but I really have no idea.

> [DS Bennett stared fixedly into Humphrey's eyes. Humphrey did not flinch.]

The interview went on and on, covering ground that had already been covered, going back to what Humphrey had said to the uniformed officers at his house and returning to what he had already told the detectives several times over. At last DS Bennett said: 'The time is 20:08 hours. We are suspending the interview at this time.'

53. Interview 2

Humphrey tried to sleep a little but his dozing was dream-wracked. There was no narrative, just crowded, leering faces floating in at him. The hard bed seemed to press up through the thin mattress and assault every bone and joint in his body. And all the time there was inescapable noise.

He had no idea how much time had passed when Tom Sinclair was let into his cell.

'You're doing very well, Humphrey,' he said. 'Don't let them get to you. As far as I can see, they've got nothing on you. Just hearsay and speculation. They'll try to invite you to contradict yourself. Don't rise to it. Just answer briefly and to the point. Don't evade anything but don't help them out by giving expansive answers either. They can't keep you more than twenty-four hours without charging you, but they can keep you for a further twelve if they apply to a magistrate for an extension.

'And don't worry. I'm staying with you.'

'Did they raid my home?' said Humphrey.

'They did. They had a warrant, but don't worry about that now. You've enough on your plate.

Humphrey & Jack

Soon they were taken to the same interview room and the tape was started. For a long time they covered ground that Humphrey believed had been amply covered before, sometimes phrased differently, but often put to him in exactly the same words. Humphrey remembered Tom's counsel and hid his impatience.

Eventually DS Bennett moved into a new phase.

DS Bennett: I want to talk to you now about your friendship with your protégé, Jack. Is that how you pronounce it - protégé?

Humphrey: Yes, that is correct.

DS Bennett: Thank you. Tell us how you first met?

Humphrey: You must have all that on record. We met through a programme of restorative justice organised by PCSO Thompson.

DS Bennett: Ah, but you see there's a difficulty with that. PCSO Thompson went far beyond his brief in allowing Jack to build a fence for you. What the scheme is supposed to offer in lieu of prosecution is some sort of community project, agreed with the victim, not one recommended by the victim. PCSO Thompson is no longer operating from this police station. So let's begin the story afresh, shall we? How did you first meet Jack Lis?

Humphrey explained carefully how, two years before, Jack and his gang disturbed Humphrey regularly with their loud music; how Humphrey had complained to the police; how in revenge the boys had thrown litter from the park all over Humphrey's lawn, and how the PCSO had agreed that, in reparation, Jack should build a fence between Humphrey's property and Mrs Bellingham's.

DC Amis: Why particularly did you want a fence built? Wasn't there already one there?

Humphrey: I wanted a taller one.

DC Amis: Why was that?

Humphrey & Jack

Humphrey: To be honest, Mrs Bellingham and I didn't always see eye to eye. I wanted a bit more privacy. I also wanted to stop her cat coming into my garden and defecating in my flowerbeds. There was a gap in the fence that she refused to repair.

DC Amis: You didn't see 'eye to eye'? Wouldn't it be fairer to say that you were having a running feud with Mrs Bellingham?

Humphrey: Yes, you could say that that's more accurate.

DS Bennett: We may come back to that later. Tell us about the first time you invited Jack into the house.

Humphrey: Well, in the first instance, I had no intention of inviting him into the house. Why would I? Up till now I had only found him particularly offensive. However, I was in my study one day and I noticed through the window that a storm was brewing up. I thought I'd better call Jack in before he got drenched. However, I was too late. By the time I got down to the garden door, he was soaked to the skin.

DS Bennett: So you took him upstairs and asked him to take his clothes off?

Humphrey: No, I did not, DS Bennett. I told him to take off his clothes in the downstairs bathroom and put on a bathrobe. Then I told him to go upstairs whilst I put his clothes into the washing machine on the drying cycle.

DS Bennett: Why did you tell him to go upstairs?

Humphrey: Because I didn't want him in a damp bathrobe in my sitting room. You must remember, that as far as I was concerned at the time, he was a disagreeable felon. And I didn't want him in the kitchen because there's a clear view of it from the road.

DS Bennett: You were ashamed of having a half-naked boy in the house?

Humphrey: Not a bit of it. I simply did not want there to be grounds for any misinterpretation. My neighbour is a very nosy woman, DS Bennett.

DS Bennett: To the extent of peering through your kitchen window?

Humphrey & Jack

Humphrey: I wouldn't have put it past her. Anyway I'd been working in my study. I wanted to go back there.

DC Amis: You made the boy coffee?

Humphrey: I did.

DC Amis: Why?

DS Bennett: You wanted to keep the boy with you? You wanted to begin a relationship? Do you know what grooming is, Humphrey?

Humphrey: Well, if you mean…

DS Bennett: I don't mean haircuts.

Humphrey: I know precisely what you mean. No. I was not grooming the boy. I was later to groom him academically. And by grooming here, I mean 'nurturing'. Let's have that clearly understood.

DS Bennett: Why did you offer him coffee?

Humphrey: Because it was a civilised thing to do. Because I wanted something to do while his clothes were drying. Because I'm not very good at conversation, or at least, I wasn't then, and I was trying to avoid it.

DC Amis: Wasn't it a little odd to leave him in your study? It seems very trusting under the circumstances.

Humphrey: The thought did cross my mind.

DC Amis: What happened when he went back upstairs?

Humphrey: He was watching the thunderstorm at the window. I joined him. It seems we both like thunderstorms. Then I went downstairs to check if his clothes were dry and when I came back he was reading one of my books. Look, I may not have things in exactly the right order. We're talking about two years ago, don't forget.

DC Amis: What was the book?

Humphrey: It was an illustrated medieval history. He was looking at a chapter about Poland in the Middle Ages. And that's how our friendship began. You see I am a medievalist and this intrigued me. I saw signs of a good intellect in him and I began to mentor him. Eventually he got into Durham University. I'm not saying he wasn't capable of doing this on his own but things were going wrong for him, especially at home. He was full of anger. I offered him a refuge. And he's not been one of your customers since, has he?

DS Bennett: Let's not rush things, shall we? Jack was more to you than just a student, wasn't he?

Humphrey: Yes, he quickly became a friend.

DS Bennett: A secret friend.

Humphrey: Not especially, no.

DS Bennett: So why did you tell Mrs Bellingham that he was working for the council?

Humphrey laughed.

Humphrey: I didn't. Jack did.

DS Bennett: And you thought it appropriate to collude with a teenager in mocking an elderly neighbour?

Humphrey: It's not a criminal offence, is it? And yes, I thought it quite appropriate: her nosying and interfering and busy-bodying was tantamount to harassment, which *is* an offence I believe?

Humphrey felt Tom's hand on his wrist for a moment and he nodded in acknowledgement.

DC Amis: What do you mean by harassment, Humphrey?

Humphrey: She was always watching us, coming and going, watching us from her upstairs bedroom when we ate outside. She even came round to the house pretending she was looking for her cat. It was so obvious. She just wanted to know if Jack was there.

DS Bennett: And she saw him at the top of the stairs dressed only in a bathrobe, didn't she?

Humphrey: Did she? Perhaps he had just had a bath. I've already explained to you that my bedroom and bathroom are on the ground floor.

Humphrey & Jack

Unexpectedly, a uniformed officer came into the room and took DS Bennett on one side and whispered something to him. Abruptly, DS Bennett suspended the interview and the detectives left the room.

'What's going on?' said Humphrey.

'Not sure. The clock is ticking,' Tom said. 'They may be going to apply to a magistrate for extension of custody which means you would have to appear in court. In theory, they could apply to keep you for ninety-six hours but given how flimsy their so-called evidence is, they'll be lucky to keep you for another twelve.'

Soon, the detectives returned, the tape was started and the questioning resumed.

DC Amis: can we go back to talking about your relationship with Jack?

Humphrey: Of course.

DS Bennett: Did you not think that there was anything odd about the relationship? Were you not concerned about what other people might think?

Humphrey: No. What do you mean by 'odd'?

DS Bennett: Unusual? Strange? Weird? Queer?

Humphrey: Unusual, certainly. I dare even say surprising. But so what? The opinions of other people don't interest me much. Apart from a few friends.

DS Bennett: Your friends in The Seven Stars, for example? The Four Evangelists?

That sounded silly coming from a police officer. But who had been talking, Humphrey wondered. Cora? Surely not. Garth Porter? Possibly. Second-hand Sue? Not unlikely.

Humphrey: Well, since you seem to know about all these people: Hector Podowski approved of my attempts to help the boy; Norman Retford was, I think, indifferent but he is pretty insipid anyway; Garth Porter was against it but he is a contrarian and a bag of wind and a hypocrite to boot. Anyway, at the time, I didn't have many friends.

DC Amis: You said you had keys to the property cut for him? Is that correct?

Humphrey: It is.

DC Amis: With respect wasn't that a bit naive, especially when you knew that the boy was known to the police?

Humphrey: That would be fair enough but it was also the point. I wanted Jack to feel trusted. I just had an instinct that he never trusted anybody because nobody had ever trusted him. It was a risk I was prepared to take. I also wanted him to feel that he could come and go as he pleased.

DC Amis: It wasn't some kind of reward for something Jack had done for you, was it?

Humphrey: What kind of thing?

DC Amis: I don't know. Anything. Some kind of favour?

Humphrey: No, it wasn't. I meant it to signify a rite of passage. When I was young you'd get the key of the door when you were twenty-one.

DC Amis: But Jack wasn't twenty-one, was he?

Humphrey: Thank you. I am aware that the age of majority hasn't been twenty-one for some time now. Jack had just become eighteen.

DC Amis: What is the age difference between you and Jack, Humphrey?

Humphrey: Forty-seven years.

DC Amis: Forty-seven years?

Humphrey: Yes.

[Pause]

DS Bennett: Tell me, when did Jack start staying overnight at your house?

Humphrey & Jack

Humphrey: Perhaps you'd better ask Mrs Bellingham. She seems to have kept you remarkably well-informed about my private life.

DS Bennett: But I'm asking you, Humphrey. When did Jack start staying overnight at your house?

Humphrey: He arrived at my house one evening badly beaten up. I couldn't turn him away, could I?

DS Bennett: And who had beaten him up? Did he tell you?

Humphrey: Yes, he did. It was his father.

DS Bennett: You treated his injuries, yes?

Humphrey: I did.

DS Bennett: Were they serious?

Humphrey: Not life threatening but he was a mess. There were cuts which I thought needed stitches.

DS Bennett: Why didn't you take him to A & E?

Humphrey: Because he refused to go.

DS Bennett: He told you he'd been assaulted. Why was it not reported to the police?

Humphrey: Because Jack said he didn't want any fuss. I think he was trying to protect his father who was in enough trouble already. He was probably wondering what would happen to him if his father went down.

DS Bennett: I think you wanted to keep your relationship a secret. I think you wanted to create a closer bond between you.

Humphrey: That's a very unpleasant thing to say.

DC Amis: You suggested he stay the night.

Humphrey: I did. In my view I was offering him a refuge. I couldn't send him back to his violent father.

DC Amis: Where did he sleep?

Humphrey: In the guest bedroom.

DC Amis: And is that close to your bedroom?

Humphrey: In a sense yes. It's immediately above. And it has an en-suite bathroom, as I showed the officers who came to my house. He had total privacy, if that's what you're getting at.

Humphrey & Jack

DS Bennett: Did you visit Jack that night?

Humphrey: No.

DS Bennett: Did he visit you?

Humphrey: No.

DC Amis: He stayed with you often after that, didn't he?

Humphrey: He did. When his father was sent to prison it seemed sensible. It gave him a base where he could be safe and continue his studies peacefully. When he went off to University, the house he had been living in with his father was repossessed. Technically, he had nowhere to live. It seemed sensible for him to come to me. And he came to stay during vacations.

DS Bennett: Where is Jack now, Humphrey?

Humphrey: I don't know.

DS Bennett: Come on, Humphrey. You're such good friends aren't you?

Humphrey: He was never a good correspondent. I haven't heard from him for a while. I know that he's in Poland and that he's backpacking around the country during the Easter vacation.

DC Amis: How do you usually communicate?

Humphrey: Through Facebook Messenger.

DC Amis: And when did you last hear from him?

Humphrey: I'm not sure. About a fortnight ago? Ten days ago?

DS Bennett: About the time Marek went missing?

Humphrey: Coincidentally, yes, I suppose so.

DS Bennett: I'm going to suggest that Jack isn't in Poland. I'm going to suggest he's back in England and I think you know where he is. And I think you know where Marek is.

Humphrey: That's nonsense.

DS Bennett: The only reason Jack has not been reported as missing is because he's an adult. Are you aware that Jack has not only failed to communicate with you but that he has not communicated with anybody since Marek went missing? What does that suggest to you?

Humphrey & Jack

Humphrey: It suggests to me that you are attempting to implicate me in a *cum hoc ergo propter hoc* logical fallacy.

DS Bennett: For the benefit of those of us who have not had the privilege of an expensive education, I'm going to have to ask you to explain that.

Humphrey: It means that you're mistaking correlation for causation. In other words, because two things happened at the same time, it doesn't mean that one was the cause of the other. Mark has gone missing and I am sorry about that, even though I didn't like the boy. Jack is incommunicado because that's how he wants things. In fact, he suggested as much the last time we were in contact. The two things may have happened around the same time but they are not necessarily connected. Because Mark has gone missing doesn't mean I have abducted Jack.

DS Bennett: Did I say anything about abducting Jack?

Humphrey: I believe you implied it.

DS Bennett: Nevertheless, you *are* in custody on suspicion of abducting Marek. You were seen talking to him by the coffee machine at Radcester College on several occasions. What were you talking about?

Humphrey: I really can't remember.

DC Amis: Were you making arrangements to meet?

Humphrey: No.

DC Amis: You accepted Marek as a Facebook friend and then you suddenly deleted him. Why was that?

Humphrey: I don't know why I accepted his request in the first place. I think subconsciously it was a way of staying in contact with Jack.

DC Amis: Do you realise that makes you sound like a stalker?

Humphrey: Actually, yes, I do and I'm rather ashamed of it. That's why I deleted him.

DC Amis: It wasn't to cover your tracks?

Humphrey: I don't know what you mean but, no.

Humphrey & Jack

DS Bennett: Humphrey, you don't want to be here and neither do we. This is no place for an intelligent man. So if you know anything about the disappearance of Marek Kapel, now would be a very good time to tell us.

Humphrey: I keep telling you that I know nothing about the disappearance of this boy.

DS Bennett: The time is 22:36 hours and I am suspending this interview.

The detective sergeant stopped the tape and said: 'Right, Humphrey, we'll take a short break and then we'll resume.'

Once again, Humphrey was offered a choice between two bland microwaveable meals but he refused them both. He felt bilious. He knew that if he attempted as much as a mouthful he would throw up.

55. Interview 3

Tom Sinclair was allowed to speak to Humphrey before the interview resumed.

'Are you all right, Humphrey?' he said. 'You look terrible.'

'Is it surprising?' said Humphrey.

'No, of course not,' said Tom. 'But you really do look ill. Did they give you something to eat?'

'Yes,' said Humphrey, 'but I didn't feel like it. I just want to get out of here and go home.'

'Just stick with it,' said Tom. 'Tell yourself: "This too shall pass". They will have to charge you by first thing tomorrow morning or let you go.'

Humphrey groaned.

'Oh God, not a night in here. I don't think I can bear it.'

'It may not come to that,' Tom said. 'But you have to brace yourself for the fact that they have the right to keep you in custody till then. Now listen carefully.'

Humphrey & Jack

'I'm listening,' said Humphrey.

'They're getting quite frustrated that they're not getting anywhere. A case like this excites a lot of press attention. When a child is missing there is pressure on the police to come up with miracles. They need a culprit and they need one quickly. There is also the idea in the public mind that, if the child is not found alive and a body is subsequently found, then the police are to blame. Our friends are looking for a conviction, Humphrey, and I'm afraid you'll do. You fit a pattern for them: single, very private, eccentric, often at odds with the world, a grudge bearer.'

'But I'm not like that. Or at least not any more,' said Humphrey. 'I don't bear grudges.'

'Yes you do,' said Tom. 'I'm sorry to talk to you like this but you need to be prepared. They are getting frustrated that they can't pin you down and I suspect that they're going to get a bit rough. Once again don't rise to it. Keep your answers as short as possible and resist the temptation to offer them a narrative. The more you say, the easier it is for them to twist it.

'And Humphrey, please try to avoid sarcasm. They don't like it. They really don't. And don't show off.'

'Show off? What do you mean?'

'Oh Humphrey, don't be obtuse. The Latin? The lesson in logic? Just don't.'

'Oh I'm sorry,' Humphrey said, 'I just couldn't help it. They treat me as if I were as dim as they are.'

The next interview began on that very note.

DS Bennett: Are you all right, Humphrey?

Humphrey: I'm fine.

DS Bennett: Only you look a bit rough.

Humphrey: I'm fine. Don't worry about it. Can we just get on with it, please?

DS Bennett: Very well. What can you tell me about this photograph?

Humphrey & Jack

He pushed toward Humphrey a grainy photograph of a boy on Humphrey's lawn with his back to the camera and his trousers round his knees. He was bending over and his head was turned around to leer at the camera.

Humphrey: I didn't take this photograph. It was taken by my CCTV camera. Look at the date. It's from ages ago. I hadn't even met Jack by then. It was taken on the night they strewed rubbish all over my garden. I put the photos on Facebook and passed them on to the police.

DS Bennett: Oh yes, Humphrey. We have all the evidence that you sent to us. Listen to me now. I'd like to divest you of an assumption you may have made. My colleague and I may not speak fluent Latin and we may not dwell up in the airy towers of Academia. But we are not stupid, Humphrey. We are members of a team of highly qualified people, and all of them are working on your case. Some of them are forensic scientists who are just as qualified as you are. Some of them are experienced policemen who have been talking to a lot of people you know. Together, we want to get the truth and together we want to find this boy as soon as possible. His safety is our primary concern. So let's have no more smart-arsery, Humphrey, and then we'll get on fine. Is that understood?

Humphrey: Yes of course, I'm sorry.

DS Bennett: You see, I know perfectly well that the photograph is a CCTV image taken when Jack Lis trespassed in your garden, aided and abetted by Marek Kapel. But what I want to know is why you did not submit this image to the police along with all the others and why you kept it?

Humphrey: I haven't looked at that image since I collected screen shots to send on to you. I didn't even know it was still on my computer.

DS Bennett: Why did you keep it then?

Humphrey & Jack

Humphrey: I don't really know. I think I had some vague idea that I would hold it in reserve in case the police thought they needed further evidence of malicious intent.

DS Bennett: But you supplied us with plenty of evidence and we acted on it. Why would you want to keep this particular image?

Humphrey: I've already told you that I had some half-baked idea that I might use it against the boy at some future time. It possibly doesn't make a lot of sense, but I was very angry with the boys at the time and I wasn't thinking straight. I kept the image and forgot all about it.

DS Bennett: Are you sure you didn't keep the image for some other purpose?

Tom Sinclair: Detective Sergeant Bennett, my client has answered your question. I don't see what is to be gained by pressing it any further.

DS Bennett: Humphrey, how would you describe yourself?

Humphrey: Good lord, I've no idea.

DS Bennett: Please. Oblige me. Have a try.

Humphrey: Well, up until the last couple of years, I would have described myself as a failure.

DC Amis: But your CV suggests that you are a successful academic. So how can you think you're a failure?

Humphrey: Oh, the academic stuff was never really that important to me. I mean a failure socially... personally... getting on with people... forming relationships. All that stuff. I've always been a loner. I was irritable all the time. I made enemies all over the place. I was totally negative about everything and my only meagre pleasure was meeting up with like-minded sods a couple of times a week to moan about things. Sad, isn't it? I was a saddo. Sad sad sad.

DC Amis: You put all that in the past tense. What changed?

Humphrey: Whatever you might think of it, my friendship with Jack changed things. It gave me a purpose in life. It gave me something to do. It gave me something to believe in. It gave me some sort of ambition. In fact, you could say the relationship was symbiotic.

Humphrey & Jack

DC Amis: Come again.

Humphrey: I'm sorry. I'm not showing off. It just happens to be the right word to describe the relationship. I was of use to Jack as an academic mentor and as a source of support, practically and financially. I was of use to him as a moral and psychological fixed point. He was of use to me because he supplied me with a motive to pull myself out of the ditch of despondency in which I'd been living.

DS Bennett: You said previously that you were not a violent man. Is that right?

Humphrey: It is.

DS Bennett: But you have violent thoughts, don't you?

Humphrey: Doesn't everybody?

DC Amis: Have you ever threatened to kill anyone?

Humphrey: Of course I haven't.

DC Amis: Didn't you threaten to kill Mrs Bellingham's cat?

Humphrey: I don't think so. If I did it was only in jest.

DC Amis: [consulting notes] You were overheard in The Seven Stars saying that you would get a gun and shoot it, or trap it and strangle it with your bare hands, or blow it up with gunpowder, or poison it.

Good God, Humphrey thought, where did they dig this up from and how? Flake and Secondhand Sue! Flake with his books and his notepads! He and Secondhand Sue had not just been eavesdropping: Flake had been writing things down. What a grimy little pair.

DC Amis: Did you say these things?

Humphrey: I may have done. But, come on! I was clearly joking. I'm sometimes prone to exaggeration. I would never have harmed the thing.

DC Amis: You were seen throwing stones at the cat.

Humphrey: Olives.

Tom Sinclair: Is this relevant?

Humphrey & Jack

DS Bennett: We are trying to establish what kind of person Dr Icke is.

Tom Sinclair harrumphed.

DS Bennett: Humphrey, did you also threaten to kill Mrs Bellingham?

Humphrey: If I did it would have been in the same hyperbolic vein. I would never have done it. I mean it's ridiculous. I don't have a violent bone in my body.

DS Bennett: Really? You were involved in a common pub brawl recently, were you not, Humphrey? We have a statement from a Mr Garth Porter saying you threw an unprovoked punch at his face. Is this true?

Humphrey: Yes it is. But it was hardly unprovoked. He had been goading me beyond endurance. In any case, I came off much worse.

DC Amis: But you started it?

Humphrey: If you mean did I strike the first blow physically, yes, I did. You have no idea of the kind of abuse I was being subjected to. Anyway, this was the first and only fight I have ever been involved in.

DS Bennett: Your solicitor seems to think it's insignificant, but with your forbearance, Mr Sinclair, I'd like to ask Humphrey a couple of questions about Mrs Bellingham's cat.

Tom Sinclair rolled his eyes but gave a cursory nod.

DS Bennett: Did you entice the cat into the house?

Humphrey: No, it came in of its own accord. It had taken a fancy to Jack, you see. In fact it worshipped him and followed him all over the place.

DS Bennett: Did you feed it?

Humphrey: No... yes.

DS Bennett: So you did entice it into the house?

Humphrey & Jack

Humphrey: Well, yes, if you put it like that, I suppose I did.

DS Bennett: Why?

Humphrey: Jack was fond of the beast so I sort of encouraged it. It's true.

DS Bennett: Isn't it also true that you were intent on tormenting Mrs Bellingham?

Humphrey: To a degree.

DS Bennett: To very great degree?

Humphrey: Yes.

DS Bennett: And then you killed it.

Humphrey: It was an accident. It shot out in front of the car. There was no way I could avoid it.

DS Bennett: You said you'd kill it and you did. Just to annoy an elderly lady you found irritating, you killed a dumb animal by running over it.

Humphrey [agitated]: No, It wasn't like that at all. It was an accident, I tell you.

[Pause]

DC Amis: Do you take any illegal drugs?

Humphrey: I do not.

DC Amis: Do you take heroin?

Humphrey: No.

DC Amis: Do you take cocaine?

Humphrey: No.

DC Amis: So let's talk about drink. When was the last time you were drunk?

Humphrey: Do you mean falling-over-bumping-into-things drunk? Not since the night when refuse was tipped into my garden. I'd been to a pub quiz and drunk too much Guinness. I think blind rage could've contributed.

DS Bennett: Not since then?

Humphrey & Jack

Humphrey: Not like that, no.

DS Bennett: How much would you say you drink, in a week, say?

Humphrey: It's hard to say. I'm no good at totting up those unit things.

DS Bennett: Too much, would you say?

Humphrey: Probably, yes.

DS Bennett: Have people ever said to you that you drink too much?

Humphrey: Yes.

DS Bennett: And how do you react to that?

Humphrey: I think that people should mind their own business.

DS Bennett: Has your doctor ever told you to cut down?

Humphrey: He has.

DS Bennett: And have you?

Humphrey: I always mean to.

DC Amis: Does your drinking have a significant impact on your day-to-day life?

Humphrey: Not really. If I know I'm going anywhere in the car I don't drink. I have it under control to that extent. I don't drink myself to oblivion. I seem to have a naturally high resistance to alcohol.

DC Amis: That's not necessarily a good sign.

Oh is that so, you smug little tapeworm? thought Humphrey. How old are you anyway? About 12?

Humphrey: I sometimes forget things.

DC Amis: What sort of things?

Humphrey: Nothing important. Dentist's appointments. Where I put the car keys. Passwords.

DS Bennett: No blackouts at all?

Humphrey: No, no blackouts.

DS Bennett: Do you ever find you've done something and have no recall of doing it?

Humphrey & Jack

    Humphrey: That's not uncommon, is it? Especially at my age.
    DS Bennett: I mean something you deeply regret doing? Something dreadful?
    Humphrey: No. Not really. Not since I was a teenager at any rate.
    DS Bennett: Tell us about it.

Sorrowfully, Humphrey told them all about the vodka-fuelled night at Rowntrees and the moonlit dingle in the woods by the gurgling stream where Janet Dobbs had forced him to put his hands on her prodigious boobies and then slapped her hand onto his unresponsive privates. And he told them about poor Minty Cresswell and her violent lover and how damaged she was and how she curtailed his clumsy attempt to make love to her.

    DC Amis: And since then? Have there been other lovers?
    Humphrey: No.
    DC Amis: Are you in a relationship now?
    Humphrey: What do you mean by relationship?
    DS Bennett: Let's not play semantic games, Humphrey. You know what DC Amis means.
    Humphrey: With respect, I'm not sure that I do.
    Tom Sinclair: I don't think Humphrey is playing semantic games, gentlemen. Could you define precisely what you're asking?
    DC Amis: Are you in a sexual relationship at the moment?
    Humphrey: No. I hardly know any women. And those I know are just friends or professional colleagues.
    DS Bennett: Are you in a sexual relationship with a male person?

Tom Sinclair slapped the table in frustration.

    Humphrey: No, I am not.

Humphrey & Jack

DS Bennett: Are you or have you been in a relationship, a sexual relationship, with Jack Lis?

Humphrey: No.

DS Bennett: Are you a homosexual, Humphrey?

Humphrey: I don't think so.

DS Bennett: You don't think so?

Humphrey: I think I may be asexual. I was going to ask my doctor about it but I bottled out.

DS Bennett: Do you have any sexual feelings for Marek Kapel?

Humphrey: Absolutely not.

DS Bennett: The time is 00:15 hours and we are suspending this interview.

Tom Sinclair put both hands on the table with his elbows pointing outwards and said: 'DS Bennett, are you seriously going to continue to question my client? He has answered your questions patiently and with great candour. It should be quite clear to any rational person that there is nothing to be gained by pressurising him any further. He is clearly not a sexual predator. He is a victim of gossip and the fallout from petty feuds in which, to be sure, he is a not entirely innocent party.

'Look at him. He is ageing and overweight and clearly incapable of physically restraining one fit youth, let alone two.

'He is guilty of nothing more than altruism and a certain naivety.

'You have no tangible evidence whatsoever that this shattered man abducted the boy. You know you cannot bring a case based on insinuation and tittle-tattle. What you have tried to imply is tendentious in the extreme.

'There is also the question of certain procedural anomalies which are cause for concern.

'You can also see that he's ill. A night in the cells would only exacerbate that. You must release him by four in the morning in any case. Unless you have a credible new line of questioning, I can only see you going over the same ground again. I think you must either charge Dr Icke or release him.'

The two detectives stood and left the room without a comment.

Very shortly afterwards, Humphrey was released on police bail.

56. News from Poland

'What an unconscionable shambles,' said Tom Sinclair in the car which had been waiting for Humphrey. 'They didn't have a scintilla of real evidence. The pathetic case they were trying to make would be thrown out of court in derision. There are too many cases where a scapegoat is found to appease a jabbering and slavering press. I am going to go for these guys. I've been waiting for a case like this.'

The car was being driven by Hector. Tom sat beside him.

'Where to, Humphrey?' Hector said.

'I just want to go home,' Humphrey said.

'You don't, Humphrey. You really don't,' Althea said.

'Here's a better plan,' said Hector. 'It can be as short-term or as long-term as you want. You're very welcome to stay with us but there are the children. They're good girls, as you know, but they're quite boisterous, which is only natural. And then there's the baby. You might find it trying.

'Or Althea is very happy to have you. She has plenty of room and you'll have time and space to get better.'

'I'd like to have you stay, Humphrey darling,' Althea said, 'if you don't mind a rather bohemian ménage.'

'Please. I just want to go home. Please take me home.'

'Okay, okay', said Hector. 'We'll take you home but you'll see what we mean.'

As soon as he could, Hector did a U-turn on the Ring Road and they were soon on Burdock Hill and turning into Upper Bishop's Lane. When they got out of the car, Humphrey could see blue-and-white tape festooned everywhere. It said: Police Do Not Enter.

Humphrey & Jack

Tom pulled it away from the front door. Humphrey opened it with the keys which had been returned to him. The scene within was one of devastation: books had been taken from shelves and left in piles; cupboards had been emptied; papers were scattered everywhere; the beds in the bedrooms had been stripped and the bed linen lay on the floor. The loft hatch was open and the ladder was still extended. His study was a scene of particular havoc. Books and papers were strewn everywhere but worst of all, sketches for the *Medieval Book of Manners* lay on the floor.

'But surely,' Humphrey said, 'they have to clear this up if I'm not charged?'

'I'm sorry,' Tom said, 'but they're under no legal obligation.'

Humphrey stood with his arms by his side and his head on the doorjamb and wept.

The others stood by helplessly. Humphrey wept for a long time, choking sobs from deep inside him. Suddenly, he began retching and he made a dash for the bathroom. He only just made it in time.

When he rejoined the others, the tracks of tears could still be seen on his cheeks.

'Oh, Humphrey darling, look at you!' said Althea. 'What have they done to you? Come to mine, love. I'll look after you.'

'If you'll have me,' Humphrey said in a very quiet voice.

'Sweetheart, it'll be a privilege.'

'Just a minute,' Humphrey said and he went back to the open door of the study.

'Where's my computer?'

'The police have it,' said Tom, and any other electronic devices you may have. I'm afraid that they don't have a very good record of returning these things promptly but I'll get on to them about it.'

'Don't worry about it,' said Althea. 'You can use mine but first of all you need a proper meal and a good long sleep.'

'I'm not hungry,' said Humphrey.

Humphrey & Jack

Nevertheless, at Althea's home by the river, he ate a small bowl of pasta.

'I'll look in tomorrow,' said Hector, 'see how you're doing.'

'I have to get back to London at sparrowfart,' said Tom, 'but I'll be back at the weekend and we'll talk about where to go from there.'

'You must tell me what I owe you,' Humphrey said.

'Won't hear of it, man,' Tom said. '*Pro bono publico*, eh? For the public good. And that's a bit of Latin that is allowed. We should be looking for compensation but let's not talk about it now. I'll see you on Friday. Now get some rest, there's a good fellow.'

Soon Humphrey was put to bed in a room smelling of cinnamon. He fell asleep as soon as his head hit the pillow.

He emerged the next day shortly after noon. He had slept deeply and dreamlessly and felt much refreshed. Althea prescribed a long hot soak and said that in the meantime she would prepare brunch. Once upon a time Humphrey would have cringed at the word but now he was pathetically grateful. All the same, he could only eat half of the enormous full English breakfast that Althea had cooked.

'I'm sorry,' he said.

'No worries,' Althea said. 'I'm sure you'll soon get your appetite back.'

'Indeed,' said Humphrey. 'Thank you. Althea, do you think I could use your computer now?'

'Dear man, of course you can,' she said.

She installed him in her study, turned on the computer and set him up as a guest user. Humphrey logged into Facebook.

There were two notifications. One was from Mrs Price, wondering what on earth was going on, when would he be back and should she start tidying up. She was worried about the police cordon. Humphrey thanked her for the enquiry and asked her to do nothing for the moment. He would have instructions for her soon.

The other notification was from Jack. It read:

Humphrey & Jack

Hi Humphrey, wtf is going on. I've been hitch-hiking in the Warmia Forest away from any signal. Just got to Reszel and saw the Brit news. You're all over it. You've been arrested?

> Jack, I am so glad to hear from you. I'm out now. It's been incredibly distressing. Mark's gone missing and they think I had something to do with it.

But that's bollocks! He's been with me. I told him I was planning to go backpacking around the countryside and he said he'd saved up some money and could he join me. I said sure it sounded kinda fun. So I borrowed a friend's car and met him at the airport. And we went off trekking around Warmia.

> But he didn't tell anybody where he was going. He certainly didn't tell his mother. Christ knows why the police thought I had anything to do with it but they put me through hell.

Shit. I'm really sorry about that, Humphrey, but I didn't get your last message till just now. As for his not letting anybody know he was joining me, tell me about it. Turns out he hadn't saved up diddly squat. He stole the money from his mother and made his way over here without a freaking word to anybody.

> Is he still with you?

Nah, as soon as I found out he'd robbed his mother I lent the stupid bastard some money and sent him home. I doubt I'll ever see that again. Is he not back yet?

Humphrey & Jack

No, he isn't. Look Jack, I need to let the police know about this but I need to speak to you some more. Can we arrange a specific time to chat this evening?

Sure. When?

At seven o'clock?

Well, we're an hour ahead of you here, so I'll FaceTime you at eight. Is that okay? Give me your number.

No, not FaceTime I don't like it. Just contact me on Messenger at eight your time then.

Definitely.

Don't let me down, Jack. It's been a nightmare.

I can imagine. Don't worry.

Humphrey went downstairs to the kitchen as fast as his knees would allow. Hector had arrived and was drinking coffee with Althea.

'He's been with Jack all along. In Poland. Devious little shit,' said Humphrey.

'Who has? said Althea.

'Mark. Marek. Whatever.'

And he told them everything Jack had said.

Instantly, the room was a hive of activity.

'That's spankingly good news,' said Hector. 'It exonerates you completely. And it sounds as if the wretched boy is safe. O frabjous day! Come to my arms, my beamish boy!'

Humphrey & Jack

And he gave Humphrey a bear hug which made him feel very uncomfortable.

'Now,' Hector said, 'the police must be told immediately.'

'Yes, I suppose I'd better'... Humphrey began.

'No, I'll do it. You've spent enough time in the company of our gallant bobbies. Besides, with respect, it will sound more objective coming from me. Althea, my fragrant one, do you have such a thing as a spare memory stick floating around?'

'I've got a pack of them as it happens,' said Althea. 'They were for the art class. A project that never happened.'

'Splendiferous,' said Hector. 'Now, Humphrey, we need to take a screenshot of your conversation with Jack and put it on the USB. Then I will drive like Batman out of hell to the police station and they can begin to do something useful instead of terrorising timid and harmless senior citizens.'

'But I don't want Jack compromised,' said Humphrey.

'I'm deeply sorry,' said Hector, 'but I suspect that they are going to want to talk to Jack at some stage. But it will be routine, I should think. I can't see that he could possibly be in any kind of trouble. On the contrary, since he told the boy to come back.

'Anyway, it's okay. We only need to do a screen capture of the relevant part of your conversation with Jack, nothing else. I'm sure he wouldn't mind surrendering a fragment of his privacy if he knew it would lead to the boy being found safe and secure.'

'I suppose... ' said Humphrey.

'While you do that,' Althea said, 'I'll ring Tom.'

'Good idea,' said Hector.

When they came back down, Althea said: 'He was very excited. He'll be coming up from London tomorrow on the 16:13 and heading straight here for supper.'

Hector held up the memory stick in the fingertips of both hands.

Humphrey & Jack

'Behold I give you a mystery,' he said. 'Behold the Holy Grail! In this sacred vessel is that which will liberate Humphrey from his tormentors and discover the missing boy and return him to his grieving Lady Mother!'

'You are such a sad twat,' said Althea. 'Come on, gird up your loins. I'm coming with you.'

'Would you mind if I don't?' said Humphrey.

'Oh I don't think it would be a good idea anyway, my precious,' said Hector. 'I don't think it's time for you to go back out into the world yet.'

'What do you mean?' Humphrey said.

'I'm afraid the press demonised you pretty thoroughly,' Althea said. 'But we'll talk about it when we get back.'

Humphrey sank into a carver at the kitchen table in a mixture of confusion, fatigue and relief.

'Do you think I could possibly have a drink?' he said.

'But of course you can, sweetheart. I wasn't thinking. The dining room is through there. The drinks cupboard is in the corner. Just help yourself to whatever you want. I've no idea how long this is going to take but if you're hungry just raid the fridge. Come on Hecky-Thump, let's get this show on the road.'

When the door banged shut after them, the house was filled with a quiet that Humphrey had not known since before his arrest. He found the applewood corner cabinet in the dining room. It was well stocked. He took a tumbler from the nearby dresser and pulled himself a large measure of Irish. He seated himself at the dining room table to drink in great draughts of silence and of whiskey.

57. Hall of Mirrors

Humphrey sat in a kind of daze at the dining room table for a while and then had a look around the house.

There could be no doubt that this was the home of an artist. Paintings, sketches and photographs covered every wall in a haphazard kind of way. Each item of furniture was beautiful in itself but nothing matched. The dining room had a gothic air. The living room was low-level with beanbags here and there and a voluptuously battered sofa was covered with throws in exotic fabrics in geometric patterns. Everywhere there were staring dolls and pictures of clowns and ballerinas. A stuffed greyhound stood in the hallway.

The only room which was furnished in any way agreeable to Humphrey's taste was the large conservatory. A rattan sofa and chairs were scattered with tapestry cushions. There was also a white colonial-style dining table with six chairs upholstered in oatmeal. There were a number of white bookcases crammed with art books, and there were several Victorian oil lamps about the room. His picture of an emperor in purple robes hung above one of the bookcases.

The plate glass windows looked out on to a well-kept lawn which sloped down to the riverbank. Willow trees were already in leaf in the late April sunshine. Humphrey settled in here, bringing the whiskey bottle with him.

A brave punter glided by. He was wearing a T-shirt even though it was still quite chilly. Because of the height of the bank at the bottom of the lawn, he was only visible from the waist upwards and so the effect as he slid by swinging the pole was quite surreal.

It was late afternoon before a clattering in the hallway and animated chatter announced that Hector and Althea were back. Humphrey was quite mellow by now.

'I'm in here!' he shouted.

'They've put out an alert to all the ports and airports,' Althea said. 'They are bound to intercept him as soon as he sets foot in the country. They'll want to question him, of course, but there is now no reason to suppose that he's in any kind of danger. His mother has been told what has happened and she's overjoyed, naturally. I think we can expect some news very soon.'

Humphrey & Jack

'Thank God for that,' Humphrey said. 'She will not be the only one to be overjoyed.'

'Oh, look, I'm sorry. I'm afraid I've given this whiskey a bit of a caning. I'll replace it obviously.'

'Don't be silly. Don't worry about that. Now listen. Hector and I were having a bit of a think in the car. If you carry on wearing the same clothes you'll begin to pong. What say you make a list of things you need, clothes and toiletries, that sort of thing. Hector will zap round to your house and pick them up for you. I'm afraid everything was on the floor but we can easily pop stuff in the washing machine. You'll feel so much better with fresh clobber. And in the meantime I will get on with making some supper.'

'Bless you both,' said Humphrey. 'I don't know what I would've done without you.'

'Oh stuff and nonsense, my old turnip,' said Hector. 'Now, are you sober enough to write that list?'

'Get stuffed,' said Humphrey. 'Just bring me the writing thingies.'

'It's nice in here, isn't it?' said Althea. 'Why don't we have supper in here tonight? It's so cosy with the lamps lit. We'll have champagne.'

Later Hector returned with a suitcase full of clothes. They were perfectly clean, if a little crumpled. Althea pressed a pair of trousers and a jumper whilst the chicken casserole was cooking and filling the house with the fragrance of wine and herbs.

Humphrey did indeed feel much better in fresh clothing. The stink of the prison cell with all its grim associations had seemed to cling to the clothes he had been wearing and it was a relief to be able to hand them over to Althea to be washed.

The casserole was as tasty as it smelt and Althea had been right, the oil lamps created a charming atmosphere replicated as they were in the conservatory's black window panes. The receding reflections seemed to hang suspended in chains across the lawn.

Humphrey & Jack

All the same, Humphrey could eat but little, though he drank several glasses of champagne. At seven o'clock, he retired to the study to continue his conversation with Jack.

Jack was on time.

Hi, Humphrey. How's it going? Is he back yet?

No, do you know what route he's taken?

No I don't. I drove him to Warsaw airport but I was so cross with him I didn't go into the terminal. He's fucked up my holiday and now all this mess. I had no idea of the trouble he's got you into, which is just as well or I would have decked him. He'll have got a flight with EasyJet or some other cut-price airline.

Well, I'm afraid he's going to find the police are waiting for him.

Serve him right, the clown.

I think they may want to speak to you at some stage.

That's all right. Will I have to come back to England, though?

I've no idea. But if it comes to that, don't worry about money. It'll be a case of here and back again and I don't want you missing out on your studies.

That's cool. But how are you?

Humphrey & Jack

I'm fine. I'm staying at Althea's for the moment. The police made a bit of a mess of the house while they were searching it.

Whatever made the muppets think that you could be involved? You're hardly a gay Humbert Humbert are you?

That's what they seemed to think.

Jesus!

Anyway I don't want to talk about it. When are you back? Sometime in June, isn't it? That's what you said.

Ah yes, well about that…

What?

Promise you won't go ape at me.

I promise I won't go ape at you. What?

Thing is, I've got a job over the summer teaching English. It'll probably be well boring but it pays incredibly well. It means I can stay in Poland longer which will give me an advantage in my finals year. And if I save the money it will give me a hell of a lot more independence. Hey, I'm really sorry to be so disappointing, Humphrey.

I'll live.

Humphrey & Jack

Don't be like that. I know I promised to be back in June but it's such an opportunity. I'll definitely be back in September.

Jack, if you ever come to think of coming to see me as a duty, it'll be time to call a halt to our friendship. September is good. I look forward to September. Let me know in good time and we'll make arrangements to transport your luggage.

You're a star.

Look, I gotta go now. Let me know the minute Marek touches down, will you?

You look after yourself, Humphrey. I feel I ought to fly straight back to look after you but you see how it is.

I can look after myself. Take care.

Talk soon, mój drogi przyjacielu!

Humphrey had had such a dismal time of late that the postponement of his reunion with Jack was just a dull shock rather than the keener cut it might otherwise have been. Perhaps he would feel it later.

He cut and pasted the fragment of Polish into Google Translate and discovered that it meant 'my dear friend'. It lifted his spirits even more than clean clothes, chicken casserole, and champagne.

***

Neither Humphrey nor Althea would have dreamed of watching breakfast television under normal circumstances, but these were not normal times, and the little TV set in Althea's kitchen jabbered away as she prepared breakfast for them.

The early morning news bulletin came on and they stopped everything to watch.

When images of Mark arriving at Luton airport in the early hours and being intercepted by the police appeared on the screen, Althea screamed, knocked over her orange juice and began jumping up and down. Humphrey drummed on the table with his knife and fork.

'Look at the smug little swine,' said Humphrey. 'He's so full of himself.'

Indeed, he seemed to be greeting the flashes of the press photographers as if he were some megastar returning to his native land after an international gig.

'I've a feeling that very soon the police are going to knock that smile from off his face,' said Althea.

'But how did the press get there?' Humphrey said. 'How did they know which airport?'

'Oh they are everywhere. They breed in shit like flies,' said Althea. 'The police will have checked the passenger lists for incoming flights and then tipped off the hacks.'

Humphrey finished his scrambled eggs and then had several slices of toast with ginger marmalade. Later, Althea heard him being noisily sick in the upstairs loo, though she said nothing.

While she cleared the table, he said he would like to read for a while and he found a promising book of short stories on one of Althea's shelves. She said he might like to read in the garden. There was growing warmth in the sunshine and if he wrapped up warmly he would come to no harm. The air would be good for him, she said, after his recent incarceration. She set him up in a comfortable garden chair at the top of the lawn and laid a travel blanket over his lap.

'O for heaven's sake,' he said. 'Don't fuss, woman. You make me feel like an invalid.'

Humphrey & Jack

'Well, so you are in a way,' Althea said. 'Don't think I haven't heard you throwing up. I'm very worried about you. I really think you should see your doctor.'

'Oh God, no, he'll sermonise at me and tell me off about my lifestyle. It's totally counter-productive, you know. When he tells me to get more exercise, I just want to lie on a chaise longue and eat grapes. And when he tells me to cut down on the drinking, I develop a thirst like a dredger. The Grim Reaper will come for me when he's ready, and not before. And nothing I can do about it will make the slightest bit of difference.'

'Oh well, at least you're getting your grumpiness back.'

'I am not grumpy,' Humphrey snapped.

***

The early evening brought Tom back from town. Hector had already arrived at teatime. Tom joined them in the kitchen rubbing his hands and immediately took charge of the party as was his wont.

'Now here's the cunning plan,' he said. 'I propose that we have an *apéro* here and then pootle along to The Swan with Two Necks for dinner. It is time Humphrey ventured out into the world which has treated him so badly but it must be in disguise. Althea, what do you have in your dressing up box?'

'Well now, we could dress him up as a washerwoman,' she said, 'or an Albanian warrior, or we could put him in full drag as Cleopatra. What do you think?'

'You will do no such thing,' said Humphrey. 'Why do I need a disguise anyway?'

'Oh, Humphrey, you innocent child,' said Hector. 'You have indeed lived a sheltered life. I'm afraid the press has made your face as well-known as Her Majesty's. If you go out as you are, you will be mobbed.'

Humphrey & Jack

'But surely now they know that I'm innocent the press will vindicate me?'

'And admit they were wrong? Dear Lord,' said Tom, 'now you really are being naive. Just now they're all over the story of the return of the prodigal and you are already a mere footnote. They're not going to declare publicly that they made a serious boo-boo in hounding you – not until I make them, that is. You will fade from their pages into your former anonymity.

'However, mud sticks, and for a while the good people of England will remember your face and what you were supposed to have done as if you had actually done it. Gradually they will forget until the predators of the press turn their spotlights on some other poor skunk who is involved in a sex scandal with a lonely housewife, an earl's daughter or a chubby chorister.'

'So you see, Humperdinck,' said Hector, 'a low profile would be a very good idea though I think that full drag would be taking it a little too far.'

'Oh what a shame,' Althea said. 'I was so looking forward to painting your fingernails. I've got a lovely new magenta which would just suit your colouring.'

Humphrey muttered an obscenity under his breath.

'So,' said Tom. 'Does my proposal that we adjourn to The Swan with Two Necks meet with your approval? My Lords, are you content or not content?'

They were unanimously content.

'That's just as well,' said Tom, 'because I've already booked it. Time for a snifter first, and then we can be off.'

As the evenings were still chilly, Humphrey put on his overcoat and the tartan scarf which Jack had bought him in Edinburgh. Althea found him a hat with a wide brim which she pulled over his face. Humphrey protested that he was sure it made him look like Quentin Crisp.

Humphrey & Jack

Together they strolled along the tow path where he and Jack had walked the previous summer.

Tom had reserved for them a small wood-panelled booth at the back of the pub where they could be private. When they had ordered, Humphrey said: 'What I want to know is what were the press saying about me whilst I was locked up?'

'Are you sure you're ready for this?' said Tom.

'I'm going to find out sooner or later, aren't I?' said Humphrey. 'So you might as well tell me now.'

Tom showed him several pages from tabloid newspapers which he'd copied on to his phone. Humphrey had prepared himself for a very unpleasant experience but he was quite taken aback by the nastiness of what he saw. He recoiled at some of the headlines:

MISSING BOY: 'GRUMPY OLD MAN' ARRESTED

Dr Humphrey Icke (67), a retired lecturer at the University of Radcester, was arrested in a raid on his house in the early hours of this morning on suspicion of abducting Marek Kapel (15) who has been missing for five days.

BOYS WINED AND DINED IN THE HOUSE BY THE PARK

Dr Humphrey Icke (67), in police custody on suspicion of abducting Marek Kapel, entertained young boys at his wealthy home near Alexandra Park. His neighbour, Iolanthe Bellingham, told *The Globe* that young boys were seen coming and going from the house. One of them was Marek Kapel, missing for a week. 'One of them even had keys to the house,' she said.

WEIRDO KILLED MY CAT

Humphrey Icke, in custody on suspicion of abducting missing teen, Marek Kapel, killed his neighbour's cat, during a long and vicious feud, it was alleged today. 'He was a thoroughly nasty man,' said Iolanthe Bellingham, a neighbour.

'He would play loud music at night in his garden and if he saw me turn my bedroom light on he would turn it up.'

'He was also very abusive and foul-mouthed. Not what I would call a gentleman. He deliberately killed my cat by driving over it. I had to move out of my house because of his behaviour.'

I DON'T BELIEVE IT!
RETIRED LECTURER IN PUB BRAWL

Vile-tempered ex-lecturer, Humphrey Icke, dubbed 'Victor Meldrew', and implicated in the disappearance of Marek Kapel (15), was frequently drunk, a former colleague said today. Garth Porter (52), a history lecturer at the University of Radcester where Icke once taught, said that Icke threw 'a vicious punch' at him.

'It came out of the blue,' he said, 'and was quite unprovoked. I was just saying that his association with young boys was unwise and he tried to hit me. I knew no good would come of this.'

MISSING BOY VISITED 'VICTOR MELDREW'S' HOUSE

Marek Kapel (15), missing for seven days, was known to have visited the opulent home of Humphrey Icke (67), known as 'Victor Meldrew' because of his eccentricity and miserable personality.

LOUD MUSIC AND LATE NIGHT PARTIES IN 'VICTOR MELDREW'S' GARDEN

Humphrey Icke, known as 'Victor Meldrew' because of his cantankerous character, is being questioned by police for a second day following his arrest on suspicion of abducting missing college student, Marek Kapel.

'One night, he sat up till the small hours with this other boy playing loud music and drinking,' his neighbour Iolanthe Bellingham said. 'When I went to my bedroom window, they just waved at me.'

Humphrey & Jack

'It was disgraceful.'

The other boy is thought to be Jack Lis (20) who is also missing. Police want to question him on Marek's disappearance but have not yet managed to trace him.

WAS MISSING BOY LOCKED IN THE ATTIC?
Fingerprints found at 'Meldrew Mansion'

Humphrey handed the phone back and for a while he stared at the crayfish cocktail which had just been put in front of him.

'I didn't know she was called Iolanthe,' he said.

The others laughed with a kind of relief.

'I rather dreaded showing you these,' said Tom. 'I thought they might completely knock you for six and send you spiralling into depression.'

'Oh no,' said Humphrey. 'I'm not depressed, except at the degrading spectacle of human nature gorging on manufactured carrion like hyenas. But fortunately I never had a particularly high opinion of human nature anyway. With certain honourable exceptions. I am angry however, bloody seething, in fact. How can they justify this filth?'

'They will claim that they published the stories in the public interest. Now that is a very slippery term indeed. They will claim that the purpose of the stories was to provide information to the public in the hope that people would come forward with information which would help the police to find the missing boy.

'You'll find that there is nothing in there that is actually a lie. But the stories are not true either. There are facts there certainly but they don't conduce to any kind of objectivity. Take for instance the statement that boys were seen coming and going from your house. Well that's true. But the prurient suggestion is that streams of lewd laddies were queueing up on Upper Bishop's Lane to do you pleasure in your very own molly house. Now we know that there were only two boys and that nothing even the tiniest bit naughty ever happened. Which narrative do you think a salivating public would rather believe?

'You see, not even in the poshest broadsheets will you find the naked truth about anything. It's all mediated. The baying mob does not want mere information. They want entertainment. They want to jeer at the tumbrils; they want to do their self-righteous knitting by the guillotine; they want Barabbas released, and they want you crucified with a placard around your neck saying 'Deviant'. They have captured you in their hall of mirrors and claim that every distorted image is the real you.

'That is how they work. But they are not going to get away with it this time. Their collusion with the police, whose incompetence has been breathtaking, is full of legal holes. We're going to take them for all they've got, Humphrey. There could be substantial damages. Are you up for it?'

'Will that put me in the public eye again?' said Humphrey. 'I'm not sure I want that.'

'Probably. But this time as victim rather than villain. You'll have to trust me, Humphrey. But I promise I will do nothing without your say-so.'

'Okay, go ahead,' said Humphrey. 'Just keep me informed.'

During the meal Humphrey told them about the plans he'd been incubating during the day. He would stay with Althea for a while longer if that was okay.

'In a few days,' he said, 'I will go home and meet up with Mrs Price. We'll pack my books and papers into boxes in an orderly fashion and put them into storage. And then I will have the whole house re-decorated. By the time that is done, I hope the whole affair will have faded, probably superseded by some new scandal, as Tom suggested.

'I will not be driven out of my own home but a new start should help me put the trauma behind me. I might even take a holiday before I move back in. What do you think? Does that make sense?'

Humphrey's friends thought it was a good plan and Humphrey thought it was a good thing to have friends.

Humphrey & Jack

As they were eating, he said: 'One thing I don't understand. Mark's mother must have discovered pretty quickly that he had stolen money from her. Why didn't she tell the police?'

'Good question,' said Tom. 'Your answer is in *The Metro*. I picked up a copy on the train. Apparently the police got him to admit he stole a debit card from her purse. He'd seen her use it at cash machines and memorised the pin. He drew £250 and replaced the card. She would not have known about it until her next statement. But in any case, you should never underestimate a mother's love for her cub. Even if she'd known, she might still have concealed it.'

Humphrey refused a pudding and excused himself to go to the gents.

He was away for a long time.

58. The Fall

Humphrey's plan to refurbish the house was going swimmingly.

When he met Mrs Price to begin sorting out his papers, she seemed very shy of him.

'Look, I hope you're not angry with me, Dr Icke. I had to talk to the police. They came to my house and made me answer their questions, see. I only told them the truth about young Jack staying here, like. They were suggesting terrible things but I told them it was a load of rubbish and that they should be ashamed of themselves.'

'Good for you, Mrs Price. And don't worry - I'm not cross with you. You've been a treasure.'

Removal boxes had been ordered and delivered and between them they packed up everything that Humphrey wanted out of the way during the decoration. It took most of the day to tidy up and at tea time the van arrived to take the boxes away into storage.

Mrs Price said she would clean the house from top to bottom before the decorators arrived. Humphrey tried to suggest that it would be more logical to do the cleaning after they'd finished but she was having none of it and said she would clean up the house afterwards as well.

The next time Humphrey went round there, the men were at work in what had been Jack's room. There was a drugget on the floor and drapes over the furniture. Humphrey had chosen a fresh green for the walls and there were to be new curtains in a regency style. Humphrey thought Jack would approve.

The decorators said that they thought the whole house would be ready for him to move in by the end of May.

One morning in the middle of the month, Humphrey and Althea were having breakfast.

'I'm worried about you, Humphrey darling,' she said. 'Have you noticed that the whites of your eyes are yellowish? Go and look in the mirror. And I swear your skin has a yellow tint too. You really must make an appointment with your doctor. I insist, Humphrey. Or you're out on your ear.'

'Don't fuss. It's probably nothing. I'll ring after breakfast,' Humphrey said.

'He can't see me till Wednesday,' Humphrey shouted downstairs from the study door later.

'Did you tell him it was urgent?'

'But I don't think it is urgent,' Humphrey said. 'It'll be fine. And don't fuss. I've told you once.'

When Althea came home from college the following evening, Tuesday, the twenty-third of May, she found Humphrey lying unconscious at the foot of the stairs, his left leg twisted under him.

Humphrey & Jack

NOAH

59. Noah

Noah is on the early shift, 5 am till 2 pm. Even at this early hour, in mid-August, it is already very hot. The security guard at the gatehouse greets him with a cheery wave. In the month since he's been working here, Noah's affable disposition has commended him to everyone.

He lets himself into the Blackwell Building using the security keypad and turns right into the locker room where he changes. In his locker, there are two freshly laundered white tunics. He takes one from its sealed package and puts it on. It is crisply starched, with buttons down the side, and its peach coloured epaulettes designate him as an auxiliary nurse.

The Blackwell Building houses the geriatric unit. Noah climbs the three flights of stairs which take him up to Tourneur Ward. The pungent reek of urine and faeces greets him on the stairs as it does every morning. It will be a large part of his job to do something about it.

This is Priestcliffe Memorial Hospital which stands just outside the village of Questwell, two miles from Radcester. It is a private hospital, allegedly very expensive. This means it can boast a quality of care beyond the dreams of even the very best NHS hospitals.

Noah is an undergraduate at Christ's College, Cambridge, and he's working at the hospital during the long vacation. His aunt is the Senior

Nursing Officer and offered him the job when he said he was looking to earn some money during the holiday.

'You'll need a strong stomach, Noah, and I'm afraid the pay is not particularly good but you should find it rewarding in ways you could not possibly imagine,' she had said.

Noah was pleased to have the chance even though this didn't sound too promising. If it was grim, at least he had the knowledge that he would be returning to Cambridge at the beginning of October. He had gained a first in his second year exams and had been awarded a scholarship, with the coveted privilege of rooms in First Court in his final year.

He had checked out the rooms at the end of term. They were right at the top of a narrow staircase. The sitting room looked out onto St Andrew's Church and its most remarkable features were a sloping ceiling with strange cupboards in it and a colossal table covered with the graffiti of ages. There was a separate, if rather poky bedroom, which was good news, and a small pantry with a refrigerator, which was definitely a bonus. If he did well in his finals he would fill it with champagne for May Week. Noah felt proud: he would be living and working in the same court where Darwin had lived.

Tourneur Ward is a far cry from his future ivory tower. Noah goes into the clean storage area in the sluice room and takes a new disposable plastic apron and a pair of disposable gloves from a drawer.

Staff Nurse Britten meets him as he emerges.

'Ah Noah, good man. Can you help Mr Lang onto the commode. He's been asking for about half an hour but I've been run off my feet. Mind you, this will be his eighth time tonight. Then if you can help out Nurse Austin for now. When Sister Kent comes on shift at six she'll tell you what needs doing next.'

Noah knows very well what will need doing: patients who have soiled themselves will need to be cleaned up. This is a part of the job that Noah had dreaded but, surprisingly, it had become routine very quickly, like changing a baby, he supposed. Here, at the other end of life, the same quality of care is just as necessary. The smell, the physical nastiness, and the bleak nakedness of old people takes some getting used to, but the necessity of restoring some measure of dignity is always paramount.

What is still hard to take is the sense of shame and humiliation that some of the patients feel, and there is little Noah and the nurses can do about that except to be aware of it.

The soiled bed linen has to be taken away and the beds made up again. Some patients have to be turned at intervals to avoid getting bedsores and those patients already awake might be given a bed bath to save time later when the ward is at its busiest. All this requires a great deal of lifting and patients are often a dead weight. Nurse Austin says she likes working with Noah because he is so strong. This makes him blush.

Bedpans and urine bottles will need taking to the sluice room to be emptied and cleaned in the pressure washer machines.

He must not forget Mr Lang, who will need wiping and putting back into bed. Noah has discovered that Mr Lang is much more mobile than he pretends to be and Noah will be able to sort him out without any help.

The ward is in a horse shoe shape with male patients' beds down one leg of the horseshoe and female patients' beds down the other. The nurses' station is at the crown of the bend. Noah's work is mostly with the men though he is sometimes called to help out with the women. He was shy of their nakedness at first, but that too became routine.

One morning a woman with emphysema took off her oxygen mask and grabbed him by the balls.

'I'm ninety-two and I don't care,' she managed to wheeze.

He'd laughed with the other nurses in the common room later although her grip had been very tight and had brought tears to his eyes.

All the patients have been woken now. There are temperature and blood pressure checks. Sister Kent is on duty by now and there is the morning medication round. Soon Noah will be asked to help patients who cannot feed themselves with their breakfast.

Humphrey & Jack

The cleaners arrive to wash floors and Sister Kent stands watching with her arms folded to make sure that not even a square centimetre is missed.

The changing of beds continues and Noah is getting quite proud of his hospital corners. Everything must be clean and shipshape for the doctors' rounds later in the morning, and the patients need to be made to look their best for visiting times soon afterwards.

Noah has brought in a modest innovation which has met with Sister Kent's approval, something not easily earned. Normally the nurses are so busy that they can only afford the time to offer the men a shave with an electric razor. One primitive razor has to do for the whole ward. It is fairly ineffectual against the rough stubble it has to contend with. Noah has bought a cheap sponge bag, disposable razors and shaving soap and brush, so that he can give the men a wet shave. This has to be done on a rotational basis when Noah can be spared from his other duties but it is much appreciated by the patients.

Sister Kent says that she's very pleased that Noah has already learnt one of the first principles of geriatric nursing and that is to work constantly towards building up the patients' self-respect. Nevertheless, she suggests that Noah take home the bottle of Lynx aftershave which he has brought in and she replaces it at her own expense with a bottle of expensive, unscented, toilet water.

One afternoon, on the twelve till nine shift, when the pressure is a little less intense, Sister Kent sends Noah to a private room and instructs him to shave a patient. Noah thinks this is a little odd but does as he is told. It doesn't do to question Sister Kent. As always the patient is very appreciative.

'Smooth as a baby's bum,' he says, as he splashes on the toilet water which Noah has handed to him. 'Wow! that stings. Never mind. I feel fresh as a daisy and ready for love.'

Later, back in Tourneur Ward, Sister Kent says to Noah: 'I thought I asked you to shave Mr Leamington?'

Humphrey & Jack

'But I did,' says Noah, and then the ludicrous truth dawns on him. He was supposed to shave Mr Leamington's pubic hair ready for an operation. When he returns to do the job properly, Mr Leamington is laughing merrily. Noah realises that he knew all along what was supposed to happen.

'Right, you… ' says Noah, brandishing the razor.

'Smooth as a baby's bum,' Mr Leamington cackles.

The story has the other nurses in convulsions for there are no secrets in schools or in hospitals. Even Sister Kent, who had seemed very frosty, had been seen chuckling heartily in her office when she sent him off to the private room a second time.

Laughter is a coping mechanism in the unit.

Mrs Guest has dementia and is permitted to wander the ward. She shuffles the length of the women's section close to the wall, her fingertips trailing along it. She rounds the curve until she can see the men's beds. As if affronted, she turns and retraces her footsteps. She will do this all day, if allowed.

'Unless she gets underfoot, leave her, leave her,' says Sister Kent. 'She's doing no harm.'

One afternoon, Mrs Guest finds her way into the sluice room. There is a small drum tumbler dryer in one corner. Lifting the lid, she defecates into it copiously. She stands up and, without putting the lid down, she presses the start button which she takes to be the flush.

Noah is the first on the scene when he hears her screaming. She stands there in her nightie covered in her own excrement, as are the walls and ceiling. She is led away wailing by two student nurses to be cleaned up and consoled.

Only a week later and Noah draws the short straw again. He is on the morning shift and, just before breakfast, a ripple of outrage runs through the ward. Someone has stolen the patients' false teeth. Men as well as women are complaining that their dentures have disappeared in the night. Noah is put on the case and finally discovers a cache of falsies grinning at him from Ms Butterfield's locker.

Humphrey & Jack

Now Noah must reunite them with their owners. Fortunately, they have been labelled with a marker pen and the numbers recorded but one pair has escaped the system and can only be returned to their owner by a process of elimination. The situation is complicated by the fact that Mr Cooper refuses to accept that the teeth he has been offered are his own despite the labelling and the evidence of the record book. He makes such a hullabaloo that it takes Sister Kent herself to convince him. She cleans them in front of him and persuades him to pop them in his mouth, 'just to see'. Mr Cooper is astounded to discover that they are a perfect fit.

Ms. Butterfield is a tiny birdlike woman. She must have been very cunning and nimble to escape the vigilance of the nurses on night duty and probably made several forays. Staff Nurse Britten tells her that she has been very naughty and won't be allowed out of bed if she misbehaves again. Noah sees the old woman flick a V sign at her as soon as her back is turned.

These stories and many others are told and retold in the sluice room and in the nurses' common room and no matter how many times they are told they still elicit the same screams of laughter. They would not dream of laughing in front of the patients; Sister Kent would flay them alive. So there is a sense of relief in the chortling and guffawing, and perhaps a touch of hysteria.

The nurses laugh so that they can avoid crying, though there are tears enough some mornings when the nurses come on shift, Noah among them, and the bed of a favoured patient is found empty.

Tourneur Ward is the terminal ward.

Most deaths occur in the night.

60. Kraków

Hector is in Kraków. He is looking for Jack to take him back to England for Humphrey is dying and cannot last long now. Hector knows that Jack is very bad at replying to messages and cannot be relied on to open his inbox,

Humphrey & Jack

sometimes for days on end. He cannot countenance the risk of such a delay and so he has come to Poland in person.

He goes first to the Collegium Novum in the Jagiellonian University. Its Neo-gothic facade is impressive but he is not here as a tourist, though the Vistula reflects the stainless blue of the sky on this August afternoon, and the majestic Cloth Hall in the Main Square and the Basilica on Wawel Hill gleam in the sunshine.

The receptionist is charming and helpful and searches for Jack's details on her computer. The fact that Hector speaks Polish speeds things up. Yes, she has an address for him. Fortunately, it is close by and she gives directions. It is perhaps a twenty minute walk to Tenczyńska, the street where Jack lives.

It is very humid and Hector is sweating by the time he has climbed six floors to the top of a well-appointed tenement building. There are lots of polished doors with brass fittings though the lift isn't working.

He's let into a tiny studio flat with a sloping roof and a huge dormer window by a strikingly pretty girl. She introduces herself as Zofia. She says she is Jack's girlfriend and they share the flat. Hector explains the situation and its urgency. Zofia says that Jack is taking an adult English class at the Liceum around the corner and that she expects him back within half an hour. While they wait she serves him with iced tea and raspberries.

Hector takes in his surroundings. The dormer window opens out onto the tops of broad-leaved trees. There is a beaded shawl on one wall and a *Solidarność* poster from the strikes of the eighties on another. The low couch, which is presumably also their bed, is covered with a patchwork throw. A healthy weeping fig stands in a corner and beside it is a mirror framed with a mosaic of tiny purple and gold tiles. The kitchen, separated off by a beaded curtain, is no more than a cupboard. Hector feels too large for the room as he sits in a blue rocking chair with his tea.

When Jack arrives he is delighted, but astonished, to see Hector sitting with his girlfriend. At first he is as exuberant as a puppy dog but as Hector explains his mission he becomes very solemn.

Humphrey & Jack

'But of course I'll come,' he says. 'My God, I feel so guilty. I hardly look at Facebook these days. I've been so tied up with uni work, the English teaching, and well… with Zofia' – he smiles at her – 'that I feel I belong in Kraków now. I don't even think of England much. Oh God, what kind of shit friend am I?'

'Don't beat yourself up about it,' Hector says. 'I'm sure we all have regrets of one kind or another.'

Jack makes a few phone calls, throws a few things into a holdall, and kisses Zofia goodbye. Hector books a taxi to the airport. In less than half an hour, they are on their way.

Once there, timetables are in disarray. Weeks of intense heat over Europe are generating thunderstorms. Flights are delayed everywhere. The direct flight to Heathrow that Hector had booked for them has been cancelled. In the end, Hector purchases fresh tickets for a Brussels Airlines flight, leaving just before midnight, with stops at Frankfurt and Brussels. The delay at Frankfurt is three hours but it cannot be helped.

There is plenty of time to kill and time becomes viscous and congeals when you're in a hurry. Kraków is a small airport. They have been warned not to go through security too early as there is nothing on the other side and, equally, they have been warned not to leave it too late as processing can be slow and rather chaotic.

They find a restaurant called The Suitcase Bar and over a couple of beers, Hector explains what's been happening to Humphrey.

Since his fall at Althea's house at the end of May, things have been going very badly for him. He was lucky not to have broken any bones although the serious bruising that he sustained would not heal. He also seemed rather confused. His short-term memory was impaired. He wouldn't be able to tell you, for instance, what he had eaten for breakfast, even half an hour later.

There was some suggestion at the hospital that he might have suffered a stroke but in any case they wanted to admit him for tests. The bruising was particularly worrying.

Humphrey & Jack

The results revealed conclusively that Humphrey was suffering from cirrhosis of the liver. Hector learnt that Humphrey may have had this condition for some time. Apparently, a patient may present no symptoms for years and then go into rapid and fatal decline. Humphrey's feelings of nausea, his itchy skin, general fatigue and bruising all conduced to this diagnosis. However, the yellowing of the whites of his eyes and the deepening yellow tint of his skin confirmed jaundice, a concomitant of the disease.

Through June and July, Humphrey's condition worsened. He was desperate to go home. The decoration was now complete but he couldn't be trusted to look after himself and it now seemed impossible that he would ever see his home again. He had been allowed to go back to Althea's house but he collapsed on the second day there and was rushed back to hospital, this time to Webster Ward in the geriatric unit.

He complained of terrible itching. There was swelling in his legs and abdomen due to fluid build-up. He was barely eating at all and had lost a great deal of weight. At the end of July it became clear that he was not responding to any treatment and he was moved up to Tourneur Ward where he would be given palliative care only.

His mental deterioration accelerated. When he woke up he became very agitated because he couldn't remember where he was. Often, he couldn't remember who the nurses were though he saw them several times a day. He remembered Sister Kent but thought she was his mother, although his mother died decades ago. He recognised Althea intermittently but sometimes thought she was a nurse. Sadly, he didn't recognise Hector at all and gave every indication of being very frightened of him, trying to get out of bed and ripping the drip tube from the cannula in his hand.

This distressed Hector very much. Sister Kent told him that he must not take it personally.

'It's not your old friend who is rejecting you. You must remember that. It's a distorted and diminished version of him. After all, what is our identity but a sequencing of memories and without our memories we no longer really exist? You must try to stick to memories of happier times. That is where your friendship exists now.'

Hector was deeply impressed by the wisdom of this diminutive woman with her stiff white hair, outwardly so fierce and authoritarian, inwardly so profoundly perceptive and compassionate.

It had not been confirmed but Sister Kent told Hector that she suspected that Humphrey was suffering from Korsakoff's Syndrome, a chronic memory disorder caused by severe deficiency of thiamine, most commonly triggered by prolonged alcohol abuse. Common symptoms included substantial blackouts in the patient's personal history and the kind of short-term memory loss that Humphrey was displaying. Often patients would retain very sharp memories of long-ago events and, in conversation with him, Sister Kent had found this to be the case with Humphrey.

Since then, Hector continues to visit but sits outside in the corridor while Althea goes in.

Tom Sinclair comes up from London from time to time to say that the actions against the police and the press are in preparation and going well but, though Humphrey chats to him happily, he has no idea who he is nor what he is talking about.

Jack's eyes fill with tears as he listens to Hector's account.

'He might not recognise me,' he says.

'Yes, true. I'm afraid there is no guarantee that he will,' Hector says softly.

'And all this will be quite pointless,' Jack whispers.

'Perhaps. But then again he might. Whatever happens, you'd know you tried, Jack. You would know.'

61. This Afternoon

Noah is shaving Humphrey.

Sister Kent telephoned him early in the morning to ask if he would like some overtime. One of the student nurses has let her down and she has

Humphrey & Jack

not been able to secure an agency nurse until much later. Could he work from ten till nine? She could do with a reliable pair of hands.

Noah says he can. The money will be handy although his feet will be killing him by the end of the shift. However, he has an advanced sense of team spirit and is flattered that Sister Kent has thought of him.

Sister Kent has been known to grumble about student nurses. They don't have the stamina of earlier generations, she says. They all want to work in paediatric wards, she says. They cannot know how very much harder it is to endure the suffering and death of children.

Noah's first task has been to help Staff Nurse Britten to give Humphrey a bed bath. Then she asks him to trim Humphrey's nails. Noah goes further and gives Humphrey's feet a thorough wash, especially between the toes. He dries them thoroughly and dusts them with a medicated talc. The toenails are horny and overgrown and it is a tough job. Now he tackles the fingernails, being careful with the drip. Noah feels a pang of compassion as he holds Humphrey's shrivelled yellow hands.

Now, he has brought fresh hot water and is shaving him.

'Thank you so much, Jack,' he says. 'I can't thank you enough for coming all this way to see me. And it's good of you to do this for me. I feel so much fresher. I've had a bad night to be honest.'

Staff Nurse Britten has already told Noah this. Humphrey slept little and brought up a lot of blood in the small hours.

'Listen, Jack, I wonder if you could do me a favour,' he says. 'Could you bring me a bottle of beer? A bottle of Doom Bar ideally but it doesn't really matter.'

'Ah, I'm not sure about that, Humphrey,' Noah says.

Humphrey has insisted Noah use his first name. He's a little uncomfortable with it but sister Kent insists that when it comes to forms of address the patient's wishes must always be respected.

'I think Sister Kent would kill me if I were caught smuggling alcohol into the ward.'

'Who will kill you?' says Humphrey, bemused.

Humphrey & Jack

'It doesn't matter. I will ask. I mean, I'll see what I can do.'

'I wouldn't ask only I've been very ill, Jack, and I'm so tired. I think it will be this afternoon. And I'd like a glass of beer before I go. I don't want to trouble you but it's not a lot to ask is it?'

'Don't talk like that, Humphrey. We'll soon have you feeling more comfortable. Perhaps even move you to the ward upstairs?'

Noah has heard Sister Kent use this euphemism to dying patients. There is no ward upstairs.

'Of course you can get him a beer,' says sister Sister Kent when Noah speaks to her later. 'I don't know if they do Doom Bar at The Lemon Tree but you can try when you have your break. Just be discreet.'

'He says he's going to die this afternoon. How weird is that? Freaks me out a bit.'

'It's not unusual. Patients sometimes appear to feel reconciled towards the end and they have a premonition that the time has come. Last requests are not uncommon too. Sometimes it's as simple as a cup of tea. I'm afraid it's misuse of alcohol that's killing him, Noah, but it is going to make no difference now, is it?'

'He keeps calling me Jack.'

'I know. Someone called Jack must have been very important to him. Humour him. It is a kindness.'

Noah looks nothing like Jack. He is handsome certainly, but he has red hair and green eyes and there is a strawberry birthmark that covers much of his right cheek.

Sister Kent knows about this someone called Jack. From time to time, in the relatively quiet hour after visiting, she has gone to sit with Humphrey and encouraged him to talk as she has done with countless other patients over the long years of her career.

She is fascinated by the fact that where Jack is concerned Humphrey's recall is exact, although he is a little confused about who she is and he calls her Althea at one point. He talks in great detail about a trip to London and a walk along the river where there were swans.

Humphrey & Jack

***

Hector and Jack pass the long wait at Frankfurt airport with another beer and an early breakfast. Neither of them has been able to sleep on the plane.

At Brussels, they have to walk the whole length of the L-shaped terminal to go through passport control. Their flight to Heathrow is delayed for an hour because of the thunderstorms but at last a shuttle bus takes them all the way along the outside of the L shape almost to where they started.

They board the plane but it is another age before it begins to taxi towards the runway.

***

The morning is exceptionally busy in Tourneur Ward. There are several admissions and Noah is chuffed when Sister Kent lets him conduct one of them on his own for the first time. The ambulance men are, as always, jocular and entertain themselves by calling Noah 'Matron'. Noah blushes.

At one-thirty Sister Kent tells Noah to take his lunch break.

'And no more than a shandy for you, young man,' she says.

'Of course not,' says Noah.

It is not the first time he's been in The Lemon Tree. Recently a patient from Kydd Ward managed to outwit everyone and escaped via an alleyway beyond the visitors' car park. From there he made his way to the pub. The landlord bought him half a pint and rang the hospital. Noah was sent to collect him. And there he was, sitting at the bar in his pyjamas, chatting away and telling salty jokes as if he did this every day of his life.

Today Noah and the landlord have a laugh about this. The pub does stock Doom Bar ale and Noah comes away with a half-litre bottle.

Humphrey & Jack

Later in the afternoon, Sister Kent says to Noah: 'You can take Dr Icke his beer now. I want you to sit with him for a while. Let him talk to you. Just pull the curtains. Oh, and not a paper cup. Here's a proper glass.
'Oh, and Noah…'
'Yes, Sister.'
'Don't sit on the bed.'
Sitting on a patient's bed is a cardinal sin in Sister Kent's eyes.

***

Jack and Hector reach Heathrow at about eleven in the morning. They take the Heathrow Express to Paddington and reach Euston by 12:30.
Jack curses the fact that Radcester is so out of the way. They will have to change and there are not many connexions outside peak periods. However, they manage to book seats on a direct train to Birmingham leaving at one o'clock.

***

The beds in Tourneur Ward are in bays of four. Humphrey's bed was moved to a place by a window two days ago. He can see trees and clouds and there is a blind which can be pulled down so that the sun does not shine directly into his eyes.
Noah leans Humphrey forward, taking his weight against his own chest. He raises the head of the bed and sorts out the pillows so that Humphrey can sit up and drink.
Noah pours the beer for him. Humphrey is too weak to hold the glass himself and Noah holds it for him as one would with a child. Humphrey gulps at first, which makes him cough, but then he begins to take sips.
'Is that good?' says Noah.
'It's very good.'

Humphrey & Jack

Humphrey manages about two thirds of the beer and then lies back and begins to talk.

He talks about his garden and about the bees in the lavender and the golden rod. He talks about a little blackbird he once tried to befriend. He talks about the majestic ash tree at the bottom of the garden. He talks about the smell of the leaves and the flowers after rain.

'And do you remember, Jack,' he says, 'when we once sat outside all night one summer, drinking port and listening to music? And when we got up the next morning we had been devoured by mosquitoes or midges?'

'I remember very well,' says Noah and the lie comes easily.

Humphrey puts out his ravaged hand and Noah takes it into his own healthy one and he begins to stroke the back of it with his thumb in little circles.

'You wouldn't recognise the fence now, Jack,' Humphrey says. 'It's weathered beautifully and there are climbing roses all over it.'

Humphrey continues to turn over memories of his early friendship with this someone called Jack. Noah can tell that Humphrey is experiencing them in high resolution.

'And do you remember the thunderstorm?' says Humphrey.

'As if it were yesterday,' says Noah. 'It was a belter, wasn't it?'

'It was.'

***

There are further delays at Birmingham New Street. Thieves have been at work on the Radcester line and cable has been stolen. Jack and Hector sit despondently on a bench watching the departure board. Their eyes prickle with exhaustion and they're too tired even to talk to each other.

The estimated departure time on the board climbs in increments to an intolerable two hours and then the figures disappear altogether and are replaced by the one word: 'cancelled'.

Humphrey & Jack

***

'I think I should like to sleep a little now,' says Humphrey.

Noah lowers the head of the bed and plumps up the pillows again and Humphrey lies back.

Noah continues to sit by him still holding his hand.

Humphrey drifts off. Gradually his breathing becomes very faint and his hand begins to feel cool.

Noah continues to stroke the back of it with little circular motions of his thumb.

Acknowledgements

I have had the inexpressible privilege and good fortune to have had two editors at work on this book at the same time: Julie Dexter in Vermont, USA and Peter Cheshire in London, England. Julie's microscopically close eye helped weed out any number of typos and punctuation gaffes but, even more importantly, her instinctive empathy with what I was trying to say helped me to improve the fluency of my text so often. Her ear is as good as her eye. It has been an exciting and invaluable collaboration and I can't thank her enough. It has been delightful to make friends during the process. My most excellent and learned friend, Peter, exercised peerless pedantry in his scrutiny of the manuscript and was brilliant at spotting anomalies. I am particularly grateful for the way in which he researched all manner of details to confirm (or deny) their authenticity. His encouragement has been a great boon when I have been seized by self-doubt. Without these two midwives, *Humphrey & Jack* would never have been brought to term.

Thanks too must go to Helen Brace for her sinister cover photograph and to Indy Poole and Harry Marcus, who were her models. Julie Fox kindly acted as chaperone. I would also like to show my appreciation to Helen for succour and support during a trying time.

Once again, Gavin Smith lent his expertise to a critical reading of the police scenes. Christopher Gunning checked my (otherwise ignorant) references to cricket. To Piotr Ulfig for help with the fragments of Polish, and to Marek Sledziewski for help with the topography of Poland - dzięki! Eileen Barclay kindly checked the Durham chapters for authenticity.

The case of Christopher Jefferies, the Bristol schoolmaster, falsely arrested for the murder in 2010 of Joanna Yeates, was an oblique inspiration for the latter part of my novel. A valuable reminder of the details has been the film: *The Lost Honour of Christopher Jefferies*, Carnival Film and Television, 2014, Peter Morgan (Writer), Kevin Loader (Producer) and Roger Michell (Director) - first aired on ITV in 2014. I have also been helped by *The Crime Writer's Casebook, A Reference Guide to Police Investigation Past and Present*, by Steven Wade and Stuart Gibbon, Straightforward Publishing, 2017.

Should any errors remain in this book, the fault is mine alone.

Ian Thomson
Lincoln

Postscript: I am ineffably grateful to Michael Rogers who has squirrelled away at my text to unearth errors which were overlooked previously and have been corrected in this new edition.

Praise for other works by Ian Thomson
A selection of Amazon Reviews

Martin
A Novel

'Ian Thomson's novel is a diamond as black as coal. His sparkling and vivid prose helps him pull off an impressive feat: to make the reader care about a cruel and capricious sociopath, Robert Reith, and his vengeful, erotic obsession.

'The writer is adept at living within the skin of his subject and the novel feels authentic - even biographical - throughout. Sexually, socially and geographically, Reith lives on the margins. As a northern, working-class grammar-school boy who happens to like boys, Reith is the perennial outsider who never dares stop using his wit as a pitchfork, despite the collateral damage.

'Ian Thomson adroitly balances sympathy, suspense and morbid fascination when Reith starts to wreak havoc. From a northern fishing village to elite academia, from the Dark Web to the mortuary, this novel remains grimly compelling.

For me, this is a love story with a brutal caveat. Without giving too much away, Mr Thomson takes a clinical and compelling look at the greedy, selfish and destructive underbelly of what we lazily refer to as "love".'

***

'An extraordinarily brilliant book. Too often today, novels are not about people but about "issues", with the result that they treat their characters as the contents of income brackets rather than as people. No character in Martin is typical. They are individuals whose characters emerge through Thomson's superb use of the English language. He is a writer who knows his craft, and this is evident in his brilliantly witty language which flows poetically, and often hilariously, across the page. It made me laugh out loud, and which I read voraciously though I wanted to savour it. There aren't many books like that being published now.'

***

'Ian Thomson's first novel *Martin* is compelling from the very outset, as Robert Reith, the narrator-protagonist, drunk, his life for reasons as yet unknown on the rocks, seeks to enlist the support of us, his readers. It soon becomes clear that he will be spiky but entertaining company, capable of wistfulness for sure, but often cynical, opinionated and seemingly amoral. But at least you can say that he is ruthlessly honest about his own shortcomings.

'His journey from a traditional working-class childhood as the son of a trawlerman in the fictional fishing port of Quex Quay to the rarefied world of the Oxbridge don is charted in vivid and evocative language and with a superb eye for detail.

'Of the many problematical relationships in the novel, in some ways the most interesting is that between the narrator and his reader. In his unflinching honesty he seems almost excessively keen to present himself as a reliable guide to the unfolding events. And so when he blithely assumes that we will accept and understand his main proposition: that the memory of a love from the distant past is enough to justify an elaborate scheme of vengeance which, as he admits, will lay waste to three lives including his own, for a moment we catch ourselves going along with this and we struggle to recapture our moral perspective.

'Not that Reith is in any way ingratiating towards his reader. At one point he asks us Who are you, anyway? But when he writes Do I feel remorse? No, categorically no…I was merely an innocent catalyst…my position is unimpeachable, we have to ask ourselves who it is that he is trying to convince.

'And yet, in the novel's final pages, which are genuinely touching, we find ourselves once again sympathising with Reith, for all his monstrous amorality, and wondering, if only for a moment, whether love does not indeed redeem all things.

'Robert Reith's life spirals out of control because he is so controlling and calculating. The novel on the other hand unleashes its considerable power on us precisely because its author has structured it so carefully and marshals his forces so brilliantly.'

Cherries
And Other Tales

'None of the stories in this little collection goes where you expect it to. Sometimes you want to kick yourself for not seeing it in advance. Even in the stories where there is a dark ending, there is mischievous humour. I liked the story of The Wrong Dog in *The Pier* and daft Betty in *Cold Sweat*. *Mansfield Retail Park* is hilarious and as camp as a pantomime. In all the stories the dialogue rings true, whether it's the kids in *Cardigan*, or the freaky conversation between the lady and the beggar in *Cherries*.'

***

'This is a perfect little confection for Halloween. Three of the tales feature the black humour for which Thomson has often been noted. *The Pier* begins innocently enough with the romancing of Meg, a retired teacher, by Captain Quinn, an engaging old fraud who runs The Sea Horse. The middle story, *Cold Sweat*, is overtly scary and you wonder whether Tanya's life is falling apart because of some external agency or whether it's all in her head. The ending is a tour de force and quite unexpected. The last story, *Cherries*, set in Avignon, also has a final twist, where an act of kindness goes horribly wrong. By contrast, the other two stories are quite charming. *Cardigan* conjures up the hormonal torments of adolescence and the ecstasy and the heartache of first love. Comic distancing gives the tale piquancy. *Mansfield Retail Park* is hilarious – a romantic pastiche where Jane Austen and Charlotte Bronte meet Victoria Wood.'

The Mouse Triptych

'Thomson's words dance over the pages and I am enthralled and captivated.'

***

'What a delight these three little stories are. Very different in tone and style, each relates how the worlds of mice and men intersect and how the mice sometimes have the upper hand. I'm not usually a fan of anthropomorphised animals and am rarely won over by the playful in fiction, but Thomson's facility with words and his darkly comic take on the somewhat surrealistic scenarios he introduces us to both amused and quite captivated me. Very well-written and very enjoyable. Highly recommended.'

***

'Dark, humorous, very well-written. I am very glad I bought *The Mouse Triptych*. It's not often that I read a book at one sitting.'

***

'*The Mouse Triptych* is a trio dessert that leaves the reader feeling light as air. A surreal collection of short stories, with a common theme of small creatures making a big impact. Refreshingly, one is encouraged to leave all preconceptions behind and embrace a childlike journey behind cabinets, along skirting boards and under fridges.'

***

'Humorous yet shocking and intriguing. It is one of those books which you find yourself remembering elements of for many years. It holds your attention and I loved the link between the three stories. This book is a keeper and I look forward to rereading again and again.'

The Swan Diptych

'*How the Dean Angered the Swans* is an historical fantasy, set in Richard II's Lincoln. We discover how the Cathedral clergy's conceit leads to the city's ruin. It is both scholarly and slapstick. I laughed out loud at how the swans effect the Dean's demise. *The Patronal Feast* takes us across the Fens to Cambridge, and through time to the reign of Elizabeth I. It is an altogether richer dish, and whilst there is still a deal of comedy to be found, the mood is much darker. Again, we have a story in which there are few likeable characters, again the author's scholarship is in evidence, but it is never superfluous. The details about conditions in a 16th century Cambridge college kitchen are essential to the unravelling of the mystery. The plot is well-constructed, and the mixture of characters' letters and an omniscient narrator make for a page-turner of a story.'

***

'His research seems impeccable to me but, as in all the best historical writing, it is worn lightly. The two stories in this diptych, linked by the central motif of swans, work on many levels. For a start, and perhaps most importantly, they work as a really good read. Historical detective fiction, crime fiction, murder mystery, a little fantasy thrown in for good measure, all these combine to create a really compelling and entertaining tale. There's wit, black humour and erudition aplenty here. The first short story is set in medieval Lincoln, the second, longer novella in Tudor Cambridge. I believed in both these places. I believed that what happens could indeed have happened. I was kept guessing right to the end and the conclusion in both stories is deeply satisfying.'

***

'Superb. Both stories are excellent and compelling, so much so that I had to read the final couple of chapters at my desk as I couldn't leave it unfinished on arrival at the office! They are as well researched and written as the historic fiction of well-known authors like Sansom and Scarrow.'

***

'In both stories, Thomson takes the reader to Vanity Fair, where people of all ages and levels of society misspend their time and abilities on self-aggrandisement, which, as in all fables, is in vain.

'While the subjects and themes are serious, the stories are masterfully told with a thoroughly readable mixture of wit, erudition, irony and black humour. One can imagine the author chuckling, Hitchcock-like, at his typewriter with each innocent adultery and virtuous vice. These qualities make *The Swan Diptych* accessible, entertaining and thought-provoking.'

***

'Fascinating and joyous!'

Come Away, O Human Child
A collection of four unrelated short stories

'*Hibernation* is a comically dark story, reminiscent of Roald Dahl, about a boy and two family pets – one of them, highly unconventional. Dancing in the background are questions of truth, fantasy, parental responsibility and the current trend of taking things too seriously. It's well-crafted, witty and thoroughly enjoyable.

'*Duck* is a far more serious tale that looks at the complexity of relationships, love, death and memory. Told with great sensitivity, *Duck* is the most realistic and substantial story of the collection.

'*Just a Little Kitchen Supper* is "the most awful dinner party in the history of civilisation as we know it." It makes *Abigail's Party* look like the event *sans pareil* of the social season. Like the best comedy, it builds a series of logical premises until stability is lost and chaos ensues. The worrying part is how many of the constituent events of this disaster one recognises from personal experience.

'*Come Away, O Human Child* is a metaphysical story; not real, and not science fiction, it is a grim fairy tale with no happy ever after. What gives the story its special edge is the matter-of-fact manner in which it is related and the similar way that the inhabitants of the story accept what's going on. Thomson peppers the pages with clues as to what he is thinking, and it is told with his customary wit and stylistic aplomb.'

Non-Fiction

Mr Thomson's Diary

For Release in 2019

Humphrey and Jack

Printed in Great Britain
by Amazon